FROM THE PAGES OF *A PORTRAIT*
OF THE ARTIST AS A YOUNG MAN

It pained him that he did not know well what politics meant and that he did not know where the universe ended. He felt small and weak. When would he be like the fellows in Poetry and Rhetoric? They had big voices and big boots and they studied trigonometry. That was very far away. (page 13)

His eyes were dimmed with tears and, looking humbly up to heaven, he wept for the innocence he had lost. (page 121)

To merge his life in the common tide of other lives was harder for him than any fasting or prayer, and it was his constant failure to do this to his own satisfaction which caused in his soul at last a sensation of spiritual dryness together with a growth of doubts and scruples.

(page 132)

He was unheeded, happy, and near to the wild heart of life. He was alone and young and wilful and wildhearted, alone amid a waste of wild air and brackish waters and the seaharvest of shells and tangle and veiled grey sunlight and gayclad lightclad figures of children and girls and voices childish and girlish in the air. (page 150)

—The artist, like the God of the creation, remains within or behind or beyond or above his handiwork, invisible, refined out of existence, indifferent, paring his fingernails. (page 191)

I will not serve that in which I no longer believe, whether it call itself my home, my fatherland or my church: and I will try to express myself in some mode of life or art as freely as I can and as wholly as I can, using for my defence the only arms I allow myself to use, silence, exile and cunning. (page 219)

FROM THE PAGES OF *DUBLINERS*

I kept her brown figure always in my eye and, when we came near the point at which our ways diverged, I quickened my pace and passed her. This happened morning after morning. I had never spoken to her, except for a few casual words, and yet her name was like a summons to all my foolish blood. (from "Araby," page 250)

The car steered out slowly for Grafton Street while the two young men pushed their way through the knot of gazers. They walked northward with a curious feeling of disappointment in the exercise, while the city hung its pale globes of light above them in a haze of summer evening. (from "After the Race," page 262)

For the first time in his life he felt superior to the people he passed. For the first time his soul revolted against the dull inelegance of Capel Street. There was no doubt about it: if you wanted to succeed you had to go away. You could do nothing in Dublin. (from "A Little Cloud," page 287)

A few light taps upon the pane made him turn to the window. It had begun to snow again. He watched sleepily the flakes, silver and dark, falling obliquely against the lamplight. The time had come for him to set out on his journey westward. Yes, the newspapers were right: snow was general all over Ireland. It was falling on every part of the dark central plain, on the treeless hills, falling softly upon the Bog of Allen and, farther westward, softly falling into the dark mutinous Shannon waves. It was falling, too, upon every part of the lonely churchyard on the hill where Michael Furey lay buried. It lay thickly drifted on the crooked crosses and headstones, on the spears of the little gate, on the barren thorns. His soul swooned slowly as he heard the snow falling faintly through the universe and faintly falling, like the descent of their last end, upon all the living and the dead. (from "The Dead," page 412)

A PORTRAIT OF THE ARTIST AS A YOUNG MAN
and
DUBLINERS

JAMES JOYCE

With an Introduction and Notes
by Kevin J. H. Dettmar

GEORGE STADE
CONSULTING EDITORIAL DIRECTOR

BARNES & NOBLE CLASSICS
NEW YORK

ß

BARNES & NOBLE CLASSICS
NEW YORK

Published by Barnes & Noble Books
122 Fifth Avenue
New York, NY 10011

www.barnesandnoble.com/classics

Dubliners was first published in 1914. *A Portrait of the Artist as a Young Man* was published in *The Egoist* between 1914 and 1915, and in volume form in 1916.

Published in 2004 by Barnes & Noble Classics with new Introduction, Notes, Biography, Note on the Texts, Note on Currency and Coinage, Inspired By, Comments & Questions, and For Further Reading.

A Portrait of the Artist as a Young Man and *Dubliners*
ISBN-13: 978-1-59308-031-0
ISBN-10: 1-59308-031-X
LC Control Number 2004101078

Produced and published in conjunction with:
Fine Creative Media, Inc.
322 Eighth Avenue
New York, NY 10001
Michael J. Fine, President & Publisher

Printed in the United States of America
QM
10 12 14 16 18 20 19 17 15 13 11

JAMES JOYCE

Irish novelist James Joyce was born on February 2, 1882, in Dublin. The eldest of ten children, James spent his early years in a solvent, middle-class Catholic household. At age six, he enrolled in prestigious Clongowes Wood College, but three years later his father's spending habits and failed investments had depleted the family's modest fortune. James was taken out of the costly Jesuit school, and the family was forced into more affordable housing, ultimately moving to a poor neighborhood on Dublin's south side. Following a brief enrollment in a Christian Brothers school for the Irish poor, James was admitted, without fees, to another Jesuit school, Belevedere College. In the fall of 1898, he entered University College Dublin, where he studied languages, read widely, and was influenced by Yeats, Thomas Aquinas, and, especially, the plays of Henrik Ibsen. A devout Catholic in his youth, Joyce would break with the Church during his years at University College. In 1900 he published his first essay, a review of Ibsen's *When We Dead Awaken*, in the London journal the *Fortnightly Review*.

After graduation in 1902, Joyce left Ireland for Paris, supposedly to study medicine. Instead, he worked as a teacher and journalist and spent much of his time in the library. He returned to Ireland in April 1903 to visit his dying mother. The following year, he fell in love with an uneducated girl from Galway, Nora Barnacle, who would become his lifelong companion and the inspiration for the character Molly Bloom in his great novel *Ulysses* (1922). (Joyce would later immortalize the day they met, June 16, as Bloomsday—the day on which *Ulysses* takes place.) During this time he began work on an early version of *A Portrait of the Artist as a Young Man*, entitled *Stephen Hero*. He also began writing, under the nom de plume Stephen Dedalus, the stories that would later appear as *Dubliners*. Joyce persuaded Nora to move to the Continent, and after some misadventures and displacement, in 1905 the couple settled in Trieste, where they would remain for fifteen years. Scarcity of money did not affect Joyce's productivity: He published a book of poetry, *Chamber Music* (1907), and completed *Dubliners* (1914), *A Portrait of the Artist as a Young Man* (1916), the play *Exiles* (1918), and large passages of *Ulysses*. The American poet Ezra Pound sponsored publication of his work and introduced him to the literary salons of Paris, while bookstore owner Sylvia Beach and publisher Harriet Shaw Weaver assisted Joyce with publication and patronage.

Joyce had at first conceived *Ulysses* as a short story, but he expanded it into a novel that he published in installments starting in 1918 and until it was banned for obscenity in 1920. Joyce and his family weathered World War I in Zurich and, after a brief return to Trieste, resettled in Paris in 1920. The full text of *Ulysses* was published in Paris in 1922, but the book continued to be banned in England and America. Joyce spent the next seventeen years writing *Finnegans Wake*, which would be published in 1939. The author's growing literary success during this period eased the family's financial burdens, but tragedy loomed in the background. Joyce's vision troubles were acute, and his daughter, Lucia, diagnosed with schizophrenia, suffered a mental breakdown. In 1934 *Ulysses* was published in the United States, accompanied by a landmark obscenity decision; in 1936 it was published in England. Once again war struck, and Joyce returned to Zurich, where he died on January 13, 1941. James Joyce is widely regarded as among the most important writers of the twentieth century.

TABLE OF CONTENTS

1882 James Augustine Aloysius Joyce is born on February 2 in the
      Dublin suburb of Rathgar to Mary Jane Murray Joyce and John
      Stanislaus Joyce. Virginia Woolf is born.

1884 Nora Barnacle is born in Galway on March 21. Stanislaus
      Joyce, James's brother, is born on December 17.

1887 The Joyce family moves to the seaside town of Bray.

1888 James enters Clongowes Wood College, a Jesuit school known
      as the Eton of Ireland.

1891 James withdraws from Clongowes because his father can no
      longer afford the tuition; for the next two years he is informally
      educated at home. Irish political leader Charles Stewart Parnell
      dies. James writes the poem "Et Tu, Healy" about Parnell's be-
      trayal.

1893 James enrolls in a Christian Brothers school. Soon after, he and
      Stanislaus are admitted, without fees, to Belvedere College, a
      Jesuit grammar school in Dublin.

1898 Joyce enters University College Dublin, where he studies mod-
      ern languages. He is influenced by Yeats and Ibsen, and studies
      Dano-Norwegian in order to read Ibsen's original work.

1899 Ibsen's symbolic drama *When We Dead Awaken* is published.

1900 The *Fortnightly Review*, in London, publishes "Ibsen's New
      Drama," Joyce's review of *When We Dead Awaken*.

1901 At his own expense, Joyce publishes "The Day of the Rabble-
      ment," an essay critical of the parochialism of the Irish Literary
      Theatre (later to become the Abbey Theatre).

1902 Joyce graduates from University College and leaves Dublin for
      Paris with the intention of studying medicine.

1903 In April, Joyce returns to Dublin when his mother is diagnosed
      with cancer; she dies in the summer. Joyce resides for a short
      time in the Martello Tower at Sandycove.

1904 He has his first date with Nora Barnacle on June 16, a date he
      went on to memorialize as the setting for his novel *Ulysses*
      (1922); with the publication of *Ulysses*, June 16 will come to be
      known as Bloomsday. He has begun the autobiographical novel

Stephen Hero, which later will become *A Portrait of the Arist as a Young Man*. He takes time away from working on *Stephen Hero* to write the first stories in the collection that will become *Dubliners*. In October, James and Nora leave Dublin and settle in Pola, Austria-Hungary.

1905   Foreigners are expelled from Pola, and the Joyces move to Trieste, Italy, where Joyce works at a Berlitz school. He submits an early version of *Dubliners* for publication. He meets and tutors then unknown novelist Italo Svevo, whose work he helps to publish. The Joyces' son, Giorgio, is born on July 27. The Sinn Fein Party is organized in Dublin. George Bernard Shaw's *Mrs. Warren's Profession* opens in New York but is closed by the police censor after one performance.

1906   Joyce moves his family to Rome, where he works in a bank. Although their financial situation improves, Joyce is unhappy, and the family returns to Trieste after eight months. Henrik Ibsen dies.

1907   The couple's daughter, Lucia, is born on July 26. Joyce completes "The Dead" and begins revising *Stephen Hero* as *A Portrait of the Artist as a Young Man*. His first collection of poems, *Chamber Music*, is published.

1909   Joyce returns to Dublin and opens the city's first movie theater, the Volta; the venture fails. J. M. Synge writes *Deirdre of the Sorrows*; he dies later this year.

1910   Joyce returns to Trieste.

1912   He makes his final visit to Ireland to deal with problems in the publishing of *Dubliners*.

1913   D. H. Lawrence publishes *Sons and Lovers*. Shaw's *Pygmalion* is first performed in Vienna.

1914   The *Egoist* begins serialization of *A Portrait of the Artist as a Young Man*. *Dubliners* is published in London. World War I begins.

1915   Italy enters World War I. The Joyces move from Trieste to Zurich. D. H. Lawrence's *The Rainbow* is published.

1916   Patrick Pearse (Joyce's former Irish teacher) and the Irish Republicans declare independence with the Easter Rising on April 24. Five hundred people are killed during the failed rebellion, and Pearse and fourteen other leaders are executed; Yeats writes "Easter 1916" to commemorate the event. C. G. Jung's *Psychology of the Unconscious*, published in German in 1912, is published in English translation. *A Portrait of the Artist as a Young Man* is published in the United States.

1917   Joyce undergoes the first of twenty-five operations for eye diseases, including glaucoma and cataracts. The feminist and activist editor of the *Egoist*, Harriet Shaw Weaver, begins her patronage of Joyce. T. S. Eliot publishes *Prufrock and Other Observations*.

1918   Chapters of *Ulysses* begin to be published in the American journal the *Little Review*.

1919   The U.S. Post Office seizes and burns copies of the January and June issues of the *Little Review*. Joyce's play *Exiles* is published in England and the United States. Following the war, the Joyces return to Trieste.

1920   The U.S. Post Office seizes and burns copies of the January issue of the *Little Review*, and the *Little Review*'s publication of *Ulysses* is halted by court order with half the book published. The Joyce family relocates to Paris. Edith Wharton's *The Age of Innocence* is published.

1922   The Irish Free State achieves independence. Northern Ireland remains under British rule. American expatriate Sylvia Beach, owner of the bookshop Shakespeare and Company in Paris, publishes *Ulysses* on February 2. The U.S. Post Office burns a shipment of 500 copies. T. S. Eliot publishes *The Waste Land* and founds the literary journal the *Criterion*. Joyce begins work on *Finnegans Wake*; his final novel, it will take seventeen years to complete.

1923   Italo Svevo publishes *La coscienza di Zeno* (*Confessions of Zeno*). Yeats is awarded the Nobel Prize for Literature.

1924   The first piece of *Finnegans Wake* is published in Paris in the *Transatlantic Review*.

1925   In London, the *Criterion* publishes a second piece from *Finnegans Wake*.

1927   A second volume of poems by Joyce, *Pomes Penyeach*, is published. Publication of the seven volumes of Marcel Proust's *À la recherche du temps perdu* (*Remembrance of Things Past*), begun in 1913, is completed. Virginia Woolf's *To the Lighthouse* is published.

1928   D. H. Lawrence's *Lady Chatterley's Lover*, Virginia Woolf's *Orlando*, and Yeats's *The Tower* are published.

1930   W. H. Auden's *Poems* and T. S. Eliot's *Ash Wednesday* are published. D. H. Lawrence dies.

1931   James and Nora marry for legal reasons. Joyce's father dies.

1932   Lucia Joyce is hospitalized and diagnosed as schizophrenic.

1933   United States District Judge John Woolsey lifts the ban on *Ulysses* and, in his decision, writes a legal definition of obscenity.

1934   The first authorized edition of *Ulysses* is published in the United States.

1936   *Ulysses* is published in the United Kingdom.

1939   *Finnegans Wake* is published. World War II begins. W. B. Yeats dies.

1940   As France is invaded, the Joyces obtain visas for Switzerland and return to Zurich in December.

1941   Joyce dies of a perforated ulcer on January 13.

INTRODUCTION

Now that the dust of the previous century has settled, there seems little doubt that James Joyce was the most significant, the most influential English-language prose writer of the twentieth century. His one short-story collection, three novels, one play, and two volumes of poems have won him the devoted attention of students, scholars, and general readers alike; in scholarly terms alone, Joyce is now the second most densely explicated of English-language authors, after only Shakespeare. He has become, in both the public and scholarly imagination, the bespectacled (or sometimes eye-patched) public face of modern literature, in all its difficulty and hard-won pleasures.

Such a fate was far from evident in the early reaction to his writing: Both his collection of fifteen short stories, *Dubliners* (1914), and his autobiographically based first novel, *A Portrait of the Artist as a Young Man* (1916), very nearly never saw the light of day. The eventual publisher of *Dubliners*, London-based Grant Richards, first issued Joyce a contract for the book in February 1906; the collection itself wasn't published until more than eight years later, however, and after a running battle with a series of publishers and printers that Joyce described in an open letter, "A Curious History," which he later proposed Richards publish as a preface to the book. At issue, first and foremost, were questions of obscenity and libel—epiphenomena of the realism of Joyce's stories—for which publishers believed they would be prosecuted. Joyce's indiscretions are, by contemporary standards, quite tame: A man conducting an adulterous affair is described as having "two establishments to keep up"; King Edward VII is called by one character "a bit of a rake"; and the obscene colloquialism "bloody" pops up with uncomfortable frequency in the second half of the collection. At the same time, as Joyce peevishly pointed out in a 1906 letter to Richards, the much grosser obscenity of stories like "An Encounter" and "The Boarding House" had been completely overlooked. Richards replied, by return mail, that "On consideration, I should *like* to leave out altogether 'The [sic] Encounter.'" Censors very rarely have a sense of humor.

In "A Curious History," Joyce throws in the towel:

I wrote this book seven years ago and, as I cannot see in any quarter a chance that my rights will be protected, I hereby give Messrs Maunsel publicly permission to publish this story ["Ivy Day in the Committee Room"] with what changes or deletions they may please to make and shall hope that what they may publish may resemble that to the writing of which I gave thought and time. . . . I, as a writer, protest against the systems (legal, social and ceremonious) which have brought me to this pass (James Joyce, *Letters*, edited by Stuart Gilbert and Richard Ellmann, New York: Viking Press, 1957–1966; vol. 2, p. 293).

The pre-publication difficulties of *Dubliners* mark a minor episode in the larger struggle over censorship that was waged by early twentieth-century writers like D. H. Lawrence and Radclyffe Hall, and was fought most memorably over Joyce's own 1922 masterpiece *Ulysses*. As it turns out, Joyce's "A Curious History" was curiously proleptic, however: It was written in August 1911, when the book's strange odyssey was barely half done. A Dublin edition of the stories, having been set in type by Maunsel & Co., was summarily destroyed by a scrupulous printer in September 1912. On the back of the annulled contract Joyce wrote a broadside poem, "Gas from a Burner"; it opens with these lines, spoken by a figure compounded of Maunsel's manager, George Roberts, and the scandalized printer, John Falconer:

> Ladies and gents, you are here assembled
> To hear why earth and heaven trembled
> Because of the black and sinister arts
> Of an Irish writer in foreign parts.
> He sent me a book ten years ago.
> I read it a hundred times or so,
> Backwards and forwards, down and up,
> Through both ends of a telescope.
> I printed it all to the very last word
> But by the mercy of the Lord
> The darkness of my mind was rent
> And I saw the writer's foul intent (Joyce, *Critical Writings*,
> pp. 242–243; see "For Further Reading").

As Joyce's poem closes, the heretical work goes up in flames, as all heretics must: "I'll burn the book, so help me devil. / I'll sing a psalm as I watch it burn" (p. 245). While Joyce's martyr imagination believed his book to have been burned, in fact the print run was probably just cut and pulped; having come this close to fruition, however, the book's publication was thus delayed by another twenty-one months, until Grant Richards stepped back into the fray and brought the book out in June 1914.

Even while *Dubliners* was fitfully slouching toward London to be born, Joyce was at work on his first novel, *A Portrait of the Artist as a Young Man* (as well as his first volume of poems, *Chamber Music*, published in 1907). Conceptually, *Portrait* is the earlier book: Its germ is to be found in a 2,500 word essay that Joyce wrote on January 7, 1904, "A Portrait of the Artist," whereas the earliest of the *Dubliners* stories, "The Sisters," was not begun until six months later. Like *Dubliners*, *Portrait* nearly went up in flames before it found its readership: In a famous story, the unfinished manuscript was snatched from the fireplace by Joyce's sister Eileen in 1911, after Joyce had thrown it on the flames in a fit of despair.

This rescued manuscript had already gone through an intermediate stage, in which the short essay "A Portrait" was expanded into an unfinished novel of twenty-six chapters; the remaining portions of that earlier version were published after Joyce's death as *Stephen Hero*, though the manuscript is said to have been rejected by twenty different publishers before Joyce began its wholesale revision as *Portrait*. Even with the novel in its final form, however, and with both *Chamber Music* and *Dubliners* already in print, Joyce had a great deal of difficulty finding a home for *Portrait*. In what is surely a characteristic opinion, the reader's report prepared for the publisher Duckworth & Co. in June 1916 found both Joyce's social realism and his narrative experimentation a bit too much to contend with:

> James Joyce's "Portrait of the Artist as a Young Man" wants going through carefully from start to finish. There are many "longueurs" [boring passages]. Passages which, though the publisher's reader may find them entertaining, will be tedious to the ordinary man among the reading public. . . . It is too discursive, formless, unrestrained, and ugly things, ugly words, are too prominent; indeed at times they seem to be shoved in one's face, on purpose, unnecessarily. . . .
>
> The author shows us he has art, strength and originality, but this MS. wants time and trouble spent on it, to make it a more finished piece of work, to shape it more carefully as the product of the craftsmanship, mind and imagination of the artist (James Joyce, *A Portrait*

of the Artist as a Young Man: Text, Criticism, and Notes, edited by
Chester G. Anderson, New York: Viking Press, 1968, p. 320).

Having worked on the novel by turns for more than twelve years, Joyce
cannot have been pleased to read that the manuscript was in need of
"time and trouble spent on it." Although the author of the report acknowledged that some of "the old conventions" concerning fiction were
then falling away, he could not yet discern the larger outlines of Joyce's
narrative experiment, in which great "time and trouble" were spent precisely in honing the novel's continually evolving prose—blurring his
protagonist's ultimate fate and the novel's plot trajectory, as Joseph
Conrad had done in *Heart of Darkness*, in a healthy dose of narrative
fog.

    While Joyce struggled against what, in "A Curious History," he
called "legal, social and ceremonious" systems in order to get *Dubliners*
published, his vision for the stories seems not to have changed significantly from his earliest conception: It was from the beginning to be a
collection written "to betray the soul of that hemiplegia [partial paral-
ysis] or paralysis which many consider a city," written "for the most part
in a style of scrupulous meanness." In writing *Portrait*, on the other
hand—his troubles with publishers notwithstanding—Joyce's main
hurdles were personal and artistic, not public. In the 1904 essay, he
writes with dissatisfaction about the conventions of autobiography, in
which the "features of infancy" are presented only in their "iron, me-
morial aspect": Youth is narrated only from the hindsight of maturity,
and with a false confidence that betrays the real uncertainty of those
early years. Joyce states as a goal—though one he is unable satisfacto-
rily to accomplish in the early essay—an autobiographical style that
would present the past as "a fluid succession of presents, the development of an entity of which our actual present is a phase only." The
essay's opening, manifesto-like paragraph concludes with the statement
that for those exceptional individuals for whom an autobiography is a
worthwhile undertaking, "a portrait is not an identificative paper but
rather the curve of an emotion."

    Joyce thus sought to forge (a word that plays an interesting role in
Portrait, as we'll see) a style of shifting emphases and perspectives,
drawing its imagery and vocabulary from different sources during different periods of his protagonist's life—a technique we might today, in
light of the nearly simultaneous work in narrative technique being carried out in England by writers like Conrad and Ford Madox Ford, call

"impressionism." Joyce's "Portrait" essay is certainly impressionistic—nearly to the point of incomprehensibility; his impressionism in presentation is combined with a preciosity of style, rendering the resultant text narrowly self-involved. Over the years of its genesis, however—and because of, not merely in spite of, its trials and persecutions—this first "Portrait" became *A Portrait of the Artist as a Young Man*, achieving a nearly perfect accommodation of style to mood and thought—"the curve of an emotion," precisely. In the much-discussed 1997 Random House poll that named Joyce's *Ulysses* the number-one novel of the twentieth century, *Portrait* came in a close third, behind F. Scott Fitzgerald's *The Great Gatsby*; this novel that nearly arrived stillborn has now been confirmed as a twentieth-century classic and has been installed as a mainstay of high school and college curricula in English-speaking countries around the world.

Though written very nearly in tandem, *Dubliners* and *A Portrait of the Artist as a Young Man* have very different agendas, and represent very different reading experiences, as well. We might, for purposes of illustration, think of Joyce's first two works of fiction as representing critiques of two rather different literary genres: *Dubliners*, a critique of the short story as Joyce had inherited it, in which complicated psychological struggles are simplified and resolved in the course of three thousand words; and *Portrait*, a critique of the deeply romantic legacy of the *Bildungsroman* (novel of education and maturation) and its close relative the *Kunstlerroman* (which focuses on the development of the artist), forms that perpetuated a notion of heroism wholly unsuited to the realities of life and art in the twentieth century.

If early readers and critics of *Dubliners* were taken aback by Joyce's unflinching reportage of the sordid details of modern urban life, contemporary readers are more often struck by the stories' very abrupt endings: Time and again they seem merely to stop, dead in their tracks, rather than properly ending. The first three stories, in this regard, are representative. "The Sisters" ends while one of the eponymous sisters is in mid-conversation, mid-sentence: "So then, of course, when they saw that, that made them think that there was something gone wrong with him. . . . " The ellipsis that closes the story is just one of twenty sets in this very elliptical three-thousand-word story, in which meaning seems to lie just behind the words, in between the words, peeking out at us but ultimately eluding us. At the close of the second story, "An Encounter," our narrator calls for help to his friend Mahoney, but this message is relayed along with confession of a sin we cannot understand, or even guess at: "And I was penitent; for in my heart I had always despised him a little." Hence, rather than the sort of closure a short story is supposed to provide, "An Encounter" opens up, vertiginously, on a host of other issues just when it should be shutting down new possibilities. The beautifully lyrical ending of "Araby" has been much analyzed, and to read the criticism, one would think that there's nothing at all out of the way about the narrator's sudden outburst in his closing sentence: "Gazing up into the darkness I saw myself as a creature driven and derided by vanity; and my eyes burned with anguish and anger." What—? Revelation, it seems, arrives from out of the blue (or black), but we readers can neither see it coming nor figure out with any certainty whither it will lead our protagonist.

These three stories—and many others in the collection besides, including "Eveline," "Two Gallants," "The Boarding House," "Clay," "A Painful Case," "Ivy Day in the Committee Room," and "The Dead"— focus on the moment of sudden revelation that Joyce called, after the traditions of the Catholic Church, an "epiphany." A full description of the epiphany is one of the elements that Joyce stripped out of *Stephen Hero* in making *Portrait*; if we turn back to that earlier text, however, we discover the following explanation of the place of the epiphany in Stephen Dedalus's evolving aesthetic philosophy:

> This triviality [of a banal conversation he has overheard] made him think of collecting many such moments together in a book of epiphanies. By an epiphany he meant a sudden spiritual manifestation, whether in the vulgarity of speech or of gesture or in a memorable phase of the mind itself. He believed that it was for the man of letters to record these epiphanies with extreme care, seeing that they themselves are the most delicate and evanescent of moments (James Joyce, Stephen Hero, edited by John J. Slocum and Herbert Cahoon, second edition, New York: New Directions, 1963, p. 211).

This insistence on the importance of the trivial plays throughout both *Dubliners* and *Portrait*; and a great deal of scholarly attention has been paid over the years to the concept of the epiphany. Without rehearsing in detail that voluminous scholarship, we might pause here to note that the terse description given in *Stephen Hero* describes a locus for the epiphany (in "everyday life") and an agent of the epiphany (the writer); if much of public life consists of playing some kind of role, wearing a mask, an epiphany is one of those rare moments when the mask slips, and we see past convention, past language, and glimpse some fundamental truth about human nature. But the question of for whom the timeless human truth of the situation is suddenly made manifest, apart from the writer who records it, is left somewhat ambiguous.

In the first three stories, our narrator is also the story's protagonist; hence if the narrator experiences a "sudden spiritual manifestation," we know that perforce our protagonist has, too. Things get much messier in the remaining twelve stories, though, in which characters are not left to tell their own tales; what confidence do we have that Mr. James Duffy in "A Painful Case," for instance, has in fact come to terms with the revealed human bankruptcy of his life? The proper understanding of these epiphanies, and their proper role in an overall understanding of the *Dubliners* stories, is still a matter of some debate; it might help to suggest the richness of these stories, though, if we note only that truth can certainly be made manifest—to an author, his narrator, even his readers—without that truth ever quite penetrating the thick psychological defenses of his characters. One interesting index of this possible refusal of their epiphanies by various of the *Dubliners* characters is the image of the mirror: Think of Bob Doran, Mrs. Mooney, and her daughter Polly, as each comports him- or herself at the mirror in "The Boarding House"; think of Mr. Duffy, as he is confronted with the image of himself in the laborious, droning train "winding out of Kingsbridge Station"; think, perhaps, of Gabriel Conroy in "The Dead," eschewing light and avoiding mirrors in the Gresham Hotel as his story builds to its tragic climax. Joyce borrowed his term for these dramatically revealing moments from the apparition of the Christ child to the Magi, from the account in the Gospel of Matthew; part of what Joyce so disturbingly suggests, time and again in *Dubliners*, is that contemporary magi would sooner deny the reality of what they had seen, would, like Mr. Duffy, sooner "doubt the reality of what memory" tells them, than come to terms with the difficult changes their revelations would seem to demand of them.

This skepticism about human beings' willingness, or ability, to change is of a piece with Joyce's stylistic regimen, what he called "a style of scrupulous meanness": a style, in other words, that places an absolute moral value on truth-telling. Given the aesthetic detachment from ethical and political concerns evidenced by much twentieth-century literature, Joyce's early remarks about *Dubliners* sound almost naive: He writes to Grant Richards, for instance, that "my intention was to write a chapter of the moral history of my country" (*Letters*, vol. 2, p. 134), and later that "I believe that in composing my chapter of moral history in exactly the way that I have composed it I have taken the first step towards the spiritual liberation of my country" (*Letters*, vol. 1, pp. 62–63). A month later, Joyce further opines that should Richards decide not to publish the book, "I seriously believe that you will retard the course of civilisation in Ireland by preventing the Irish people from having one good look at themselves in my nicely polished looking-glass" (*Letters*, vol. 1, p. 64). Surely comments like these, even as they confirm some of the worst stereotypes of artistic egotism, stand as a healthy corrective to the common depiction of the modernist writers as disaffected aesthetes, unconcerned about the moral or political dimension of their work.

Concerned as he is with the moral paralysis of the people of Dublin—a diagnosis which, Joyce knew well enough, applied equally to the denizens of any modern city—the stories of *Dubliners* at the same time explore the special responsibilities of the man of letters in general, and the artist in particular. The volume's last and greatest story, "The Dead," stands as a case in point; in it, Joyce explores the death-in-life of a handful of Dubliners, but most poignantly, perhaps, that of the story's protagonist, Gabriel Conroy: a figure of what Joyce feared he might have become, had he not left Dublin permanently for the continent in 1904. Gabriel is intelligent, well-educated, a man of the world; he vacations in Belgium, not the west of Ireland, teaches and reviews books, makes learned allusions to Greek mythology and the poetry of Robert Browning in his after-dinner remarks—he even wears galoshes! Yet he is, for all that, another paralytic soul: His nose is put out of joint three different times before dinner is even served, as minor resistance from other guests at his aunts' party (Lily, his wife Gretta, and Molly Ivors) put in peril his oversize yet fragile male ego. He proceeds to use his speech to take revenge on a college friend no longer at the party, and parades his own learning at the expense of his aunts' pleasure; and in the climactic scene at the Gresham Hotel, which includes one of the best known and most beautiful passages in all of modern literature, Gabriel's petulant anger (fueled by a frustrated "pang of lust") ruins an opportunity to know his wife yet more intimately and honestly than hitherto he ever has.

In *Dubliners*, a handful of writers and would-be writers make up a supporting cast: The protagonist-narrators in the first three stories clearly have literary pretensions, as do Little Chandler ("A Little

Cloud"), Mr. Duffy ("A Painful Case"), Joe Hynes ("Ivy Day in the Committee Room"), and Gabriel Conroy. In *A Portrait of the Artist as a Young Man*, of course, a would-be artist is at the absolute center of the novel's action and narration: a presence so central that, in ways that were being fleshed out in physics and astrophysics at the very time Joyce was writing *Portrait,* all other objects are more or less deformed in his field. In the novel, the competing claims of religion and art are laid out, and in chapters 3 and 4, especially, we see them at war: One thing not often remarked upon in the criticism of *Portrait,* however, is that within the novel's pages, it is far from clear that art comes out on top. In the sermons of chapter 3, a poetic and rhetorical inventiveness is brought to bear that dwarfs anything our young artist himself musters; the mystic, scholar, and writer Thomas Merton, for instance, converted to Catholicism as a result of reading them. By comparison, the writing that Stephen himself produces during the course of the novel is pale and bloodless; we read *about* a poem rehearsing romantic platitudes on "the maiden lustre of the moon," for instance, and his artistic production for the period covered in the novel culminates in his "Villanelle of the Temptress," which represents an advance only in that Stephen is parroting fin-de-siècle rather than earlier-century clichés.

The scene describing the writing of Stephen's first poem, in the second "scene" of chapter 2, is instructive. In a passage recalling the discussion of epiphany in *Stephen Hero,* Joyce describes Stephen Dedalus's habits of attention: "He chronicled with patience what he saw, detaching himself from it and testing its mortifying flavour in secret" (p. 58)." What follows, though not labeled as such in the text, are precisely three epiphanies: Two of them, in fact, are based on incidents recorded in Joyce's own epiphany notebook. Like the *Dubliners* stories, these vignettes are spare, closely observed, and slightly mysterious; and the third, describing the tram ride back from Harold's Cross in which Stephen's intials-only love interest E— C— seems eminently embraceable but remains unembraced, is the provocation for the poem Stephen then attempts to write. These three brief prose sketches—based on what we see in *Dubliners,* for instance, as well as the mature prose sections of *Portrait*—represent something like what Joyce thought twentieth-century literature ought to be accomplishing, that "style of scrupulous meanness" he saw as a kind of moral ideal.

In explicit contrast, Stephen's poem is . . . well, strictly speaking, it's just not there at all. We watch Stephen write; but we're shown no writing. Just when it seems that his attempts to write the poem will fail, even by Stephen's standards, he pushes forward by "brooding" on the tram incident, and in the process of writing the poem,

> all those elements which he deemed common and insignificant fell out of the scene. There remained no trace of the tram itself nor of the trammen nor of the horses: nor did he and she appear vividly. The verses told only of the night and the balmy breeze and the maiden lustre of the moon. Some undefined sorrow was hidden in the hearts of the protagonists as they stood in silence beneath the leafless trees and when the moment of farewell had come the kiss, which had been withheld by one, was given by both (p. 6).

Whereas Joyce's own practice insists on focusing on the actual details of a scene until they come starkly into view—chronicling with patience what one sees—his artist "as a young man" instead "broods" (never a good sign, in Joyce) until everything real falls away, and all that's left is a sodden lump of romantic clichés. A sharply observant prose like that of the *Dubliners* stories is written about Stephen's experience, but he himself can write only a vaporous and derivative poetry. (Joyce emphasizes the schoolboy quality of the poem by having Stephen write it in a school exercise book, with the motto *Ad Majoram Dei Gloriam* ["to the greater glory of God"] at the head and *Laus Deo Semper* ["praise to God always"] at its close, the obligatory topoi of his classroom writing exercises under the Jesuits.) As if the point were not yet clear, the paragraph concludes: "Having hidden the book, he went into his mother's bedroom and gazed at his face for a long time in the mirror of her dressing table." A very Narcissus in Dublin.

In the course of this scene, and others beside (compare, for instance, the prose describing the "bird girl" in chapter 5 with the jejune villanelle he makes out of the same episode), Joyce seems to be suggesting that if poetry had been the leading edge of literary innovation in the nineteenth century, it would be prose that would lead the way in the twentieth. (On the far side of the twentieth century now, we can't help but be impressed by Joyce's prescience.) As long as Stephen fetishizes writers like George Gordon, Lord Byron, Percy Bysshe Shelley, and Algernon Charles Swinburne, the authentic literary voice of the twentieth century, the modern world, will remain gagged. As a young writer Joyce first thought of himself as a poet, though had his reputation depended on his poems, his name would now be forgotten: A perusal of Joyce's own first volume of poems, *Chamber Music*, quickly confirms that his prose was as avant-garde as his poetry was derriere-garde. Thus the move from poet to prose writer was one that Joyce knew something about, for it was a move he himself had already made by the time he wrote *Portrait*. As the example of Stephen's first poem makes clear, *Portrait* supports a very complicated narrative structure: It is an autobiographical novel about a former self—a self about whom the author now has some misgivings, even feels some embarrassment. But in strict accordance with what critic Maud Ellmann has called modernism's "poetics of impersonality" (her book bears this title), Joyce forbids himself anything like explicit, third-person commentary on Stephen's beliefs, positions, and actions: The novel contains only dramatic "showing," no authorial "telling," and the aesthetically calculated juxtaposition (the prose and poetic versions of Stephen's tram ride, for instance) is the most explicit commentary Joyce will allow himself. This stealthy mode of criticizing his protagonist, providing a kind of ironic counterpoint, differentiates *Portrait* from the abortive draft *Stephen Hero*, in which Joyce did indulge, in small doses at least, in commentary on the callowness of his protagonist. In *Stephen Hero*, when Stephen flies a bit too high, for instance, the narrative calls him a "fantastic idealist"; in *Portrait*, this kind of criticism must remain always unspoken, merely implied, so that, for example, Stephen believes the most sublime and transcendent moment of *The Count of Monte Cristo* to be Dantes's utterance of his "sadly proud gesture of refusal": "—Madam, I never eat muscatel grapes."

Hence the overarching structural irony of *Portrait*, which has made the tone of the book so very hard for so very many readers over the years to discern: It's a novel about a devotee of an anachronistic literary cult, written by a writer who has himself outgrown his infatuation with that same cult but who writes with a conviction that the only legitimate form of critique is precisely the patient and detached description found in Stephen's epiphanies. Joyce's reluctance to "weigh in" has made for an interesting reception history; as in *Dubliners*, in *Portrait* Joyce seeks to hold up his finely polished looking-glass to us for our inspection. But since we readers tend to identify with, rather than criticize, the aspirations and idealism of Stephen Dedalus—because his foibles are so nearly our own—we have tended not to see Joyce's understated criticism. This, finally, is what makes Joyce's writing in *Dubliners* and *Portrait* so powerful for so many readers: We're never allowed simply to sit in judgment of their characters, but must instead recognize that their follies are our own. We are drawn, propulsively, into an imaginative identification with these characters and their plights. The reader whose heart doesn't respond to Stephen Dedalus's high-flown aspirations ("I go to encounter for the millionth time the reality of experience" [p. 225]), or who doesn't fervently hope that Eveline Hill will get on that ship with Frank, hasn't truly engaged these texts in the spirit with which they were written. Regarding his most famous protagonist, the nineteenth-century French novelist Gustave Flaubert wrote, "Madame Bovary, c'est moi": Flaubert held himself neither superior to, nor different in kind from, his deeply flawed character. And like Flaubert, the reader of *Dubliners* and *Portrait* must be able to say, when she has come to the end: "Gabriel Conroy, c'est moi," and "Stephen Dedalus, c'est moi." For in the letter quoted above, Joyce promises not (as Shakespeare does, in *Hamlet*) to "hold . . . the mirror up to nature"—but instead, much more menacingly, he holds the mirror up before his readers, that they might "[have] one good look at themselves in [his] nicely polished looking-glass."

Portrait, in other words, moves the *Bildungsroman* and the *Kunstlerroman* into the twentieth century, although in the process it drags along with it a resolutely nineteenth-century protagonist. In one of his last diary entries Stephen attempts to outdo his fellow countryman and poet William Butler Yeats. Yeats, who had referred to himself as one of Ireland's "last romantics," expresses the desire through his character Michael Robartes to "press / My heart upon the loveliness / That has long faded from the world" (W. B. Yeats, "He Remembers Forgotten Beauty," *The Wind Among the Reeds*, New York: J. Lane, The Bodley Head, 1899); with even more romantic hunger than Robartes's nostalgic longing betrays, Stephen expresses his desire "to press in my arms the loveliness which has not yet come into the world" (p. 224). While Joyce does not allow the narrative of *Portrait* to level any explicit criticism at Stephen, other characters are free to do so, and seeing the great gulf opened up between Joyce's prose and Stephen's poetry, we might sympathize with Lynch's closing comment on Stephen's discourse on aesthetic philosophy: "—What do you mean, Lynch asked surlily, by prating about beauty and the imagination in this miserable God forsaken island?" (p. 191). What, indeed?

One point upon which these two books agree is the absolutely fundamental role that language plays in our being-in-the-world; in both *Dubliners* and *Portrait*, Joyce forces us to pay careful attention to the language in which we cast our dreams, and to which we perforce bend our realities. Here again Joyce anticipates new discoveries made in the sciences, in this case the human science of linguistics. The idea, called in one of its early formulations the "Whorfian hypothesis," is that we never use language without language at the same time using us: Language is not merely descriptive of, but in fact constitutive of, what we know as "reality." Words, Joyce realized early on, always drag along with them the history of their prior associations and usages; words, in one sense, are never purely aesthetic objects, "certain good" in Yeats's phrase, but are always already political objects. Stephen recognizes this, if inchoately, when he muses on the English-born dean of studies' condescending attention to Stephen's use of the word "tundish":

—The language in which we are speaking is his before it is mine. How different are the words home, Christ, ale, master, on his lips and on mine! I cannot speak or write these words without unrest of spirit. His language, so familiar and so foreign, will always be for me an acquired speech. I have not made or accepted its words. My voice holds them at bay. My soul frets in the shadow of his language (p. 167).

While Stephen may desire to press in his arms "the loveliness which has not yet come into the world," there is an awareness at the textual level, if not perhaps at a conscious level, for Stephen, that he has not "made or accepted" the words of any human tongue, but must instead accept them at second hand. And this hand-me-down language, Stephen can't help but notice from the very earliest pages of the novel, is always somewhat shopworn. Stephen's vision of pure artistic creation from nothing (*ex nihilo*), something completely fresh and new, requires a pristine and univocal language: And yet everywhere, language equivocates. In the same conversation with the dean of studies, Stephen calls attention to this problem, using as his example the various connotations of the word "detain"; and confirming his worst fears, the dean misunderstands Stephen's point initially because his own usage is loose and sloppy. In *Alice in Wonderland* (a text that enthralled Joyce, as *Finnegans Wake* clearly evidences), Humpty Dumpty insists to Alice that "When I use a word it means just what I choose it to mean"; like Humpty Dumpty, Stephen would like to exert complete mastery over language and meaning, but his experience consistently brings home the fact that none of us has such power. He may complain, in *Ulysses*, that "history is a nightmare from which I am trying to awake," but he realizes that he must do so in a language conditioned by that very history.

The inherently equivocal structure of language (and to be clear, this is the structure of all human languages, not just English)—language's consistent difference from itself—has both this historical dimension and another, ahistorical component. The words upon which Stephen muses while talking with the dean of studies, "home," "Christ," "ale," and "master," all resonate differently for Stephen owing to the history of colonial subjection of Ireland by Great Britain; for the ambiguity of these words, to quote the Englishman Haines in *Ulysses*, "it seems history is to blame." But even if this history could be factored out, language is always at odds with itself. The French philosopher Jacques Derrida has termed this frustrating and elusive structure of language *différence*; it means that the momentum of writing is always centrifugal, always toward what Derrida calls the "dissemination" of meaning, rather than its consolidation, as the idealized will of its author, in a text. In his best-known example, Derrida examines the way that the word "supplement" (which he comes across in a passage from Jean-Jacques Rousseau) means both "surplus" and "remedy for a deficit": The supplement is the surplus that (inadvertently) betrays a lack. Such, according to Derrida, is the fundamental structure of all human language.

Though no linguist, Joyce seems intuitively to have had a sense of this dynamic; this principle is observable on both the level of the individual word, and on the larger level of phrases, sentences, and narrative units, in all of Joyce's writing. (In an early example, Joyce punningly titled his first volume of poems *Chamber Music*, betraying both the poems' delicate beauty and invoking the sound of urine in a chamberpot.) The truth of language's inherent slipperiness is first made manifest to Stephen Dedalus just a couple of pages into *Portrait*. Stephen, cold while playing football in the fall air,

> kept his hands in the side pockets of his belted grey suit. That was a belt round his pocket. And belt was also to give a fellow a belt. One day a fellow had said to Cantwell:
> —I'd give you such a belt in a second (p. 6).

Belt as security, belt as violence: "belt," it would seem, is an especially paradoxical word, something like its own antonym. In truth, however, as Stephen soon discovers, language is full of similarly slippery terms: In quick succession he is given to contemplating the mystery of words like "suck," "queer," and most famously of all, "smugging." Indeed at the very close of the novel, which the diary-entry form suggests that Stephen himself has written, the final formulation of his artistic credo

is undermined by just such a slippage: "Welcome, O life! I go to encounter for the millionth time the reality of experience and to forge in
the smithy of my soul the uncreated conscience of my race" (p. 225).
"Forge," like the good old English word "cleave," is its own antonym.
Using the metaphor of a blacksmith working metal, Stephen promises
to "forge . . . the uncreated conscience of his race," by heating and ham-
mering the red-hot metal of the English language, bending it to his
will. But to forge is also, of course, to counterfeit: Forgery, whether in
one's smithy or in one's basement, is an act of criminal deception, an attempt to pass off the ersatz as the genuine article. Is Stephen aware of
the equivocation in his declaration, the *différence* between intention and
utterance, the dissemination of his meaning every which way? We cannot know the answer to this question; the next sentence is the text's last,
as Stephen invokes the protection and aid of his mythic forebear, the
Dædalus of the novel's epigraph. But there may be, too, a meaningful
difference between Stephen's own awareness of his writing's betrayal, or
lack thereof, and our understanding as readers. Perhaps, even if Stephen
has not, we are able to enjoy a kind of hard-won epiphany; and while
our "artist as a young man" wrestles to make an intractable language
conform to his meaning, his author instead focuses our attention on the
stubborn materiality and historicity of language. A wiser writer—like
Joyce, perhaps—would learn to work in accord with language's stubborn resistances, rather than trying in vain to master them.

As suggested earlier, it's not simply individual words that slip—as if
that weren't bad enough. But phrases, too, sometimes carry with them
untoward baggage, refusing to mean simply what they appear to say.
On an early page of the novel, for instance, the affluence of one of
Stephen's classmates at Clongowes Wood School is invoked: "Rody
Kickham had greaves in his number and a hamper in the refectory." A
hamper in the refectory means simply that Rody Kickham has a private
supply of food available to him in the dining hall—a luxury that
Stephen's family certainly cannot afford for him. The phrase "greaves in
his number," however, is a bit more layered. The standard annotations
will tell us that it means "shin-guards in his locker," suggesting the possibility that shin-guards are not issued to all the boys at Clongowes as
standard equipment: Again, the Kickham family's wealth buys young
Rody a degree of luxury that Stephen cannot afford, and when playing
football Rody gets kicked in the greaves, while Stephen takes it in the
shins. However, a look into the historical *Oxford English Dictionary*
suggests a further dimension: The word "greaves" is quite rare, out of

use since the late nineteenth century, and the *OED* gives as its literary exemplars passages from an obscure poem of Lord Byron, "The Bride of Abydos," as well as a passage from a far more familiar poem of Alfred, Lord Tennyson, "The Lady of Shallot": "The sun came dazzling thro' the leaves, / And flamed upon the brazen greaves / Of bold Sir Lancelot." Hence "greaves" isn't just any old word for shin-guards, but a particularly literary one (the *OED* also tells us that the word "shin-guards" was in use back in the 1880s); further, it's not just literary language, but language retaining the flavor of its earlier usage in Tennyson: an identifiably Tennysonian affectation on Stephen's part (if, as is common in the criticism, we assume Stephen's consciousness to be shaping, if not exactly writing, the prose of this section). With this Tennyson connection unearthed, it's easy to look back to a sentence earlier in the paragraph and find Tennyson's fingerprints there, too: "The evening air was pale and chilly and after every charge and thud of the foot-ballers the greasy leather orb flew like a heavy bird through the grey light" sounds a lot more like something from *Idylls of the King* or "The Charge of the Light Brigade" or even "The Lady of Shallot" once we're alerted to Tennyson's lurking presence in the passage. Further, the early flirtation with Tennyson that lingers around these images and archaisms sheds an interesting light on a later episode in the novel, when Stephen is beaten up by his classmate Heron and his goons for suggesting that Byron is a better poet than the "rhymster" Tennyson. Stephen's Tennysonianism suggests he had not always thought so.

Moving up one level, we witness Stephen's growing attraction to the story of the "dark avenger" of *The Count of Monte Cristo* throughout the first two chapters of the novel. Stephen's grasp on the specifics of the plot seem somewhat shaky, but one thing he knows for certain:

He wanted to meet in the real world the unsubstantial image [of the love interest in *Monte Cristo*, Mercedes] which his soul so constantly beheld. He did not know where to seek it or how but a premonition which led him on told him that this image would, without any overt act of his, encounter him. They would meet quietly as if they had known each other and had made their tryst, perhaps at one of the gates or in some more secret place. They would be alone, surrounded by darkness and silence: and in that moment of supreme tenderness he would be transfigured. He would fade into something impalpable under her eyes and then in a moment, he would be transfigured. Weakness and timidity and inexperience would fall from him in that magic moment (p. 56).

While Stephen seems to be imagining some sort of amorous tryst, his imagination has not yet been fed any of the stark details of actual, physical sex: Like his poem about riding the tram home with E— C— just a few pages later, his inexperience leads him here to the brink of a scene that he is unable to imagine. *The Count of Monte Cristo*, too, is evasive on these questions; and precisely because the story he wishes to act out has skirted the issue, Stephen's imagination runs into a kind of wall when the actual moment of his "fall" is to take place.

Stephen's fall from sexual innocence into experience takes place in the closing pages of chapter 2; and when he wanders into the red-light Nighttown district of Dublin, and ends up in the bed of a prostitute, every feature of his earlier fantasy centering on Mercedes is ironically fulfilled. Not knowing where to look for Mercedes, his feet seemingly of their own accord take him "into a maze of narrow and dirty streets." He knows that his role in his encounter with his Mercedes will be entirely passive, and in his transaction with the prostitute, Stephen "would not bend to kiss her," and later "swoons" or perhaps, less poetically, passes out. He does indeed "fade into something impalpable under her eyes"; but this is *Monte Cristo* with an ironic difference. With the veil of a romantic fantasy interposing itself between Stephen and the prostitute, it's almost as if he's not present at his own deflowering. The narrative, in this case, both trumps and dictates the real.

One lesson, then, that we might take away from these two exquisitely well written books is that narrative in particular, and language in general, is in a sense the "prison-house" that German philosopher Friedrich Nietzsche, another near-contemporary of Joyce's, claimed that it was: Reality, or "the reality of experience," is unavailable to human vessels excepting through the somewhat distorting vehicle of human language. Some, like young Stephen Dedalus, might expend their energies wishing for, working for, a language that would escape all such limitations: a sort of pre-Babel super-language, infinitely adaptable to the infinitely shifting shapes of the real. Another response suggests itself, however—one that Joyce was to work out in greater detail, and with greater care, in his next novel, *Ulysses*: that if stories are the only means we have to "encounter reality," it matters very much which stories we carry around in our heads. *Dubliners* and *A Portrait of the Artist as a Young Man*, both stories that, on one level, counsel caution about the stories with which we furnish our imaginations, make a very good start.

Kevin J. H. Dettmar is Professor of modern British and Irish literary and cultural studies at Southern Illinois University at Carbondale. He has published a study of James Joyce and the stylistics of postmodernism and has edited or coedited three volumes of essays: on modernism's relationship to commodity culture, on the intersections of literary modernism and postmodernism, and on theoretical approaches to contemporary popular music. He also serves as coeditor of the twentieth-century materials for the *Longman Anthology of British Literature,* and as a chapter coordinator for the *James Joyce's "Ulysses" in Hypermedia* project. He is past president and member of the Executive Board for the international Modernist Studies Association.

Dettmar is currently researching and writing two studies that reflect the range of his scholarly interests: one, a book on the cultural history of the notion that "rock is dead," and the other, a study of James Joyce's relationship to the Great Books tradition.

NOTE ON CURRENCY AND COINAGE

During the early years of the twentieth century, during which the events of the *Dubliners* stories and *A Portrait of the Artist as a Young Man* take place, Ireland was part of the United Kingdom and used British money.

Until Great Britain switched to a decimal system for its money in 1971, with 100 pence to the pound, British money followed a somewhat idiosyncratic system. The chart below gives the primary denominations of pre-1971 British money, along with any slang terms, and the approximate buying power these denominations would have represented in 1910, given in current (2004) U.S. dollars.

Coin or note	Abbrev.	Equivalency	Slang	Current U.S. dollar equivalent
Farthing	1/4d.	1/4 pence	copper	$0.10
Half penny	1/2d.	1/2 pence	ha'penny; copper	$0.20
Pence *or* penny	1d.	1 penny	copper	$0.39
Twopence	2d.	2 pence	copper	$0.78
Threepence	3d.	3 pence	thruppenny bit	$1.17
Sixpence	6d.	6 pence	sixpenny bit; tanner	$2.34
Shilling	1s.	12d. = 1 shilling	bob	$4.68
Florin	2s.	2 shillings		$9.36
Half crown	2s. 6d.	2 shillings, 6 pence		$11.70
Double florin	4s.	4 shillings		$18.72
Crown	5s.	5 shillings		$23.40
Half pound	10s.	10 shillings		$46.80
Pound	1£	240d. = 20s. = 1 pound	quid	$93.60
Sovereign (coin)	1£	1 pound		$93.60
Guinea	1£ 1s.	1 pound, 1 shilling		$98.28

NOTE ON THE TEXTS

The copy text for our edition of *Dubliners* is the 1914 first edition (first printing), published in London by Grant Richards; that for *A Portrait of the Artist as a Young Man*, the 1916 first edition (fifth printing, 1922) published in New York by W. B. Huebsch. Many factors have contributed to the appearance of errors in these early editions; Joyce complained to Richards, for instance, that he read the page proofs of *Dubliners* very quickly because he expected to be sent a second set of proofs, which never materialized. For this edition obvious errors have been silently emended.

The punctuation of direct speech in Joyce's fiction is an area that has attracted a good deal of scholarly attention over the years. In standard British usage—and though an Irishman, Joyce wrote as a (somewhat reluctant) British subject until Irish independence was granted in 1922—direct speech is ordinarily indicated by enclosure between single quotation marks, or inverted commas:

'He was too scrupulous always,' she said.

Joyce thought this convention unsightly; he referred jokingly to the punctuation as "perverted commas," and pleaded with the London publisher of *Dubliners* to use dashes instead to indicate direct speech. As it was first typeset, *Dubliners* did in fact indicate direct speech by enclosing it between em-dashes:

—He was too scrupulous always,—she said.

But this edition, printed for Maunsel & Co. in Dublin, was destroyed before being distributed, and this typography never saw the light of day (Maunsel feared being sued for obscenity and/or libel). When the book was re-set for the Richards publication, the dashes were changed back to the conventional inverted commas.

With *A Portrait*, however, Joyce got something closer to his wishes. The Huebsch edition indicates direct speech with an introductory dash:

—O, Stephen will apologise.

But the convention in this edition is employed inconsistently; indeed, the very next quotation on the same page uses not just a single introductory dash, but a closing dash as well:

—O, if not, the eagles will come and pull out his eyes.—

For the most part, the first half of the novel punctuates direct speech with a single, introductory dash; but halfway through the novel, the convention switches to both introductory and closing dashes, with no apparent textual logic to support the switch.

Finally, British publishing conventions dictate that for a quotation embedded within direct speech, double quotation marks be enclosed within single quotation marks:

'Annoyed! Not he! "Manly little chap!" he said.'

In the early printings of *Portrait*, however, in which dashes are used to introduce direct speech, italics are (irregularly) used to indicate a quotation within direct speech, and that convention has been adopted in this edition:

—Annoyed! Not he! *Manly little chap,* he said.

Given this hodgepodge of editorial decisions—and with little sense of which of these conventions Joyce finally preferred—we have chosen to punctuate direct speech uniformly with the single introductory dash, a technique that we know Joyce favored by the time *Ulysses* was published in 1922. In that novel, it is clear that Joyce valued the ambiguity a single introductory dash lent to a paragraph that might begin with direct speech but then wander off into interior monologue or even third-person narration, with these different registers of discourse remaining unmarked. While the clues to Joyce's preferred style early in his career are somewhat contradictory, by the time he was in a position to have his texts set in the way he wanted, he chose to indicate where a quotation began, but not where it ended. This willful ambiguity is altogether characteristic of the slippery stylistics of the greatest English prose writer of the twentieth century.

LIST OF MAPS

A PORTRAIT OF THE ARTIST
AS A YOUNG MAN

Et ignotas animum dimittit in artes.

Ovid, Metamorphoses, VIII, 188*

---

*And he applies his mind to obscure arts (Latin); said of Dædalus, who, in a Greek myth, made wings for himself and his son, Icarus, to escape the labyrinth of the Minotaur.

CHAPTER I

ONCE UPON A TIME and a very good time it was there was a moocow coming down along the road and this moocow that was down along the road met a nicens little boy named baby tuckoo. . . .

His father told him that story: his father looked at him through a glass:* he had a hairy face.

He was baby tuckoo. The moocow came down the road where Betty Byrne lived: she sold lemon platt.†

> O, the wild rose blossoms
> On the little green place.‡

He sang that song. That was his song.

> O, the green wothe botheth.

When you wet the bed, first it is warm then it gets cold. His mother put on the oilsheet.§ That had the queer‖ smell.

His mother had a nicer smell than his father. She played on the piano the sailor's hornpipe# for him to dance. He danced:

> Tralala lala,
> Tralala tralaladdy,
> Tralala lala,
> Tralala lala.

---

*Monocle.
†Candy.
‡From the song "Lily Dale"; in this bowdlerized version, the word "grave" in the second line is replaced with "place."
§Waterproof sheet used in cases of bedwetting.
‖Strange.
#Dance tune.

Uncle Charles and Dante* clapped. They were older than his father and mother but Uncle Charles was older than Dante.

Dante had two brushes in her press.† The brush with the maroon velvet back was for Michael Davitt and the brush with the green velvet back was for Parnell.[1] Dante gave him a cachou‡ every time he brought her a piece of tissue paper.

The Vances lived in number seven. They had a different father and mother. They were Eileen's father and mother. When they were grown up he was going to marry Eileen. He hid under the table. His mother said:

—O, Stephen will apologise.

Dante said:

—O, if not, the eagles will come and pull out his eyes.

> *Pull out his eyes,*
> *Apologise,*
> *Apologise,*
> *Pull out his eyes.*

> *Apologise,*
> *Pull out his eyes,*
> *Pull out his eyes,*
> *Apologise.*

* * * *

The wide playgrounds were swarming with boys. All were shouting and the prefects§ urged them on with strong cries. The evening air was pale and chilly and after every charge and thud of the foot-ballers the greasy leather orb flew like a heavy bird through the grey light. He kept on the fringe of his line,‖ out of sight of his prefect, out of the reach of the rude feet, feigning to run now and then. He felt his body small and weak amid the throng of players and his eyes were weak and watery. Rody Kickham was not like that: he would be captain of the third line all the fellows said.

---

*Stephen's childish pronunciation of "auntie."
†Cupboard or cabinet.
‡Lozenge.
§Teachers.
‖His age- and grade-level cohort in the school.

Chapter 1

Howth.

Dublin Bay

Kingstown (now Dun Laoghaire)

Dalkey

Blackrock

Dublin

Poolbeg Point

Grand Canal

Ennisterry

Bray

Brayhead

Greystones

Newtown Mt. Kennedy

Roundwood

Vartry Reservoir

Lough

Wicklow

D u b l i n   o r
W i c k l o w   M o u n t a i n s

Lughill

Hill of Lyons at 651'

Celbridge Wood College

Straffan House

Leixlip

Maynooth

Kilcock

Clane

Sallins

Naas

Blessington

Lackan Reservoir

Eustace

River Liffey

Kilcullen

Railway (Dublin to Cork)

Hill of Allen at 676'

Grand Canal

Kildare

Athy

Scale   2 1 0   2   4   6 miles

Rody Kickham was a decent fellow but Nasty Roche was a stink. Rody Kickham had greaves in his number* and a hamper in the refectory. Nasty Roche had big hands. He called the Friday pudding dog-in-the-blanket. And one day he had asked:

—What is your name?

Stephen had answered: Stephen Dedalus.

Then Nasty Roche had said:

—What kind of a name is that?

And when Stephen had not been able to answer Nasty Roche had asked:

—What is your father?

Stephen had answered:

—A gentleman.

Then Nasty Roche had asked:

—Is he a magistrate?

He crept about from point to point on the fringe of his line, making little runs now and then. But his hands were bluish with cold. He kept his hands in the side pockets of his belted grey suit. That was a belt round his pocket. And belt was also to give a fellow a belt. One day a fellow had said to Cantwell:

—I'd give you such a belt in a second.

Cantwell had answered:

—Go and fight your match. Give Cecil Thunder a belt. I'd like to see you. He'd give you a toe in the rump for yourself.

That was not a nice expression. His mother had told him not to speak with the rough boys in the college.† Nice mother! The first day in the hall of the castle‡ when she had said goodbye she had put up her veil double to her nose to kiss him: and her nose and eyes were red. But he had pretended not to see that she was going to cry. She was a nice mother but she was not so nice when she cried. And his father had given him two five-shilling pieces for pocket money. And his father had told him if he wanted anything to write home to him and, whatever he did, never to peach§ on a fellow. Then at the door of the castle the rector‖

---

*Football shin-guards in his locker.

†Here, not a post-secondary institution but a private boys' preparatory school.

‡Clongowes Wood College, which still operates today, is housed in buildings originally constructed as a castle.

§To inform; to "fink" or "rat" on someone.

‖Chief administrator of the college.

had shaken hands with his father and mother, his soutane* fluttering in the breeze, and the car had driven off with his father and mother on it. They had cried to him from the car, waving their hands:

—Good-bye, Stephen, goodbye!

—Good-bye, Stephen, goodbye!

He was caught in the whirl of a scrimmage and, fearful of the flashing eyes and muddy boots, bent down to look through the legs. The fellows were struggling and groaning and their legs were rubbing and kicking and stamping. Then Jack Lawton's yellow boots dodged out the ball and all the other boots and legs ran after. He ran after them a little way and then stopped. It was useless to run on. Soon they would be going home for the holidays. After supper in the study hall he would change the number pasted up inside his desk from seventyseven to seventysix.

It would be better to be in the study hall than out there in the cold. The sky was pale and cold but there were lights in the castle. He wondered from which window Hamilton Rowan[†] had thrown his hat on the haha[‡] and had there been flowerbeds at that time under the windows. One day when he had been called to the castle the butler had shown him the marks of the soldiers' slugs in the wood of the door and had given him a piece of shortbread that the community[§] ate. It was nice and warm to see the lights in the castle. It was like something in a book. Perhaps Leicester Abbey[||] was like that. And there were nice sentences in Doctor Cornwell's Spelling Book. They were like poetry but they were only sentences to learn the spelling from.

> *Wolsey died in Leicester Abbey*
> *Where the abbots buried him.*
> *Canker is a disease of plants,*
> *Cancer one of animals.*

It would be nice to lie on the hearthrug before the fire, leaning his head upon his hands, and think on those sentences. He shivered as if

---

*Long, black gown worn by the Jesuits.
†Irish patriot and friend of Irish republican Wolfe Tone (see footnote on p. 162) who sought shelter in the castle in 1794 when wanted by the British authorities.
‡Barrier, such as a fence, set within a ditch.
§Religious group—in this case, the Jesuits.
||Abbey 100 miles northwest of London; Cardinal Thomas Wolsey (1475–1530) died there.

he had cold slimy water next his skin. That was mean of Wells to shoulder him into the square ditch* because he would not swop his little snuffbox for Wells's seasoned hacking chestnut,† the conqueror of forty. How cold and slimy the water had been! A fellow had once seen a big rat jump into the scum. Mother was sitting at the fire with Dante waiting for Brigid to bring in the tea. She had her feet on the fender‡ and her jewelly slippers were so hot and they had such a lovely warm smell! Dante knew a lot of things. She had taught him where the Mozambique Channel was and what was the longest river in America and what was the name of the highest mountain in the moon. Father Arnall knew more than Dante because he was a priest but both his father and Uncle Charles said that Dante was a clever woman and a wellread woman. And when Dante made that noise after dinner and then put up her hand to her mouth: that was heartburn.

A voice cried far out on the playground:

—All in!

Then other voices cried from the lower and third lines:

—All in! All in!

The players closed around, flushed and muddy, and he went among them, glad to go in. Rody Kickham held the ball by its greasy lace. A fellow asked him to give it one last: but he walked on without even answering the fellow. Simon Moonan told him not to because the prefect was looking. The fellow turned to Simon Moonan and said:

—We all know why you speak. You are McGlade's suck.§

Suck was a queer word. The fellow called Simon Moonan that name because Simon Moonan used to tie the prefect's false sleeves behind his back and the prefect used to let on to be angry. But the sound was ugly. Once he had washed his hands in the lavatory of the Wicklow Hotel‖ and his father pulled the stopper up by the chain after and the dirty water went down through the hole in the basin. And when it had all gone down slowly the hole in the basin had made a sound like that: suck. Only louder.

To remember that and the white look of the lavatory made him feel

---

*Open cesspool on the school grounds.
†Chestnut used in a children's game, in which one chestnut was swung by an attached string against another until one was destroyed.
‡Protective metal guard in front of a fireplace.
§Obsequious favorite; we would say "teacher's pet."
‖Hotel in downtown Dublin.

cold and then hot. There were two cocks that you turned and water came out: cold and hot. He felt cold and then a little hot: and he could see the names printed on the cocks. That was a very queer thing.

And the air in the corridor chilled him too. It was queer and wettish. But soon the gas would be lit and in burning it made a light noise like a little song. Always the same: and when the fellows stopped talking in the playroom you could hear it.

It was the hour for sums. Father Arnall wrote a hard sum on the board and then said:

—Now then, who will win? Go ahead, York! Go ahead, Lancaster!*

Stephen tried his best but the sum was too hard and he felt confused. The little silk badge with the white rose on it that was pinned on the breast of his jacket began to flutter. He was no good at sums but he tried his best so that York might not lose. Father Arnall's face looked very black but he was not in a wax:† he was laughing. Then Jack Lawton cracked his fingers and Father Arnall looked at his copybook and said:

Right. Bravo Lancaster! The red rose wins. Come on now, York! Forge ahead!

Jack Lawton looked over from his side. The little silk badge with the red rose on it looked very rich because he had a blue sailor top on. Stephen felt his own face red too, thinking of all the bets about who would get first place in Elements,‡ Jack Lawton or he. Some weeks Jack Lawton got the card for first and some weeks he got the card for first. His white silk badge fluttered and fluttered as he worked at the next sum and heard Father Arnall's voice. Then all his eagerness passed away and he felt his face quite cool. He thought his face must be white because it felt so cool. He could get out the answer for the sum but it did not matter. White roses and red roses: those were beautiful colours to think of. And the cards for first place and third place were beautiful colours too: pink and cream and lavender. Lavender and cream and pink roses were beautiful to think of. Perhaps a wild rose might be like those colours and he remembered the song about the wild rose blossoms on the little green place. But you could not have a green rose. But perhaps somewhere in the world you could.

---

*The houses (families) York and Lancaster were the opponents in the Wars of the Roses (1455–1485).
†Fit of anger.
‡Early schooling in spelling, arithmetic, geography, history, Latin, and writing.

The bell rang and then the classes began to file out of the rooms and along the corridors towards the refectory. He sat looking at the two prints of butter on his plate but could not eat the damp bread. The tablecloth was damp and limp. But he drank off the hot weak tea which the clumsy scullion, girt with a white apron, poured into his cup. He wondered whether the scullion's apron was damp too or whether all white things were cold and damp. Nasty Roche and Saurin drank cocoa that their people sent them in tins. They said they could not drink the tea; that it was hogwash. Their fathers were magistrates, the fellows said.

All the boys seemed to him very strange. They had all fathers and mothers and different clothes and voices. He longed to be at home and lay his head on his mother's lap. But he could not: and so he longed for the play and study and prayers to be over and to be in bed.

He drank another cup of hot tea and Fleming said:

—What's up? Have you a pain or what's up with you?

—I don't know, Stephen said.

—Sick in your bread basket, Fleming said, because your face looks white. It will go away.

—O yes, Stephen said.

But he was not sick there. He thought that he was sick in his heart if you could be sick in that place. Fleming was very decent to ask him. He wanted to cry. He leaned his elbows on the table and shut and opened the flaps of his ears. Then he heard the noise of the refectory every time he opened the flaps of his ears. It made a roar like a train at night. And when he closed the flaps the roar was shut off like a train going into a tunnel. That night at Dalkey* the train had roared like that and then, when it went into the tunnel, the roar stopped. He closed his eyes and the train went on, roaring and then stopping; roaring again, stopping. It was nice to hear it roar and stop and then roar out of the tunnel again and then stop.

Then the higher line[2] fellows began to come down along the matting in the middle of the refectory, Paddy Rath and Jimmy Magee and the Spaniard who was allowed to smoke cigars and the little Portuguese who wore the woolly cap. And then the lower line tables and the tables of the third line. And every single fellow had a different way of walking.

---

*Affluent suburb on the coast south of Dublin, in County Wicklow.

He sat in a corner of the playroom pretending to watch a game of dominos and once or twice he was able to hear for an instant the little song of the gas. The prefect was at the door with some boys and Simon Moonan was knotting his false sleeves. He was telling them something about Tullabeg.*

Then he went away from the door and Wells came over to Stephen and said:

—Tell us, Dedalus, do you kiss your mother before you go to bed?

Stephen answered:

—I do.

Wells turned to the other fellows and said:

—O, I say, here's a fellow says he kisses his mother every night before he goes to bed.

The other fellows stopped their game and turned round, laughing. Stephen blushed under their eyes and said:

—I do not.

Wells said:

—O, I say, here's a fellow says he doesn't kiss his mother before he goes to bed.

They all laughed again. Stephen tried to laugh with them. He felt his whole body hot and confused in a moment. What was the right answer to the question? He had given two and still Wells laughed. But Wells must know the right answer for he was in third of grammar. He tried to think of Wells's mother but he did not dare to raise his eyes to Wells's face. He did not like Wells's face. It was Wells who had shouldered him into the square ditch the day before because he would not swop his little snuffbox for Wells's seasoned hacking chestnut, the conqueror of forty. It was a mean thing to do; all the fellows said it was. And how cold and slimy the water had been! And a fellow had once seen a big rat jump plop into the scum.

The cold slime of the ditch covered his whole body; and, when the bell rang for study and the lines filed out of the playrooms, he felt the cold air of the corridor and staircase inside his clothes. He still tried to think what was the right answer. Was it right to kiss his mother or wrong to kiss his mother? What did that mean, to kiss? You put your face up like that to say goodnight and then his mother put her face down. That was to kiss. His mother put her lips on his cheek; her lips

---

*County Offaly location of the Jesuit novitiate.

were soft and they wetted his cheek; and they made a tiny little noise: kiss. Why did people do that with their two faces?

Sitting in the study hall he opened the lid of his desk and changed the number pasted up inside from seventyseven to seventysix. But the Christmas vacation was very far away: but one time it would come because the earth moved round always.

There was a picture of the earth on the first page of his geography: a big ball in the middle of clouds. Fleming had a box of crayons and one night during free study he had coloured the earth green and the clouds maroon. That was like the two brushes in Dante's press, the brush with the green velvet back for Parnell and the brush with the maroon velvet back for Michael Davitt. But he had not told Fleming to colour them those colours. Fleming had done it himself.

He opened the geography to study the lesson; but he could not learn the names of places in America. Still they were all different places that had different names. They were all in different countries and the countries were in continents and the continents were in the world and the world was in the universe.

He turned to the flyleaf of the geography and read what he had written there: himself, his name and where he was.

> *Stephen Dedalus*
> *Class of Elements*
> *Clongowes Wood College*
> *Sallins*
> *County Kildare*
> *Ireland*
> *Europe*
> *The World*
> *The Universe*

That was in his writing: and Fleming one night for a cod had written on the opposite page:

> *Stephen Dedalus is my name,*
> *Ireland is my nation.*
> *Clongowes is my dwellingplace*
> *And heaven my expectation.*

He read the verses backwards but then they were not poetry. Then he read the flyleaf from the bottom to the top till he came to his own name. That was he: and he read down the page again. What was after the universe? Nothing. But was there anything round the universe to show where it stopped before the nothing place began? It could not be a wall but there could be a thin thin line there all round everything. It was very big to think about everything and everywhere. Only God could do that. He tried to think what a big thought that must be but he could think only of God. God was God's name just as his name was Stephen. *Dieu* was the French for God and that was God's name too; and when anyone prayed to God and said Dieu then God knew at once that it was a French person that was praying. But though there were different names for God in all the different languages in the world and God understood what all the people who prayed said in their different languages still God remained always the same God and God's real name was God.

It made him very tired to think that way. It made him feel his head very big. He turned over the flyleaf and looked wearily at the green round earth in the middle of the maroon clouds. He wondered which was right, to be for the green or for the maroon, because Dante had ripped the green velvet back off the brush that was for Parnell one day with her scissors and had told him that Parnell was a bad man. He wondered if they were arguing at home about that. That was called politics. There were two sides in it: Dante was on one side and his father and Mr. Casey were on the other side but his mother and Uncle Charles were on no side. Every day there was something in the paper about it.

It pained him that he did not know well what politics meant and that he did not know where the universe ended. He felt small and weak. When would he be like the fellows in Poetry and Rhetoric? They had big voices and big boots and they studied trigonometry. That was very far away. First came the vacation and then the next term and then vacation again and then again another term and then again the vacation. It was like a train going in and out of tunnels and that was like the noise of the boys eating in the refectory when you opened and closed the flaps of the ears. Term, vacation; tunnel, out; noise, stop. How far away it was! It was better to go to bed to sleep. Only prayers in the chapel and then bed. He shivered and yawned. It would be lovely in bed after the sheets got a bit hot. First they were so cold to get into. He shivered to think how cold they were first. But then they got hot and then he could sleep. It was lovely to be tired. He yawned again. Night prayers and then bed: he shivered and wanted to yawn. It would be lovely in a few minutes. He felt a warm glow creeping up from the cold shivering sheets, warmer and warmer till he felt warm all over, ever so warm and yet he shivered a little and still wanted to yawn.

The bell rang for night prayers and he filed out of the study hall after the others and down the staircase and along the corridors to the chapel. The corridors were darkly lit and the chapel was darkly lit. Soon all would be dark and sleeping. There was cold night air in the chapel and the marbles were the colour the sea was at night. The sea was cold day and night: but it was colder at night. It was cold and dark under the seawall beside his father's house. But the kettle would be on the hob* to make punch.†

The prefect of the chapel prayed above his head and his memory knew the responses:

> *O Lord, open our lips*
> *And our mouths shall announce Thy praise.*
> *Incline unto our aid, O God!*
> *O Lord, make haste to help us!*‡

There was a cold night smell in the chapel. But it was a holy smell. It was not like the smell of the old peasants who knelt at the back of the chapel at Sunday mass. That was a smell of air and rain and turf§ and corduroy. But they were very holy peasants. They breathed behind him on his neck and sighed as they prayed. They lived in Clane,‖ a fellow said: there were little cottages there and he had seen a woman standing at the halfdoor of a cottage with a child in her arms, as the cars# had come past from Sallins. It would be lovely to sleep for one night in that cottage before the fire of smoking turf, in the warm dark, breathing the smell of the peasants, air and rain and turf and corduroy. But, O, the road there between the trees was dark! You would be lost in the dark. It made him afraid to think of how it was.

---

*Shelf within a fireplace.
†Hot whiskey punch, or "toddy."
‡The opening lines of matins, early-morning prayers.
§Peat, dried and burned as fuel.
‖Village near Clongowes.
#Horse-drawn hackney coaches, or "hacks."

He heard the voice of the prefect of the chapel saying the last prayer.
He prayed it too against the dark outside under the trees.

*Visit, we beseech Thee, O Lord, this habitation and drive away from it all
the snares of the enemy. May Thy holy angels dwell herein to preserve us
in peace and may Thy blessing be always upon us through Christ our Lord.
Amen.**

His fingers trembled as he undressed himself in the dormitory. He
told his fingers to hurry up. He had to undress and then kneel and say
his own prayers and be in bed before the gas was lowered so that he
might not go to hell when he died. He rolled his stockings off and put
on his nightshirt quickly and knelt trembling at his bedside and repeated his prayers quickly, fearing that the gas would go down. He felt
his shoulders shaking as he murmured:

God bless my father and my mother and spare them to me!
God bless my little brothers and sisters and spare them to me!
God bless Dante and Uncle Charles and spare them to me!

He blessed himself and climbed quickly into bed and, tucking the
end of the nightshirt under his feet, curled himself together under the
cold white sheets, shaking and trembling. But he would not go to hell
when he died; and the shaking would stop. A voice bade the boys in the
dormitory goodnight. He peered out for an instant over the coverlet
and saw the yellow curtains round and before his bed that shut him off
on all sides. The light was lowered quietly.

The prefect's shoes went away. Where? Down the staircase and
along the corridors or to his room at the end? He saw the dark. Was it
true about the black dog that walked there at night with eyes as big as
carriagelamps? They said it was the ghost of a murderer. A long shiver
of fear flowed over his body. He saw the dark entrance hall of the castle. Old servants in old dress were in the ironing room above the staircase. It was long ago. The old servants were quiet. There was a fire there
but the hall was still dark. A figure came up the staircase from the hall.
He wore the white cloak of a marshal; his face was pale and strange; he
held his hand pressed to his side. He looked out of strange eyes at the

---

*Prayer near the close of compline, the last prayer session of the day.

old servants. They looked at him and saw their master's face and cloak
and knew that he had received his death wound. But only the dark was
where they looked: only dark silent air. Their master had received his
death wound on the battlefield of Prague far away over the sea. He was
standing on the field; his hand was pressed to his side; his face was pale
and strange and he wore the white cloak of a marshal.

O how cold and strange it was to think of that! All the dark was cold
and strange. There were pale strange faces there, great eyes like carriagelamps. They were the ghosts of murderers, the figures of marshals
who had received their death wound on battlefields far away over the
sea. What did they wish to say that their faces were so strange?

*Visit, we beseech Thee, O Lord, this habitation and drive away from it
all . . .*

Going home for the holidays! That would be lovely: the fellows had
told him. Getting up on the cars in the early wintry morning outside
the door of the castle. The cars were rolling on the gravel. Cheers for
the rector!

Hurray! Hurray! Hurray!

The cars drove past the chapel and all caps were raised. They drove
merrily along the country roads. The drivers pointed with their whips
to Bodenstown.* The fellows cheered. They passed the farmhouse of
the Jolly Farmer. Cheer after cheer after cheer. Through Clane they
drove, cheering and cheered. The peasant women stood at the half-
doors, the men stood here and there. The lovely smell there was in the
wintry air: the smell of Clane: rain and wintry air and turf smouldering
and corduroy.

The train was full of fellows: a long long chocolate train with cream
facings. The guards went to and fro opening, closing, locking, unlock-
ing the doors. They were men in dark blue and silver; they had silvery
whistles and their keys made a quick music: click, click: click, click.

And the train raced on over the flat lands and past the Hill of Allen.†
The telegraph poles were passing, passing. The train went on and on.
It knew. There were lanterns in the hall of his father's house and ropes

---

*Parish, including Sallins, in which Irish republican Wolfe Tone (see footnote on p.
162) is buried.
†Hill near the Sallins railway station.

of green branches. There were holly and ivy round the pierglass and holly and ivy, green and red, twined round the chandeliers. There were red holly and green ivy round the old portraits on the walls. Holly and ivy for him and for Christmas.

Lovely . . .

All the people. Welcome home, Stephen! Noises of welcome. His mother kissed him. Was that right? His father was a marshal now: higher than a magistrate. Welcome home, Stephen!

Noises . . .

There was a noise of curtainrings running back along the rods, of water being splashed in the basins. There was a noise of rising and dressing and washing in the dormitory: a noise of clapping of hands as the prefect went up and down telling the fellows to look sharp. A pale sunlight showed the yellow curtains drawn back, the tossed beds. His bed was very hot and his face and body were very hot.

He got up and sat on the side of his bed. He was weak. He tried to pull on his stocking. It had a horrid rough feel. The sunlight was queer and cold.

Fleming said:

—Are you not well?

He did not know; and Fleming said:

—Get back into bed. I'll tell McGlade you're not well.

—He's sick.

—Who is?

—Tell McGlade.

—Get back into bed.

—Is he sick?

A fellow held his arms while he loosened the stocking clinging to his foot and climbed back into the hot bed.

He crouched down between the sheets, glad of their tepid glow. He heard the fellows talk among themselves about him as they dressed for mass. It was a mean thing to do, to shoulder him into the square ditch, they were saying.

Then their voices ceased; they had gone. A voice at his bed said:

—Dedalus, don't spy on us, sure you won't?

Wells's face was there. He looked at it and saw that Wells was afraid.

—I didn't mean to. Sure you won't?

His father had told him, whatever he did, never to peach on a fellow. He shook his head and answered no and felt glad.

Wells said:

—I didn't mean to, honour bright. It was only for cod.* I'm sorry.

The face and the voice went away. Sorry because he was afraid. Afraid that it was some disease. Canker was a disease of plants and cancer one of animals: or another different. That was a long time ago then out on the playgrounds in the evening light, creeping from point to point on the fringe of his line, a heavy bird flying low through the grey light. Leicester Abbey lit up. Wolsey died there. The abbots buried him themselves.

It was not Wells's face, it was the prefect's. He was not foxing.† No, no: he was sick really. He was not foxing. And he felt the prefect's hand on his forehead; and he felt his forehead warm and damp against the prefect's cold damp hand. That was the way a rat felt, slimy and damp and cold. Every rat had two eyes to look out of. Sleek slimy coats, little little feet tucked up to jump, black slimy eyes to look out of. They could understand how to jump. But the minds of rats could not understand trigonometry. When they were dead they lay on their sides. Their coats dried then. They were only dead things.

The prefect was there again and it was his voice that was saying that he was to get up, that Father Minister‡ had said he was to get up and dress and go to the infirmary. And while he was dressing himself as quickly as he could the prefect said:

—We must pack off to Brother Michael because we have the collywobbles!

He was very decent to say that. That was all to make him laugh. But he could not laugh because his cheeks and lips were all shivery: and then the prefect had to laugh by himself.

The prefect cried:

—Quick march! Hayfoot! Strawfoot!

They went together down the staircase and along the corridor and past the bath. As he passed the door he remembered with a vague fear the warm turf-coloured bogwater, the warm moist air, the noise of plunges, the smell of the towels, like medicine.

Brother Michael was standing at the door of the infirmary and from the door of the dark cabinet on his right came a smell like medicine. That came from the bottles on the shelves. The prefect spoke to

*A practical joke.
†Malingering.
‡The vice-rector of Clongowes.

Brother Michael and Brother Michael answered and called the prefect sir. He had reddish hair mixed with grey and a queer look. It was queer that he would always be a brother. It was queer too that you could not call him sir because he was a brother* and had a different kind of look. Was he not holy enough or why could he not catch up on the others?

There were two beds in the room and in one bed there was a fellow: and when they went in he called out:

—Hello! It's young Dedalus! What's up?

—The sky is up, Brother Michael said.

He was a fellow out of the third of grammar and, while Stephen was undressing, he asked Brother Michael to bring him a round of buttered toast.

—Ah, do! he said.

—Butter you up! said Brother Michael. You'll get your walking papers in the morning when the doctor comes.

—Will I? the fellow said. I'm not well yet.

Brother Michael repeated:

—You'll get your walking papers. I tell you.

He bent down to rake the fire. He had a long back like the long back of a tramhorse. He shook the poker gravely and nodded his head at the fellow out of third of grammar.

Then Brother Michael went away and after a while the fellow out of third of grammar turned in towards the wall and fell asleep.

That was the infirmary. He was sick then. Had they written home to tell his mother and father? But it would be quicker for one of the priests to go himself to tell them. Or he would write a letter for the priest to bring.

Dear Mother,
    I am sick. I want to go home. Please come and take me home. I am in the infirmary.

                                                        Your fond son,
                                                        Stephen.

How far away they were! There was cold sunlight outside the window. He wondered if he would die. You could die just the same on a sunny day. He might die before his mother came. Then he would have

---

*Member of the Jesuit order who has not taken priestly orders.

a dead mass in the chapel like the way the fellows had told him it was when Little had died. All the fellows would be at the mass, dressed in black, all with sad faces. Wells too would be there but no fellow would look at him. The rector would be there in a cope* of black and gold and there would be tall yellow candles on the altar and round the catafalque.† And they would carry the coffin out of the chapel slowly and he would be buried in the little graveyard of the community off the main avenue of limes. And Wells would be sorry then for what he had done. And the bell would toll slowly.

He could hear the tolling. He said over to himself the song that Brigid had taught him.

> *Dindong! The castle bell!*
> *Farewell, my mother!*
> *Bury me in the old churchyard*
> *Beside my eldest brother.*
> *My coffin shall be black,*
> *Six angels at my back,*
> *Two to sing and two to pray*
> *And two to carry my soul away.*‡

How beautiful and sad that was! How beautiful the words were where they said *Bury me in the old churchyard!* A tremor passed over his body. How sad and how beautiful! He wanted to cry quietly but not for himself: for the words, so beautiful and sad, like music. The bell! The bell! Farewell! O farewell!

The cold sunlight was weaker and Brother Michael was standing at his bedside with a bowl of beeftea.§ He was glad for his mouth was hot and dry. He could hear them playing in the playgrounds. And the day was going on in the college just as if he were there.

Then Brother Michael was going away and the fellow out of third of grammar told him to be sure and come back and tell him all the news in the paper. He told Stephen that his name was Athy and that his father kept a lot of racehorses that were spiffing jumpers and that his fa-

---

*Long cloak made from a semicircle of cloth.
†Raised platform upon which the body of the deceased is laid.
‡Anonymous nursery rhyme.
§Beef bouillon.

ther would give a good tip to Brother Michael any time he wanted it because Brother Michael was very decent and always told him the news out of the paper they got every day up in the castle. There was every kind of news in the paper: accidents, shipwrecks, sports and politics.

—Now it is all about politics in the papers, he said. Do your people talk about that too?

—Yes, Stephen said.

—Mine too, he said.

Then he thought for a moment and said:

—You have a queer name, Dedalus, and I have a queer name too, Athy. My name is the name of a town.* Your name is like Latin.

Then he asked:

—Are you good at riddles?

Stephen answered:

—Not very good.

Then he said:

—Can you answer me this one? Why is the county of Kildare like the leg of a fellow's breeches?

Stephen thought what could be the answer and then said:

—I give it up.

—Because there is a thigh in it, he said. Do you see the joke? Athy is the town in the county Kildare, and a thigh is the other thigh.

—O, I see, Stephen said.

—That's an old riddle, he said.

After a moment he said:

—I say!

—What? asked Stephen.

—You know, he said, you can ask that riddle another way.

—Can you? said Stephen.

—The same riddle, he said. Do you know the other way to ask it?

—No, said Stephen.

—Can you not think of the other way? he said.

He looked at Stephen over the bedclothes as he spoke. Then he lay back on the pillow and said:

—There is another way but I won't tell you what it is.

Why did he not tell it? His father, who kept the racehorses, must be a magistrate too like Saurin's father and Nasty Roche's father. He

---

*Athy, in County Kildare, is about 26 miles from Clongowes.

thought of his own father, of how he sang songs while his mother played and of how he always gave him a shilling when he asked for sixpence and he felt sorry for him that he was not a magistrate like the other boys' fathers. Then why was he sent to that place with them? But his father had told him that he would be no stranger there because his granduncle had presented an address to the Liberator* there fifty years before. You could know the people of that time by their old dress. It seemed to him a solemn time: and he wondered if that was the time when the fellows in Clongowes wore blue coats with brass buttons and yellow waistcoats and caps of rabbit-skin and drank beer like grownup people and kept greyhounds of their own to course the hares with.

He looked at the window and saw that the daylight had grown weaker. There would be cloudy grey light over the playgrounds. There was no noise on the playgrounds. The class must be doing the themes[†] or perhaps Father Arnall was reading out of the book.

It was queer that they had not given him any medicine. Perhaps Brother Michael would bring it back when he came. They said you got stinking stuff to drink when you were in the infirmary. But he felt better now than before. It would be nice getting better slowly. You could get a book then. There was a book in the library about Holland. There were lovely foreign names in it and pictures of strange-looking cities and ships. It made you feel so happy.

How pale the light was at the window! But that was nice. The fire rose and fell on the wall. It was like waves. Someone had put coal on and he heard voices. They were talking. It was the noise of the waves. Or the waves were talking among themselves as they rose and fell.

He saw the sea of waves, long dark waves rising and falling, dark under the moonless night. A tiny light twinkled at the pierhead where the ship was entering: and he saw a multitude of people gathered by the waters' edge to see the ship that was entering their harbour. A tall man stood on the deck, looking out towards the flat dark land: and by the light at the pierhead he saw his face, the sorrowful face of Brother Michael.

He saw him lift his hand towards the people and heard him say in a loud voice of sorrow over the waters:

---

*Daniel O'Connell (1775–1847), chief architect of Catholic Emancipation (the return of civil rights to Catholics) in 1829.

†Essays written to set topics.

—He is dead. We saw him lying upon the catafalque. A wail of sorrow went up from the people.

—Parnell! Parnell! He is dead!*

They fell upon their knees, moaning in sorrow.

And he saw Dante in a maroon velvet dress and with a green velvet mantle hanging from her shoulders walking proudly and silently past the people who knelt by the waters' edge.

A great fire, banked high and red, flamed in the grate and under the ivy twined branches of the chandelier the Christmas table was spread. They had come home a little late and still dinner was not ready: but it would be ready in a jiffy, his mother had said. They were waiting for the door to open and for the servants to come in, holding the big dishes covered with their heavy metal covers.

All were waiting: Uncle Charles, who sat far away in the shadow of the window, Dante and Mr Casey, who sat in the easy chairs at either side of the hearth, Stephen, seated on a chair between them, his feet resting on the toasted boss.† Mr Dedalus looked at himself in the pierglass‡ above the mantelpiece, waxed out his moustache ends and then, parting his coat tails, stood with his back to the glowing fire: and still from time to time he withdrew a hand from his coat tail to wax out one of his moustache ends. Mr Casey leaned his head to one side and, smiling, tapped the gland of his neck with his fingers. And Stephen smiled too for he knew now that it was not true that Mr Casey had a purse of silver in his throat. He smiled to think how the silvery noise which Mr Casey used to make had deceived him. And when he had tried to open Mr Casey's hand to see if the purse of silver was hidden there he had seen that the fingers could not be straightened out: and Mr Casey had told him that he had got those three cramped fingers making a birthday present for Queen Victoria.[3]

Mr Casey tapped the gland of his neck and smiled at Stephen with sleepy eyes: and Mr Dedalus said to him:

—Yes. Well now, that's all right. O, we had a good walk, hadn't we, John? Yes . . . I wonder if there's any likelihood of dinner this evening.

---

*Irish nationalist leader Charles Stewart Parnell (see endnote 1) died on October 6, 1891.

†Footstool.

‡Long, narrow mirror.

Yes. . . . O, well now, we got a good breath of ozone round the Head*
today. Ay, bedad.

He turned to Dante and said:

—You didn't stir out at all, Mrs Riordan?

Dante frowned and said shortly:

—No.

Mr Dedalus dropped his coat tails and went over to the sideboard.
He brought forth a great stone jar of whisky from the locker and filled
the decanter slowly, bending now and then to see how much he had
poured in. Then replacing the jar in the locker he poured a little of the
whisky into two glasses, added a little water and came back with them
to the fireplace.

—A thimbleful, John, he said, just to whet your appetite.

Mr Casey took the glass, drank, and placed it near him on the mantelpiece. Then he said:

—Well, I can't help thinking of our friend Christopher manufacturing . . .

He broke into a fit of laughter and coughing and added:

— . . . manufacturing that champagne† for those fellows.

Mr Dedalus laughed loudly.

—Is it Christy? he said. There's more cunning in one of those warts
on his bald head than in a pack of jack foxes.

He inclined his head, closed his eyes, and, licking his lips profusely,
began to speak with the voice of the hotel keeper.

—And he has such a soft mouth when he's speaking to you, don't
you know. He's very moist and watery about the dewlaps,‡ God bless
him.

Mr Casey was still struggling through his fit of coughing and laughter. Stephen, seeing and hearing the hotel keeper through his father's
face and voice, laughed.

Mr Dedalus put up his eyeglass and, staring down at him, said quietly and kindly:

—What are you laughing at, you little puppy, you?

The servants entered and placed the dishes on the table. Mrs
Dedalus followed and the places were arranged.

—Sit over, she said.

---

*Bray Head, geographic landmark at the southern end of Dublin Bay.
†Mr. Casey may be referring to the manufacture of explosives for terrorist violence.
‡Folds of loose skin under the throat.

Mr Dedalus went to the end of the table and said:

—Now, Mrs Riordan, sit over. John, sit you down, my hearty.

He looked round to where Uncle Charles sat and said:

—Now then, sir, there's a bird here waiting for you.

When all had taken their seats he laid his hand on the cover and then said quickly, withdrawing it:

—Now, Stephen.

Stephen stood up in his place to say the grace before meals:

*Bless us, O Lord, and these Thy gifts which through Thy bounty we are about to receive through Christ our Lord. Amen.**

All blessed themselves and Mr Dedalus with a sigh of pleasure lifted from the dish the heavy cover pearled around the edge with glistening drops.

Stephen looked at the plump turkey which had lain, trussed and skewered, on the kitchen table. He knew that his father had paid a guinea for it in Dunn's of D'Olier Street and that the man had prodded it often at the breastbone to show how good it was: and he remembered the man's voice when he had said:

—Take that one, sir. That's the real Ally Daly.

Why did Mr Barrett in Clongowes call his pandybat† a turkey? But Clongowes was far away: and the warm heavy smell of turkey and ham and celery rose from the plates and dishes and the great fire was banked high and red in the grate and the green ivy and red holly made you feel so happy and when dinner was ended the big plum pudding would be carried in, studded with peeled almonds and sprigs of holly, with bluish fire running around it and a little green flag flying from the top.

It was his first Christmas dinner and he thought of his little brothers and sisters who were waiting in the nursery, as he had often waited, till the pudding came. The deep low collar and the Eton jacket‡ made him feel queer and oldish: and that morning when his mother had brought him down to the parlour, dressed for mass, his father had cried.

---

*Common Catholic grace said before meals.

†Small club, similar to the "blackjack," made of a hard core of whalebone covered in leather.

‡Waist-length black jacket with wide lapels; worn by the boys at Eton College preparatory school in England.

That was because he was thinking of his own father. And Uncle Charles had said so too.

Mr Dedalus covered the dish and began to eat hungrily. Then he said:

—Poor old Christy, he's nearly lopsided now with roguery.

—Simon, said Mrs Dedalus, you haven't given Mrs Riordan any sauce.

Mr Dedalus seized the sauceboat.

—Haven't I? he cried. Mrs Riordan, pity the poor blind.

Dante covered her plate with her hands and said:

—No, thanks.

Mr Dedalus turned to Uncle Charles.

—How are you off, sir?

—Right as the mail, Simon.

—You, John?

—I'm all right. Go on yourself.

—Mary? Here, Stephen, here's something to make your hair curl.

He poured sauce freely over Stephen's plate and set the boat again on the table. Then he asked Uncle Charles was it tender. Uncle Charles could not speak because his mouth was full but he nodded that it was.

—That was a good answer our friend made to the canon.* What? said Mr Dedalus.

—I didn't think he had that much in him, said Mr Casey.

—*I'll pay your dues, father, when you cease turning the house of God into a polling-booth.*

—A nice answer, said Dante, for any man calling himself a catholic to give to his priest.

—They have only themselves to blame, said Mr Dedalus suavely. If they took a fool's advice they would confine their attention to religion.

—It is religion, Dante said. They are doing their duty in warning the people.

—We go to the house of God, Mr Casey said, in all humility to pray to our Maker and not to hear election addresses.

—It is religion, Dante said again. They are right. They must direct their flocks.

—And preach politics from the altar, is it? asked Mr Dedalus.

—Certainly, said Dante. It is a question of public morality. A priest

---

*Member of a religious order.

would not be a priest if he did not tell his flock what is right and what is wrong.

Mrs Dedalus laid down her knife and fork, saying:

—For pity sake and for pity sake let us have no political discussion on this day of all days in the year.

—Quite right, ma'am, said Uncle Charles. Now Simon, that's quite enough now. Not another word now.

—Yes, yes, said Mr Dedalus quickly.

He uncovered the dish boldly and said:

—Now then, who's for more turkey?

Nobody answered. Dante said:

—Nice language for any catholic to use!

—Mrs Riordan, I appeal to you, said Mrs Dedalus, to let the matter drop now.

Dante turned on her and said:

—And am I to sit here and listen to the pastors of my church being flouted?

—Nobody is saying a word against them, said Mr Dedalus, so long as they don't meddle in politics.

—The bishops and priests of Ireland have spoken, said Dante, and they must be obeyed.

—Let them leave politics alone, said Mr Casey; or the people may leave their church alone.

—You hear? said Dante turning to Mrs Dedalus.

—Mr Casey! Simon! said Mrs Dedalus, let it end now.

—Too bad! Too bad! said Uncle Charles.

—What? cried Mr Dedalus. Were we to desert him at the bidding of the English people?

—He was no longer worthy to lead, said Dante. He was a public sinner.

—We are all sinners and black sinners, said Mr Casey coldly.

—Woe be to the man by whom the scandal cometh! said Mrs Riordan. *It would be better for him that a millstone were tied about his neck and that he were cast into the depths of the sea rather than that he should scandalise one of these, my least little ones.** That is the language of the Holy Ghost.

—And very bad language if you ask me, said Mr Dedalus coolly.

---

*Reference to the Bible, Luke 17:1–2.

—Simon! Simon! said Uncle Charles. The boy.

—Yes, yes, said Mr Dedalus. I meant about the . . . I was thinking about the bad language of that railway porter. Well now, that's all right. Here, Stephen, show me your plate, old chap. Eat away now. Here.

He heaped up the food on Stephen's plate and served Uncle Charles and Mr Casey to large pieces of turkey and splashes of sauce. Mrs Dedalus was eating little and Dante sat with her hands in her lap. She was red in the face. Mr Dedalus rooted with the carvers at the end of the dish and said:

—There's a tasty bit here we call the pope's nose.* If any lady or gentleman . . .

He held a piece of fowl up on the prong of the carvingfork. Nobody spoke. He put it on his own plate, saying:

—Well, you can't say but you were asked. I think I had better eat it myself because I'm not well in my health lately.

He winked at Stephen and, replacing the dish-cover, began to eat again.

There was a silence while he ate. Then he said:

—Well now, the day kept up fine after all. There were plenty of strangers down too.

Nobody spoke. He said again:

—I think there were more strangers down than last Christmas.

He looked round at the others whose faces were bent towards their plates and, receiving no reply, waited for a moment and said bitterly:

—Well, my Christmas dinner has been spoiled anyhow.

—There could be neither luck nor grace, Dante said, in a house where there is no respect for the pastors of the church.

Mr Dedalus threw his knife and fork noisily on his plate.

—Respect! he said. Is it for Billy with the lip or for the tub of guts up in Armagh?† Respect!

—Princes of the church, said Mr Casey with slow scorn.

—Lord Leitrim's coachman,‡ yes, said Mr Dedalus.

---

*Fatty flap of skin over the rump of a roasted fowl.
†Stephen's father is referring to William J. Walsh, archbishop of Dublin, and Michael Logue, archbishop of Armagh, in the province of Ulster, northern Ireland.
‡A conservative politician and landlord, Leitrim was murdered in 1877 in County Donegal by a vengeful tenant farmer; his coachman attempted to defend him from the attack. The reference is to one who aids his oppressor.

—They are the Lord's anointed, Dante said. They are an honour to their country.

—Tub of guts, said Mr Dedalus coarsely. He has a handsome face, mind you, in repose. You should see that fellow lapping up his bacon and cabbage of a cold winter's day. O Johnny!

He twisted his features into a grimace of heavy bestiality and made a lapping noise with his lips.

—Really, Simon, you should not speak that way before Stephen. It's not right.

—O, he'll remember all this when he grows up, said Dante hotly— the language he heard against God and religion and priests in his own home.

—Let him remember too, cried Mr Casey to her from across the table, the language with which the priests and the priests' pawns broke Parnell's heart and hounded him into his grave. Let him remember that too when he grows up.

—Sons of bitches! cried Mr Dedalus. When he was down they turned on him to betray him and rend him like rats in a sewer. Lowlived dogs! And they look it! By Christ, they look it!

—They behaved rightly, cried Dante. They obeyed their bishops and their priests. Honour to them!

—Well, it is perfectly dreadful to say that not even for one day in the year, said Mrs Dedalus, can we be free from these dreadful disputes!

Uncle Charles raised his hands mildly and said:

—Come now, come now, come now! Can we not have our opinions whatever they are without this bad temper and this bad language? It is too bad surely.

Mrs Dedalus spoke to Dante in a low voice but Dante said loudly:

—I will not say nothing. I will defend my church and my religion when it is insulted and spit on by renegade catholics.

Mr Casey pushed his plate rudely into the middle of the table and, resting his elbows before him, said in a hoarse voice to his host:

—Tell me, did I tell you that story about a very famous spit?

—You did not, John, said Mr Dedalus.

—Why then, said Mr Casey, it is a most instructive story. It happened not long ago in the county Wicklow where we are now.

He broke off and, turning towards Dante, said with quiet indignation:

—And I may tell you, ma'am, that I, if you mean me, am no renegade catholic. I am a catholic as my father was and his father before him and his father before him again when we gave up our lives rather than sell our faith.

—The more shame to you now, Dante said, to speak as you do.

—The story, John, said Mr Dedalus smiling. Let us have the story anyhow.

—Catholic indeed! repeated Dante ironically. The blackest protestant in the land would not speak the language I have heard this evening.

Mr Dedalus began to sway his head to and fro, crooning like a country singer.

—I am no protestant, I tell you again, said Mr Casey flushing.

Mr Dedalus, still crooning and swaying his head, began to sing in a grunting nasal tone:

> *O, come all you Roman catholics*
> *That never went to mass.*

He took up his knife and fork again in good humour and set to eating, saying to Mr Casey:

—Let us have the story, John. It will help us to digest.

Stephen looked with affection at Mr Casey's face which stared across the table over his joined hands. He liked to sit near him at the fire, looking up at his dark fierce face. But his dark eyes were never fierce and his slow voice was good to listen to. But why was he then against the priests? Because Dante must be right then. But he had heard his father say that she was a spoiled nun and that she had come out of the convent in the Alleghanies* when her brother had got the money from the savages for the trinkets and the chainies.† Perhaps that made her severe against Parnell. And she did not like him to play with Eileen because Eileen was a protestant and when she was young she knew children that used to play with protestants and the protestants used to make fun of the litany of the Blessed Virgin. *Tower of Ivory,* they used to say, *House of Gold!*‡ How could a woman be a tower of ivory or a house of gold? Who was right then? And he remembered the

---

*Part of the Appalachian mountain range in the eastern United States.

†Another word for trinkets.

‡The litany often forms part of evening prayers; "tower of ivory," "house of gold," and "morning star" are among the phrases used to describe the Blessed Virgin's glories.

evening in the infirmary in Clongowes, the dark waters, the light at the pierhead and the moan of sorrow from the people when they had heard.

—Eileen had long white hands. One evening when playing tig* she had put her hands over his eyes: long and white and thin and cold and soft. That was ivory: a cold white thing. That was the meaning of *Tower of Ivory*.

—The story is very short and sweet, Mr Casey said. It was one day down in Arklow,† a cold bitter day, not long before the chief‡ died. May God have mercy on him!

He closed his eyes wearily and paused. Mr Dedalus took a bone from his plate and tore some meat from it with his teeth, saying:

—Before he was killed, you mean.

Mr Casey opened his eyes, sighed and went on:

—He was down in Arklow one day. We were down there at a meeting and after the meeting was over we had to make our way to the railway station through the crowd. Such booing and baaing, man, you never heard. They called us all the names in the world. Well there was one old lady, and a drunken old harridan§ she was surely, that paid all her attention to me. She kept dancing along beside me in the mud bawling and screaming into my face: *Priest hunter! The Paris Funds! Mr Fox! Kitty O'Shea!*[4]

—And what did you do, John? asked Mr Dedalus.

—I let her bawl away, said Mr. Casey. It was a cold day and to keep up my heart I had (saving your presence, ma'am) a quid of Tullamore‖ in my mouth and sure I couldn't say a word in any case because my mouth was full of tobacco juice.

—Well, John?

—Well. I let her bawl away, to her heart's content, *Kitty O'Shea* and the rest of it till at last she called that lady a name that I won't sully this Christmas board# nor your ears, ma'am, nor my own lips by repeating.

He paused. Mr Dedalus, lifting his head from the bone, asked:

—And what did you do, John?

—Do! said Mr Casey. She stuck her ugly old face up at me when she

---

*Tag.
†25 miles south of Bray on the eastern coast of Ireland.
‡Charles Stewart Parnell (see endnote 1).
§Hag.
‖Chewing tobacco.
#Table; hospitality.

said it and I had my mouth full of tobacco juice. I bent down to her and *Phth!* says I to her like that.

He turned aside and made the act of spitting.

—Phth! says I to her like that, right into her eye.

He clapped a hand to his eye and gave a hoarse scream of pain.

—*O Jesus, Mary and Joseph!* says she. *I'm blinded! I'm blinded and drownded!*

He stopped in a fit of coughing and laughter, repeating:

—*I'm blinded entirely.*

Mr Dedalus laughed loudly and lay back in his chair while Uncle Charles swayed his head to and fro.

Dante looked terribly angry and repeated while they laughed:

—Very nice! Ha! Very nice!

It was not nice about the spit in the woman's eye.

But what was the name the woman had called Kitty O'Shea that Mr Casey would not repeat? He thought of Mr Casey walking through the crowds of people and making speeches from a wagonette. That was what he had been in prison for and he remembered that one night Sergeant O'Neill had come to the house and had stood in the hall, talking in a low voice with his father and chewing nervously at the chinstrap of his cap. And that night Mr Casey had not gone to Dublin by train but a car had come to the door and he had heard his father say something about the Cabinteely* road.

He was for Ireland and Parnell and so was his father: and so was Dante too for one night at the band on the esplanade she had hit a gentleman on the head with her umbrella because he had taken off his hat when the band played *God save the Queen*† at the end.

Mr Dedalus gave a snort of contempt.

—Ah, John, he said. It is true for them. We are an unfortunate priestridden race and always were and always will be till the end of chapter.

Uncle Charles shook his head, saying:

—A bad business! A bad business!

Mr Dedalus repeated:

—A priestridden Godforsaken race!

---

*Village near Killiney Hill, in County Wicklow.

†Ireland was still part of the United Kingdom and Queen Victoria her queen. Mrs. Riordan ("Dante") showed her Irish nationalist streak by attacking this show of loyalty to the crown.

He pointed to the portrait of his grandfather on the wall to his right.

—Do you see that old chap up there, John? he said. He was a good Irishman when there was no money in the job. He was condemned to death as a whiteboy.* But he had a saying about our clerical friends, that he would never let one of them put his two feet under his mahogany.†

Dante broke in angrily:

—If we are a priestridden race we ought to be proud of it! They are the apple of God's eye. *Touch them not,* says Christ, *for they are the apple of My eye.*‡

— And can we not love our country then? asked Mr Casey. Are we not to follow the man that was born to lead us?

—A traitor to his country! replied Dante. A traitor, an adulterer! The priests were right to abandon him. The priests were always the true friends of Ireland.

—Were they, faith? said Mr Casey.

He threw his fist on the table and, frowning angrily, protruded one finger after another.

—Didn't the bishops of Ireland betray us in the time of the union when Bishop Lanigan presented an address of loyalty to the Marquess Cornwallis? Didn't the bishops and priests sell the aspirations of their country in 1829 in return for catholic emancipation? Didn't they denounce the fenian movement from the pulpit and in the confession box? And didn't they dishonour the ashes of Terence Bellew Mac-Manus?[5]

His face was glowing with anger and Stephen felt the glow rise to his own cheek as the spoken words thrilled him. Mr Dedalus uttered a guffaw of coarse scorn.

—O, by God, he cried, I forgot little old Paul Cullen!§ Another apple of God's eye!

Dante bent across the table and cried to Mr Casey:

—Right! Right! They were always right! God and morality and religion come first.

Mrs Dedalus, seeing her excitement, said to her:

---

*The Whiteboys were an eighteenth-century group of oppressed tenants organized against the abuses of British absentee landlords.

†Dining table.

‡Mrs. Riordan misattributes this Old Testament passage (Zacharias 2:8) to Christ.

§(1803–1878); first Irishman named to the College of Cardinals; an ardent anti-nationalist.

—Mrs Riordan, don't excite yourself answering them.

—God and religion before everything! Dante cried. God and religion before the world!

Mr Casey raised his clenched fist and brought it down on the table with a crash.

—Very well, then, he shouted hoarsely, if it comes to that, no God for Ireland!

—John! John! cried Mr Dedalus, seizing his guest by the coat sleeve.

Dante stared across the table, her cheeks shaking. Mr Casey struggled up from his chair and bent across the table towards her, scraping the air from before his eyes with one hand as though he were tearing aside a cobweb.

—No God for Ireland! he cried. We have had too much God in Ireland. Away with God!

—Blasphemer! Devil! screamed Dante, starting to her feet and almost spitting in his face.

Uncle Charles and Mr Dedalus pulled Mr Casey back into his chair again, talking to him from both sides reasonably. He stared before him out of his dark flaming eyes, repeating:

—Away with God, I say!

Dante shoved her chair violently aside and left the table, upsetting her napkinring which rolled slowly along the carpet and came to rest against the foot of an easychair. Mrs Dedalus rose quickly and followed her towards the door. At the door Dante turned round violently and shouted down the room, her cheeks flushed and quivering with rage:

—Devil out of hell! We won! We crushed him to death! Fiend!

The door slammed behind her.

Mr Casey, freeing his arms from his holders, suddenly bowed his head on his hands with a sob of pain.

—Poor Parnell! he cried loudly. My dead king!

He sobbed loudly and bitterly.

Stephen, raising his terrorstricken face, saw that his father's eyes were full of tears.

*   *   *   *

The fellows talked together in little groups.

One fellow said:

—They were caught near the Hill of Lions.*

---

*3 miles from Cellbridge, in County Wicklow.

—Who caught them?

—Mr Gleeson and the minister. They were on a car.

The same fellow added:

—A fellow in the higher line told me.

Fleming asked:

—But why did they run away, tell us?

—I know why, Cecil Thunder said. Because they had fecked* cash out of the rector's room.

—Who fecked it?

—Kickham's brother. And they all went shares in it.

But that was stealing. How could they have done that?

—A fat lot you know about it, Thunder! Wells said. I know why they scut.†

—Tell us why.

—I was told not to, Wells said.

—O, go on, Wells, all said. You might tell us. We won't let it out.

Stephen bent forward his head to hear. Wells looked round to see if anyone was coming. Then he said secretly:

—You know the altar wine they keep in the press in the sacristy?‡

—Yes.

—Well, they drank that and it was found out who did it by the smell. And that's why they ran away, if you want to know.

And the fellow who had spoken first said:

—Yes, that's what I heard too from the fellow in the higher line.

The fellows were all silent. Stephen stood among them, afraid to speak, listening. A faint sickness of awe made him feel weak. How could they have done that? He thought of the dark silent sacristy. There were dark wooden presses there where the crimped surplices§ lay quietly folded. It was not the chapel but still you had to speak under your breath. It was a holy place. He remembered the summer evening he had been there to be dressed as boat-bearer,‖ the evening of the procession to the little altar in the wood. A strange and holy place. The boy that held the censer had swung it gently to and fro near the door with the

---

*Stolen.

†Ran away.

‡In a church, the storage area for sacred vessels and vestments.

§White vestments with loose sleeves, worn by those presiding over church services.

‖Server at a Mass who carries the receptacle containing the incense to be burned in the censer.

silvery cap lifted by the middle chain to keep the coals lighting. That
was called charcoal: and it had burned quietly as the fellow had swung
it gently and had given off a weak sour smell. And then when all were
vested he had stood holding out the boat to the rector and the rector
had put a spoonful of incense in and it had hissed on the red coals.

The fellows were talking together in little groups here and there on
the playground. The fellows seemed to him to have grown smaller: that
was because a sprinter had knocked him down the day before, a fellow
out of second of grammar. He had been thrown by the fellow's machine
lightly on the cinderpath and his spectacles had been broken in three
pieces and some of the grit of the cinders had gone into his mouth.

That was why the fellows seemed to him smaller and farther away
and the goalposts so thin and far and the soft grey sky so high up. But
there was no play on the football grounds for cricket was coming: and
some said that Barnes would be the prof and some said it would be
Flowers. And all over the playgrounds they were playing rounders and
bowling twisters and lobs.* And from here and from there came the
sounds of the cricket bats through the soft grey air. They said: pick,
pack, pock, puck: little drops of water in a fountain slowly falling in the
brimming bowl.

Athy, who had been silent, said quietly:

—You are all wrong.

All turned towards him eagerly.

—Why?

—Do you know?

—Who told you?

—Tell us, Athy.

Athy pointed across the playground to where Simon Moonan was
walking by himself kicking a stone before him.

—Ask him, he said.

The fellows looked there and then said:

—Why him?

—Is he in it?

Athy lowered his voice and said:

—Do you know why those fellows scut? I will tell you but you must
not let on you know.

—Tell us, Athy. Go on. You might if you know.

---

*Terms for various types of cricket bowls.

He paused for a moment and then said mysteriously:

—They were caught with Simon Moonan and Tusker Boyle in the square* one night.

The fellows looked at him and asked:

—Caught?

—What doing?

Athy said:

—Smugging.†

All the fellows were silent: and Athy said:

—And that's why.

Stephen looked at the faces of the fellows but they were all looking across the playground. He wanted to ask somebody about it. What did that mean about the smugging in the square? Why did the five fellows out of the higher line run away for that? It was a joke, he thought. Simon Moonan had nice clothes and one night he had shown him a ball of creamy sweets that the fellows of the football fifteen had rolled down to him along the carpet in the middle of the refectory when he was at the door. It was the night of the match against the Bective Rangers and the ball was made just like a red and green apple only it opened and it was full of the creamy sweets. And one day Boyle had said that an elephant had two tuskers instead of two tusks and that was why he was called Tusker Boyle but some fellows called him Lady Boyle because he was always at his nails, paring them.

Eileen had long thin cool white hands too because she was a girl. They were like ivory; only soft. That was the meaning of *Tower of Ivory* but protestants could not understand it and made fun of it. One day he had stood beside her looking into the hotel grounds. A waiter was running up a trail of bunting on the flagstaff and a fox terrier was scampering to and fro on the sunny lawn. She had put her hand into his pocket where his hand was and he had felt how cool and thin and soft her hand was. She had said that pockets were funny things to have: and then all of a sudden she had broken away and had run laughing down the sloping curve of the path. Her fair hair had streamed out behind her like gold in the sun. *Tower of Ivory. House of Gold.* By thinking of things you could understand them.

---

*Open latrines.

†Said to be slang for a form of homosexual petting; what seems more significant here is the way it both names and refuses to name some form of forbidden activity, so that Stephen's imagination is left to its own devices.

But why in the square? You went there when you wanted to do something. It was all thick slabs of slate and water trickled all day out of tiny pinholes and there was a queer smell of stale water there. And behind the door of one of the closets* there was a drawing in red pencil of a bearded man in a Roman dress with a brick in each hand and underneath was the name of the drawing:

Balbus† was building a wall.

Some fellows had drawn it there for a cod. It had a funny face but it was very like a man with a beard. And on the wall of another closet there was written in backhand in beautiful writing:

Julius Cæsar wrote The Calico Belly.

Perhaps that was why they were there because it was a place where some fellows wrote things for cod. But all the same it was queer what Athy said and the way he said it. It was not a cod because they had run away. He looked with the others across the playground and began to feel afraid.

At last Fleming said:

—And we are all to be punished for what other fellows did?

—I won't come back, see if I do, Cecil Thunder said. Three days' silence in the refectory and sending us up for six and eight‡ every minute.

—Yes, said Wells. And old Barrett has a new way of twisting the note so that you can't open it and fold it again to see how many ferulæ§ you are to get. I won't come back too.

—Yes, said Cecil Thunder, and the prefect of studies‖ was in second of grammar this morning.

—Let us get up a rebellion, Fleming said. Will we?

All the fellows were silent. The air was very silent and you could hear the cricket bats but more slowly than before: pick, pock.

Wells asked:

—What is going to be done to them?

—Simon Moonan and Tusker are going to be flogged, Athy said, and the fellows in the higher line got their choice of flogging or being expelled.

---

*Water closets; toilets.
†Figure in Caesar's text on the Gallic wars, *De Bello Gallico*.
‡A beating on the palms of the hands: six strokes on each, followed by eight on each.
§Strokes.
‖Assistant to the rector, responsible for academic oversight of the school.

—And which are they taking? asked the fellow who had spoken first.

—All are taking expulsion except Corrigan, Athy answered. He's going to be flogged by Mr Gleeson.

—I know why, Cecil Thunder said. He is right and the other fellows are wrong because a flogging wears off after a bit but a fellow that has been expelled from college is known all his life on account of it. Besides Gleeson won't flog him hard.

—It's best of his play* not to, Fleming said.

—I wouldn't like to be Simon Moonan and Tusker, Cecil Thunder said. But I don't believe they will be flogged. Perhaps they will be sent up for twice nine.†

—No, no, said Athy. They'll both get it on the vital spot.

Wells rubbed himself and said in a crying voice:

—Please, sir, let me off!

Athy grinned and turned up the sleeves of his jacket, saying:

> *It can't be helped;*
> *It must be done.*
> *So down with your breeches*
> *And out with your bum.*

The fellows laughed; but he felt that they were a little afraid. In the silence of the soft grey air he heard the cricket bats from here and from there: pock. That was a sound to hear but if you were hit then you would feel a pain. The pandybat made a sound too but not like that. The fellows said it was made of whalebone and leather with lead inside: and he wondered what was the pain like. There were different kinds of sounds. A long thin cane would have a high whistling sound and he wondered what was that pain like. It made him shivery to think of it and cold: and what Athy said too. But what was there to laugh at in it? It made him shivery: but that was because you always felt like a shiver when you let down your trousers. It was the same in the bath when you undressed yourself. He wondered who had to let them down, the master or the boy himself. O how could they laugh about it that way?

He looked at Athy's rolled-up sleeves and knuckly inky hands. He

---

*In his best interest.
†Nine strokes on each hand—the maximum allowed.

had rolled up his sleeves to show how Mr Gleeson would roll up his sleeves. But Mr Gleeson had round shiny cuffs and clean white wrists and fattish white hands and the nails of them were long and pointed. Perhaps he pared them too like Lady Boyle. But they were terribly long and pointed nails. So long and cruel they were though the white fattish hands were not cruel but gentle. And though he trembled with cold and fright to think of the cruel long nails and of the high whistling sound of the cane and of the chill you felt at the end of your shirt when you undressed yourself yet he felt a feeling of queer quiet pleasure inside him to think of the white fattish hands, clean and strong and gentle. And he thought of what Cecil Thunder had said; that Mr Gleeson would not flog Corrigan hard. And Fleming had said he would not because it was best of his play not to. But that was not why.

A voice from far out on the playground cried:

—All in!

And other voices cried:

—All in! All in!

During the writing lesson he sat with his arms folded, listening to the slow scraping of the pens. Mr Harford went to and fro making little signs in red pencil and sometimes sitting beside the boy to show him how to hold his pen. He had tried to spell out the headline for himself though he knew already what it was for it was the last of the book. *Zeal without prudence is like a ship adrift.* But the lines of the letters were like fine invisible threads and it was only by closing his right eye tight tight and staring out of the left eye that he could make out the full curves of the capital.

But Mr Harford was very decent and never got into a wax. All the other masters got into dreadful waxes. But why were they to suffer for what fellows in the higher line did? Wells had said that they had drunk some of the altar wine out of the press in the sacristy and that it had been found out who had done it by the smell. Perhaps they had stolen a monstrance* to run away with it and sell it somewhere. That must have been a terrible sin, to go in there quietly at night, to open the dark press and steal the flashing gold thing into which God was put on the altar in the middle of flowers and candles at benediction† while the incense went up in clouds at both sides as the fellow swung the censer

---

*Gold or silver vessel in which the host is displayed during the part of the Mass known as the Eucharist (Communion).

†The part of the Catholic Mass in which the priest shows the eucharistic host to those in attendance and blesses them with it.

and Dominic Kelly sang the first part by himself in the choir. But God was not in it of course when they stole it. But still it was a strange and a great sin even to touch it. He thought of it with deep awe; a terrible and strange sin: it thrilled him to think of it in the silence when the pens scraped lightly. But to drink the altar wine out of the press and be found out by the smell was a sin too: but it was not terrible and strange. It only made you feel a little sickish on account of the smell of the wine. Because on the day when he had made his first holy communion in the chapel he had shut his eyes and opened his mouth and put out his tongue a little: and when the rector had stooped down to give him the holy communion he had smelt a faint winy smell off the rector's breath after the wine of the mass. The word was beautiful: wine. It made you think of dark purple because the grapes were dark purple that grew in Greece outside houses like white temples. But the faint smell off the rector's breath had made him feel a sick feeling on the morning of his first communion. The day of your first communion was the happiest day of your life. And once a lot of generals had asked Napoleon what was the happiest day of his life. They thought he would say the day he won some great battle or the day he was made an emperor. But he said:

—Gentlemen, the happiest day of my life was the day on which I made my first holy communion.*

Father Arnall came in and the Latin lesson began and he remained still leaning on the desk with his arms folded. Father Arnall gave out the theme-books and he said that they were scandalous and that they were all to be written out again with the corrections at once. But the worst of all was Fleming's theme because the pages were stuck together by a blot: and Father Arnall held it up by a corner and said it was an insult to any master to send him up such a theme. Then he asked Jack Lawton to decline the noun *mare*† and Jack Lawton stopped at the ablative singular and could not go on with the plural.

—You should be ashamed of yourself, said Father Arnall sternly. You, the leader of the class!

Then he asked the next boy and the next and the next. Nobody knew. Father Arnall became very quiet, more and more quiet as each boy tried to answer it and could not. But his face was black looking and his eyes were staring though his voice was so quiet. Then he asked

---

*This bit of school lore is almost certainly false, since Napoleon had renounced the Church.
†The sea (Latin).

Fleming and Fleming said that that word had no plural. Father Arnall suddenly shut the book and shouted at him:

—Kneel out there in the middle of the class. You are one of the idlest boys I ever met. Copy out your themes again the rest of you.

Fleming moved heavily out of his place and knelt between the two last benches. The other boys bent over their theme-books and began to write. A silence filled the classroom and Stephen, glancing timidly at Father Arnall's dark face, saw that it was a little red from the wax he was in.

Was that a sin for Father Arnall to be in a wax or was he allowed to get into a wax when the boys were idle because that made them study better or was he only letting on to be in a wax? It was because he was allowed because a priest would know what a sin was and would not do it. But if he did it one time by mistake what would he do to go to confession? Perhaps he would go to confession to the minister. And if the minister did it he would go to the rector: and the rector to the provincial: and the provincial to the general* of the jesuits. That was called the order: and he had heard his father say that they were all clever men. They could all have become high-up people in the world if they had not become jesuits. And he wondered what Father Arnall and Paddy Barrett would have become and what Mr McGlade and Mr Gleeson would have become if they had not become jesuits.† It was hard to think what because you would have to think of them in a different way with different coloured coats and trousers and with beards and moustaches and different kinds of hats.

The door opened quietly and closed. A quick whisper ran through the class: the prefect of studies. There was an instant of dead silence and then the loud crack of a pandybat on the last desk. Stephen's heart leapt up in fear.

—Any boys want flogging here, Father Arnall? cried the prefect of studies. Any lazy idle loafers that want flogging in this class?

He came to the middle of the class and saw Fleming on his knees.

—Hoho! he cried. Who is this boy? Why is he on his knees? What is your name, boy?

—Fleming, sir.

—Hoho, Fleming! An idler of course. I can see it in your eye. Why is he on his knees, Father Arnall?

---

*The text describes the chain of command within the Jesuit order.
†The Society of Jesus, an order within the Catholic Church founded by Ignatius Loyola (1491 1556); its members are known especially for their learning

—He wrote a bad Latin theme, Father Arnall said, and he missed all the questions in grammar.

—Of course he did! cried the prefect of studies, of course he did! A born idler! I can see it in the corner of his eye.

He banged his pandybat down on the desk and cried:

—Up, Fleming! Up, my boy!

Fleming stood up slowly.

—Hold out!* cried the prefect of studies.

Fleming held out his hand. The pandybat came down on it with a loud smacking sound: one, two, three, four, five, six.

—Other hand!

The pandybat came down again in six loud quick smacks.

—Kneel down! cried the prefect of studies.

Fleming knelt down squeezing his hands under his armpits, his face contorted with pain, but Stephen knew how hard his hands were because Fleming was always rubbing rosin into them. But perhaps he was in great pain for the noise of the pandybat was terrible. Stephen's heart was beating and fluttering.

—At your work, all of you! shouted the prefect of studies. We want no lazy idle loafers here, lazy idle little schemers. At your work, I tell you. Father Dolan will be in to see you every day. Father Dolan will be in tomorrow.

He poked one of the boys in the side with the pandybat, saying:

—You, boy! When will Father Dolan be in again?

—Tomorrow, sir, said Tom Furlong's voice.

—Tomorrow and tomorrow and tomorrow,† said the prefect of studies. Make up your minds for that. Every day Father Dolan. Write away. You, boy, who are you?

Stephen's heart jumped suddenly.

—Dedalus, sir.

—Why are you not writing like the others?

—I . . . my . . .

He could not speak with fright.

—Why is he not writing, Father Arnall?

—He broke his glasses, said Father Arnall, and I exempted him from work.

---

*That is, hold out your hands for disciplining; the Latin word for this phrase, *pande*, gives the pandybat and pandying their names.

†Quotation from William Shakespeare's *Macbeth* (act 5, scene 5).

—Broke? What is this I hear? What is this? Your name is? said the prefect of studies.

—Dedalus, sir.

—Out here, Dedalus. Lazy little schemer. I see schemer in your face. Where did you break your glasses?

Stephen stumbled into the middle of the class, blinded by fear and haste.

—Where did you break your glasses? repeated the prefect of studies.

—The cinderpath, sir.

—Hoho! The cinderpath! cried the prefect of studies. I know that trick.

Stephen lifted his eyes in wonder and saw for a moment Father Dolan's whitegrey not young face, his baldy whitegrey head with fluff at the sides of it, the steel rims of his spectacles and his no-coloured eyes looking through the glasses. Why did he say he knew that trick?

—Lazy idle little loafer! cried the prefect of studies. Broke my glasses! An old schoolboy trick! Out with your hand this moment!

Stephen closed his eyes and held out in the air his trembling hand with the palm upwards. He felt the prefect of studies touch it for a moment at the fingers to straighten it and then the swish of the sleeve of the soutane as the pandybat was lifted to strike. A hot burning stinging tingling blow like the loud crack of a broken stick made his trembling hand crumple together like a leaf in the fire: and at the sound and the pain scalding tears were driven into his eyes. His whole body was shaking with fright, his arm was shaking and his crumpled burning livid hand shook like a loose leaf in the air. A cry sprang to his lips, a prayer to be let off. But though the tears scalded his eyes and his limbs quivered with pain and fright he held back the hot tears and the cry that scalded his throat.

—Other hand! shouted the prefect of studies.

Stephen drew back his maimed and quivering right arm and held out his left hand. The soutane sleeve swished again as the pandybat was lifted and a loud crashing sound and a fierce maddening tingling burning pain made his hand shrink together with the palms and fingers in a livid quivering mass. The scalding water burst forth from his eyes and, burning with shame and agony and fear, he drew back his shaking arm in terror and burst out into a whine of pain. His body shook with a palsy of fright and in shame and rage he felt the scalding cry come from his throat and the scalding tears falling out of his eyes and down his flaming cheeks.

—Kneel down! cried the prefect of studies.

Stephen knelt down quickly pressing his beaten hands to his sides. To think of them beaten and swollen with pain all in a moment made him feel so sorry for them as if they were not his own but someone else's that he felt sorry for. And as he knelt, calming the last sobs in his throat and feeling the burning tingling pain pressed into his sides, he thought of the hands which he had held out in the air with the palms up and of the firm touch of the prefect of studies when he had steadied the shaking fingers and of the beaten swollen reddened mass of palm and fingers that shook helplessly in the air.

—Get at your work, all of you, cried the prefect of studies from the door. Father Dolan will be in every day to see if any boy, any lazy idle little loafer wants flogging. Every day. Every day.

The door closed behind him.

The hushed class continued to copy out the themes. Father Arnall rose from his seat and went among them, helping the boys with gentle words and telling them the mistakes they had made. His voice was very gentle and soft. Then he returned to his seat and said to Fleming and Stephen:

—You may return to your places, you two.

Fleming and Stephen rose and, walking to their seats, sat down. Stephen, scarlet with shame, opened a book quickly with one weak hand and bent down upon it, his face close to the page.

It was unfair and cruel because the doctor had told him not to read without glasses and he had written home to his father that morning to send him a new pair. And Father Arnall had said that he need not study till the new glasses came. Then to be called a schemer before the class and to be pandied when he always got the card for first or second and was the leader of the Yorkists! How could the prefect of studies know that it was a trick? He felt the touch of the prefect's fingers as they had steadied his hand and at first he had thought he was going to shake hands with him because the fingers were soft and firm: but then in an instant he had heard the swish of the soutane sleeve and the crash. It was cruel and unfair to make him kneel in the middle of the class then: and Father Arnall had told them both that they might return to their places without making any difference between them. He listened to Father Arnall's low and gentle voice as he corrected the themes. Perhaps he was sorry now and wanted to be decent. But it was unfair and cruel. The prefect of studies was a priest but that was cruel and unfair. And his whitegrey face and the no-coloured eyes behind the steel rimmed spectacles were cruel looking because he had steadied the hand first with his firm soft fingers and that was to hit it better and louder.

—It's a stinking mean thing, that's what it is, said Fleming in the corridor as the classes were passing out in file to the refectory, to pandy a fellow for what is not his fault.

—You really broke your glasses by accident, didn't you? Nasty Roche asked.

Stephen felt his heart filled by Fleming's words and did not answer.

—Of course he did! said Fleming. I wouldn't stand it. I'd go up and tell the rector on him.

—Yes, said Cecil Thunder eagerly, and I saw him lift the pandybat over his shoulder and he's not allowed to do that.

—Did they hurt much? Nasty Roche asked.

—Very much, Stephen said.

—I wouldn't stand it, Fleming repeated, from Baldyhead or any other Baldyhead. It's a stinking mean low trick, that's what it is. I'd go straight up to the rector and tell him about it after dinner.

—Yes, do. Yes, do, said Cecil Thunder.

—Yes, do. Yes, go up and tell the rector on him, Dedalus, said Nasty Roche, because he said that he'd come in tomorrow again and pandy you.

—Yes, yes. Tell the rector, all said.

And there were some fellows out of second of grammar listening and one of them said:

—The senate and the Roman people declared that Dedalus had been wrongly punished.

It was wrong; it was unfair and cruel: and, as he sat in the refectory, he suffered time after time in memory the same humiliation until he began to wonder whether it might not really be that there was something in his face which made him look like a schemer and he wished he had a little mirror to see. But there could not be; and it was unjust and cruel and unfair.

He could not eat the blackish fish fritters they got on Wednesdays in Lent* and one of his potatoes had the mark of the spade in it. Yes, he would do what the fellows had told him. He would go up and tell the rector that he had been wrongly punished. A thing like that had been done before by somebody in history, by some great person whose head was in the books of history. And the rector would declare that he had been wrongly punished because the senate and the Roman people always declared that the men who did that had been wrongly punished.

---

*Period of preparation for Easter, beginning with Ash Wednesday and comprising the forty weekdays before Easter.

Those were the great men whose names were in Richmal Magnall's Questions. History was all about those men and what they did and that was what Peter Parley's Tales about Greece and Rome were all about. Peter Parley himself was on the first page in a picture. There was a road over a heath with grass at the side and little bushes: and Peter Parley had a broad hat like a protestant minister and a big stick and he was walking fast along the road to Greece and Rome.

It was easy what he had to do. All he had to do was when the dinner was over and he came out in his turn to go on walking but not out to the corridor but up the staircase on the right that led to the castle. He had nothing to do but that; to turn to the right and walk fast up the staircase and in half a minute he would be in the low dark narrow corridor that led through the castle to the rector's room. And every fellow had said that it was unfair, even the fellow out of second of grammar who had said that about the senate and the Roman people.

What would happen? He heard the fellows of the higher line stand up at the top of the refectory and heard their steps as they came down the matting: Paddy Rath and Jimmy Magee and the Spaniard and the Portuguese and the fifth was big Corrigan who was going to be flogged by Mr Gleeson. That was why the prefect of studies had called him a schemer and pandied him for nothing: and, straining his weak eyes, tired with the tears, he watched big Corrigan's broad shoulders and big hanging black head passing in the file. But he had done something and besides Mr Gleeson would not flog him hard: and he remembered how big Corrigan looked in the bath. He had skin the same colour as the turf-coloured bogwater in the shallow end of the bath and when he walked along the side his feet slapped loudly on the wet tiles and at every step his thighs shook a little because he was fat.

The refectory was half empty and the fellows were still passing out in file. He could go up the staircase because there was never a priest or a prefect outside the refectory door. But he could not go. The rector would side with the prefect of studies and think it was a schoolboy trick and then the prefect of studies would come in every day the same, only it would be worse because he would be dreadfully waxy at any fellow going up to the rector about him. The fellows had told him to go but they would not go themselves. They had forgotten all about it. No, it was best to forget all about it and perhaps the prefect of studies had only said he would come in. No, it was best to hide out of the way because when you were small and young you could often escape that way.

The fellows at his table stood up. He stood up and passed out among them in the file. He had to decide. He was coming near the door. If he went on with the fellows he could never go up to the rector because he could not leave the playground for that. And if he went and was pandied all the same all the fellows would make fun and talk about young Dedalus going up to the rector to tell on the prefect of studies.

He was walking down along the matting and he saw the door before him. It was impossible: he could not. He thought of the baldy head of the prefect of studies with the cruel no-coloured eyes looking at him and he heard the voice of the prefect of studies asking him twice what his name was. Why could he not remember the name when he was told the first time? Was he not listening the first time or was it to make fun out of the name? The great men in the history had names like that and nobody made fun of them. It was his own name that he should have made fun of if he wanted to make fun. Dolan: it was like the name of a woman who washed clothes.

He had reached the door and, turning quickly up to the right, walked up the stairs; and, before he could make up his mind to come back, he had entered the low dark narrow corridor that led to the castle. And as he crossed the threshold of the door of the corridor he saw, without turning his head to look, that all the fellows were looking after him as they went filing by.

He passed along the narrow dark corridor, passing little doors that were the doors of the rooms of the community. He peered in front of him and right and left through the gloom and thought that those must be portraits. It was dark and silent and his eyes were weak and tired with tears so that he could not see. But he thought they were the portraits of the saints and great men of the order who were looking down on him silently as he passed: Saint Iganatius Loyola holding an open book and pointing to the words *Ad Majorem Dei Gloriam* in it, saint Francis Xavier* pointing to his chest, Lorenzo Ricci† with his berretta on his head like one of the prefects of the lines, the three patrons of holy youth, saint Stanislaus Kostka, saint Aloysius Gonzaga and Blessed John Berchmans,‡ all with young faces because they died when

---

*One of the first to join Ignatius Loyola in the Society of Jesus.
†Eighteenth-century general of the Jesuits.
‡Kostka, Gonzaga, and Berchmans, all Jesuits, were patrons of the sodality of the Blessed Virgin Mary

they were young, and Father Peter Kenny* sitting in a chair wrapped in a big cloak.

He came out on the landing above the entrance hall and looked about him. That was where Hamilton Rowan had passed and the marks of the soldiers' slugs were there. And it was there that the old servants had seen the ghost in the white cloak of a marshal.

An old servant was sweeping at the end of the landing. He asked him where was the rector's room and the old servant pointed to the door at the far end and looked after him as he went on to it and knocked.

There was no answer. He knocked again more loudly and his heart jumped when he heard a muffled voice say:

—Come in!

He turned the handle and opened the door and fumbled for the handle of the green baize† door inside. He found it and pushed it open and went in.

He saw the rector sitting at a desk writing. There was a skull on the desk and a strange solemn smell in the room like the old leather of chairs.

His heart was beating fast on account of the solemn place he was in and the silence of the room: and he looked at the skull and at the rector's kind-looking face.

—Well, my little man, said the rector, what is it?

Stephen swallowed down the thing in his throat and said:

—I broke my glasses, sir.

The rector opened his mouth and said:

—O!

Then he smiled and said:

—Well, if we broke our glasses we must write home for a new pair.

—I wrote home, sir, said Stephen, and Father Arnall said I am not to study till they come.

—Quite right! said the rector.

Stephen swallowed down the thing again and tried to keep his legs and his voice from shaking.

—But, sir . . .

—Yes?

---

*He purchased Clongowes for the Jesuits in 1813.
†Felt-like fabric.

—Father Dolan came in today and pandied me because I was not writing my theme.

The rector looked at him in silence and he could feel the blood rising to his face and the tears about to rise to his eyes.

The rector said:

—Your name is Dedalus, isn't it?

—Yes, sir.

—And where did you break your glasses?

—On the cinderpath, sir. A fellow was coming out of the bicycle house and I fell and they got broken. I don't know the fellow's name.

The rector looked at him again in silence. Then he smiled and said:

—O, well, it was a mistake, I am sure Father Dolan did not know.

—But I told him I broke them, sir, and he pandied me.

—Did you tell him that you had written home for a new pair? the rector asked.

—No, sir.

—O well then, said the rector, Father Dolan did not understand. You can say that I excuse you from your lessons for a few days.

Stephen said quickly for fear his trembling would prevent him:

—Yes, sir, but Father Dolan said he will come in tomorrow to pandy me again for it.

—Very well, the rector said, it is a mistake and I shall speak to Father Dolan myself. Will that do now?

Stephen felt the tears wetting his eyes and murmured:

—O yes sir, thanks.

The rector held his hand across the side of the desk where the skull was and Stephen, placing his hand in it for a moment, felt a cool moist palm.

—Good day now, said the rector, withdrawing his hand and bowing.

—Good day, sir, said Stephen.

He bowed and walked quietly out of the room, closing the doors carefully and slowly.

But when he had passed the old servant on the landing and was again in the low narrow dark corridor he began to walk faster and faster. Faster and faster he hurried on through the gloom excitedly. He bumped his elbow against the door at the end and, hurrying down the staircase, walked quickly through the two corridors and out into the air.

He could hear the cries of the fellows on the playgrounds. He broke into a run and, running quicker and quicker, ran across the cinderpath and reached the third line playground, panting.

The fellows had seen him running. They closed round him in a ring, pushing one against another to hear.

—Tell us! Tell us!

—What did he say?

—Did you go in?

—What did he say?

—Tell us! Tell us!

He told them what he had said and what the rector had said and, when he had told them, all the fellows flung their caps spinning up into the air and cried:

—Hurroo!

They caught their caps and sent them up again spinning skyhigh and cried again:

—Hurroo! Hurroo!

They made a cradle of their locked hands and hoisted him up among them and carried him along till he struggled to get free. And when he had escaped from them they broke away in all directions, flinging their caps again into the air and whistling as they went spinning up and crying:

—Hurroo!

And they gave three groans for Baldyhead Dolan and three cheers for Conmee and they said he was the decentest rector that was ever in Clongowes.

The cheers died away in the soft grey air. He was alone. He was happy and free: but he would not be anyway proud with Father Dolan. He would be very quiet and obedient: and he wished that he could do something kind for him to show him that he was not proud.

The air was soft and grey and mild and evening was coming. There was the smell of evening in the air, the smell of the fields in the country where they digged up turnips to peel them and eat them when they went out for a walk to Major Barton's, the smell there was in the little wood beyond the pavilion where the gallnuts* were.

The fellows were practising long shies† and bowling lobs and slow twisters. In the soft grey silence he could hear the bump of the balls: and from here and from there through the quiet air the sound of the cricket bats: pick, pack, pock, puck: like drops of water in a fountain falling softly in the brimming bowl.

---

*Hard knots produced in tree branches by boring insects.

†In cricket, long throws to return batted balls.

CHAPTER II

UNCLE CHARLES SMOKED SUCH black twist* that at last his nephew suggested to him to enjoy his morning smoke in a little outhouse at the end of the garden.

—Very good, Simon. All serene, Simon, said the old man tranquilly. Anywhere you like. The outhouse will do me nicely: it will be more salubrious.

—Damn me, said Mr Dedalus frankly, if I know how you can smoke such villainous awful tobacco. It's like gunpowder, by God.

—It's very nice, Simon, replied the old man. Very cool and mollifying.

Every morning, therefore, uncle Charles repaired to his outhouse but not before he had creased and brushed scrupulously his back hair and brushed and put on his tall hat. While he smoked the brim of his tall hat and the bowl of his pipe were just visible beyond the jambs of the outhouse door. His arbour, as he called the reeking outhouse which he shared with the cat and the garden tools, served him also as a soundingbox: and every morning he hummed contentedly one of his favourite songs: *O, twine me a bower* or *Blue eyes and golden hair* or *The Groves of Blarney*† while the grey and blue coils of smoke rose slowly from his pipe and vanished in the pure air.

During the first part of the summer in Blackrock‡ uncle Charles was Stephen's constant companion. Uncle Charles was a hale old man with a well tanned skin, rugged features and white side whiskers. On week days he did messages between the house in Carysfort Avenue and those shops in the main street of the town with which the family dealt. Stephen was glad to go with him on these errands for uncle Charles helped him very liberally to handfuls of whatever was exposed in open boxes and barrels outside the counter. He would seize a handful of

*Smoking tobacco.
†Three popular late-eighteenth-century and nineteenth-century Irish songs.
‡Seaside community south of Dublin, between the city and Dun Laoghaire.

grapes and sawdust or three or four American apples and thrust them generously into his grandnephew's hand while the shopman smiled uneasily; and, on Stephen's feigning reluctance to take them, he would frown and say:

—Take them, sir. Do you hear me, sir? They're good for your bowels.

When the order list had been booked the two would go on to the park where an old friend of Stephen's father, Mike Flynn, would be found seated on a bench, waiting for them. Then would begin Stephen's run round the park. Mike Flynn would stand at the gate near the railway station, watch in hand, while Stephen ran round the track in the style Mike Flynn favoured, his head high lifted, his knees well lifted and his hands held straight down by his sides. When the morning practice was over the trainer would make his comments and sometimes illustrate them by shuffling along for a yard or so comically in an old pair of blue canvas shoes. A small ring of wonderstruck children and nursemaids would gather to watch him and linger even when he and uncle Charles had sat down again and were talking athletics and politics. Though he had heard his father say that Mike Flynn had put some of the best runners of modern times through his hands Stephen often glanced at his trainer's flabby stubble-covered face, as it bent over the long stained fingers through which he rolled his cigarette, and with pity at the mild lustreless blue eyes which would look up suddenly from the task and gaze vaguely into the blue distance while the long swollen fingers ceased their rolling and grains and fibres of tobacco fell back into the pouch.

On the way home uncle Charles would often pay a visit to the chapel and, as the font was above Stephen's reach, the old man would dip his hand and then sprinkle the water briskly about Stephen's clothes and on the floor of the porch. While he prayed he knelt on his red handkerchief and read above his breath from a thumb blackened prayer-book wherein catchwords* were printed at the foot of every page. Stephen knelt at his side respecting, though he did not share, his piety. He often wondered what his granduncle prayed for so seriously. Perhaps he prayed for the souls in purgatory or for the grace of a happy death or perhaps he prayed that God might send him back a part of the big fortune he had squandered in Cork.†

On Sundays Stephen with his father and his granduncle took their

---

*Guide words indicating the first or last word in the text of a page.
†Large port city in County Munster.

constitutional. The old man was a nimble walker in spite of his corns and often ten or twelve miles of the road were covered. The little village of Stillorgan was the parting of the ways. Either they went to the left towards the Dublin mountains or along the Goatstown road and thence into Dundrum, coming home by Sandyford.* Trudging along the road or standing in some grimy wayside public house his elders spoke constantly of the subjects nearer their hearts, of Irish politics, of Munster and of the legends of their own family, to all of which Stephen lent an avid ear. Words which he did not understand he said over and over to himself till he had learnt them by heart: and through them he had glimpses of the real world about him. The hour when he too would take part in the life of that world seemed drawing near and in secret he began to make ready for the great part which he felt awaited him the nature of which he only dimly apprehended.

His evenings were his own; and he pored over a ragged translation of *The Count of Monte Cristo.*[6] The figure of that dark avenger stood forth in his mind for whatever he had heard or divined in childhood of the strange and terrible. At night he built up on the parlour table an image of the wonderful island cave out of transfers and paper flowers and coloured tissue paper and strips of the silver and golden paper in which chocolate is wrapped. When he had broken up this scenery, weary of its tinsel, there would come to his mind the bright picture of Marseilles, of sunny trellises and of Mercedes.

Outside Blackrock, on the road that led to the mountains, stood a small whitewashed house in the garden of which grew many rosebushes: and in this house, he told himself, another Mercedes lived. Both on the outward and on the homeward journey he measured distance by this landmark: and in his imagination he lived through a long train of adventures, marvellous as those in the book itself, towards the close of which there appeared an image of himself, grown older and sadder, standing in a moonlit garden with Mercedes who had so many years before slighted his love, and with a sadly proud gesture of refusal, saying:

—Madam, I never eat muscatel grapes.

He became the ally of a boy named Aubrey Mills and founded with him a gang of adventurers in the avenue. Aubrey carried a whistle dangling from his buttonhole and a bicycle lamp attached to his belt while

---

*Stillorgan, Goatstown, Dundrum, and Sandyford are villages in and along the Dublin mountains, south of the city center.

the others had short sticks thrust daggerwise through theirs. Stephen, who had read of Napoleon's plain style of dress, chose to remain unadorned and thereby heightened for himself the pleasure of taking counsel with his lieutenant before giving orders. The gang made forays into the gardens of old maids or went down to the castle and fought a battle on the shaggy weedgrown rocks, coming home after it weary stragglers with the stale odours of the foreshore in their nostrils and the rank oils of the seawrack upon their hands and in their hair.

Aubrey and Stephen had a common milkman and often they drove out in the milk car to Carrickmines* where the cows were at grass. While the men were milking the boys would take turns in riding the tractable mare round the field. But when autumn came the cows were driven home from the grass: and the first sight of the filthy cowyard at Stradbrook with its foul green puddles and clots of liquid dung and steaming bran troughs sickened Stephen's heart. The cattle which had seemed so beautiful in the country on sunny days revolted him and he could not even look at the milk they yielded.

The coming of September did not trouble him this year for he was not to be sent back to Clongowes. The practice in the park came to an end when Mike Flynn went into hospital. Aubrey was at school and had only an hour or two free in the evening. The gang fell asunder and there were no more nightly forays or battles on the rocks. Stephen sometimes went round with the car which delivered the evening milk: and these chilly drives blew away his memory of the filth of the cowyard and he felt no repugnance at seeing the cow hairs and hayseeds on the milkman's coat. Whenever the car drew up before a house he waited to catch a glimpse of a well scrubbed kitchen or of a softly lighted hall and to see how the servant would hold the jug and how she would close the door. He thought it should be a pleasant life enough, driving along the roads every evening to deliver milk, if he had warm gloves and a fat bag of gingernuts in his pocket to eat from. But the same foreknowledge which had sickened his heart and made his legs sag suddenly as he raced round the park, the same intuition which had made him glance with mistrust at his trainer's flabby stubblecovered face as it bent heavily over his long stained fingers, dissipated any vision of the future. In a vague way he understood that his father was in trouble and that this was the reason why he himself had not been sent back to Clon-

*Community 3 miles south of Blackrock.

gowes. For some time he had felt the slight change in his house; and those changes in what he had deemed unchangeable were so many slight shocks to his boyish conception of the world. The ambition which he felt astir at times in the darkness of his soul sought no outlet. A dusk like that of the outer world obscured his mind as he heard the mare's hoofs clattering along the tramtrack on the Rock Road and the great can swaying and rattling behind him.

He returned to Mercedes and, as he brooded upon her image, a strange unrest crept into his blood. Sometimes a fever gathered within him and led him to rove alone in the evening along the quiet avenue. The peace of the gardens and the kindly lights in the windows poured a tender influence into his restless heart. The noise of children at play annoyed him and their silly voices made him feel, even more keenly than he had felt at Clongowes, that he was different from others. He did not want to play. He wanted to meet in the real world the unsubstantial image which his soul so constantly beheld. He did not know where to seek it or how but a premonition which led him on told him that this image would, without any overt act of his, encounter him. They would meet quietly as if they had known each other and had made their tryst, perhaps at one of the gates or in some more secret place. They would be alone, surrounded by darkness and silence: and in that moment of supreme tenderness he would be transfigured. He would fade into something impalpable under her eyes and then in a moment, he would be transfigured. Weakness and timidity and inexperience would fall from him in that magic moment.

*   *   *   *

Two great yellow caravans had halted one morning before the door and men had come tramping into the house to dismantle it. The furniture had been hustled out through the front garden which was strewn with wisps of straw and rope ends and into the huge vans at the gate. When all had been safely stowed the vans had set off noisily down the avenue: and from the window of the railway carriage, in which he had sat with his red eyed mother, Stephen had seen them lumbering along the Merrion Road.

The parlour fire would not draw that evening and Mr Dedalus rested the poker against the bars of the grate to attract the flame. Uncle Charles dozed in a corner of the half furnished uncarpeted room and near him the family portraits leaned against the wall. The lamp on the table shed a weak light over the boarded floor, muddied by the feet of the vanmen.

Stephen sat on a footstool beside his father listening to a long and incoherent monologue. He understood little or nothing of it at first but he
became slowly aware that his father had enemies and that some fight was
going to take place. He felt, too, that he was being enlisted for the fight,
that some duty was being laid upon his shoulders. The sudden flight from
the comfort and revery of Blackrock, the passage through the gloomy
foggy city, the thought of the bare cheerless house in which they were
now to live made his heart heavy: and again an intuition, a foreknowledge of the future came to him. He understood also why the servants had
often whispered together in the hall and why his father had often stood
on the hearthrug, with his back to the fire, talking loudly to uncle
Charles who urged him to sit down and eat his dinner.

—There's a crack of the whip left in me yet, Stephen, old chap, said
Mr Dedalus, poking at the dull fire with fierce energy. We're not dead
yet, sonny. No, by the Lord Jesus (God forgive me) nor half dead.

Dublin was a new and complex sensation. Uncle Charles had grown
so witless that he could no longer be sent out on errands and the disorder in settling in the new house left Stephen freer than he had been
in Blackrock. In the beginning he contented himself with circling
timidly round the neighbouring square or, at most, going half way
down one of the side streets but when he had made a skeleton map of
the city in his mind he followed boldly one of its central lines until he
reached the Custom House.* He passed unchallenged among the docks
and along the quays† wondering at the multitude of corks that lay bob-
bing on the surface of the water in a thick yellow scum, at the crowds
of quay porters and the rumbling carts and the ill-dressed bearded policeman. The vastness and strangeness of the life suggested to him by
the bales of merchandise stocked along the walls or swung aloft out of
the holds of steamers wakened again in him the unrest which had sent
him wandering in the evening from garden to garden in search of Mercedes. And amid this new bustling life he might have fancied himself
in another Marseilles but that he missed the bright sky and the sun-
warmed trellises of the wineshops. A vague dissatisfaction grew up
within him as he looked on the quays and on the river and on the lowering skies and yet he continued to wander up and down day after day
as if he really sought someone that eluded him.

---

*Beautiful civic building on the north side of the Liffey, the river running west to
east through downtown Dublin, dividing it into south and north.
†Commercial stretches of road alongside the river.

He went once or twice with his mother to visit their relatives: and though they passed a jovial array of shops lit up and adorned for Christmas his mood of embittered silence did not leave him. The causes of his embitterment were many, remote and near. He was angry with himself for being young and the prey of restless foolish impulses, angry also with the change of fortune which was reshaping the world about him into a vision of squalor and insincerity. Yet his anger lent nothing to the vision. He chronicled with patience what he saw, detaching himself from it and testing its mortifying flavour in secret.

He was sitting on the backless chair in his aunt's kitchen. A lamp with a reflector hung on the japanned* wall of the fireplace and by its light his aunt was reading the evening paper that lay on her knees. She looked a long time at a smiling picture that was set in it and said musingly:

—The beautiful Mabel Hunter!

A ringletted girl stood on tiptoe to peer at the picture and said softly:

—What is she in, mud?†

—In a pantomime, love.

The child leaned her ringletted head against her mother's sleeve, gazing on the picture and murmured as if fascinated:

—The beautiful Mabel Hunter!

As if fascinated, her eyes rested long upon those demurely taunting eyes and she murmured devotedly:

—Isn't she an exquisite creature?

And the boy who came in from the street, stamping crookedly under his stone of coal,‡ heard her words. He dropped his load promptly on the floor and hurried to her side to see. He mauled the edges of the paper with his reddened and blackened hands, shouldering her aside and complaining that he could not see.

He was sitting in the narrow breakfast room high up in the old dark windowed house. The firelight flickered on the wall and beyond the window a spectral dusk was gathering upon the river. Before the fire an old woman was busy making tea and, as she bustled at the task, she told in a low voice of what the priest and the doctor had said. She told too

---

*Coated in thick varnish, in the Japanese manner.

†Term of endearment.

‡A 14-pound bag of coal; in the British system of measurement, a stone is 14 pounds.

of certain changes they had seen in her of late and of her odd ways and sayings. He sat listening to the words and following the ways of adventure that lay open in the coals, arches and vaults and winding galleries and jagged caverns.

Suddenly he became aware of something in the doorway. A skull appeared suspended in the gloom of the doorway. A feeble creature like a monkey was there, drawn there by the sound of voices at the fire. A whining voice came from the door asking:

—Is that Josephine?

The old bustling woman answered cheerily from the fireplace:

—No, Ellen, it's Stephen.

—O . . . O, good evening, Stephen.

He answered the greeting and saw a silly smile break over the face in the doorway.

—Do you want anything, Ellen? asked the old woman at the fire.

But she did not answer the question and said:

—I thought it was Josephine. I thought you were Josephine, Stephen.

And, repeating this several times, she fell to laughing feebly.

He was sitting in the midst of a children's party at Harold's Cross.* His silent watchful manner had grown upon him and he took little part in the games. The children, wearing the spoils of their crackers,† danced and romped noisily and, though he tried to share their merriment, he felt himself a gloomy figure amid the gay cocked hats and sunbonnets.

But when he had sung his song‡ and withdrawn into a snug corner of the room he began to taste the joy of his loneliness. The mirth, which in the beginning of the evening had seemed to him false and trivial, was like a soothing air to him, passing gaily by his senses, hiding from other eyes the feverish agitation of his blood while through the circling of the dancers and amid the music and laughter her glance travelled to his corner, flattering, taunting, searching, exciting his heart.

In the hall the children who had stayed latest were putting on their things: the party was over. She had thrown a shawl about her and, as they went together towards the tram, sprays of her fresh warm breath

---

*Neighborhood at the southern edge of Dublin.

†Paper-wrapped party favors.

‡In this Irish tradition, men and women have one song for which they are known and which they are prepared to perform at gatherings.

flew gaily above her cowled head and her shoes tapped blithely on the glassy road.

It was the last tram. The lank brown horses knew it and shook their bells to the clear night in admonition. The conductor talked with the driver, both nodding often in the green light of the lamp. On the empty seats of the tram were scattered a few coloured tickets. No sound of footsteps came up or down the road. No sound broke the peace of the night save when the lank brown horses rubbed their noses together and shook their bells.

They seemed to listen, he on the upper step and she on the lower. She came up to his step many times and went down to hers again between their phrases and once or twice stood close beside him for some moments on the upper step, forgetting to go down, and then went down. His heart danced upon her movements like a cork upon a tide. He heard what her eyes said to him from beneath their cowl and knew that in some dim past, whether in life or revery, he had heard their tale before. He saw her urge her vanities, her fine dress and sash and long black stockings, and knew that he had yielded to them a thousand times. Yet a voice within him spoke above the noise of his dancing heart, asking him would he take her gift to which he had only to stretch out his hand. And he remembered the day when he and Eileen had stood looking into the Hotel Grounds, watching the waiters running up a trail of bunting on the flagstaff and the fox terrier scampering to and fro on the sunny lawn, and how, all of a sudden, she had broken out into a peal of laughter and had run down the sloping curve of the path. Now, as then, he stood listlessly in his place, seemingly a tranquil watcher of the scene before him.

—She too wants me to catch hold of her, he thought. That's why she came with me to the tram. I could easily catch hold of her when she comes up to my step: nobody is looking. I could hold her and kiss her.

But he did neither: and, when he was sitting alone in the deserted tram he tore his ticket into shreds and stared gloomily at the corrugated footboard.

The next day he sat at his table in the bare upper room for many hours. Before him lay a new pen, a new bottle of ink and a new emerald exercise.* From force of habit he had written at the top of the first page the initial letters of the jesuit motto: A.M.D.G.† On the first line

---

*Bound composition notebook.

†*Ad Majorem Dei Gloriam,* Latin for "for the greater glory of God": the Jesuit motto.

of the page appeared the title of the verses he was trying to write: To E—— C——.* He knew it was right to begin so for he had seen similar titles in the collected poems of Lord Byron.† When he had written this title and drawn an ornamental line underneath he fell into a day dream and began to draw diagrams on the cover of the book. He saw himself sitting at his table in Bray the morning after the discussion at the Christmas dinner table, trying to write a poem about Parnell on the back of one of his father's second moiety notices.‡ But his brain had then refused to grapple with the theme and, desisting, he had covered the page with the names and addresses of certain of his classmates:

> Roderick Kickham
> John Lawton
> Anthony MacSwiney
> Simon Moonan

Now it seemed as if he would fail again but, by dint of brooding on the incident, he thought himself into confidence. During this process all those elements which he deemed common and insignificant fell out of the scene. There remained no trace of the tram itself nor of the trammen nor of the horses: nor did he and she appear vividly. The verses told only of the night and the balmy breeze and the maiden lustre of the moon. Some undefined sorrow was hidden in the hearts of the protagonists as they stood in silence beneath the leafless trees and when the moment of farewell had come the kiss, which had been withheld by one, was given by both. After this the letters L. D. S.§ were written at the foot of the page and, having hidden the book, he went into his mother's bedroom and gazed at his face for a long time in the mirror of her dressing table.

But his long spell of leisure and liberty was drawing to its end. One evening his father came home full of news which kept his tongue busy all through dinner. Stephen had been awaiting his father's return for there had been mutton hash that day and he knew that his father would

---

*In the draft version of the novel, published as *Stephen Hero* after Joyce's death, Stephen's love interest is named Emma Clery.

†George Gordon (1788–1824), leading poet and charismatic figure in British Romantic poetry.

‡Notices of debts owed.

§*Laus Deo Semper,* Latin for "praise to God always."

make him dip his bread in the gravy. But he did not relish the hash for the mention of Clongowes had coated his palate with a scum of disgust.

—I walked bang into him, said Mr Dedalus for the fourth time, just at the corner of the square.

—Then I suppose, said Mrs Dedalus, he will be able to arrange it. I mean about Belvedere.

—Of course, he will, said Mr Dedalus. Don't I tell you he's provincial of the order now?

—I never liked the idea of sending him to the christian brothers* myself, said Mrs Dedalus.

—Christian brothers be damned! said Mr Dedalus. Is it with Paddy Stink and Mickey Mud? No, let him stick to the jesuits in God's name since he began with them. They'll be of service to him in after years. Those are the fellows that can get you a position.

—And they're a very rich order, aren't they, Simon?

—Rather. They live well, I tell you. You saw their table at Clongowes. Fed up, by God, like gamecocks.

Mr Dedalus pushed his plate over to Stephen and bade him finish what was on it.

—Now then, Stephen, he said, you must put your shoulder to the wheel, old chap. You've had a fine long holiday.

—O, I'm sure he'll work very hard now, said Mrs Dedalus, especially when he has Maurice with him.

—O, Holy Paul, I forgot about Maurice, said Mr Dedalus. Here, Maurice! Come here, you thick-headed ruffian! Do you know I'm going to send you to a college where they'll teach you to spell c.a.t. cat. And I'll buy you a nice little penny handkerchief to keep your nose dry. Won't that be grand fun?

Maurice grinned at his father and then at his brother. Mr Dedalus screwed his glass into his eye and stared hard at both of his sons. Stephen mumbled his bread without answering his father's gaze.

—By the bye, said Mr Dedalus at length, the rector or provincial rather, was telling me that story about you and Father Dolan. You're an impudent thief, he said.

—O, he didn't, Simon!

—Not he! said Mr Dedalus. But he gave me a great account of the

---

*Brotherhood of Catholic laymen, founded in Waterford, in County Munster, in 1802 by Edmund Ignatius Rice; the Christian Brothers ran inexpensive day schools that emphasized practical learning.

whole affair. We were chatting, you know, and one word borrowed another. And, by the way, who do you think he told me will get that job in the corporation?* But I'll tell you that after. Well, as I was saying, we were chatting away quite friendly and he asked me did our friend here wear glasses still and then he told me the whole story.

—And was he annoyed, Simon?

—Annoyed! Not he! *Manly little chap!* he said.

Mr Dedalus imitated the mincing nasal tone of the provincial.

—Father Dolan and I, when I told them all at dinner about it, Father Dolan and I had a great laugh over it. *You better mind yourself, Father Dolan,* said I, *or young Dedalus will send you up for twice nine.* We had a famous laugh together over it. Ha! Ha! Ha!

Mr Dedalus turned to his wife and interjected in his natural voice:

—Shows you the spirit in which they take the boys there. O, a jesuit for your life, for diplomacy!

He reassumed the provincial's voice and repeated:

—I told them all at dinner about it and Father Dolan and I and all of us we all had a hearty laugh together over it. Ha! Ha! Ha!

The night of the Whitsuntide† play had come and Stephen from the window of the dressing room looked out on the small grassplot across which lines of Chinese lanterns were stretched. He watched the visitors come down the steps from the house and to the theatre. Stewards in evening dress, old Belvedereans, loitered in groups about the entrance to the theatre and ushered in the visitors with ceremony. Under the sudden glow of a lantern he could recognise the smiling face of a priest.

The Blessed Sacrament had been removed from the tabernacle‡ and the first benches had been driven back so as to leave the daïs of the altar and the space before it free. Against the walls stood companies of barbells and Indian clubs; the dumb bells were piled in one corner: and in the midst of countless hillocks of gymnasium shoes and sweaters and singlets in untidy brown parcels there stood the stout leatherjacketed vaulting horse waiting its turn to be carried up on the stage and set in the middle of the winning team at the end of the gymnastic display.

Stephen, though in deference to his reputation for essay writing he had been elected secretary to the gymnasium, had had no part in the first section of the programme, but in the play which formed the sec-

---

*The Dublin Corporation, the city's governing body.
†The week beginning on Pentecost, the seventh Sunday after Easter.
‡Vessel containing the eucharistic host.

ond section he had the chief part, that of a farcical pedagogue. He had been cast for it on account of his stature and grave manners for he was now at the end of his second year at Belvedere and in number two.*

A score of the younger boys in white knickers and singlets came pattering down from the stage, through the vestry and into the chapel. The vestry and chapel were peopled with eager masters and boys. The plump bald sergeant major was testing with his foot the spring board of the vaulting horse. The lean young man in a long overcoat, who was to give a special display of intricate club swinging, stood near watching with interest, his silver coated clubs peeping out of his deep sidepockets. The hollow rattle of the wooden dumb bells was heard as another team made ready to go up on the stage: and in another moment the excited prefect was hustling the boys through the vestry like a flock of geese, flapping the wings of his soutane nervously and crying to the laggards to make haste. A little troop of Neapolitan peasants were practising their steps at the end of the chapel, some circling their arms above their heads, some swaying their baskets of paper violets and curtseying. In a dark corner of the chapel at the gospel side of the altar a stout old lady knelt amid her copious black skirts. When she stood up a pink dressed figure, wearing a curly golden wig and an old fashioned straw sunbonnet, with black pencilled eyebrows and cheeks delicately rouged and powdered, was discovered. A low murmur of curiosity ran round the chapel at the discovery of this girlish figure. One of the prefects, smiling and nodding his head, approached the dark corner and, having bowed to the stout old lady, said pleasantly:

—Is this a beautiful young lady or a doll that you have here, Mrs Tallon?

Then, bending down to peer at the smiling painted face under the leaf of the bonnet, he exclaimed:

—No! Upon my word I believe it's little Bertie Tallon after all!

Stephen at his post by the window heard the old lady and the priest laugh together and heard the boys' murmurs of admiration behind him as they passed forward to see the little boy who had to dance the sunbonnet dance by himself. A movement of impatience escaped him. He let the edge of the blind fall and, stepping down from the bench on which he had been standing, walked out of the chapel.

He passed out of the schoolhouse and halted under the shed that

---

*The penultimate year of studies.

flanked the garden. From the theatre opposite came the muffled noise of the audience and sudden brazen clashes of the soldiers' band. The light spread upwards from the glass roof making the theatre seem a festive ark, anchored among the hulks of houses, her frail cables of lanterns looping her to her moorings. A side door of the theatre opened suddenly and a shaft of light flew across the grassplots. A sudden burst of music issued from the ark, the prelude of a waltz: and when the side door closed again the listener could hear the faint rhythm of the music. The sentiment of the opening bars, their languor and supple movement, evoked the incommunicable emotion which had been the cause of all his day's unrest and of his impatient movement of a moment before. His unrest issued from him like a wave of sound: and on the tide of flowing music the ark was journeying, trailing her cables of lanterns in her wake. Then a noise like dwarf artillery broke the movement. It was the clapping that greeted the entry of the dumb bell team on the stage.

At the far end of the shed near the street a speck of pink light showed in the darkness and as he walked towards it he became aware of a faint aromatic odour. Two boys were standing in the shelter of a doorway, smoking, and before he reached them he had recognised Heron by his voice.

—Here comes the noble Dedalus! cried a high throaty voice. Welcome to our trusty friend!

This welcome ended in a soft peal of mirthless laughter as Heron salaamed* and then began to poke the ground with his cane.

—Here I am, said Stephen, halting and glancing from Heron to his friend.

The latter was a stranger to him but in the darkness, by the aid of the glowing cigarette tips, he could make out a pale dandyish face, over which a smile was travelling slowly, a tall overcoated figure and a hard hat. Heron did not trouble himself about an introduction but said instead:

—I was just telling my friend Wallis what a lark it would be tonight if you took off the rector in the part of the schoolmaster. It would be a ripping good joke.

Heron made a poor attempt to imitate for his friend Wallis the rector's pedantic bass and then, laughing at his failure, asked Stephen to do it.

---

*Performed an Islamic form of low bow.

—Go on, Dedalus, he urged, you can take him off rippingly. *He that will not hear the churcha let him be to theea as the heathena and the publicana.*

The imitation was prevented by a mild expression of anger from Wallis in whose mouthpiece the cigarette had become too tightly wedged.

—Damn this blankety blank holder, he said, taking it from his mouth and smiling and frowning upon it tolerantly. It's always getting stuck like that. Do you use a holder?

—I don't smoke, answered Stephen.

—No, said Heron, Dedalus is a model youth. He doesn't smoke and he doesn't go to bazaars and he doesn't flirt and he doesn't damn anything or damn all.

Stephen shook his head and smiled in his rival's flushed and mobile face, beaked like a bird's. He had often thought it strange that Vincent Heron had a bird's face as well as a bird's name. A shock of pale hair lay on the forehead like a ruffled crest: the forehead was narrow and bony and a thin hooked nose stood out between the closeset prominent eyes which were light and inexpressive. The rivals were school friends. They sat together in class, knelt together in the chapel, talked together after beads* over their lunches. As the fellows in number one were undistinguished dullards Stephen and Heron had been during the year the virtual heads of the school. It was they who went up to the rector together to ask for a free day or to get a fellow off.

—O by the way, said Heron suddenly, I saw your governor going in.

The smile waned on Stephen's face. Any allusion made to his father by a fellow or by a master put his calm to rout in a moment. He waited in timorous silence to hear what Heron might say next. Heron, however, nudged him expressively with his elbow and said:

—You're a sly dog.

—Why so? said Stephen.

—You'd think butter wouldn't melt in your mouth, said Heron. But I'm afraid you're a sly dog.

—Might I ask you what you are talking about? said Stephen urbanely.

—Indeed you might, answered Heron. We saw her, Wallis, didn't we? And deucedly pretty she is too. And inquisitive! *And what part does Stephen take, Mr Dedalus? And will Stephen not sing, Mr Dedalus?* Your governor was staring at her through that eyeglass of his for all he was

---

*Slang for a session of praying the rosary, a devotion whose progress is marked on a string of beads.

worth so that I think the old man has found you out too. I wouldn't care a bit, by Jove. She's ripping, isn't she, Wallis?

—Not half bad, answered Wallis quietly as he placed his holder once more in a corner of his mouth.

A shaft of momentary anger flew through Stephen's mind at these indelicate allusions in the hearing of a stranger. For him there was nothing amusing in a girl's interest and regard. All day he had thought of nothing but their leavetaking on the steps of the tram at Harold's Cross, the stream of moody emotions it had made to course through him, and the poem he had written about it. All day he had imagined a new meeting with her for he knew that she was to come to the play. The old restless moodiness had again filled his breast as it had done on the night of the party but had not found an outlet in verse. The growth and knowledge of two years of boyhood stood between then and now, forbidding such an outlet: and all day the stream of gloomy tenderness within him had started forth and returned upon itself in dark courses and eddies, wearying him in the end until the pleasantry of the prefect and the painted little boy had drawn from him a movement of impatience.

—So you may as well admit, Heron went on, that we've fairly found you out this time. You can't play the saint on me any more, that's one sure five.

A soft peal of mirthless laughter escaped from his lips and, bending down as before, he struck Stephen lightly across the calf of the leg with his cane, as if in jesting reproof.

Stephen's movement of anger had already passed. He was neither flattered nor confused but simply wished the banter to end. He scarcely resented what had seemed to him a silly indelicateness for he knew that the adventure in his mind stood in no danger from these words: and his face mirrored his rival's false smile.

—Admit! repeated Heron, striking him again with his cane across the calf of the leg.

The stroke was playful but not so lightly given as the first one had been. Stephen felt the skin tingle and glow slightly and almost painlessly; and, bowing submissively, as if to meet his companion's jesting mood, began to recite the *Confiteor*.* The episode ended well for both Heron and Wallis laughed indulgently at the irreverence.

The confession came only from Stephen's lips and, while they spoke

---

*A prayer, part of the traditional Catholic Mass, in which one confesses having sinned (the word is Latin for "I confess") and asks God's forgiveness.

the words, a sudden memory had carried him to another scene called
up, as if by magic, at the moment when he had noted the faint cruel
dimples at the corners of Heron's smiling lips and had felt the familiar
stroke of the cane against his calf and had heard the familiar word of
admonition:
—Admit.

It was towards the close of his first term in the college when he was
in number six. His sensitive nature was still smarting under the lashes
of an undivined and squalid way of life. His soul was still disquieted and
cast down by the dull phenomenon of Dublin. He had emerged from a
two years' spell of reverie to find himself in the midst of a new scene,
every event and figure of which affected him intimately, disheartened
him or allured and, whether alluring or disheartening, filled him always
with unrest and bitter thoughts. All the leisure which his school life left
him was passed in the company of subversive writers whose gibes and
violence of speech set up a ferment in his brain before they passed out
of it into his crude writings.

The essay was for him the chief labour of his week and every Tuesday, as he marched from home to the school, he read his fate in the incidents of the way, pitting himself against some figure ahead of him and
quickening his pace to outstrip it before a certain goal was reached or
planting his steps scrupulously in the spaces of the patchwork of the
pathway and telling himself that he would be first and not first in the
weekly essay.

On a certain Tuesday the course of his triumphs was rudely broken.
Mr Tate the English master, pointed his finger at him and said bluntly:
—This fellow has heresy in his essay.

A hush fell on the class. Mr Tate did not break it but dug with his
hand between his thighs while his heavily starched linen creaked about
his neck and wrists. Stephen did not look up. It was a raw spring morning and his eyes were still smarting and weak. He was conscious of failure and of detection, of the squalor of his own mind and home, and felt
against his neck the raw edge of his turned and jagged collar.

A short loud laugh from Mr Tate set the class more at ease.
—Perhaps you didn't know that, he said.
—Where? asked Stephen.

Mr Tate withdrew his delving hand and spread out the essay.
—Here. It's about the Creator and the soul. Rrm . . . rrm . . .

rrm . . . Ah! *without a possibility of ever approaching nearer.* That's heresy.

Stephen murmured:

—I meant *without a possibility of ever reaching.*[7]

It was a submission and Mr Tate, appeased, folded up the essay and passed it across to him, saying:

—O . . . Ah! *ever reaching.* That's another story.

But the class was not so soon appeased. Though nobody spoke to him of the affair after class he could feel about him a vague general malignant joy.

A few nights after this public chiding he was walking with a letter along the Drumcondra Road when he heard a voice cry:

—Halt!

He turned and saw three boys of his own class coming towards him in the dusk. It was Heron who had called out and, as he marched forward between his two attendants, he cleft the air before him with a thin cane, in time to their steps. Boland, his friend, marched beside him, a large grin on his face, while Nash came on a few steps behind, blowing from the pace and wagging his great red head.

As soon as the boys had turned into Clonliffe Road together they began to speak about books and writers, saying what books they were reading and how many books there were in their fathers' bookcases at home. Stephen listened to them in some wonderment for Boland was the dunce and Nash the idler of the class. In fact after some talk about their favourite writers Nash declared for Captain Marryat* who, he said, was the greatest writer.

—Fudge! said Heron. Ask Dedalus. Who is the greatest writer, Dedalus?

Stephen noted the mockery in the question and said:

—Of prose do you mean?

—Yes.

—Newman, I think.

—Is it Cardinal Newman?[8] asked Boland.

—Yes, answered Stephen.

The grin broadened on Nash's freckled face as he turned to Stephen and said:

—And do you like Cardinal Newman, Dedalus?

---

*Frederick Marryat (1792–1848), an author whose best-known works include *Japhet in Search of a Father* (1836) and *The Children of the New Forest* (1847).

—O, many say that Newman has the best prose style, Heron said to the other two in explanation; of course he's not a poet.

—And who is the best poet, Heron? asked Boland.

—Lord Tennyson,* of course, answered Heron.

—O, yes, Lord Tennyson, said Nash. We have all his poetry at home in a book.

At this Stephen forgot the silent vows he had been making and burst out:

—Tennyson a poet! Why, he's only a rhymester!

—O, get out! said Heron. Everyone knows that Tennyson is the greatest poet.

—And who do you think is the greatest poet? asked Boland, nudging his neighbour.

—Byron, of course, answered Stephen.

Heron gave the lead and all three joined in a scornful laugh.

—What are you laughing at? asked Stephen.

—You, said Heron. Byron the greatest poet! He's only a poet for uneducated people.

—He must be a fine poet! said Boland.

—You may keep your mouth shut, said Stephen, turning on him boldly. All you know about poetry is what you wrote up on the slates in the yard and were going to be sent to the loft for.

Boland, in fact, was said to have written on the slates in the yard a couplet about a classmate of his who often rode home from the college on a pony:

> *As Tyson was riding into Jerusalem*
> *He fell and hurt his Alec Kafoozelum.*

This thrust put the two lieutenants to silence but Heron went on:

—In any case Byron was a heretic and immoral too.

—I don't care what he was, cried Stephen hotly.

—You don't care whether he was a heretic or not? said Nash.

—What do you know about it? shouted Stephen. You never read a line of anything in your life except a trans† or Boland either.

—I know that Byron was a bad man, said Boland.

---

*Alfred, Lord Tennyson (1809–1892), poet laureate (1850–1892); author of *In Memoriam* (1850) and *Idylls of the King* (1859).

†"Crib," or study aid.

—Here, catch hold of this heretic, Heron called out.

In a moment Stephen was a prisoner.

—Tate made you buck up the other day, Heron went on, about the heresy in your essay.

—I'll tell him tomorrow, said Boland.

—Will you? said Stephen. You'd be afraid to open your lips.

— Afraid?

—Ay. Afraid of your life.

—Behave yourself! cried Heron, cutting at Stephen's legs with his cane.

It was the signal for their onset. Nash pinioned his arms behind while Boland seized a long cabbage stump which was lying in the gutter. Struggling and kicking under the cuts of the cane and the blows of the knotty stump Stephen was borne back against a barbed wire fence.

—Admit that Byron was no good.

—No.

—Admit.

—No.

—Admit.

—No. No.

At last after a fury of plunges he wrenched himself free. His tormentors set off towards Jones's Road, laughing and jeering at him, while he, half blinded with tears, stumbled on, clenching his fists madly and sobbing.

While he was still repeating the *Confiteor* amid the indulgent laughter of his hearers and while the scenes of that malignant episode were still passing sharply and swiftly before his mind he wondered why he bore no malice now to those who had tormented him. He had not forgotten a whit of their cowardice and cruelty but the memory of it called forth no anger from him. All the description of fierce love and hatred which he had met in books had seemed to him therefore unreal. Even that night as he stumbled homewards along Jones's Road he had felt that some power was divesting him of that sudden woven anger as easily as a fruit is divested of its soft ripe peel.

He remained standing with his two companions at the end of the shed listening idly to their talk or to the bursts of applause in the theatre. She was sitting there among the others perhaps waiting for him to appear. He tried to recall her appearance but could not. He could remember only that she had worn a shawl about her head like a cowl and that her dark eyes had invited and unnerved him. He wondered had he been in her thoughts or she had been in his. Then in the dark and unseen by the other two he rested the tips of the fingers of one hand upon the palm of the other hand, scarcely touching it lightly. But the pressure of her fingers had been lighter and steadier: and suddenly the memory of their touch traversed his brain and body like an invisible wave.

A boy came towards them, running along under the shed. He was excited and breathless.

—O, Dedalus, he cried, Doyle is in a great bake* about you. You're to go in at once and get dressed for the play. Hurry up, you better.

—He's coming now, said Heron to the messenger with a haughty drawl, when he wants to.

The boy turned to Heron and repeated:

—But Doyle is in an awful bake.

—Will you tell Doyle with my best compliments that I damned his eyes? answered Heron.

—Well, I must go now, said Stephen, who cared little for such points of honour.

—I wouldn't, said Heron, damn me if I would. That's no way to send for one of the senior boys. In a bake, indeed! I think it's quite enough that you're taking a part in his bally old play.

This spirit of quarrelsome comradeship which he had observed lately in his rival had not seduced Stephen from his habits of quiet obedience. He mistrusted the turbulence and doubted the sincerity of such comradeship which seemed to him a sorry anticipation of manhood. The question of honour here raised was, like all such questions, trivial to him. While his mind had been pursuing its intangible phantoms and turning in irresolution from such pursuit he had heard about him the constant voices of his father and of his masters, urging him to be a gentleman above all things and urging him to be a good catholic above all things. These voices had now come to be hollow sounding in his ears. When the gymnasium had been opened he had heard another voice urging him to be strong and manly and healthy and when the movement towards national revival had begun to be felt in the college yet another voice had bidden him be true to his country and help to raise up her language and tradition.† In the profane world, as he foresaw, a worldly voice would bid him raise up his father's fallen state by his

---

*Fit of anger.

†Allusion to the work of the Gaelic League (established in 1893), which sought to revive the Irish language, literature in Irish, and traditional Irish culture.

labours and, meanwhile, the voice of his school-comrades urged him to be a decent fellow, to shield others from blame or to beg them off and to do his best to get free days for the school. And it was the din of all these hollowsounding voices that made him halt irresolutely in the pursuit of phantoms. He gave them ear only for a time but he was happy only when he was far from them, beyond their call, alone or in the company of phantasmal comrades.

In the vestry a plump freshfaced jesuit and an elderly man, in shabby blue clothes, were dabbling in a case of paints and chalks. The boys who had been painted walked about or stood still awkwardly, touching their faces in a gingerly fashion with their furtive fingertips. In the middle of the vestry a young jesuit, who was then on a visit to the college, stood rocking himself rhythmically from the tips of his toes to his heels and back again, his hands thrust well forward into his side pockets. His small head set off with glossy red curls and his newly shaven face agreed well with the spotless decency of his soutane and with his spotless shoes.

As he watched this swaying form and tried to read for himself the legend of the priest's mocking smile there came into Stephen's memory a saying which he had heard from his father before he had been sent to Clongowes, that you could always tell a jesuit by the style of his clothes. At the same moment he thought he saw a likeness between his father's mind and that of this smiling welldressed priest: and he was aware of some desecration of the priest's office or of the vestry itself whose silence was now routed by loud talk and joking and its air pungent with the smells of the gasjets and the grease.

While his forehead was being wrinkled and his jaws painted black and blue by the elderly man he listened distractedly to the voice of the plump young jesuit which bade him speak up and make his points clearly. He could hear the band playing *The Lily of Killarney** and knew that in a few moments the curtain would go up. He felt no stage fright but the thought of the part he had to play humiliated him. A remembrance of some of his lines made a sudden flush rise to his painted cheeks. He saw her serious alluring eyes watching him from among the audience and their image at once swept away his scruples, leaving his will compact. Another nature seemed to have been lent him: the infection of the excitement and youth about him entered into and trans-

---

*From the opera based on Dion Boucicault's *The Colleen Bawn* (1860).

Chapter II

- - - Stephen's Route after the Play

Mountjoy Square

Belvedere College

Gt. Denmark Street

Gt. George's St. N.

Rutland (Parnell) Square

Marlborough Street

O'Connell Street

Dublin City Morgue

Mechanics Institute (later, The Abbey Theatre)

Custom House

Abbey Street Old

Lotts

River Liffey

formed his moody mistrustfulness. For one rare moment he seemed to be clothed in the real apparel of boyhood: and, as he stood in the wings among the other players, he shared the common mirth amid which the drop scene was hauled upwards by two ablebodied priests with violent jerks and all awry.

A few moments after he found himself on the stage amid the garish gas and the dim scenery, acting before the innumerable faces of the void. It surprised him to see that the play which he had known at rehearsals for a disjointed lifeless thing had suddenly assumed a life of its own. It seemed now to play itself, he and his fellow actors aiding it with their parts. When the curtain fell on the last scene he heard the void filled with applause and, through a rift in a side scene, saw the simple body before which he had acted magically deformed, the void of faces breaking at all points and falling asunder into busy groups.

He left the stage quickly and rid himself of his mummery* and passed out through the chapel into the college garden. Now that the play was over his nerves cried for some further adventure. He hurried onwards as if to overtake it. The doors of the theatre were all open and the audience had emptied out. On the lines which he had fancied the moorings of an ark a few lanterns swung in the night breeze, flickering cheerlessly. He mounted the steps from the garden in haste, eager that some prey should not elude him, and forced his way through the crowd in the hall and past the two jesuits who stood watching the exodus and bowing and shaking hands with the visitors. He pushed onward nervously, feigning a still greater haste and faintly conscious of the smiles and stares and nudges which his powdered head left in its wake.

When he came out on the steps he saw his family waiting for him at the first lamp. In a glance he noted that every figure of the group was familiar and ran down the steps angrily.

—I have to leave a message down in George's Street, he said to his father quickly. I'll be home after you.

Without waiting for his father's questions he ran across the road and began to walk at breakneck speed down the hill. He hardly knew where he was walking. Pride and hope and desire like crushed herbs in his heart sent up vapours of maddening incense before the eyes of his mind. He strode down the hill amid the tumult of suddenrisen vapours

---

*Pantomime performance.

of wounded pride and fallen hope and baffled desire. They streamed upwards before his anguished eyes in dense and maddening fumes and passed away above him till at last the air was clear and cold again.

A film still veiled his eyes but they burned no longer. A power, akin to that which had often made anger or resentment fall from him, brought his steps to rest. He stood still and gazed up at the sombre porch of the morgue and from that to the dark cobbled laneway at its side. He saw the word *Lotts** on the wall of the lane and breathed slowly the rank heavy air.

—That is horse piss and rotted straw, he thought. It is a good odour to breathe. It will calm my heart. My heart is quite calm now. I will go back.

*   *   *   *

Stephen was once again seated beside his father in the corner of a railway carriage at Kingsbridge.† He was travelling with his father by the night mail to Cork. As the train steamed out of the station he recalled his childish wonder of years before and every event of his first day at Clongowes. But he felt no wonder now. He saw the darkening lands slipping away past him, the silent telegraphpoles passing his window swiftly every four seconds, the little glimmering stations, manned by a few silent sentries, flung by the mail behind her and twinkling for a moment in the darkness like fiery grains flung backwards by a runner.

He listened without sympathy to his father's evocation of Cork and of scenes of his youth—a tale broken by sighs or draughts from his pocket flask whenever the image of some dead friend appeared in it, or whenever the evoker remembered suddenly the purpose of his actual visit. Stephen heard, but could feel no pity. The images of the dead were all strangers to him save that of Uncle Charles, an image which had lately been fading out of memory. He knew, however, that his father's property was going to be sold by auction and in the manner of his own dispossession he felt the world give the lie rudely to his phantasy.

At Maryborough‡ he fell asleep. When he awoke the train had passed out of Mallow§ and his father was stretched asleep on the other

---

*Short laneway on the northern quays of the Liffey.
†Terminal for trains departing to the south.
‡50 miles from Dublin on the route to Cork.
§115 miles from Dublin; 19 miles outside Cork.

seat. The cold light of the dawn lay over the country, over the unpeopled fields and the closed cottages. The terror of sleep fascinated his mind as he watched the silent country or heard from time to time his father's deep breath or sudden sleepy movement. The neighbourhood of unseen sleepers filled him with strange dread, as though they could harm him, and he prayed that the day might come quickly. His prayer, addressed neither to God nor saint, began with a shiver, as the chilly morning breeze crept through the chink of the carriage door to his feet, and ended in a trail of foolish words which he made to fit the insistent rhythm of the train; and silently, at intervals of four seconds, the telegraphpoles held the galloping notes of the music between punctual bars. This furious music allayed his dread and, leaning against the window ledge, he let his eyelids close again.

They drove in a jingle across Cork while it was still early morning and Stephen finished his sleep in a bedroom of the Victoria Hotel. The bright warm sunlight was streaming through the window and he could hear the din of traffic. His father was standing before the dressingtable, examining his hair and face and moustache with great care, craning his neck across the water jug and drawing it back sideways to see the better. While he did so he sang softly to himself with quaint accent and phrasing:

> *'Tis youth and folly*
> *Makes young men marry,*
> *So here, my love, I'll*
> *No longer stay.*
> *What can't be cured, sure,*
> *Must be injured, sure,*
> *So I'll go to Amerikay.*

> *My love she's handsome,*
> *My love she's bonny:*
> *She's like good whisky*
> *When it is new;*
> *But when 'tis old*
> *And growing cold*
> *It fades and dies like*
> *The mountain dew.*

The consciousness of the warm sunny city outside his window and the tender tremors with which his father's voice festooned the strange sad happy air, drove off all the mists of the night's ill humour from Stephen's brain. He got up quickly to dress and, when the song had ended, said:

—That's much prettier than any of your other *come-all-yous*.[*]

—Do you think so? asked Mr Dedalus.

—I like it, said Stephen.

—It's a pretty old air,[†] said Mr Dedalus, twirling the points of his moustache. Ah, but you should have heard Mick Lacy sing it! Poor Mick Lacy! He had little turns for it, grace notes he used to put in that I haven't got. That was the boy who could sing a *come-all-you*, if you like.

Mr Dedalus had ordered drisheens[‡] for breakfast and during the meal he cross-examined the waiter for local news. For the most part they spoke at cross purposes when a name was mentioned, the waiter having in mind the present holder and Mr Dedalus his father or perhaps his grandfather.

Well, I hope they haven't moved the Queen's College[§] anyhow, said Mr Dedalus, for I want to show it to this youngster of mine.

Along the Mardyke[||] the trees were in bloom. They entered the grounds of the college and were led by the garrulous porter across the quadrangle. But their progress across the gravel was brought to a halt after every dozen or so paces by some reply of the porter's—

—Ah, do you tell me so? And is poor Pottlebelly dead?

—Yes, sir. Dead, sir.

During these halts Stephen stood awkwardly behind the two men, weary of the subject and waiting restlessly for the slow march to begin again. By the time they had crossed the quadrangle his restlessness had risen to fever. He wondered how his father, whom he knew for a shrewd suspicious man, could be duped by the servile manners of the porter; and the lively southern speech which had entertained him all the morning now irritated his ears.

---

[*]Popular ballads that often begin with the phrase "Come all you [for example, Irish men]," etc. Mr. Dedalus begins a satiric "come-all-you" during the Christmas dinner scene (p. 30): "O, come all you Roman catholics / That never went to mass."
[†]Tune or melody.
[‡]Type of blood sausage.
[§]Opened in 1849.
[||]A promenade.

They passed into the anatomy theatre* where Mr Dedalus, the porter aiding him, searched the desks for his initials. Stephen remained in the background, depressed more than ever by the darkness and silence of the theatre and by the air it wore of jaded and formal study. On the desk he read the word *Fœtus* cut several times in the dark stained wood. The sudden legend startled his blood: he seemed to feel the absent students of the college about him and to shrink from their company. A vision of their life, which his father's words had been powerless to evoke, sprang up before him out of the word cut in the desk. A broad shouldered student with a moustache was cutting in the letters with a jack knife, seriously. Other students stood or sat near him laughing at his handiwork. One jogged his elbow. The big student turned on him, frowning. He was dressed in loose grey clothes and had tan boots.

Stephen's name was called. He hurried down the steps of the theatre so as to be as far away from the vision as he could be and, peering closely at his father's initials, hid his flushed face.

But the word and the vision capered before his eyes as he walked back across the quadrangle and towards the college gate. It shocked him to find in the outer world a trace of what he had deemed till then a brutish and individual malady of his own mind. His monstrous reveries came thronging into his memory. They too had sprung up before him, suddenly and furiously, out of mere words. He had soon given in to them, and allowed them to sweep across and abase his intellect, wondering always where they came from, from what den of monstrous images, and always weak and humble towards others, restless and sickened of himself when they had swept over him.

- -Ay, bedad! And there's the Groceries sure enough! cried Mr Dedalus. You often heard me speak of the Groceries, didn't you, Stephen. Many's the time we went down there when our names had been marked, a crowd of us, Harry Peard and little Jack Mountain and Bob Dyas and Maurice Moriarty, the Frenchman, and Tom O'Grady and Mick Lacy that I told you of this morning and Joey Corbet and poor little good hearted Johnny Keevers of the Tantiles.

The leaves of the trees along the Mardyke were astir and whispering in the sunlight. A team of cricketers passed, agile young men in flannels and blazers, one of them carrying the long green wicket bag. In a quiet by street a German band of five players in faded uniforms and

---

*Classroom.

with battered brass instruments was playing to an audience of street arabs* and leisurely messenger boys. A maid in a white cap and apron was watering a box of plants on a sill which shone like a slab of limestone in the warm glare. From another window open to the air came the sound of a piano, scale after scale rising into the treble.

Stephen walked on at his father's side, listening to stories he had heard before, hearing again the names of the scattered and dead revellers who had been the companions of his father's youth. And a faint sickness sighed in his heart. He recalled his own equivocal position in Belvedere, a free boy, a leader afraid of his own authority, proud and sensitive and suspicious, battling against the squalor of his life and against the riot of his mind. The letters cut in the stained wood of the desk stared upon him, mocking his bodily weakness and futile enthusiasms and making him loathe himself for his own mad and filthy orgies. The spittle in his throat grew bitter and foul to swallow and the faint sickness climbed to his brain so that for a moment he closed his eyes and walked on in darkness.

He could still hear his father's voice.

—When you kick out for yourself, Stephen—as I daresay you will one of those days—remember, whatever you do, to mix with gentlemen. When I was a young fellow I tell you I enjoyed myself. I mixed with fine decent fellows. Everyone of us could do something. One fellow had a good voice, another fellow was a good actor, another could sing a good comic song, another was a good oarsman or a good racket player, another could tell a good story and so on. We kept the ball rolling anyhow and enjoyed ourselves and saw a bit of life and we were none the worse of it either. But we were all gentlemen, Stephen—at least I hope we were—and bloody good honest Irishmen too. That's the kind of fellows I want you to associate with, fellows of the right kidney.† I'm talking to you as a friend, Stephen. I don't believe a son should be afraid of his father. No, I treat you as your grandfather treated me when I was a young chap. We were more like brothers than father and son. I'll never forget the first day he caught me smoking. I was standing at the end of the South Terrace one day with some maneens‡ like myself and sure we thought we were grand fellows because we had pipes stuck in the corners of our mouths. Suddenly the governor

---

*Street urchins or beggars.
†Temperament, disposition.
‡Little men (Anglo-Irish).

passed. He didn't say a word, or stop even. But the next day, Sunday, we were out for a walk together and when we were coming home he took out his cigar case and said: *By the by, Simon, I didn't know you smoked,* or something like that. Of course I tried to carry it off as best I could. *If you want a good smoke, he said, try one of these cigars. An American captain made me a present of them last night in Queenstown.*[*]

Stephen heard his father's voice break into a laugh which was almost a sob.

—He was the handsomest man in Cork at that time, by God he was! The women used to stand to look after him in the street.

He heard the sob passing loudly down his father's throat and opened his eyes with a nervous impulse. The sunlight breaking suddenly on his sight turned the sky and clouds into a fantastic world of sombre masses with lakelike spaces of dark rosy light. His very brain was sick and powerless. He could scarcely interpret the letters of the signboards of the shops. By his monstrous way of life he seemed to have put himself beyond the limits of reality. Nothing moved him or spoke to him from the real world unless he heard in it an echo of the infuriated cries within him. He could respond to no earthly or human appeal, dumb and insensible to the call of summer and gladness and companionship, wearied and dejected by his father's voice. He could scarcely recognise as his his own thoughts, and repeated slowly to himself:

—I am Stephen Dedalus. I am walking beside my father whose name is Simon Dedalus. We are in Cork, in Ireland. Cork is a city. Our room is in the Victoria Hotel. Victoria and Stephen and Simon. Simon and Stephen and Victoria. Names.

The memory of his childhood suddenly grew dim. He tried to call forth some of its vivid moments but could not. He recalled only names. Dante, Parnell, Clane, Clongowes. A little boy had been taught geography by an old woman who kept two brushes in her wardrobe. Then he had been sent away from home to a college, he had made his first communion and eaten slim jim[†] out of his cricket cap and watched the firelight leaping and dancing on the wall of a little bedroom in the infirmary and dreamed of being dead, of mass being said for him by the rector in a black and gold cope, of being buried then in the little graveyard of the community off the main avenue of lines. But he had not died then. Parnell had died. There had been no mass for the dead in the

---

[*]Cork's primary seaport, now called again by its Irish name, Cobh.
[†]Candy confection.

chapel, and no procession. He had not died but he had faded out like a film in the sun. He had been lost or had wandered out of existence for he no longer existed. How strange to think of him passing out of existence in such a way, not by death, but by fading out in the sun or by being lost and forgotten somewhere in the universe! It was strange to see his small body appear again for a moment: a little boy in a grey belted suit. His hands were in his side pockets and his trousers were tucked in at the knees by elastic bands.

On the evening of the day on which the property was sold Stephen followed his father meekly about the city from bar to bar. To the sellers in the market, to the barmen and barmaids, to the beggars who importuned him for a lob* Mr Dedalus told the same tale, that he was an old Corkonian, that he had been trying for thirty years to get rid of his Cork accent up in Dublin and that Peter Pickackafax beside him was his eldest son but that he was only a Dublin jackeen.†

They had set out early in the morning from Newcombe's coffee-house, where Mr Dedalus' cup had rattled noisily against its saucer, and Stephen had tried to cover that shameful sign of his father's drinking-bout of the night before by moving his chair and coughing. One humiliation had succeeded another—the false smiles of the market sellers, the curvetings‡ and oglings of the barmaids with whom his father flirted, the compliments and encouraging words of his father's friends. They had told him that he had a great look of his grandfather and Mr Dedalus had agreed that he was an ugly likeness. They had unearthed traces of a Cork accent in his speech and made him admit that the Lee§ was a much finer river than the Liffey. One of them, in order to put his Latin to the proof, had made him translate short passages from Dilectus,‖ and asked him whether it was correct to say: *Tempora mutantur nos et mutamur in illis,* or *Tempora mutantur et nos mutamur in illis.*# Another, a brisk old man, whom Mr Dedalus called Johnny Cashman, had covered him with confusion by asking him to say which were prettier, the Dublin girls or the Cork girls.

—He's not that way built, said Mr Dedalus. Leave him alone. He's

---

*Coin.
†Young boy (Anglo-Irish).
‡Prancings.
§River that flows through Cork.
‖Popular Latin phrasebook.
#Times change and we change with them (Latin); both Latin versions are correct.

a levelheaded thinking boy who doesn't bother his head about that kind of nonsense.

—Then he's not his father's son, said the little old man.

—I don't know, I'm sure, said Mr Dedalus, smiling complacently.

—Your father, said the little old man to Stephen, was the boldest flirt in the city of Cork in his day. Do you know that?

Stephen looked down and studied the tiled floor of the bar into which they had drifted.

—Now don't be putting ideas into his head, said Mr Dedalus. Leave him to his Maker.

—Yerra, sure I wouldn't put any ideas into his head. I'm old enough to be his grandfather. And I am a grandfather, said the little old man to Stephen. Do you know that?

—Are you? asked Stephen.

—Bedad I am, said the little old man, I have two bouncing grand-children out at Sunday's Well.* Now, then! What age do you think I am! And I remember seeing your grandfather in his red coat riding out to hounds. That was before you were born.

—Ay, or thought of, said Mr Dedalus.

—Bedad I did, repeated the little old man. And, more than that, I can remember even your great grandfather, old John Stephen Dedalus, and a fierce old fire-eater he was. Now, then! There's a memory for you!

—That's three generations—four generations, said another of the company. Why, Johnny Cashman, you must be nearing the century.

—Well, I'll tell you the truth, said the little old man. I'm just twenty-seven years of age.

—We're as old as we feel, Johnny, said Mr Dedalus.

—And just finish what you have there, and we'll have another. Here, Tim or Tom or whatever your name is, give us the same again here. By God, I don't feel more than eighteen myself. There's that son of mine there not half my age and I'm a better man than he is any day of the week.

—Draw it mild now, Dedalus. I think it's time for you to take a back seat, said the gentleman who had spoken before.

—No, by God! asserted Mr Dedalus. I'll sing a tenor song against him or I'll vault a fire-barred gate against him or I'll run with him after

---

*Suburb of Cork.

the hounds across the country as I did thirty years ago along with the Kerry Boy and the best man for it.

—But he'll beat you here, said the little old man, tapping his forehead and raising his glass to drain it.

—Well, I hope he'll be as good a man as his father. That's all I can say, said Mr Dedalus.

—If he is, he'll do, said the little old man.

—And thanks be to God, Johnny, said Mr Dedalus, that we lived so long and did so little harm.

—But did so much good, Simon, said the little old man gravely. Thanks be to God we lived so long and did so much good.

Stephen watched the three glasses being raised from the counter as his father and his two cronies drank to the memory of their past. An abyss of fortune or of temperament sundered him from them. His mind seemed older than theirs: it shone coldly on their strifes and happiness and regrets like a moon upon a younger earth. No life or youth stirred in him as it had stirred in them. He had known neither the pleasure of companionship with others nor the vigour of rude male health nor filial piety. Nothing stirred within his soul but a cold and cruel and loveless lust. His childhood was dead or lost and with it his soul capable of simple joys and he was drifting amid life like the barren shell of the moon.

> *Art thou pale for weariness*
> *Of climbing heaven and gazing on the earth,*
> *Wandering companionless? . . .**

He repeated to himself the lines of Shelley's fragment. Its alternation of sad human ineffectualness with vast inhuman cycles of activity chilled him, and he forgot his own human and ineffectual grieving.

*   *   *   *

Stephen's mother and his brother and one of his cousins waited at the corner of quiet Foster Place while he and his father went up the steps and along the colonnade where the Highland sentry was parading. When they had passed into the great hall and stood at the counter Stephen drew forth his orders on the governor of the bank of Ireland for thirty and three pounds; and these sums, the moneys of his exhibi-

---

'From "To the Moon," by Percy Bysshe Shelley (1792–1822).

tion* and essay prize, were paid over to him rapidly by the teller in notes and in coin respectively. He bestowed them in his pockets with feigned composure and suffered the friendly teller, to whom his father chatted, to take his hand across the broad counter and wish him a brilliant career in after life. He was impatient of their voices and could not keep his feet at rest. But the teller still deferred the serving of others to say he was living in changed times and that there was nothing like giving a boy the best education that money could buy. Mr Dedalus lingered in the hall gazing about him and up at the roof and telling Stephen, who urged him to come out, that they were standing in the house of commons of the old Irish parliament.†

—God help us! he said piously, to think of the men of those times, Stephen, Hely Hutchinson and Flood and Henry Grattan and Charles Kendal Bushe,‡ and the noblemen we have now, leaders of the Irish people at home and abroad. Why, by God, they wouldn't be seen dead in a ten acre field with them. No, Stephen, old chap, I'm sorry to say that they are only as I roved out one fine May morning in the merry month of sweet July.

A keen October wind was blowing round the bank. The three figures standing at the edge of the muddy path had pinched cheeks and watery eyes. Stephen looked at his thinly clad mother and remembered that a few days before he had seen a mantle priced at twenty guineas in the windows of Barnardo's.§

—Well that's done, said Mr Dedalus.

—We had better go to dinner, said Stephen. Where?

—Dinner? said Mr Dedalus. Well, I suppose we had better, what?

—Some place that's not too dear, said Mrs Dedalus.

—Underdone's?

—Yes. Some quiet place.

—Come along, said Stephen quickly. It doesn't matter about the dearness.

He walked on before them with short nervous steps, smiling. They tried to keep up with him, smiling also at his eagerness.

---

*Writing contest.

†The Parliament House was made obsolete by the Act of Union in 1800; the building now houses the Bank of Ireland.

‡The men Mr. Dedalus mentions are eighteenth-century members of the Irish Parliament known for their oratorical skills.

§A furrier in Grafton Street.

—Take it easy like a good young fellow, said his father. We're not out for the half mile, are we?

For a swift season of merrymaking the money of his prizes ran through Stephen's fingers. Great parcels of groceries and delicacies and dried fruits arrived from the city. Every day he drew up a bill of fare for the family and every night led a party of three or four to the theatre to see *Ingomar** or *The Lady of Lyons*.† In his coat pockets he carried squares of Vienna chocolate for his guests while his trousers' pockets bulged with masses of silver and copper coins. He bought presents for everyone, overhauled his room, wrote out resolutions, marshalled his books up and down their shelves, pored upon all kinds of price lists, drew up a form of commonwealth for the household by which every member of it held some office, opened a loan bank for his family and pressed loans on willing borrowers so that he might have the pleasure of making out receipts and reckoning the interests on the sums lent. When he could do no more he drove up and down the city in trams. Then the season of pleasure came to an end. The pot of pink enamel paint gave out and the wainscot of his bedroom remained with its unfinished and ill plastered coat.

His household returned to its usual way of life. His mother had no further occasion to upbraid him for squandering his money. He, too, returned to his old life at school and all his novel enterprises fell to pieces. The commonwealth fell, the loan bank closed its coffers and its books on a sensible loss, the rules of life which he had drawn about himself fell into desuetude.

How foolish his aim had been! He had tried to build a breakwater of order and elegance against the sordid tide of life without him and to dam up, by rules of conduct and active interests and new filial relations, the powerful recurrence of the tide within him. Useless. From without as from within the water had flowed over his barriers: their tides began once more to jostle fiercely above the crumbled mole.

He saw clearly, too, his own futile isolation. He had not gone one step nearer the lives he had sought to approach nor bridged the restless shame and rancour that had divided him from mother and brother and

---

*Probably a work, originally by German dramatist E. F. J. von Münch-Bellinghausen, that was translated into English by Maria Lovell and performed as *Ingomar the Barbarian* in 1851.

†Drama (1838) by Edward Bulwer-Lytton, employing characters and situations very similar to those in *The Count of Monte Cristo*.

sister. He felt that he was hardly of the one blood with them but stood to them rather in the mystical kinship of fosterage, foster child and foster brother.

He burned to appease the fierce longings of his heart before which everything else was idle and alien. He cared little that he was in mortal sin,* that his life had grown to be a tissue of subterfuge and falsehood. Beside the savage desire within him to realise the enormities which he brooded on nothing was sacred. He bore cynically with the shameful details of his secret riots in which he exulted to defile with patience whatever image had attracted his eyes. By day and by night he moved among distorted images of the outer world. A figure that had seemed to him by day demure and innocent came towards him by night through the winding darkness of sleep, her face transfigured by a lecherous cunning, her eyes bright with brutish joy. Only the morning pained him with its dim memory of dark orgiastic riot, its keen and humiliating sense of transgression.

He returned to his wanderings. The veiled autumnal evenings led him from street to street as they had led him years before along the quiet avenues of Blackrock. But no vision of trim front gardens or of kindly lights in the windows poured a tender influence upon him now. Only at times, in the pauses of his desire, when the luxury that was wasting him gave room to a softer languor, the image of Mercedes traversed the background of his memory. He saw again the small white house and the garden of rosebushes on the road that led to the mountains and he remembered the sadly proud gesture of refusal which he was to make there, standing with her in the moonlit garden after years of estrangement and adventure. At those moments the soft speeches of Claude Melnotte† rose to his lips and eased his unrest. A tender premonition touched him of the tryst he had then looked forward to and, in spite of the horrible reality which lay between his hope of then and now, of the holy encounter he had then imagined at which weakness and timidity and inexperience were to fall from him.

Such moments passed and the wasting fires of lust sprang up again. The verses passed from his lips and the inarticulate cries and the unspoken brutal words rushed forth from his brain to force a passage. His blood was in revolt. He wandered up and down the dark slimy streets

---

*A serious, deliberately committed sin that deprives the sinner of sanctifying grace.
†Character in *The Lady of Lyons* who is roughly equivalent to Dumas's Dantes in *The Count of Monte Cristo*.

peering into the gloom of lanes and doorways, listening eagerly for any sound. He moaned to himself like some baffled prowling beast. He wanted to sin with another of his kind, to force another being to sin with him and to exult with her in sin. He felt some dark presence moving irresistibly upon him from the darkness, a presence subtle and murmurous as a flood filling him wholly with itself. Its murmur besieged his ears like the murmur of some multitude in sleep; its subtle streams penetrated his being. His hands clenched convulsively and his teeth set together as he suffered the agony of its penetration. He stretched out his arms in the street to hold fast the frail swooning form that eluded him and incited him: and the cry that he had strangled for so long in his throat issued from his lips. It broke from him like a wail of despair from a hell of sufferers and died in a wail of furious entreaty, a cry for an iniquitous abandonment, a cry which was but the echo of an obscene scrawl which he had read on the oozing wall of a urinal.

He had wandered into a maze of narrow and dirty streets. From the foul laneways he heard bursts of hoarse riot and wrangling and the drawling of drunken singers. He walked onward, undismayed, wondering whether he had strayed into the quarter of the Jews.* Women and girls dressed in long vivid gowns traversed the street from house to house. They were leisurely and perfumed. A trembling seized him and his eyes grew dim. The yellow gasflames arose before his troubled vision against the vapoury sky, burning as if before an altar. Before the doors and in the lighted halls groups were gathered arrayed as for some rite. He was in another world: he had awakened from a slumber of centuries.

He stood still in the middle of the roadway, his heart clamouring against his bosom in a tumult. A young woman dressed in a long pink gown laid her hand on his arm to detain him and gazed into his face. She said gaily:

—Good night, Willie dear!

Her room was warm and lightsome. A huge doll sat with her legs apart in the copious easychair beside the bed. He tried to bid his tongue speak that he might seem at ease, watching her as she undid her gown, noting the proud conscious movements of her perfumed head.

As he stood silent in the middle of the room she came over to him and embraced him gaily and gravely. Her round arms held him firmly

---

*Dublin's notorious "Nighttown," now redeveloped.

to her and he, seeing her face lifted to him in serious calm and feeling the warm calm rise and fall of her breast, all but burst into hysterical weeping. Tears of joy and relief shone in his delighted eyes and his lips parted though they would not speak.

She passed her tinkling hand through his hair, calling him a little rascal.

—Give me a kiss, she said.

His lips would not bend to kiss her. He wanted to be held firmly in her arms, to be caressed slowly, slowly, slowly. In her arms he felt that he had suddenly become strong and fearless and sure of himself. But his lips would not bend to kiss her.

With a sudden movement she bowed his head and joined her lips to his and he read the meaning of her movements in her frank uplifted eyes. It was too much for him. He closed his eyes, surrendering himself to her, body and mind, conscious of nothing in the world but the dark pressure of her softly parting lips. They pressed upon his brain as upon his lips as though they were the vehicle of a vague speech; and between them he felt an unknown and timid pressure, darker than the swoon of sin, softer than sound or odour.

CHAPTER III

THE SWIFT DECEMBER DUSK had come tumbling clownishly after its dull day and as he stared through the dull square of the window of the schoolroom he felt his belly crave for its food. He hoped there would be stew for dinner, turnips and carrots and bruised potatoes and fat mutton pieces to be ladled out in thick peppered flour-fattened sauce. Stuff it into you, his belly counselled him.

It would be a gloomy secret night. After early nightfall the yellow lamps would light up, here and there, the squalid quarter of the brothels. He would follow a devious course up and down the streets, circling always nearer and nearer in a tremor of fear and joy, until his feet led him suddenly round a dark corner. The whores would be just coming out of their houses making ready for the night, yawning lazily after their sleep and settling the hairpins in their clusters of hair. He would pass by them calmly waiting for a sudden movement of his own will or a sudden call to his sin-loving soul from their soft perfumed flesh. Yet as he prowled in quest of that call, his senses, stultified only by his desire, would note keenly all that wounded or shamed them; his eyes, a ring of porter froth on a clothless table or a photograph of two soldiers standing to attention on a gaudy playbill; his ears, the drawling jargon of greeting:

—Hello, Bertie, any good in your mind?

—Is that you, pigeon?

—Number ten. Fresh Nelly is waiting on you.

—Good night, husband! Coming in to have a short time?

The equation on the page of his scribbler began to spread out a widening tail, eyed and starred like a peacock's; and, when the eyes and stars of its indices had been eliminated, began slowly to fold itself together again. The indices appearing and disappearing were eyes opening and closing; the eyes opening and closing were stars being born and being quenched. The vast cycle of starry life bore his weary mind outward to its verge and inward to its centre, a distant music accompanying him outward and inward. What music? The music came nearer and he recalled the words, the words of Shelley's fragment upon the moon wandering companionless, pale for weariness. The stars began to crumble and a cloud of fine star-dust fell through space.

The dull light fell more faintly upon the page whereon another equation began to unfold itself slowly and to spread abroad its widening tail. It was his own soul going forth to experience, unfolding itself sin by sin, spreading abroad the balefire* of its burning stars and folding back upon itself, fading slowly, quenching its own lights and fires. They were quenched: and the cold darkness filled chaos.

A cold lucid indifference reigned in his soul. At his first violent sin he had felt a wave of vitality pass out of him and had feared to find his body or his soul maimed by the excess. Instead the vital wave had carried him on its bosom out of himself and back again when it receded: and no part of body or soul had been maimed, but a dark peace had been established between them. The chaos in which his ardour untinguished itself was a cold indifferent knowledge of himself. He had sinned mortally not once but many times and he knew that, while he stood in danger of eternal damnation for the first sin alone, by every succeeding sin he multiplied his guilt and his punishment. His days and works and thoughts could make no atonement for him, the fountains of sanctifying grace having ceased to refresh his soul. At most, by an alms given to a beggar whose blessing he fled from, he might hope wearily to win for himself some measure of actual grace.[9] Devotion had gone by the board. What did it avail to pray when he knew that his soul lusted after its own destruction? A certain pride, a certain awe, withheld him from offering to God even one prayer at night though he knew it was in God's power to take away his life while he slept and hurl his soul hellward ere he could beg for mercy. His great pride in his own sin, his loveless awe of God, told him that his offence was too grievous to be atoned for in whole or in part by a false homage to the Allseeing and Allknowing.

—Well now, Ennis, I declare you have a head and so has my stick! Do you mean to say that you are not able to tell me what a surd† is?

The blundering answer stirred the embers of his contempt of his fellows. Towards others he felt neither shame nor fear. On Sunday mornings as he passed the church door he glanced coldly at the worshippers who stood bareheaded, four deep, outside the church, morally present

---

*Funeral pyre or signal fire.
†An irrational number.

at the mass which they could neither see nor hear. Their dull piety and the sickly smell of the cheap hair oil with which they had anointed their heads repelled him from the altar they prayed at. He stooped to the evil of hypocrisy with others, sceptical of their innocence which he could cajole so easily.

On the wall of his bedroom hung an illuminated scroll, the certificate of his prefecture in the college of the sodality of the Blessed Virgin Mary. On Saturday mornings when the sodality met in the chapel to recite the little office* his place was a cushioned kneeling-desk at the right of the altar from which he led his wing of boys through the responses. The falsehood of his position did not pain him. If at moments he felt an impulse to rise from his post of honour and, confessing before them all his unworthiness, to leave the chapel, a glance at their faces restrained him. The imagery of the psalms of prophecy soothed his barren ride. The glories of Mary† held his soul captive: spikenard and myrrh and frankincense symbolising her royal lineage, her emblems, the late-flowering plant and late-blossoming tree, symbolising the agelong gradual growth of her cultus among men. When it fell to him to read the lesson towards the close of the office he read it in a veiled voice, lulling his conscience to its music.

> *Quasi cedrus exaltata sum in Libanon et quasi cupressus in monte Sion.*
> *Quasi palma exaltata sum in Gades et quasi plantatio rosae in Jericho.*
> *Quasi uliva speciosa in campis et quasi plantanus exaltata sum juxta*
> *aquam in plateis. Sicut cinnamomum et balsamum aromatizans odorem*
> *dedi et quasi myrrha electa dedi suavitatem odoris.*[10]

His sin, which had covered him from the sight of God, had led him nearer to the refuge of sinners. Her eyes seemed to regard him with mild pity; her holiness, a strange light glowing faintly upon her frail flesh, did not humiliate the sinner who approached her. If ever he was impelled to cast sin from him and to repent, the impulse that moved him was the wish to be her knight. If ever his soul, re-entering her

---

*An office is a form of religious observance performed at specified hours throughout the day; the reference here is to an eighth-century collection of prayers in honor of the Virgin Mary.

†Both the title of a devotional book by Saint Alphonsus Liguouri (1696–1787) and a sermon ("The Glories of Mary for the Sake of Her Son") of John Henry Cardinal Newman (see endnote 8), which Stephen recalls below (pp. 102, 121).

dwelling shyly after the frenzy of his body's lust had spent itself, was turned towards her whose emblem is the morning star, *bright and musical, telling of heaven and infusing peace,** it was when her names were murmured softly by lips whereon there still lingered foul and shameful words, the savour itself of a lewd kiss.

That was strange. He tried to think how it could be but the dusk, deepening in the schoolroom, covered over his thoughts. The bell rang. The master marked the sums and cuts[†] to be done for the next lesson and went out. Heron, beside Stephen, began to hum tunelessly.

My excellent friend Bombados.

Ennis, who had gone to the yard, came back, saying:

—The boy from the house is coming up for the rector.

A tall boy behind Stephen rubbed his hands and said:

—That's game ball. We can scut the whole hour. He won't be in till after half two. Then you can ask him questions on the catechism, Dedalus.

Stephen, leaning back and drawing idly on his scribbler, listened to the talk about him which Heron checked from time to time by saying:

—Shut up, will you. Don't make such a bally racket!

It was strange too that he found an arid pleasure in following up to the end the rigid lines of the doctrines of the church and penetrating into obscure silences only to hear and feel the more deeply his own condemnation. The sentence of Saint James[‡] which says that he who offends against one commandment becomes guilty of all had seemed to him first a swollen phrase until he had begun to grope in the darkness of his own state. From the evil seed of lust all other deadly sins[§] had sprung forth: pride in himself and contempt of others, covetousness in using money for the purchase of unlawful pleasures, envy of those whose vices he could not reach to and calumnious murmuring against the pious, gluttonous enjoyment of food, the dull glowering anger amid which he brooded upon his longing, the swamp of spiritual and bodily sloth in which his whole being had sunk.

---

*From Newman's "The Glories of Mary," quoted more fully at p. 121.

†Math problems.

‡An allusion to James 2:10. "And whosoever shall keep the whole law, but offend in one point, is become guilty of all" (Douay version).

§The seven deadly sins, all mortal sins, are lust, gluttony, greed, envy, pride, sloth, and anger.

As he sat in his bench gazing calmly at the rector's shrewd harsh face his mind wound itself in and out of the curious questions proposed to it. If a man had stolen a pound in his youth and had used that pound to amass a huge fortune how much was he obliged to give back, the pound he had stolen only or the pound together with the compound interest accruing upon it or all his huge fortune? If a layman in giving baptism pour the water before saying the words is the child baptised? Is baptism with a mineral water valid? How comes it that while the first beatitude promises the kingdom of heaven to the poor of heart, the second beatitude[11] promises also to the meek that they shall possess the land? Why was the sacrament of the eucharist instituted under the two species of bread and wine if Jesus Christ be present body and blood, soul and divinity, in the bread alone and in the wine alone? Does a tiny particle of the consecrated bread contain all the body and blood of Jesus Christ or a part only of the body and blood? If the wine change into vinegar and the host crumble into corruption after they have been consecrated, is Jesus Christ still present under their species as God and as man?

—Here he is! Here he is!

A boy from his post at the window had seen the rector come from the house. All the catechisms were opened and all heads bent upon them silently. The rector entered and took his seat on the dais. A gentle kick from the tall boy in the bench behind urged Stephen to ask a difficult question.

The rector did not ask for a catechism to hear the lesson from. He clasped his hands on the desk and said:

—The retreat will begin on Wednesday afternoon in honour of Saint Francis Xavier whose feast day is Saturday. The retreat will go on from Wednesday to Friday. On Friday confession will be heard all the afternoon after beads. If any boys have special confessors perhaps it will be better for them not to change. Mass will be on Saturday morning at nine o'clock and general communion for the whole college. Saturday will be a free day. But Saturday and Sunday being free days some boys might be inclined to think that Monday is a free day also. Beware of making that mistake. I think you, Lawless, are likely to make that mistake.

—I, sir? Why, sir?

A little wave of quiet mirth broke forth over the class of boys from the rector's grim smile. Stephen's heart began slowly to fold and fade with fear like a withering flower.

The rector went on gravely:

—You are all familiar with the story of the life of Saint Francis Xavier, I suppose, the patron of your college. He came of an old and illustrious Spanish family and you remember that he was one of the first followers of Saint Ignatius. They met in Paris where Francis Xavier was professor of philosophy at the university. This young and brilliant nobleman and man of letters entered heart and soul into the ideas of our glorious founder, and you know that he, at his own desire, was sent by Saint Ignatius to preach to the Indians. He is called, as you know, the apostle of the Indies. He went from country to country in the east, from Africa to India, from India to Japan, baptising the people. He is said to have baptised as many as ten thousand idolators in one month. It is said that his right arm had grown powerless from having been raised so often over the heads of those whom he baptised. He wished then to go to China to win still more souls for God but he died of fever on the island of Sancian.* A great Saint, Saint Francis Xavier! A great soldier of God!

The rector paused and then, shaking his clasped hands before him, went on:

—He had the faith in him that moves mountains. Ten thousand souls won for God in a single month! That is a true conqueror, true to the motto of our order: *ad majorem Dei gloriam!* A saint who has great power in heaven, remember: power to intercede for us in our grief, power to obtain whatever we pray for if it be for the good of our souls, power above all to obtain for us the grace to repent if we be in sin. A great saint, Saint Francis Xavier! A great fisher of souls!

He ceased to shake his clasped hands and, resting them against his forehead, looked right and left of them keenly at his listeners out of his dark stern eyes.

In the silence their dark fire kindled the dusk into a tawny glow. Stephen's heart had withered up like a flower of the desert that feels the simoom† coming from afar.

*   *   *   *

—*Remember only thy last things and thou shalt not sin for ever*—words taken, my dear little brothers in Christ, from the book of Ecclesiastes,

---

*Island off the coast of China.
†Hot desert wind.

seventh chapter, fortieth verse.[12] In the name of the Father and of the Son and of the Holy Ghost. Amen.

Stephen sat in the front bench of the chapel. Father Arnall sat at a table to the left of the altar. He wore about his shoulders a heavy cloak; his pale face was drawn and his voice broken with rheum. The figure of his old master, so strangely rearisen, brought back to Stephen's mind his life at Clongowes: the wide playgrounds, swarming with boys, the square ditch, the little cemetery off the main avenue of limes where he had dreamed of being buried, the firelight on the wall of the infirmary where he lay sick, the sorrowful face of Brother Michael. His soul, as these memories came back to him, became again a child's soul.

—We are assembled here today, my dear little brothers in Christ, for one brief moment far away from the busy bustle of the outer world to celebrate and to honour one of the greatest of saints, the apostle of the Indies, the patron saint also of your college, Saint Francis Xavier. Year after year for much longer than any of you, my dear little boys, can remember or than I can remember the boys of this college have met in this very chapel to make their annual retreat before the feast day of their patron saint. Time has gone on and brought with it its changes. Even in the last few years what changes can most of you not remember? Many of the boys who sat in those front benches a few years ago are perhaps now in distant lands, in the burning tropics or immersed in professional duties or in seminaries or voyaging over the vast expanse of the deep or, it may be, already called by the great God to another life and to the rendering up of their stewardship. And still as the years roll by, bringing with them changes for good and bad, the memory of the great saint is honoured by the boys of his college who make every year their annual retreat on the days preceding the feast day set apart by our Holy Mother the Church to transmit to all the ages the name and fame of one of the greatest sons of catholic Spain.

—Now what is the meaning of this word *retreat* and why is it allowed on all hands to be a most salutory practice for all who desire to lead before God and in the eyes of men a truly Christian life? A retreat, my dear boys, signifies a withdrawal for a while from the cares of our life, the cares of this workaday world, in order to examine the state of our conscience, to reflect on the mysteries of holy religion and to understand better why we are here in this world. During these few days I intend to put before you some thoughts concerning the four last things. They are, as you know from your catechism, death, judgment, hell and heaven. We shall try to understand them fully during these few days so that we may derive from the understanding of them a lasting benefit to our souls. And remember, my dear boys, that we have been sent into this world for one thing and for one thing alone: to do God's holy will and to save our immortal souls. All else is worthless. One thing alone is needful, the salvation of one's soul. What doth it profit a man to gain the whole world if he suffer the loss of his immortal soul? Ah, my dear boys, believe me there is nothing in this wretched world that can make up for such a loss.

—I will ask you therefore, my dear boys, to put away from your minds during these few days all worldly thoughts, whether of study or pleasure or ambition, and to give all your attention to the state of your souls. I need hardly remind you that during the days of the retreat all boys are expected to preserve a quiet and pious demeanour and to shun all loud unseemly pleasure. The elder boys, of course, will see that this custom is not infringed and I look especially to the prefects and officers of the sodality of Our Blessed Lady and of the sodality of the Holy Angels to set a good example to their fellow-students.

—Let us try, therefore, to make this retreat in honour of St. Francis with our whole heart and our whole mind. God's blessing will then be upon all your year's studies. But, above and beyond all, let this retreat be one to which you can look back in after years when, may be, you are far from this college and among very different surroundings, to which you can look back with joy and thankfulness and give thanks to God for having granted you this occasion of laying the first foundation of a pious honourable zealous Christian life. And if, as may so happen, there be at this moment in these benches any poor soul who has had the unutterable misfortune to lose God's holy grace and to fall into grievous sin, I fervently trust and pray that this retreat may be the turning-point in the life of that soul. I pray to God through the merits of His zealous servant Francis Xavier that such a soul may be led to sincere repentance and that the holy communion on St. Francis' day of this year may be a lasting covenant between God and that soul. For just and unjust, for saint and sinner alike, may this retreat be a memorable one.

—Help me, my dear little brothers in Christ. Help me by your pious attention, by your own devotion, by your outward demeanour. Banish from your minds all worldly thoughts, and think only of the last things, death, judgment, hell and heaven. He who remembers these things, says Ecclesiastes, shall not sin for ever. He who remembers the last things will act and think with them always before his eyes. He will live a good life and die a good death, believing and knowing that, if he has sacrificed much in this earthly life, it will be given to him a hundred-fold and a thousandfold more in the life to come, in the kingdom without end—a blessing, my dear boys, which I wish you from my heart, one and all, in the name of the Father and of the Son and of the Holy Ghost. Amen!

As he walked home with silent companions a thick fog seemed to compass his mind. He waited in stupor of mind till it should lift and reveal what it had hidden. He ate his dinner with surly appetite and when the meal was over and the grease-strewn plates lay abandoned on the table, he rose and went to the window, clearing the thick scum from his mouth with his tongue and licking it from his lips. So he had sunk to the state of a beast that licks his chaps after meat. This was the end; and a faint glimmer of fear began to pierce the fog of his mind. He pressed his face against the pane of the window and gazed out into the darkening street. Forms passed this way and that through the dull light. And that was life. The letters of the name of Dublin lay heavily upon his mind, pushing one another surily hither and thither with slow boorish insistence. His soul was fattening and congealing into a gross grease, plunging ever deeper in its dull fear into a sombre threatening dusk, while the body that was his stood, listless and dishonoured, gazing out of darkened eyes, helpless, perturbed and human for a bovine god to stare upon.

The next day brought death and judgment, stirring his soul slowly from its listless despair. The faint glimmer of fear became a terror of spirit as the hoarse voice of the preacher blew death into his soul. He suffered its agony. He felt the death-chill touch the extremities and creep onward towards the heart, the film of death veiling the eyes, the bright centres of the brain extinguished one by one like lamps, the last sweat oozing upon the skin, the powerlessness of the dying limbs, the speech thickening and wandering and failing, the heart throbbing faintly and more faintly, all but vanquished, the breath, the poor breath, the poor helpless human spirit, sobbing and sighing, gurgling and rattling in the throat. No help! No help! He—he himself—his body to which he had yielded was dying. Into the grave with it. Nail it down into a wooden box, the corpse. Carry it out of the house on the shoulders of hirelings. Thrust it out of men's sight into a long hole in the ground, into the grave, to rot, to feed the mass of its creeping worms and to be devoured by scuttling plump-bellied rats.

And while the friends were still standing in tears by the bedside the soul of the sinner was judged. At the last moment of consciousness the whole earthly life passed before the vision of the soul and, ere it had time to reflect, the body had died and the soul stood terrified before the judgment seat. God, who had long been merciful, would then be just. He had long been patient, pleading with the sinful soul, giving it time to repent, sparing it yet awhile. But that time had gone. Time was to sin and to enjoy, time was to scoff at God and at the warnings of His holy church, time was to defy His majesty, to disobey His commands, to hoodwink one's fellow men, to commit sin after sin and to hide one's corruption from the sight of men. But that time was over. Now it was God's turn: and He was not to be hoodwinked or deceived. Every sin would then come forth from its lurking-place, the most rebellious against the divine will and the most degrading to our poor corrupt nature, the tiniest imperfection and the most heinous atrocity. What did it avail then to have been a great emperor, a great general, a marvellous inventor, the most learned of the learned? All were as one before the judgment seat of God. He would reward the good and punish the wicked. One single instant was enough for the trial of a man's soul. One single instant after the body's death, the soul had been weighed in the balance. The particular judgment was over and the soul had passed to the abode of bliss or to the prison of purgatory or had been hurled howling into hell.

Nor was that all. God's justice had still to be vindicated before men: after the particular there still remained the general judgment.* The last day had come. The doomsday was at hand. The stars of heaven were falling upon the earth like the figs cast by the figtree which the wind has shaken.† The sun, the great luminary of the universe, had become as sackcloth of hair. The moon was blood red. The firmament was as a scroll rolled away. The archangel Michael, the prince of the heavenly host, appeared glorious and terrible against the sky. With one foot on the sea and one foot on the land he blew from the archangelical trumpet the brazen death of time. The three blasts of the angel filled all the universe. Time is, time was, but time shall be no more. At the last blast the souls of universal humanity throng towards the valley of Jehosaphat,‡ rich and poor, gentle and simple, wise and foolish, good and wicked. The soul of every human being that has ever existed, the souls of all those who shall yet be born, all the sons and daughters of Adam,

---

*The particular and the general judgments are, respectively, God's judgment of the individual soul at death and God's judgment of the entire world at the apocalypse.
†An allusion to the final book of the New Testament, called Apocalypse or Revelation, chapter 6, verse 13.
‡Place where, in the Bible (Joel 3), it is prophesied that God will judge all nations.

all are assembled on that supreme day. And lo, the supreme judge is coming! No longer the lowly Lamb of God, no longer the meek Jesus of Nazareth, no longer the Man of Sorrows, no longer the Good Shepherd,* He is seen now coming upon the clouds, in great power and majesty, attended by nine choirs of angels, angels and archangels, principalities, powers and virtues, thrones and dominations, cherubim and seraphim, God Omnipotent, God everlasting. He speaks: and His voice is heard even at the farthest limits of space, even in the bottomless abyss. Supreme Judge, from His sentence there will be and can be no appeal. He calls the just to His side, bidding them enter into the Kingdom, the eternity of bliss, prepared for them. The unjust He casts from Him, crying in His offended majesty: *Depart from me, ye cursed, into everlasting fire which was prepared for the devil and his angels.*† O, what agony then for the miserable sinners! Friend is torn apart from friend, children are torn from their parents, husbands from their wives. The poor sinner holds out his arms to those who were dear to him in this earthly world, to those whose simple piety perhaps he made a mock of, to those who counselled him and tried to lead him on the right path, to a kind brother, to a loving sister, to the mother and father who loved him so dearly. But it is too late: the just turn away from the wretched damned souls which now appear before the eyes of all in their hideous and evil character. O you hypocrites, O you whited sepulchres, O you who present a smooth, smiling face to the world while your soul within is a foul swamp of sin, how will it fare with you in that terrible day?

And this day will come, shall come, must come; the day of death and the day of judgment. It is appointed unto man to die, and after death the judgment. Death is certain. The time and manner are uncertain, whether from long disease or from some unexpected accident; the Son of God cometh at an hour when you little expect Him. Be therefore ready every moment, seeing that you may die at any moment. Death is the end of us all. Death and judgment, brought into the world by the sin of our first parents, are the dark portals that close our earthly existence, the portals that open into the unknown and the unseen, portals through which every soul must pass, alone, unaided save by its good works, without friend or brother or parent or master to help it, alone

---

*Four among the epithets and titles of Jesus Christ.
†Quotation from Matthew 25:41 (Douay version).

and trembling. Let that thought be ever before our minds and then we cannot sin. Death, a cause of terror to the sinner, is a blessed moment for him who has walked in the right path, fulfilling the duties of his station in life, attending to his morning and evening prayers, approaching the holy sacrament frequently and performing good and merciful works. For the pious and believing catholic, for the just man, death is no cause of terror. Was it not Addison,* the great English writer, who, when on his deathbed, sent for the wicked young earl of Warwick to let him see how a christian can meet his end. He it is and he alone, the pious and believing christian, who can say in his heart:

> *O grave, where is thy victory?*
> *O death, where is thy sting?*†

Every word of it was for him. Against his sin, foul and secret, the whole wrath of God was aimed. The preacher's knife had probed deeply into his disclosed conscience and he felt now that his soul was festering in sin. Yes, the preacher was right. God's turn had come. Like a beast in its lair his soul had lain down in its own filth but the blasts of the angel's trumpet had driven him forth from the darkness of sin into the light. The words of doom cried by the angel shattered in an instant his presumptuous peace. The wind of the last day blew through his mind; his sins, the jewel-eyed harlots of his imagination, fled before the hurricane, squeaking like mice in their terror and huddled under a mane of hair.

As he crossed the square, walking homeward, the light laughter of a girl reached his burning ear. The frail, gay sound smote his heart more strongly than a trumpetblast, and, not daring to lift his eyes, he turned aside and gazed, as he walked, into the shadow of the tangled shrubs. Shame rose from his smitten heart and flooded his whole being. The image of Emma appeared before him and under her eyes the flood of shame rushed forth anew from his heart. If she knew to what his mind had subjected her or how his brute-like lust had torn and trampled upon her innocence! Was that boyish love? Was that chivalry? Was that poetry? The sordid details of his orgies stank under his very nostrils. The sootcoated packet of pictures which he had hidden in the flue of

---

*Critic and essayist Joseph Addison (1672–1719).

†The text is from I Corinthians 15:55, though the priest here quotes it in the version of Alexander Pope (1688–1744), in "The Dying Christian to His Soul."

the fireplace and in the presence of whose shameless or bashful wantonness he lay for hours sinning in thought and deed; his monstrous dreams, peopled by apelike creatures and by harlots with gleaming jewel eyes; the foul long letters he had written in the joy of guilty confession and carried secretly for days and days only to throw them under cover of night among the grass in the corner of a field or beneath some hingeless door or in some niche in the hedges where a girl might come upon them as she walked by and read them secretly. Mad! Mad! Was it possible he had done these things? A cold sweat broke out upon his forehead as the foul memories condensed within his brain.

When the agony of shame had passed from him he tried to raise his soul from its abject powerlessness. God and the Blessed Virgin were too far from him: God was too great and stern and the Blessed Virgin too pure and holy. But he imagined that he stood near Emma in a wide land and, humbly and in tears, bent and kissed the elbow of her sleeve.

In the wide land under a tender lucid evening sky, a cloud drifting westward amid a pale green sea of heaven, they stood together, children that had erred. Their error had offended deeply God's majesty though it was the error of two children; but it had not offended her whose beauty *is not like earthly beauty, dangerous to look upon, but like the morning star which is its emblem, bright and musical.** The eyes were not offended which she turned upon him nor reproachful. She placed their hands together, hand in hand, and said, speaking to their hearts:

—Take hands, Stephen and Emma. It is a beautiful evening now in heaven. You have erred but you are always my children. It is one heart that loves another heart. Take hands together, my dear children, and you will be happy together and your hearts will love each other.

The chapel was flooded by the dull scarlet light that filtered through the lowered blinds; and through the fissure between the last blind and the sash a shaft of wan light entered like a spear and touched the embossed brasses of the candlesticks upon the altar that gleamed like the battle-worn mail armour of angels.

Rain was falling on the chapel, on the garden, on the college. It would rain for ever, noiselessly. The water would rise inch by inch, covering the grass and shrubs, covering the trees and houses, covering the monuments and the mountain tops. All life would be choked off, noiselessly: birds, men, elephants, pigs, children: noiselessly floating corpses

---

*From Newman's "The Glories of Mary."

amid the litter of the wreckage of the world. Forty days and forty nights the rain would fall till the waters covered the face of the earth.*

It might be. Why not?

—*Hell has enlarged its soul and opened its mouth without any limits*— words taken, my dear little brothers in Christ Jesus, from the book of Isaias, fifth chapter, fourteenth verse. In the name of the Father and of the Son and of the Holy Ghost. Amen.

The preacher took a chainless watch from a pocket within his soutane and, having considered its dial for a moment in silence, placed it silently before him on the table.

He began to speak in a quiet tone.

—Adam and Eve, my dear boys, were, as you know, our first parents, and you will remember that they were created by God in order that the seats in heaven left vacant by the fall of Lucifer† and his rebellious angels might be filled again. Lucifer, we are told, was a son of the morning, a radiant and mighty angel; yet he fell; he fell and there fell with him a third part of the host of heaven: he fell and was hurled with his rebellious angels into hell. What his sin was we cannot say. Theologians consider that it was the sin of pride, the sinful thought conceived in an instant: *non serviam: I will not serve.* That instant was his ruin. He offended the majesty of God by the sinful thought of one instant and God cast him out of heaven into hell for ever.

—Adam and Eve were then created by God and placed in Eden, in the plain of Damascus, that lovely garden resplendent with sunlight and colour, teeming with luxuriant vegetation. The fruitful earth gave them her bounty: beasts and birds were their willing servants: they knew not the ills our flesh is heir to, disease and poverty and death: all that a great and generous God could do for them was done. But there was one condition imposed on them by God: obedience to His word. They were not to eat of the fruit of the forbidden tree.

—Alas, my dear little boys, they too fell. The devil, once a shining angel, a son of the morning, now a foul fiend came in the shape of a serpent, the subtlest of all the beasts of the field. He envied them. He, the fallen great one, could not bear to think that man, a being of clay, should possess the inheritance which he by his sin had forfeited for ever. He came to the woman, the weaker vessel, and poured the poison

---

*Allusion to the biblical flood described in Genesis 7–8.

†See Isaiah 14:12. The most extensive account of Lucifer's pride and fall, and the basis for much of this sermon, is in John Milton's *Paradise Lost* (1667).

of his eloquence into her ear, promising her—O, the blasphemy of that promise!—that if she and Adam ate of the forbidden fruit they would become as gods, nay as God Himself. Eve yielded to the wiles of the arch tempter. She ate the apple and gave it also to Adam who had not the moral courage to resist her. The poison tongue of Satan had done its work. They fell.

—And then the voice of God was heard in that garden, calling His creature man to account: and Michael, prince of the heavenly host, with a sword of flame in his hand, appeared before the guilty pair and drove them forth from Eden into the world, the world of sickness and striving, of cruelty and disappointment, of labour and hardship, to earn their bread in the sweat of their brow. But even then how merciful was God! He took pity on our poor degraded parents and promised that in the fulness of time He would send down from heaven One who would redeem them, make them once more children of God and heirs to the kingdom of heaven: and that One, that Redeemer of fallen man, was to be God's only-begotten Son, the Second Person of the Most Blessed Trinity, the Eternal Word.

—He came. He was born of a virgin pure, Mary the virgin mother. He was born in a poor cowhouse in Judea and lived as a humble carpenter for thirty years until the hour of his mission had come. And then, filled with love for men, He went forth and called to men to hear the new gospel.

—Did they listen? Yes, they listened but would not hear. He was seized and bound like a common criminal, mocked at as a fool, set aside to give place to a public robber, scourged with five thousand lashes, crowned with a crown of thorns, hustled through the streets by the Jewish rabble and the Roman soldiery, stripped of his garments and hanged upon a gibbet* and His side was pierced with a lance and from the wounded body of our Lord water and blood issued continually.

—Yet even then, in that hour of supreme agony, Our Merciful Redeemer had pity for mankind. Yet even there, on the hill of Calvary, He founded the Holy Catholic Church against which, it is promised, the gates of hell shall not prevail. He founded it upon the rock of ages and endowed it with His grace, with sacraments and sacrifice, and promised that if men would obey the word of His Church they would still enter into eternal life, but if, after all that had been done for them, they still

---

*Gallows.

persisted in their wickedness there remained for them an eternity of torment: hell.

The preacher's voice sank. He paused, joined his palms for an instant, parted them. Then he resumed:

—Now let us try for a moment to realise, as far as we can, the nature of that abode of the damned which the justice of an offended God has called into existence for the eternal punishment of sinners. Hell is a strait* and dark and foul smelling prison, an abode of demons and lost souls, filled with fire and smoke. The straitness of this prison house is expressly designed by God to punish those who refused to be bound by His laws. In earthly prisons the poor captive has at least some liberty of movement, were it only within the four walls of his cell or in the gloomy yard of his prison. Not so in hell. There, by reason of the great number of the damned, the prisoners are heaped together in their awful prison, the walls of which are said to be four thousand miles thick, and the damned are so utterly bound and helpless that, as a blessed saint, Saint Anselm,† writes in his book on Similitudes, they are not even able to remove from the eye a worm that gnaws it.

—They lie in exterior darkness. For, remember, the fire of hell gives forth no light. As, at the command of God, the fire of the Babylonian furnace‡ lost its heat but not its light so, at the command of God, the fire of hell, while retaining the intensity of its heat, burns eternally in darkness. It is a neverending storm of darkness, dark flames and dark smoke of burning brimstone,§ amid which the bodies are heaped one upon another without even a glimpse of air. Of all the plagues with which the land of the Pharaohs was smitten one plague alone, that of darkness, was called horrible. What name, then, shall we give to the darkness of hell which is to last not for three days alone but for all eternity?

—The horror of this strait and dark prison is increased by its awful stench. All the filth of the world, all the offal and scum of the world, we are told, shall run there as to a vast reeking sewer when the terrible conflagration of the last day has purged the world. The brimstone, too, which burns there in such prodigious quantity fills all hell with its intolerable stench; and the bodies of the damned themselves exhale such

---

*Narrow.
†(1034–1109); Italian churchman.
‡An allusion to Daniel 3.
§Burning sulphur.

a pestilential odour that as Saint Bonaventure* says, one of them alone would suffice to infect the whole world. The very air of this world, that pure element, becomes foul and unbreathable when it has been long enclosed. Consider then what must be the foulness of the air of hell. Imagine some foul and putrid corpse that has lain rotting and decomposing in the grave, a jellylike mass of liquid corruption. Imagine such a corpse a prey to flames, devoured by the fire of burning brimstone and giving off dense choking fumes of nauseous loathsome decomposition. And then imagine this sickening stench, multiplied a millionfold and a millionfold again from the millions upon millions of fetid carcasses massed together in the reeking darkness, a huge and rotting human fungus. Imagine all this and you will have some idea of the horror of the stench of hell.

—But this stench is not, horrible though it is, the greatest physical torment to which the damned are subjected. The torment of fire is the greatest torment to which the tyrant has ever subjected his fellow creatures. Place your finger for a moment in the flame of a candle and you will feel the pain of fire. But our earthly fire was created by God for the benefit of man, to maintain in him the spark of life and to help him in the useful arts whereas the fire of hell is of another quality and was created by God to torture and punish the unrepentant sinner. Our earthly fire also consumes more or less rapidly according as the object which it attacks is more or less combustible so that human ingenuity has even succeeded in inventing chemical preparations to check or frustrate its action. But the sulphurous brimstone which burns in hell is a substance which is specially designed to burn for ever and for ever with unspeakable fury. Moreover our earthly fire destroys at the same time as it burns so that the more intense it is the shorter is its duration: but the fire of hell has this property that it preserves that which it burns and though it rages with incredible intensity it rages for ever.

—Our earthly fire again, no matter how fierce or widespread it may be, is always of a limited extent: but the lake of fire in hell is boundless, shoreless and bottomless. It is on record that the devil himself, when asked the question by a certain soldier, was obliged to confess that if a whole mountain were thrown into the burning ocean of hell it would be burned up in an instant like a piece of wax. And this terrible fire will not afflict the bodies of the damned only from without but each lost

---

*(1221–1274); professor of theology, general of the Franciscans, and cardinal.

soul will be a hell unto itself, the boundless fire raging in its very vitals. O, how terrible is the lot of those wretched beings! The blood seethes and boils in the veins, the brains are boiling in the skull, the heart in the breast glowing and bursting, the bowels a redhot mass of burning pulp, the tender eyes flaming like molten balls.

—And yet what I have said as to the strength and quality and boundlessness of this fire is as nothing when compared to its intensity, an intensity which it has as being the instrument chosen by divine design for the punishment of soul and body alike. It is a fire which proceeds directly from the ire of God, working not of its own activity but as an instrument of divine vengeance. As the waters of baptism cleanse the soul with the body so do the fires of punishment torture the spirit with the flesh. Every sense of the flesh is tortured and every faculty of the soul therewith: the eyes with impenetrable utter darkness, the nose with noisome odours, the ears with yells and howls and execrations, the taste with foul matter, leprous corruption, nameless suffocating filth, the touch with redhot goads and spikes, with cruel tongues of flame. And through the several torments of the senses the immortal soul is tortured eternally in its very essence amid the leagues upon leagues of glowing fires kindled in the abyss by the offended majesty of the Omnipotent God and fanned into everlasting and ever increasing fury by the breath of the anger of the Godhead.

—Consider finally that the torment of this infernal prison is increased by the company of the damned themselves. Evil company on earth is so noxious that the plants, as if by instinct, withdraw from the company of whatsoever is deadly or hurtful to them. In hell all laws are overturned—there is no thought of family or country, of ties, of relationships. The damned howl and scream at one another, their torture and rage intensified by the presence of beings tortured and raging like themselves. All sense of humanity is forgotten. The yells of the suffering sinners fill the remotest corners of the vast abyss. The mouths of the damned are full of blasphemies against God and of hatred for their fellow sufferers and of curses against those souls which were their accomplices in sin. In olden times it was the custom to punish the parricide, the man who had raised his murderous hand against his father, by casting him into the depths of the sea in a sack in which were placed a cock, a monkey and a serpent. The intention of those law-givers who framed such a law, which seems cruel in our times, was to punish the criminal by the company of hurtful and hateful beasts. But what is the fury of those dumb beasts compared with the fury of execration which bursts from the parched lips and aching throats of the damned in hell when they behold in their companions in misery those who aided and abetted them in sin, those whose words sowed the first seeds of evil thinking and evil living in their minds, those whose immodest suggestions led them on to sin, those whose eyes tempted and allured them from the path of virtue. They turn upon those accomplices and upbraid them and curse them. But they are helpless and hopeless: it is too late now for repentance.

—Last of all consider the frightful torment to those damned souls, tempters and tempted alike, of the company of the devils. These devils will afflict the damned in two ways, by their presence and by their reproaches. We can have no idea of how horrible these devils are. Saint Catherine of Siena* once saw a devil, and she has written that, rather than look again for one single instant on such a frightful monster, she would prefer to walk until the end of her life along a track of red coals. These devils, who were once beautiful angels, have become as hideous and ugly as they once were beautiful. They mock and jeer at the lost souls whom they dragged down to ruin. It is they, the foul demons, who are made in hell the voices of conscience. Why did you sin? Why did you lend an ear to the temptings of friends? Why did you turn aside from your pious practices and good works? Why did you not shun the occasions of sin? Why did you not leave that evil companion? Why did you not give up that lewd habit, that impure habit? Why did you not listen to the counsels of your confessor? Why did you not, even after you had fallen the first or the second or the third or the fourth or the hundredth time, repent of your evil ways and turn to God who only waited for your repentance to absolve you of your sins? Now the time for repentance has gone by. Time is, time was, but time shall be no more! Time was to sin in secrecy, to indulge in that sloth and pride, to covet the unlawful, to yield to the promptings of your lower nature, to live like the beasts of the field, nay worse than the beasts of the field for they, at least, are but brutes and have not reason to guide them: time was but time shall be no more. God spoke to you by so many voices but you would not hear. You would not crush out that pride and anger in your heart, you would not restore those ill-gotten goods, you would not obey the precepts of your holy church nor attend to your religious duties, you would not abandon those wicked companions, you would

---

*(1347–1380); Italian mystic.

not avoid those dangerous temptations. Such is the language of those fiendish tormentors, words of taunting and of reproach, of hatred and of disgust. Of disgust, Yes! For even they, the very devils, when they sinned, sinned by such a sin as alone was compatible with such angelical natures, a rebellion of the intellect: and they, even they, the foul devils must turn away, revolted and disgusted, from the contemplation of those unspeakable sins by which degraded man outrages and defiles the temple of the Holy Ghost,* defiles and pollutes himself.

— O, my dear little brothers in Christ, may it never be our lot to hear that language! May it never be our lot, I say! In the last day of terrible reckoning I pray fervently to God that not a single soul of those who are in this chapel today may be found among those miserable beings whom the Great Judge shall command to depart for ever from His sight, that not one of us may ever hear ringing in his ears the awful sentence of rejection: *Depart from me, ye cursed, into everlasting fire which was prepared for the devil and his angels!*

He came down the aisle of the chapel, his legs shaking and the scalp of his head trembling as though it had been touched by ghostly fingers. He passed up the staircase and into the corridor along the walls of which the overcoats and waterproofs hung like gibbeted malefactors, headless and dripping and shapeless. And at every step he feared that he had already died, that his soul had been wrenched forth of the sheath of his body, that he was plunging headlong through space.

He could not grip the floor with his feet and sat heavily at his desk, opening one of his books at random and poring over it. Every word for him! It was true. God was almighty. God could call him now, call him as he sat at his desk, before he had time to be conscious of the summons. God had called him. Yes? What? Yes? His flesh shrank together as it felt the approach of the ravenous tongues of flames, dried up as it felt about it the swirl of stifling air. He had died. Yes. He was judged. A wave of fire swept through his body: the first. Again a wave. His brain began to glow. Another. His brain was simmering and bubbling within the cracking tenement of the skull. Flames burst forth from his skull like a corolla, shrieking like voices:

—Hell! Hell! Hell! Hell! Hell!

Voices spoke near him:

—On hell.

---

*Reference to I Corinthians 6:19.

—I suppose he rubbed it into you well.

—You bet he did. He put us all into a blue funk.

—That's what you fellows want: and plenty of it to make you work.
He leaned back weakly in his desk. He had not died. God had
spared him still. He was still in the familiar world of the school. Mr
Tate and Vincent Heron stood at the window, talking, jesting, gazing
out at the bleak rain, moving their heads.

—I wish it would clear up. I had arranged to go for a spin on the
bike with some fellows out by Malahide.* But the roads must be
kneedeep.

—It might clear up, sir.

The voices that he knew so well; the common words, the quiet of the
classroom when the voices paused and the silence was filled by the
sound of softly browsing cattle as the other boys munched their lunches
tranquilly lulled his aching soul.

There was still time. O Mary, refuge of sinners, intercede for him!
O Virgin Undefiled, save him from the gulf of death!

The English lesson began with the hearing of the history. Royal persons, favourites, intriguers, bishops, passed like mute phantoms behind
their veil of names. All had died: all had been judged. What did it profit
a man to gain the whole world if he lost his soul? At last he had understood: and human life lay around him, a plain of peace whereon
antlike men laboured in brotherhood, their dead sleeping under quiet
mounds. The elbow of his companion touched him and his heart was
touched: and when he spoke to answer a question of his master he
heard his own voice full of the quietude of humility and contrition.

His soul sank back deeper into depths of contrite peace, no longer
able to suffer the pain of dread, and sending forth, as she sank, a faint
prayer. Ah yes, he would still be spared; he would repent in his heart
and be forgiven; and then those above, those in heaven, would see what
he would do to make up for the past: a whole life, every hour of life.
Only wait.

—All, God! All, all!

A messenger came to the door to say that confessions were being
heard in the chapel. Four boys left the room; and he heard others passing down the corridor. A tremulous chill blew round his heart, no
stronger than a little wind, and yet, listening and suffering silently, he

---

*Coastal village 9 miles north of Dublin

seemed to have laid an ear against the muscle of his own heart, feeling it close and quail, listening to the flutter of its ventricles.

No escape. He had to confess, to speak out in words what he had done and thought, sin after sin. How? How?

—Father, I . . .

The thought slid like a cold shining rapier into his tender flesh: confession. But not there in the chapel of the college. He would confess all, every sin of deed and thought, sincerely: but not there among his school companions. Far away from there in some dark place he would murmur out his own shame: and he besought God humbly not to be offended with him if he did not dare to confess in the college chapel: and in utter abjection of spirit he craved forgiveness mutely of the boyish hearts about him.

Time passed.

He sat again in the front bench of the chapel. The daylight without was already failing and, as it fell slowly through the dull red blinds, it seemed that the sun of the last day was going down and that all souls were being gathered for the judgment.

—*I am cast away from the sight of Thine eyes.** words taken, my dear little brothers in Christ, from the Book of Psalms, thirtieth chapter, twenty-third verse. In the name of the Father and of the Son and of the Holy Ghost. Amen.

The preacher began to speak in a quiet friendly tone. His face was kind and he joined gently the fingers of each hand, forming a frail cage by the union of their tips.

—This morning we endeavoured, in our reflection upon hell, to make what our holy founder calls in his book of spiritual exercises,† the composition of place. We endeavoured, that is, to imagine with the senses of the mind, in our imagination, the material character of that awful place and of the physical torments which all who are in hell endure. This evening we shall consider for a few moments the nature of the spiritual torments of hell.

—Sin, remember, is a twofold enormity. It is a base consent to the promptings of our corrupt nature to the lower instincts, to that which is gross and beastlike; and it is also a turning away from the counsel of

---

*Reference to Psalm 30:23 (Douay version) or the equivalent Psalm 31:22 (King James version).

†The devotional book *The Spiritual Exercises* (1548) was written by Saint Ignatius Loyola (see note on p. 42).

our higher nature, from all that is pure and holy, from the Holy God Himself. For this reason mortal sin is punished in hell by two different forms of punishment, physical and spiritual.

—Now of all these spiritual pains by far the greatest is the pain of loss, so great, in fact, that in itself it is a torment greater than all the others. Saint Thomas,* the greatest doctor of the Church, the angelic doctor, as he is called, says that the worst damnation consists in this that the understanding of man is totally deprived of Divine light and his affection obstinately turned away from the goodness of God. God, remember, is a being infinitely good and therefore the loss of such a being must be a loss infinitely painful. In this life we have not a very clear idea of what such a loss must be but the damned in hell, for their greater torment, have a full understanding of that which they have lost and understand that they have lost it through their own sins and have lost it for ever. At the very instant of death the bonds of the flesh are broken asunder and the soul at once flies towards God as towards the centre of her existence. Remember, my dear little boys, our souls long to be with God. We come from God, we live by God, we belong to God: we are His, inalienably His. God loves with a divine love every human soul and every human soul lives in that love. How could it be otherwise? Every breath that we draw, every thought of our brain, every instant of life proceed from God's inexhaustible goodness. And if it be pain for a mother to be parted from her child, for a man to be exiled from hearth and home, for friend to be sundered from friend, O think what pain, what anguish, it must be for the poor soul to be spurned from the presence of the supremely good and loving Creator Who has called that soul into existence from nothingness and sustained it in life and loved it with an immeasurable love. This, then, to be separated for ever from its greatest good, from God, and to feel the anguish of that separation, knowing full well that it is unchangeable, this is the greatest torment which the created soul is capable of bearing, *pœna damni,* the pain of loss.

—The second pain which will afflict the souls of the damned in hell is the pain of conscience. Just as in dead bodies worms are engendered by putrefaction so in the souls of the lost there arises a perpetual remorse from the putrefaction of sin, the stirs of conscience, the worm, as Pope Innocent the Third† calls it, of the triple sting. The first sting inflicted

---

*Thomas Aquinas (1225–1274), eminent medieval Christian theologian.
†Pope from 1198 to 1216.

by this cruel worm will be the memory of past pleasures. O what a dreadful memory will that be! In the lake of alldevouring flame the proud king will remember the pomps of his court, the wise but wicked man his libraries and instruments of research, the lover of artistic pleasures his marbles and pictures and other art treasures, he who delighted in the pleasures of the table his gorgeous feasts, his dishes prepared with such delicacy, his choice wines, the miser will remember his hoard of gold, the robber his illgotten wealth, the angry and revengeful and merciless murderers their deeds of blood and violence in which they revelled, the impure and adulterous the unspeakable and filthy pleasures in which they delighted. They will remember all this and loathe themselves and their sins. For how miserable will all those pleasures seem to the soul condemned to suffer in hell-fire for ages and ages. How they will rage and fume to think that they have lost the bliss of heaven for the dross of earth, for a few pieces of metal, for vain honours, for bodily comforts, for a tingling of the nerves. They will repent indeed: and this is the second sting of the worm of conscience, a late and fruitless sorrow for sins committed. Divine justice insists that the understanding of those miserable wretches be fixed continually on the sins of which they were guilty and moreover, as Saint Augustine* points out, God will impart to them His own knowledge of sin so that sin will appear to them in all its hideous malice as it appears to the eyes of God Himself. They will behold their sins in all their foulness and repent but it will be too late and then they will bewail the good occasions which they neglected. This is the last and deepest and most cruel sting of the worm of conscience. The conscience will say: You had time and opportunity to repent and would not. You were brought up religiously by your parents. You had the sacraments and graces and indulgences of the church to aid you. You had the minister of God to preach to you to call you back when you had strayed, to forgive you your sins, no matter how many, how abominable, if only you had confessed and repented. No. You would not. You flouted the ministers of holy religion, you turned your back on the confessional, you wallowed deeper and deeper in the mire of sin. God appealed to you, threatened you, entreated you to return to Him. O, what shame, what misery! The Ruler of the universe entreated you, a creature of clay, to love Him Who made you and to

---

*Augustine of Hippo (A.D. 354–430), the most important of the early Church fathers, wrote *The City of God*.

keep His law. No. You would not. And now, though you were to flood all hell with your tears if you could still weep, all that sea of repentance would not gain for you what a single tear of true repentance shed during our mortal life would have gained for you. You implore now a moment of earthly life wherein to repent: in vain. That time is gone: gone for ever.

—Such is the threefold sting of conscience, the viper which gnaws the very heart's core of the wretches in hell so that filled with hellish fury they curse themselves for their folly and curse the evil companions who have brought them to such ruin and curse the devils who tempted them in life and now mock them in eternity and even revile and curse the Supreme Being Whose goodness and patience they scorned and slighted but Whose justice and power they cannot evade.

—The next spiritual pain to which the damned are subjected is the pain of extension. Man, in this earthly life, though he be capable of many evils, is not capable of them all at once inasmuch as one evil corrects and counteracts another, just as one poison frequently corrects another. In hell, on the contrary, one torment, instead of counteracting another, lends it still greater force: and, moreover, as the internal faculties are more perfect than the external senses, so are they more capable of suffering. Just as every sense is afflicted with a fitting torment so is every spiritual faculty; the fancy with horrible images, the sensitive faculty with alternate longing and rage, the mind and understanding with an interior darkness more terrible even than the exterior darkness which reigns in that dreadful prison. The malice, impotent though it be, which possesses these demon souls is an evil of boundless extension, of limitless duration, a frightful state of wickedness which we can scarcely realise unless we bear in mind the enormity of sin and the hatred God bears to it.

—Opposed to this pain of extension and yet co-existent with it we have the pain of intensity. Hell is the centre of evils and, as you know, things are more intense at their centres than at their remotest points. There are no contraries or admixtures of any kind to temper or soften in the least the pains of hell. Nay, things which are good in themselves become evil in hell. Company, elsewhere a source of comfort to the afflicted, will be there a continual torment: knowledge, so much longed for as the chief good of the intellect, will there be hated worse than ignorance: light, so much coveted by all creatures from the lord of creation down to the humblest plant in the forest, will be loathed intensely. In this life our sorrows are either not very long or not very great because nature either overcomes them by habits or puts an end to them by sinking under their weight. But in hell the torments cannot be overcome by habit, for while they are of terrible intensity they are at the same time of continual variety, each pain, so to speak, taking fire from another and re-endowing that which has enkindled it with a still fiercer flame. Nor can nature escape from these intense and various tortures by succumbing to them for the soul is sustained and maintained in evil so that its suffering may be the greater. Boundless extension of torment, incredible intensity of suffering, unceasing variety of torture—this is what the divine majesty, so outraged by sinners, demands, this is what the holiness of heaven, slighted and set aside for the lustful and low pleasures of the corrupt flesh, requires, this is what the blood of the innocent Lamb of God, shed for the redemption of sinners, trampled upon by the vilest of the vile, insists upon.

—Last and crowning torture of all the tortures of that awful place is the eternity of hell. Eternity! O, dread and dire word. Eternity! What mind of man can understand it? And remember, it is an eternity of pain. Even though the pains of hell were not so terrible as they are yet they would become infinite as they are destined to last for ever. But while they are everlasting they are at the same time, as you know, intolerably intense, unbearably extensive. To bear even the sting of an insect for all eternity would be a dreadful torment. What must it be, then, to bear the manifold tortures of hell for ever? For ever! For all eternity! Not for a year or for an age but for ever. Try to imagine the awful meaning of this. You have often seen the sand on the seashore. How fine are its tiny grains! And how many of those tiny little grains go to make up the small handful which a child grasps in its play. Now imagine a mountain of that sand, a million miles high, reaching from the earth to the farthest heavens, and a million miles broad, extending to remotest space, and a million miles in thickness: and imagine such an enormous mass of countless particles of sand multiplied as often as there are leaves in the forest, drops of water in the mighty ocean, feathers on birds, scales on fish, hairs on animals, atoms in the vast expanse of the air: and imagine that at the end of every million years a little bird came to that mountain and carried away in its beak a tiny grain of that sand. How many millions upon millions of centuries would pass before that bird had carried away even a square foot of that mountain, how many eons upon eons of ages before it had carried away all. Yet at the end of that immense stretch of time not even one instant of eternity could be said to have ended. At the end of all those billions and trillions of years eternity would have scarcely begun. And if that mountain rose again after it had been all carried away and if the bird came again and carried it all away again grain by grain: and if it so rose and sank as many times as there are stars in the sky, atoms in the air, drops of water in the sea, leaves on the trees, feathers upon birds, scales upon fish, hairs upon animals, at the end of all those innumerable risings and sinkings of that immeasurably vast mountain not one single instant of eternity could be said to have ended; even then, at the end of such a period, after that eon of time the mere thought of which makes our very brain reel dizzily, eternity would have scarcely begun.

—A holy saint (one of our own fathers I believe it was) was once vouchsafed a vision of hell. It seemed to him that he stood in the midst of a great hall, dark and silent save for the ticking of a great clock. The ticking went on unceasingly; and it seemed to this saint that the sound of the ticking was the ceaseless repetition of the words: ever, never; ever, never. Ever to be in hell, never to be in heaven; ever to be shut off from the presence of God, never to enjoy the beatific vision; ever to be eaten with flames, gnawed by vermin, goaded with burning spikes, never to be free from those pains; ever to have the conscience upbraid one, the memory enrage, the mind filled with darkness and despair, never to escape; ever to curse and revile the foul demons who gloat fiendishly over the misery of their dupes, never to behold the shining raiment of the blessed spirits; ever to cry out of the abyss of fire to God for an instant, a single instant, of respite from such awful agony, never to receive, even for an instant, God's pardon; ever to suffer, never to enjoy; ever to be damned, never to be saved; ever, never; ever, never. O, what a dreadful punishment! An eternity of endless agony, of endless bodily and spiritual torment, without one ray of hope, without one moment of cessation, of agony limitless in intensity, of torment infinitely varied, of torture that sustains eternally that which it eternally devours, of anguish that everlastingly preys upon the spirit while it racks the flesh, an eternity, every instant of which is itself an eternity of woe. Such is the terrible punishment decreed for those who die in mortal sin by an almighty and a just God.

—Yes, a just God! Men, reasoning always as men, are astonished that God should mete out an everlasting and infinite punishment in the fires of hell for a single grievous sin. They reason thus because, blinded by the gross illusion of the flesh and the darkness of human understanding they are unable to comprehend the hideous malice of mortal sin. They reason thus because they are unable to comprehend that even venial sin is of such a foul and hideous nature that even if the omnipotent Creator could end all the evil and misery in the world the wars, the diseases, the robberies, the crime, the deaths, the murders, on condition that he allowed a single venial sin to pass unpunished, a single venial sin, a lie, an angry look, a moment of wilful sloth, He, the great omnipotent God could not do so because sin, be it in thought or deed, is a transgression of His law and God would not be God if He did not punish the transgressor.

—A sin, an instant of rebellious pride of the intellect, made Lucifer and a third part of the cohorts of angels fall from their glory. A sin, an instant of folly and weakness, drove Adam and Eve out of Eden and brought death and suffering into the world. To retrieve the consequences of that sin the Only Begotten Son of God came down to earth, lived and suffered and died a most painful death, hanging for three hours on the cross.

—O, my dear little brethren in Christ Jesus, will we then offend that good Redeemer and provoke His anger? Will we trample again upon that torn and mangled corpse? Will we spit upon that face so full of sorrow and love? Will we too, like the cruel Jews and the brutal soldiers, mock that gentle and compassionate Saviour Who trod alone for our sake the awful winepress of sorrow? Every word of sin is a wound in His tender side. Every sinful act is a thorn piercing His head. Every impure thought, deliberately yielded to, is a keen lance transfixing that sacred and loving heart. No, no. It is impossible for any human being to do that which offends so deeply the divine Majesty, that which is punished by an eternity of agony, that which crucifies again the Son of God and makes a mockery of Him.

—I pray to God that my poor words may have availed today to confirm in holiness those who are in a state of grace, to strengthen the wavering, to lead back to the state of grace the poor soul that has strayed if any such be among you. I pray to God, and do you pray with me, that we may repent of our sins. I will ask you now, all of you, to repeat after me the act of contrition,* kneeling here in this humble chapel in the presence of God. He is there in the tabernacle burning with love for mankind, ready to comfort the afflicted. Be not afraid. No matter how many or how foul the sins if only you repent of them they will be forgiven you. Let no worldly shame hold you back. God is still the merci-

---

*Prayer beginning: "Oh my God, I am heartily sorry for having offended Thee. . . ."

ful Lord who wishes not the eternal death of the sinner but rather that he be converted and live.

—He calls you to Him. You are His. He made you out of nothing. He loved you as only a God can love. His arms are open to receive you even though you have sinned against Him. Come to Him, poor sinner, poor vain and erring sinner. Now is the acceptable time. Now is the hour.

The priest rose and turning towards the altar knelt upon the step before the tabernacle in the fallen gloom. He waited till all in the chapel had knelt and every least noise was still. Then, raising his head, he repeated the act of contrition, phrase by phrase, with fervour. The boys answered him phrase by phrase. Stephen, his tongue cleaving to his palate, bowed his head, praying with his heart.

> *—O my God!—*
> *—O my God!—*
> *—I am heartily sorry—*
> *—I am heartily sorry—*
> *—for having offended Thee—*
> *—for having offended Thee—*
> *—and I detest my sins—*
> *—and I detest my sins—*
> *—above every other evil—*
> *—above every other evil—*
> *—because they displease Thee, my God—*
> *—because they displease Thee, my God—*
> *—Who art so deserving—*
> *—Who art so deserving—*
> *—of all my love—*
> *—of all my love—*
> *—and I firmly purpose—*
> *—and I firmly purpose—*
> *—by Thy Holy grace—*
> *—by Thy Holy grace—*
> *—never more to offend Thee—*
> *—never more to offend Thee—*
> *—and to amend my life—*
> *—and to amend my life—*

* * * *

He went up to his room after dinner in order to be alone with his soul: and at every step his soul seemed to sigh: at every step his soul mounted with his feet, sighing in the ascent, through a region of viscid gloom.

He halted on the landing before the door and then, grasping the porcelain knob, opened the door quickly. He waited in fear, his soul pining within him, praying silently that death might not touch his brow as he passed over the threshold, that the fiends that inhabit darkness might not be given power over him. He waited still at the threshold as at the entrance to some dark cave. Faces were there; eyes: they waited and watched.

—We knew perfectly well of course that although it was bound to come to the light he would find considerable difficulty in endeavouring to try to induce himself to try to endeavour to ascertain the spiritual plenipotentiary and so we knew of course perfectly well —

Murmuring faces waited and watched; murmurous voices filled the dark shell of the cave. He feared intensely in spirit and in flesh but, raising his head bravely, he strode into the room firmly. A doorway, a room, the same room, same window. He told himself calmly that those words had absolutely no sense which had seemed to rise murmurously from the dark. He told himself that it was simply his room with the door open.

He closed the door and, walking swiftly to the bed, knelt beside it and covered his face with his hands. His hands were cold and damp and his limbs ached with chill. Bodily unrest and chill and weariness beset him, routing his thoughts. Why was he kneeling there like a child saying his evening prayers? To be alone with his soul, to examine his conscience, to meet his sins face to face, to recall their times and manners and circumstances, to weep over them. He could not weep. He could not summon them to his memory. He felt only an ache of soul and body, his whole being, memory, will, understanding, flesh, benumbed and weary.

That was the work of devils, to scatter his thoughts and overcloud his conscience, assailing him at the gates of the cowardly and sin corrupted flesh: and, praying God timidly to forgive him his weakness, he crawled up on to the bed and, wrapping the blankets closely about him, covered his face again with his hands. He had sinned. He had sinned so deeply against heaven and before God that he was not worthy to be called God's child.

Could it be that he, Stephen Dedalus, had done those things? His conscience sighed in answer. Yes, he had done them, secretly, filthily, time after time and, hardened in sinful impenitence, he had dared to wear the mask of holiness before the tabernacle itself while his soul within was a living mass of corruption. How came it that God had not struck him dead? The leprous company of his sins closed about him, breathing upon him, bending over him from all sides. He strove to forget them in an act of prayer, huddling his limbs closer together and binding down his eyelids: but the senses of his soul would not be bound and, though his eyes were shut fast, he saw the places where he had sinned and, though his ears were tightly covered, he heard. He desired with all his will not to hear nor see. He desired till his frame shook under the strain of his desire and until the senses of his soul closed. They closed for an instant and then opened. He saw.

A field of stiff weeds and thistles and tufted nettlebunches. Thick among the tufts of rank stiff growth lay battered canisters and clots and coils of solid excrement. A faint marsh light struggling upwards from all the ordure through the bristling grey green weeds. An evil smell, faint and foul as the light, curled upwards sluggishly out of the canisters and from the stale crusted dung.

Creatures were in the field; one, three, six: creatures were moving in the field, hither and thither. Goatish creatures with human faces, horny browed, lightly bearded and grey as indiarubber. The malice of evil glittered in their hard eyes, as they moved hither and thither, trailing their long tails behind them. A rictus of cruel malignity lit up greyly their old bony faces. One was clasping about his ribs a torn flannel waistcoat, another complained monotonously as his beard stuck in the tufted weeds. Soft language issued from their spittleless lips as they swished in slow circles round and round the field, winding hither and thither through the weeds, dragging their long tails amid the rattling canisters. They moved in slow circles, circling closer and closer to enclose, to enclose, soft language issuing from their lips, their long swishing tails besmeared with stale shite, thrusting upwards their terrific faces . . .

Help!

He flung the blankets from him madly to free his face and neck. That was his hell. God had allowed him to see the hell reserved for his sins: stinking, bestial, malignant, a hell of lecherous goatish fiends. For him! For him!

He sprang from the bed, the reeking odour pouring down his throat, clogging and revolting his entrails. Air! The air of heaven! He stumbled towards the window, groaning and almost fainting with sickness. At the washstand a convulsion seized him within; and, clasping his cold forehead wildly, he vomited profusely in agony.

When the fit had spent itself he walked weakly to the window and lifting the sash, sat in a corner of the embrasure and leaned his elbow upon the sill. The rain had drawn off; and amid the moving vapours from point to point of light the city was spinning about herself a soft cocoon of yellowish haze. Heaven was still and faintly luminous and the air sweet to breathe, as in a thicket drenched with showers: and amid peace and shimmering lights and quiet fragrance he made a covenant with his heart.

He prayed:

—He once had meant to come on earth in heavenly glory but we sinned: and then He could not safely visit us but with a shrouded majesty and a bedimmed radiance for He was God. So He came Himself in weakness not in power and He sent thee, a creature in His stead, with a creature's comeliness and lustre suited to our state. And now thy very face and form, dear mother, speak to us of the Eternal; not like earthly beauty, dangerous to look upon, but like the morning star which is thy emblem, bright and musical, breathing purity, telling of heaven and infusing peace. O harbinger of day! O light of the pilgrim! Lead us still as thou hast led. In the dark night, across the bleak wilderness guide us on to our Lord Jesus, guide us home.*

His eyes were dimmed with tears and, looking humbly up to heaven, he wept for the innocence he had lost.

When evening had fallen he left the house and the first touch of the damp dark air and the noise of the door as it closed behind him made ache again his conscience, lulled by prayer and tears. Confess! Confess! It was not enough to lull the conscience with a tear and a prayer. He had to kneel before the minister of the Holy Ghost and tell over his hidden sins truly and repentantly. Before he heard again the footboard of the housedoor trail over the threshold as it opened to let him in, before he saw again the table in the kitchen set for supper he would have knelt and confessed. It was quite simple.

The ache of conscience ceased and he walked onward swiftly through the dark streets. There were so many flagstones on the footpath of that street and so many streets in that city and so many cities in

---

*From Newman's "The Glories of Mary."

the world. Yet eternity had no end. He was in mortal sin. Even once was a mortal sin. It could happen in an instant. But how so quickly? By seeing or by thinking of seeing. The eyes see the thing, without having wished first to see. Then in an instant it happens. But does that part of the body understand or what? The serpent, the most subtle beast of the field. It must understand when it desires in one instant and then prolongs its own desire instant after instant, sinfully. It feels and understands and desires. What a horrible thing! Who made it to be like that, a bestial part of the body able to understand bestially and desire bestially? Was that then he or an inhuman thing moved by a lower soul? His soul sickened at the thought of a torpid snaky life feeding itself out of the tender marrow of his life and fattening upon the slime of lust. O why was that so? O why?

He cowered in the shadow of the thought abasing himself in the awe of God Who had made all things and all men. Madness. Who could think such a thought? And, cowering in darkness and abject, he prayed mutely to his angel guardian to drive away with his sword the demon that was whispering to his brain.

The whisper ceased and he knew then clearly that his own soul had sinned in thought and word and deed wilfully through his own body. Confess! He had to confess every sin. How could he utter in words to the priest what he had done? Must, must. Or how could he explain without dying of shame? Or how could he have done such things without shame? A madman! Confess! O he would indeed to be free and sinless again! Perhaps the priest would know. O dear God!

He walked on and on through ill-lit streets, fearing to stand still for a moment lest it might seem that he held back from what awaited him, fearing to arrive at that towards which he still turned with longing. How beautiful must be a soul in the state of grace when God looked upon it with love!

Frowsy* girls sat along the curbstones before their baskets. Their dank hair hung trailed over their brows. They were not beautiful to see as they crouched in the mire. But their souls were seen by God; and if their souls were in a state of grace they were radiant to see: and God loved them, seeing them.

A wasting breath of humiliation blew bleakly over his soul to think of how he had fallen, to feel that those souls were dearer to God than

---

*Slovenly.

his. The wind blew over him and passed on to the myriads and myriads of other souls, on whom God's favour shone now more and now less, stars now brighter and now dimmer, sustained and failing. And the glimmering souls passed away, sustained and failing, merged in a moving breath. One soul was lost; a tiny soul: his. It flickered once and went out, forgotten, lost. The end: black cold void waste.

Consciousness of place came ebbing back to him slowly over a vast tract of time unlit, unfelt, unlived. The squalid scene composed itself around him; the common accents, the burning gasjets in the shops, odours of fish and spirits and wet sawdust, moving men and women. An old woman was about to cross the street, an oilcan in her hand. He bent down and asked her was there a chapel near.

—A chapel, sir? Yes, sir. Church Street chapel.

—Church?

She shifted the can to her other hand and directed him: and, as she held out her reeking withered right hand under its fringe of shawl, he bent lower towards her, saddened and soothed by her voice.

—Thank you.

—You are quite welcome sir.

The candles on the high altar had been extinguished but the fragrance of incense still floated down the dim nave. Bearded workmen with pious faces were guiding a canopy out through a side door, the sacristan aiding them with quiet gestures and words. A few of the faithful still lingered praying before one of the side-altars or kneeling in the benches near the confessionals.[13] He approached timidly and knelt at the last bench in the body, thankful for the peace and silence and fragrant shadow of the church. The board on which he knelt was narrow and worn and those who knelt near him were humble followers of Jesus. Jesus too had been born in poverty and had worked in the shop of a carpenter, cutting boards and planing them, and had first spoken of the kingdom of God to poor fishermen, teaching all men to be meek and humble of heart.

He bowed his head upon his hands, bidding his heart be meek and humble that he might be like those who knelt beside him and his prayer as acceptable as theirs. He prayed beside them but it was hard. His soul was foul with sin and he dared not ask forgiveness with the simple trust of those whom Jesus, in the mysterious ways of God, had called first to His side, the carpenters, the fishermen, poor and simple people following a lowly trade, handling and shaping the wood of trees, mending their nets with patience.

A tall figure came down the aisle and the penitents stirred: and, at the last moment glancing up swiftly, he saw a long grey beard and the brown habit of a capuchin.* The priest entered the box and was hidden. Two penitents† rose and entered the confessional at either side. The wooden slide was drawn back and the faint murmur of a voice troubled the silence.

His blood began to murmur in his veins, murmuring like a sinful city summoned from its sleep to bear its doom. Little flakes of fire fell and powdery ashes fell softly, alighting on the houses of men. They stirred, waking from sleep, troubled by the heated air.

The slide was shot back. The penitent emerged from the side of the box. The farther side was drawn. A woman entered quietly and deftly where the first penitent had knelt. The faint murmur began again.

He could still leave the chapel. He could stand up, put one foot before the other and walk out softly and then run, run, run swiftly through the dark streets. He could still escape from the shame. Had it been any terrible crime but that one sin! Had it been murder! Little fiery flakes fell and touched him at all points, shameful thoughts, shameful words, shameful acts. Shame covered him wholly like fine glowing ashes falling continually. To say it in words! His soul, stifling and helpless, would cease to be.

The slide was shot back. A penitent emerged from the farther side of the box. The near slide was drawn. A penitent entered where the other penitent had come out. A soft whispering noise floated in vaporous cloudlets out of the box. It was the woman: soft whispering cloudlets, soft whispering vapour, whispering and vanishing.

He beat his breast with his fist humbly, secretly under cover of the wooden armrest. He would be at one with others and with God. He would love his neighbour. He would love God Who had made and loved him. He would kneel and pray with others and be happy. God would look down on him and on them and would love them all.

It was easy to be good. God's yoke was sweet and light.‡ It was better never to have sinned, to have remained always a child, for God loved little children and suffered them to come to Him. It was a terrible and a sad thing to sin. But God was merciful to poor sinners who were truly sorry. How true that was! That was indeed goodness.

---

*Church Street chapel is run by members of the Capuchin order, who wear a brown robe with a cowl.

†Believers who have come to repent of their sins.

‡An allusion to Matthew 11:29–30: "And you shall find rest to your souls. For my yoke is sweet and my burden light" (Douay version).

The slide was shot to suddenly. The penitent came out. He was next. He stood up in terror and walked blindly into the box.

At last it had come. He knelt in the silent gloom and raised his eyes to the white crucifix suspended above him. God could see that he was sorry. He would tell all his sins. His confession would be long, long. Everybody in the chapel would know then what a sinner he had been. Let them know. It was true. But God had promised to forgive him if he was sorry. He was sorry. He clasped his hands and raised them towards the white form, praying with his darkened eyes, praying with all his trembling body, swaying his head to and fro like a lost creature, praying with whimpering lips.

—Sorry! Sorry! O sorry!

The slide clicked back and his heart bounded in his breast. The face of an old priest was at the grating, averted from him, leaning upon a hand. He made the sign of the cross and prayed of the priest to bless him for he had sinned.* Then, bowing his head, he repeated the *Confiteor* in fright. At the words *my most grievous fault* he ceased, breathless.

—How long is it since your last confession, my child?

—A long time, father.

—A month, my child?

—Longer, father.

—Three months, my child?

—Longer, father.

—Six months?

—Eight months, father.

He had begun. The priest asked:

—And what do you remember since that time?

He began to confess his sins: masses missed, prayers not said, lies.

—Anything else, my child?

Sins of anger, envy of others, gluttony, vanity, disobedience.

—Anything else, my child?

There was no help. He murmured:

—I . . . committed sins of impurity, father.

The priest did not turn his head.

—With yourself, my child?

—And . . . with others.

—With women, my child?

---

*Confession typically begins with these words: "Forgive me, Father, for I have sinned."

—Yes, father.

—Were they married women, my child?

He did not know. His sins trickled from his lips, one by one, trickled in shameful drops from his soul festering and oozing like a sore, a squalid stream of vice. The last sins oozed forth, sluggish, filthy. There was no more to tell. He bowed his head, overcome.

The priest was silent. Then he asked:

—How old are you, my child?

—Sixteen, father.

The priest passed his hand several times over his face. Then, resting his forehead against his hand, he leaned towards the grating and, with eyes still averted, spoke slowly. His voice was weary and old.

—You are very young, my child, he said, and let me implore of you to give up that sin. It is a terrible sin. It kills the body and it kills the soul. It is the cause of many crimes and misfortunes. Give it up, my child, for God's sake. It is dishonourable and unmanly. You cannot know where that wretched habit will lead you or where it will come against you. As long as you commit that sin, my poor child, you will never be worth one farthing to God. Pray to our mother Mary to help you. She will help you, my child. Pray to Our Blessed Lady when that sin comes into your mind. I am sure you will do that, will you not? You repent of all those sins. I am sure you do. And you will promise God now that by His holy grace you will never offend Him any more by that wicked sin. You will make that solemn promise to God, will you not?

—Yes, father.

The old and weary voice fell like sweet rain upon his quaking parching heart. How sweet and sad!

—Do so, my poor child. The devil has led you astray. Drive him back to hell when he tempts you to dishonour your body in that way—the foul spirit who hates Our Lord. Promise God now that you will give up that sin, that wretched wretched sin.

Blinded by his tears and by the light of God's mercifulness he bent his head and heard the grave words of absolution* spoken and saw the priest's hand raised above him in token of forgiveness.

—God bless you, my child. Pray for me.

He knelt to say his penance, praying in a corner of the dark nave: and his prayers ascended to heaven from his purified heart like perfume streaming upwards from a heart of white rose.

---

*Formal forgiveness of sins.

The muddy streets were gay. He strode homeward, conscious of an invisible grace pervading and making light his limbs. In spite of all he had done it. He had confessed and God had pardoned him. His soul was made fair and holy once more, holy and happy.

It would be beautiful to die if God so willed. It was beautiful to live in grace a life of peace and virtue and forbearance with others.

He sat by the fire in the kitchen, not daring to speak for happiness. Till that moment he had not known how beautiful and peaceful life could be. The green square of paper pinned round the lamp cast down a tender shade. On the dresser was a plate of sausages and white pudding and on the shelf there were eggs. They would be for the breakfast in the morning after the communion in the college chapel. White pudding and eggs and sausages and cups of tea. How simple and beautiful was life after all! And life lay all before him.

In a dream he fell asleep. In a dream he rose and saw that it was morning. In a waking dream he went through the quiet morning towards the college.

The boys were all there, kneeling in their places. He knelt among them, happy and shy. The altar was heaped with fragrant masses of white flowers: and in the morning light the pale flames of the candles among the white flowers were clear and silent as his own soul.

He knelt before the altar with his classmates, holding the altar cloth with them over a living rail of hands. His hands were trembling and his soul trembled as he heard the priest pass with the ciborium* from communicant† to communicant.

—*Corpus Domini nostri.*‡

Could it be? He knelt there sinless and timid: and he would hold upon his tongue the host§ and God would enter his purified body.

—*In vitam eternam.*|| Amen.

Another life! A life of grace and virtue and happiness! It was true. It was not a dream from which he would wake. The past was past.

—*Corpus Domini nostri.*

The ciborium had come to him.

---

*Cup or chalice containing the host, the body of Christ, in the Eucharist.
†Participant in the rite of Holy Communion.
‡The body of our Lord (Latin).
§The bread (or wafer) representing the body of Christ in the Eucharist.
||In everlasting life (Latin).

CHAPTER IV

SUNDAY WAS DEDICATED TO the mystery of the Holy Trinity,* Monday to the Holy Ghost, Tuesday to the Guardian Angels, Wednesday to Saint Joseph, Thursday to the Most Blessed Sacrament of the Altar, Friday to the Suffering Jesus, Saturday to the Blessed Virgin Mary.

Every morning he hallowed himself anew in the presence of some holy image or mystery. His day began with an heroic offering of its every moment of thought or action for the intentions of the sovereign pontiff and with an early mass. The raw morning air whetted his resolute piety; and often as he knelt among the few worshippers at the side altar, following with his interleaved prayer book the murmur of the priest, he glanced up for an instant towards the vested figure standing in the gloom between the two candles, which were the old and the new testaments, and imagined that he was kneeling at mass in the catacombs.†

His daily life was laid out in devotional areas. By means of ejaculations and prayers he stored up ungrudgingly for the souls in purgatory centuries of days and quarantines and years; yet the spiritual triumph which he felt in achieving with ease so many fabulous ages of canonical penances did not wholly reward his zeal of prayer since he could never know how much temporal punishment he had remitted by way of suffrage for the agonising souls: and, fearful lest in the midst of the purgatorial fire, which differed from the infernal only in that it was not everlasting, his penance might avail no more than a drop of moisture he drove his soul daily through an increasing circle of works of supererogation.‡

Every part of his day, divided by what he regarded now as the duties of his station in life, circled about its own centre of spiritual energy. His

---

*In Christian theology, the three persons of the godhead: the Father, the Son (Jesus Christ), and the Holy Spirit (Holy Ghost).
†Underground tombs connected by tunnels.
‡An abundance, or surplus, of good works.

life seemed to have drawn near to eternity; every thought, word and deed, every instance of consciousness could be made to revibrate radiantly in heaven: and at times his sense of such immediate repercussion was so lively that he seemed to feel his soul in devotion pressing like fingers the keyboard of a great cash register and to see the amount of his purchase start forth immediately in heaven, not as a number but as a frail column of incense or as a slender flower.

The rosaries, too, which he said constantly—for he carried his beads loose in his trousers' pockets that he might tell them as he walked the streets—transformed themselves into coronals of flowers of such vague unearthly texture that they seemed to him as hueless and odourless as they were nameless. He offered up each of his three daily chaplets* that his soul might grow strong in each of the three theological virtues, in faith in the Father Who had created him, in hope in the Son Who had redeemed him, and in love of the Holy Ghost Who had sanctified him; and this thrice triple prayer he offered to the Three Persons through Mary in the name of her joyful and sorrowful and glorious mysteries.

On each of the seven days of the week he further prayed that one of the seven gifts of the Holy Ghost† might descend upon his soul and drive out of it day by day the seven deadly sins which had defiled it in the past; and he prayed for each gift on its appointed day, confident that it would descend upon him, though it seemed strange to him at times that wisdom and understanding and knowledge were so distinct in their nature that each should be prayed for apart from the others. Yet he believed that at some future stage of his spiritual progress this difficulty would be removed when his sinful soul had been raised up from its weakness and enlightened by the Third Person of the Most Blessed Trinity. He believed this all the more, and with trepidation, because of the divine gloom and silence wherein dwelt the unseen Paraclete,‡ Whose symbols were a dove and a mighty wind, to sin against Whom was a sin beyond forgiveness, the eternal, mysterious secret Being to Whom, as God, the priests offered up mass once a year, orbed in the scarlet of the tongues of fire.

The imagery through which the nature and kinship of the Three

---

*A chaplet is one-third of a full rosary of fifteen decades (a decade is ten Hail Marys).

†Derived from Isaias 11:2–3, the gifts are wisdom, understanding, counsel, fortitude, knowledge, piety (godliness), and fear of the Lord.

‡The Holy Spirit.

Persons of the Trinity were darkly shadowed forth in the books of devotion which he read—the Father contemplating from all eternity as in a mirror His Divine Perfections and thereby begetting eternally the Eternal Son and the Holy Spirit proceeding out of Father and Son from all eternity—were easier of acceptance by his mind by reason of their august incomprehensibility than was the simple fact that God had loved his soul from all eternity, for ages before he had been born into the world, for ages before the world itself had existed.

He had heard the names of the passions of love and hate pronounced solemnly on the stage and in the pulpit, had found them set forth solemnly in books, and had wondered why his soul was unable to harbour them for any time or to force his lips to utter their names with conviction. A brief anger had often invested him, but he had never been able to make it an abiding passion and had always felt himself passing out of it as if his very body were being divested with ease of some outer skin or peel. He had felt a subtle, dark and murmurous presence penetrate his being and fire him with a brief iniquitous lust: it, too, had slipped beyond his grasp leaving his mind lucid and indifferent. This, it seemed, was the only love and that the only hate his soul would harbour.

But he could no longer disbelieve in the reality of love since God himself had loved his individual soul with divine love from all eternity. Gradually, as his soul was enriched with spiritual knowledge, he saw the whole world forming one vast symmetrical expression of God's power and love. Life became a divine gift for every moment and sensation of which, were it even the sight of a single leaf hanging on the twig of a tree, his soul should praise and thank the giver. The world for all its solid substance and complexity no longer existed for his soul save as a theorem of divine power and love and universality. So entire and unquestionable was this sense of the divine meaning in all nature granted to his soul that he could scarcely understand why it was in any way necessary that he should continue to live. Yet that was part of the divine purpose and he dared not question its use, he above all others who had sinned so deeply and so foully against the divine purpose. Meek and abased by this consciousness of the one eternal omnipresent perfect reality his soul took up again her burden of pieties, masses and prayers and sacraments and mortifications, and only then for the first time since he had brooded on the great mystery of love did he feel within him a warm movement like that of some newly born life or virtue of the soul itself. The attitude of rapture in sacred art, the raised and parted hands, the parted lips and eyes as of one about to swoon, became for him an image of the soul in prayer, humiliated and faint before her Creator.

But he had been forewarned of the dangers of spiritual exaltation and did not allow himself to desist from even the least or lowliest devotion, striving also by constant mortification to undo the sinful past rather than to achieve a saintliness fraught with peril. Each of his senses was brought under a rigorous discipline. In order to mortify the sense of sight he made it his rule to walk in the street with downcast eyes, glancing neither to right nor left and never behind him. His eyes shunned every encounter with the eyes of women. From time to time also he balked them by a sudden effort of the will, as by lifting them suddenly in the middle of an unfinished sentence and closing the book. To mortify his hearing he exerted no control over his voice which was then breaking, neither sang nor whistled and made no attempt to flee from noise which caused him painful nervous irritation such as the sharpening of knives on the knifeboard, the gathering of cinders on the fireshovel and the twigging* of the carpet. To mortify his smell was more difficult as he found in himself no instinctive repugnance to bad odours, whether they were the odours of the outdoor world such as those of dung or tar or the odours of his own person among which he had made many curious comparisons and experiments. He found in the end that the only odour against which his sense of smell revolted was a certain stale fishy stink like that of longstanding urine: and whenever it was possible he subjected himself to this unpleasant odour. To mortify the taste he practised strict habits at table, observed to the letter all the fasts of the church and sought by distraction to divert his mind from the savours of different foods. But it was to the mortification of touch that he brought the most assiduous ingenuity of inventiveness. He never consciously changed his position in bed, sat in the most uncomfortable positions, suffered patiently every itch and pain, kept away from the fire, remained on his knees all through the mass except at the gospels, left parts of his neck and face undried so that air might sting them and, whenever he was not saying his beads, carried his arms stiffly at his sides like a runner and never in his pockets or clasped behind him.

He had no temptations to sin mortally. It surprised him, however, to find that at the end of his course of intricate piety and selfrestraint he

---

*Brushing with a broom.

was so easily at the mercy of childish and unworthy imperfections. His prayers and fasts availed him little for the suppression of anger at hearing his mother sneeze or at being disturbed in his devotions. It needed an immense effort of his will to master the impulse which urged him to give outlet to such irritation. Images of the outbursts of trivial anger which he had often noted among his masters, their twitching mouths, closeshut lips and flushed cheeks, recurred to his memory, discouraging him, for all his practice of humility, by the comparison. To merge his life in the common tide of other lives was harder for him than any fasting or prayer, and it was his constant failure to do this to his own satisfaction which caused in his soul at last a sensation of spiritual dryness together with a growth of doubts and scruples. His soul traversed a period of desolation in which the sacraments themselves seemed to have turned into dried up sources. His confession became a channel for the escape of scrupulous and unrepented imperfections. His actual reception of the eucharist did not bring him the same dissolving moments of virginal self-surrender as did those spiritual communions made by him sometimes at the close of some visit to the Blessed Sacrament. The book which he used for these visits was an old neglected book written by Saint Alphonsus Liguori,* with fading characters and sere foxpapered leaves. A faded world of fervent love and virginal responses seemed to be evoked for his soul by the reading of its pages in which the imagery of the canticles† was interwoven with the communicant's prayers. An inaudible voice seemed to caress the soul, telling her names and glories, bidding her arise as for espousal and come away, bidding her look forth, a spouse, from Amana‡ and from the mountains of the leopards; and the soul seemed to answer with the same inaudible voice, surrendering herself: *Inter ubera mea commorabitur.*§

This idea of surrender had a perilous attraction for his mind now that he felt his soul beset once again by the insistent voices of the flesh which began to murmur to him again during his prayers and meditations. It gave him an intense sense of power to know that he could by

---

*(1696–1787); he founded a missionary movement, the Congregation of the Most Holy Redeemer (the Redemptorists), and wrote several devotional books.
†The collection of Old Testament love poetry also known as the Song of Songs or the Song of Solomon.
‡Mountain, near Lebanon, referred to in the Canticles.
§He shall lie betwixt my breasts (Latin); from Song of Solomon (Canticle of Canticles) 1:12 (Douay version) or 1:13 (King James version).

a single act of consent, in a moment of thought, undo all that he had done. He seemed to feel a flood slowly advancing towards his naked feet and to be waiting for the first faint timid noiseless wavelet to touch his fevered skin. Then, almost at the instant of that touch, almost at the verge of sinful consent, he found himself standing far away from the flood upon a dry shore, saved by a sudden act of the will or a sudden ejaculation: and, seeing the silver line of the floor far away and beginning again its slow advance towards his feet, a new thrill of power and satisfaction shook his soul to know that he had not yielded nor undone all.

When he had eluded the flood of temptation many times in this way he grew troubled and wondered whether the grace which he had refused to lose was not being filched from him little by little. The clear certitude of his own immunity grew dim and to it succeeded a vague fear that his soul had really fallen unawares. It was with difficulty that he won back his old consciousness of his state of grace by telling himself that he had prayed to God at every temptation and that the grace which he had prayed for must have been given to him inasmuch as God was obliged to give it. The very frequency and violence of temptations showed him at last the truth of what he had heard about the trials of the saints. Frequent and violent temptations were a proof that the citadel of the soul had not fallen and that the devil raged to make it fall.

Often when he had confessed his doubts and scruples, some momentary inattention at prayer, a movement of trivial anger in his soul or a subtle wilfulness in speech or act, he was bidden by his confessor to name some sin of his past life before absolution was given him. He named it with humility and shame and repented of it once more. It humiliated and shamed him to think that he would never be freed from it wholly, however holily he might live or whatever virtues or perfections he might attain. A restless feeling of guilt would always be present with him: he would confess and repent and be absolved, confess and repent again and be absolved again, fruitlessly. Perhaps that first hasty confession wrung from him by the fear of hell had not been good? Perhaps, concerned only for his imminent doom, he had not had sincere sorrow for his sin? But the surest sign that his confession had been good and that he had had sincere sorrow for his sin was, he knew, the amendment of his life.

—I have amended my life, have I not? he asked himself.

* * * *

The director stood in the embrasure of the window, his back to the light, leaning an elbow on the brown crossblind, and, as he spoke and smiled, slowly dangling and looping the cord of the other blind, Stephen stood before him, following for a moment with his eyes the waning of the long summer daylight above the roofs or the slow deft movements of the priestly fingers. The priest's face was in total shadow, but the waning daylight from behind him touched the deeply grooved temples and the curves of the skull. Stephen followed also with his ears the accents and intervals of the priest's voice as he spoke gravely and cordially of indifferent themes, the vacation which had just ended, the colleges of the order abroad, the transference of masters. The grave and cordial voice went on easily with its tale, and in the pauses Stephen felt bound to set it on again with respectful questions. He knew that the tale was a prelude and his mind waited for the sequel. Ever since the message of summons had come for him from the director his mind had struggled to find the meaning of the message; and during the long restless time he had sat in the college parlour waiting for the director to come in his eyes had wandered from one sober picture to another around the walls and his mind wandered from one guess to another until the meaning of the summons had almost become clear. Then, just as he was wishing that some unforeseen cause might prevent the director from coming, he had heard the handle of the door turning and the swish of a soutane.

The director had begun to speak of the Dominican and Franciscan orders[14] and of the friendship between Saint Thomas and Saint Bonaventure. The Capuchin dress, he thought, was rather too . . .

Stephen's face gave back the priest's indulgent smile and, not being anxious to give an opinion, he made a slight dubitative movement with his lips.

—I believe, continued the director, that there is some talk now among the Capuchins themselves of doing away with it and following the example of the other Franciscans.

—I suppose they would retain it in the cloisters?* said Stephen.

—O, certainly, said the director. For the cloister it is all right, but for the street I really think it would be better to do away with, don't you?

—It must be troublesome, I imagine?

—Of course it is, of course. Just imagine when I was in Belgium I

---

*Places, such as monasteries or convents, of religious seclusion.

used to see them out cycling in all kinds of weather with this thing up about their knees! It was really ridiculous. *Les jupes,** they call them in Belgium.

The vowel was so modified as to be indistinct.

—What do they call them?

—*Les jupes.*

—O!

Stephen smiled again in answer to the smile which he could not see on the priest's shadowed face, its image or spectre only passing rapidly across his mind as the low discreet accent fell upon his ear. He gazed calmly before him at the waning sky, glad of the cool of the evening and the faint yellow glow which hid the tiny flame kindling upon his cheek.

The names of articles of dress worn by women or of certain soft and delicate stuffs used in their making brought always to his mind a delicate and sinful perfume. As a boy he had imagined the reins by which horses are driven as slender silken bands and it shocked him to feel at Stradbrooke[†] the greasy leather of harness. It had shocked him, too, when he had felt for the first time beneath his tremulous fingers the brittle texture of a woman's stocking for, retaining nothing of all he read save that which seemed to him an echo or a prophecy of his own state, it was only amid softworded phrases or within rosesoft stuffs that he dared to conceive of the soul or body of a woman moving with tender life.

But the phrase on the priest's lips was disingenuous for he knew that a priest should not speak lightly on that theme. The phrase had been spoken lightly with design and he felt that his face was being searched by the eyes in the shadow. Whatever he had heard or read of the craft of jesuits he had put aside frankly as not borne out by his own experience. His masters, even when they had not attracted him, had seemed to him always intelligent and serious priests, athletic and high-spirited prefects. He thought of them as men who washed their bodies briskly with cold water and wore clean cold linen. During all the years he had lived among them in Clongowes and in Belvedere he had received only two pandies and, though these had been dealt him in the wrong, he knew that he had often escaped punishment. During all those years he had never heard from any of his masters a flippant word: it was they who had taught him christian doctrine and urged him to live a good life

---

*The skirts (French).

†Dublin suburb on the southern coast, 5½ miles from downtown.

and, when he had fallen into grievous sin, it was they who had led him back to grace. Their presence had made him diffident of himself when he was a muff* in Clongowes and it had made him diffident of himself also while he had held his equivocal position in Belvedere. A constant sense of this had remained with him up to the last year of his school life. He had never once disobeyed or allowed turbulent companions to seduce him from his habit of quiet obedience: and, even when he doubted some statement of a master, he had never presumed to doubt openly. Lately some of their judgments had sounded a little childish in his ears and had made him feel a regret and pity as though he were slowly passing out of an accustomed world and were hearing its language for the last time. One day when some boys had gathered round a priest under the shed near the chapel, he heard the priest say:

—I believe that Lord Macaulay† was a man who probably never committed a mortal sin in his life, that is to say, a deliberate mortal sin.‡

Some of the boys had then asked the priest if Victor Hugo§ were not the greatest French writer. The priest had answered that Victor Hugo had never written half so well when he had turned against the church as he had written when he was a catholic.

—But there are many eminent French critics, said the priest, who consider that even Victor Hugo, great as he certainly was, had not so pure a French style as Louis Veuillot.‖

The tiny flame which the priest's allusion had kindled upon Stephen's cheek had sunk down again and his eyes were still fixed calmly on the colourless sky. But an unresting doubt flew hither and thither before his mind. Masked memories passed quickly before him: he recognised scenes and persons yet he was conscious that he had failed to perceive some vital circumstance in them. He saw himself walking about the grounds watching the sports in Clongowes and eating chocolate out of his cricketcap. Some jesuits were walking round the cycletrack in the company of ladies. The echoes of certain expressions used in Clongowes sounded in remote caves of his mind.

---

*Failure.
†Thomas Babington Macaulay (1800–1859), English historian and man of letters.
‡A redundant statement; by definition all mortal sins are deliberate.
§(1802–1885); French romantic writer, author of *Les Misérables* (1862).
‖(1813–1883); French journalist and political activist.

His ears were listening to these distant echoes amid the silence of the parlour when he became aware that the priest was addressing him in a different voice.

—I sent for you today, Stephen, because I wished to speak to you on a very important subject.

—Yes, sir.

—Have you ever felt that you had a vocation?*

Stephen parted his lips to answer yes and then withheld the word suddenly. The priest waited for the answer and added:

—I mean have you ever felt within yourself, in your soul, a desire to join the order. Think.

—I have sometimes thought of it, said Stephen.

The priest let the blindcord fall to one side and, uniting his hands, leaned his chin gravely upon them, communing with himself.

—In a college like this, he said at length, there is one boy or perhaps two or three boys whom God calls to the religious life. Such a boy is marked off from his companions by his piety, by the good example he shows to others. He is looked up to by them; he is chosen perhaps as prefect by his fellow sodalists. And you, Stephen, have been such a boy in this college, prefect of Our Blessed Lady's sodality. Perhaps you are the boy in this college whom God designs to call to Himself.

A strong note of pride reinforcing the gravity of the priest's voice made Stephen's heart quicken in response.

—To receive that call, Stephen, said the priest, is the greatest honour that the Almighty God can bestow upon a man. No king or emperor on this earth has the power of the priest of God. No angel or archangel in heaven, no saint, not even the Blessed Virgin herself has the power of a priest of God: the power of the keys,† the power to bind and to loose from sin, the power of exorcism, the power to cast out from the creatures of God the evil spirits that have power over them, the power, the authority, to make the great God of Heaven come down upon the altar and take the form of bread and wine. What an awful power, Stephen!

A flame began to flutter again on Stephen's cheek as he heard in this proud address an echo of his own proud musings. How often had he seen himself as a priest wielding calmly and humbly the awful power of

---

*A calling to the priesthood.

†In Matthew 16:18–19, Jesus gives to Peter, the first priest of the church and first pope, "the keys to the kingdom of heaven."

which angels and saints stood in reverence! His soul had loved to muse in secret on this desire. He had seen himself, a young and silentmannered priest, entering a confessional swiftly, ascending the altarsteps, incensing, genuflecting, accomplishing the vague acts of the priesthood which pleased him by reason of their semblance of reality and of their distance from it. In that dim life which he had lived through in his musings he had assumed the voices and gestures which he had noted with various priests. He had bent his knee sideways like such a one, he had shaken the thurible only slightly like such a one, his chasuble had swung open like that of such another as he turned to the altar again after having blessed the people. And above all it had pleased him to fill the second place in those dim scenes of his imagining. He shrank from the dignity of celebrant because it displeased him to imagine that all the vague pomp should end in his own person or that the ritual should assign to him so clear and final an office. He longed for the minor sacred offices, to be vested with the tunicle of subdeacon at high mass, to stand aloof from the altar, forgotten by the people, his shoulders covered with a humeral veil, holding the paten within its folds or, when the sacrifice had been accomplished, to stand as deacon in a dalmatic cloth of gold on the step below the celebrant, his hands joined and his face towards the people, and sing the chant, *Ite missa est.** If ever he had seen himself celebrant it was as in the pictures of the mass in his child's massbook, in a church without worshippers, save for the angel of the sacrifice, at a bare altar and served by an acolyte scarcely more boyish than himself. In vague sacrificial or sacramental acts alone his will seemed drawn to go forth to encounter reality: and it was partly the absence of an appointed rite which had always constrained him to inaction whether he had allowed silence to cover his anger or pride or had suffered only an embrace he longed to give.

He listened in reverent silence now to the priest's appeal and through the words he heard even more distinctly a voice bidding him approach, offering him secret knowledge and secret power. He would know then what was the sin of Simon Magus† and what the sin against the Holy Ghost for which there was no forgiveness. He would know obscure things, hidden from others,‡ from those who were conceived and born children of wrath. He would know the sins, the sinful long-

*Go, you are dismissed (Latin).
†His sin, now called "simony" after him, involved the selling of spiritual blessings.
‡Compare the novel's opening epigraph from Ovid.

ings and sinful thoughts and sinful acts, of others, hearing them murmured into his ears in the confessional under the shame of a darkened chapel by the lips of women and of girls: but rendered immune mysteriously at his ordination by the imposition of hands his soul would pass again uncontaminated to the white peace of the altar. No touch of sin would linger upon the hands with which he would elevate and break the host; no touch of sin would linger on his lips in prayer to make him eat and drink damnation to himself not discerning the body of the Lord.* He would hold his secret knowledge and secret power, being as sinless as the innocent: and he would be a priest for ever according to the order of Melchisedec.†

—I will offer up my mass tomorrow morning, said the director, that Almighty God may reveal to you His holy will. And let you, Stephen, make a novena‡ to your holy patron saint, the first martyr who is very powerful with God, that God may enlighten your mind. But you must be quite sure, Stephen, that you have a vocation because it would be terrible if you found afterwards that you had none. Once a priest always a priest, remember. Your catechism tells you that the sacrament of Holy Orders is one of those which can be received only once because it imprints on the soul an indelible spiritual mark which can never be effaced. It is before you must weigh well, not after. It is a solemn question, Stephen, because on it may depend the salvation of your eternal soul. But we will pray to God together.

He held open the heavy hall door and gave his hand as if already to a companion in the spiritual life. Stephen passed out on to the wide platform above the steps and was conscious of the caress of mild evening air. Towards Findlater's church a quartette of young men were striding along with linked arms, swaying their heads and stepping to the agile melody of their leader's concertina. The music passed in an instant, as the first bars of sudden music always did, over the fantastic fabrics of his mind, dissolving them painlessly and noiselessly as a sudden wave dissolves the sandbuilt turrets of children. Smiling at the trivial air he raised his eyes to the priest's face and, seeing in it a mirthless reflection of the sunken day, detached his hand slowly which had acquiesced faintly in that companionship.

As he descended the steps the impression which effaced his troubled

---

*An allusion to I Corinthians 11:29.
†Reference to Hebrews 7:17–21.
‡A nine-day devotion.

selfcommunion was that of a mirthless mask reflecting a sunken day from the threshold of the college. The shadow, then, of the life of the college passed gravely over his consciousness. It was a grave and ordered and passionless life that awaited him, a life without material cares. He wondered how he would pass the first night in the *novitiate** and with what dismay he would wake the first morning in the dormitory. The troubling odour of the long corridors of Clongowes came back to him and he heard the discreet murmur of the burning gas flames. At once from every part of his being unrest began to irradiate. A feverish quickening of his pulses followed and a din of meaningless words drove his reasoned thoughts hither and thither confusedly. His lungs dilated and sank as if he were inhaling a warm moist unsustaining air, and he smelt again the moist warm air which hung in the bath in Clongowes above the sluggish turfcoloured water.

Some instinct, waking at these memories, stronger than education or piety quickened within him at every near approach to that life, an instinct subtle and hostile, and armed him against acquiescence. The chill and order of the life repelled him. He saw himself rising in the cold of the morning and filing down with the others to early mass and trying vainly to struggle with his prayers against the fainting sickness of his stomach. He saw himself sitting at dinner with the community of a college. What, then, had become of that deeprooted shyness of his which had made him loth to eat or drink under a strange roof? What had come of the pride of his spirit which had always made him conceive himself as a being apart in every order?

The Reverend Stephen Dedalus, S. J.†

His name in that new life leaped into characters before his eyes and to it there followed a mental sensation of an undefined face or colour of a face. The colour faded and became strong like a changing glow of pallid brick red: Was it the raw reddish glow he had so often seen on wintry mornings on the shaven gills of the priests? The face was eyeless and sourfavoured and devout, shot with pink tinges of suffocated anger. Was it not a mental spectre of the face of one of the jesuits whom some of the boys called Lantern Jaws and others Foxy Campbell?

He was passing at that moment before the jesuit house in Gardiner Street, and wondered vaguely which window would be his if he ever joined the order. Then he wondered at the vagueness of his wonder, at

---

*Living quarters of the novices of a religious order.
†Society of Jesus (the Jesuits)

the remoteness of his own soul from what he had hitherto imagined her sanctuary, at the frail hold which so many years of order and obedience had of him when once a definite and irrevocable act of his threatened to end forever, in time and in eternity, his freedom. The voice of the director urging upon him the proud claims of the church and the mystery and power of the priestly office repeated itself idly in his memory. His soul was not there to hear and greet it and he knew now that the exhortation he had listened to had already fallen into an idle formal tale. He would never swing the thurible before the tabernacle as priest. His destiny was to be elusive of social or religious orders. The wisdom of the priest's appeal did not touch him to the quick. He was destined to learn his own wisdom apart from others or to learn the wisdom of others himself wandering among the snares of the world.

The snares of the world were its ways of sin. He would fall.[15] He had not yet fallen but he would fall silently, in an instant. Not to fall was too hard, too hard: and he felt the silent lapse of his soul, as it would be at some instant to come, falling, falling, but not yet fallen, still unfallen, but about to fall.

He crossed the bridge over the stream of the Tolka,* and turned his eyes coldly for an instant towards the faded blue shrine of the Blessed Virgin which stood fowlwise on a pole in the middle of a hamshaped encampment of poor cottages. Then, bending to the left, he followed the lane which led up to his house. The faint sour stink of rotted cabbages came towards him from the kitchen gardens on the rising ground above the river. He smiled to think that it was this disorder, the misrule and confusion of his father's house and the stagnation of vegetable life, which was to win the day in his soul. Then a short laugh broke from his lips as he thought of that solitary farmhand in the kitchen gardens behind their house whom they had nicknamed The Man with the Hat. A second laugh, taking rise from the first after a pause, broke from him involuntarily as he thought of how The Man with the Hat worked, considering in turn the four points of the sky and then regretfully plunging his spade in the earth.

He pushed open the latchless door of the porch and passed through the naked hallway into the kitchen. A group of his brothers and sisters was sitting round the table. Tea was nearly over and only the last of the second watered tea remained in the bottoms of the small glass jars and

---

*River on the north side of Dublin.

jampots which did service for teacups. Discarded crusts and lumps of sugared bread, turned brown by the tea which had been poured over them, lay scattered on the table. Little wells of tea lay here and there on the board and a knife with a broken ivory handle was stuck through the pith of a ravaged turnover.

The sad quiet greyblue glow of the dying day came through the window and the open door, covering over and allaying quietly a sudden instinct of remorse in Stephen's heart. All that had been denied them had been freely given to him, the eldest: but the quiet glow of evening showed him in their faces no sign of rancour.

He sat near them at the table and asked where his father and mother were. One answered:

—Goneboro toboro lookboro atboro aboro houseboro.

Still another removal! A boy named Fallon, in Belvedere, had often asked him with a silly laugh why they moved so often. A frown of scorn darkened quickly his forehead as he heard again the silly laugh of the questioner.

He asked:

—Why are we on the move again, if it's a fair question?

—Becauseboro theboro landboro lordboro willboro putboro usboro outboro.

The voice of his youngest brother from the farther side of the fireplace began to sing the air "Oft in the Stilly Night."* One by one the others took up the air until a full choir of voices was singing. They would sing so for hours, melody after melody, glee after glee, till the last pale light died down on the horizon, till the first dark nightclouds came forth and night fell.

He waited for some moments, listening, before he too took up the air with them. He was listening with pain of spirit to the overtone of weariness behind their frail fresh innocent voices. Even before they set out on life's journey they seemed weary already of the way.

He heard the choir of voices in the kitchen echoed and multiplied through an endless reverberation of the choirs of endless generations of children: and heard in all the echoes an echo also of the recurring note of weariness and pain. All seemed weary of life even before entering upon it. And he remembered that Newman had heard this note also in the broken lines of Virgil *giving utterance, like the voice of Nature herself,*

---

*Poem by Irish poet Thomas Moore (1779–1852).

Dublin Bay

5 fathom line

Ben Howth

Tidal Flats

North Bull Island

Dollymount

Clontarf

Clontarf Chapel

River Liffey

Dublin

Bathing Place

Bull Wall

North Bull Light

Poolbeg Light

Pigeon House

Kingstown

Chapter IV
— Stephen's Route

*to that pain and weariness yet hope of better things which has been the experience of her children in every time.**

*   *   *   *

He could wait no longer.

From the door of Byron's public-house† to the gate of Clontarf‡ Chapel, from the gate of Clontarf Chapel to the door of Byron's public-house, and then back again to the chapel and then back again to the public-house he had paced slowly at first, planting his steps scrupulously in the spaces of the patchwork of the footpath, then timing their fall to the fall of verses. A full hour had passed since his father had gone in with Dan Crosby, the tutor, to find out for him something about the university. For a full hour he had paced up and down, waiting: but he could wait no longer.

He set off abruptly for the Bull,§ walking rapidly lest his father's shrill whistle might call him back; and in a few moments he had rounded the curve at the police barrack and was safe.

Yes, his mother was hostile to the idea, as he had read from her listless silence. Yet her mistrust pricked him more keenly than his father's pride and he thought coldly how he had watched the faith which was fading down in his soul ageing and strengthening in her eyes. A dim antagonism gathered force within him and darkened his mind as a cloud against her disloyalty: and when it passed, cloudlike, leaving his mind serene and dutiful towards her again, he was made aware dimly and without regret of a first noiseless sundering of their lives.

The university!‖ So he had passed beyond the challenge of the sentries who had stood as guardians of his boyhood and had sought to keep him among them that he might be subject to them and serve their ends. Pride after satisfaction uplifted him like long slow waves. The end he had been born to serve yet did not see had led him to escape by an unseen path: and now it beckoned to him once more and a new adventure was about to be opened to him. It seemed to him that he heard

---

*From *An Essay in Aid of a Grammar of Assent* (1870), by John Henry Cardinal Newman (see endnote 8).

†A pub, licensed for the sale and consumption of alcoholic beverages.

‡Community at the far northeastern reaches of Dublin.

§Either North Bull Island, in the mouth of the River Liffey; or the seawall that encloses it; or both.

‖University College Dublin, the city's first Catholic university.

notes of fitful music leaping upwards a tone and downwards a diminishing fourth, upwards a tone and downwards a major third, like triple-branching flames leaping fitfully, flame after flame, out of a midnight wood. It was an elfin prelude, endless and formless; and, as it grew wilder and faster, the flames leaping out of time, he seemed to hear from under the boughs and grasses wild creatures racing, their feet pattering like rain upon the leaves. Their feet passed in pattering tumult over his mind, the feet of hares and rabbits, the feet of harts and hinds and antelopes, until he heard them no more and remembered only a proud cadence from Newman:

—Whose feet are as the feet of harts and underneath the everlasting arms.*

The pride of that dim image brought back to his mind the dignity of the office he had refused. All through his boyhood he had mused upon that which he had so often thought to be his destiny and when the moment had come for him to obey the call he had turned aside, obeying a wayward instinct. Now time lay between: the oils of ordination would never anoint his body. He had refused. Why?

He turned seaward from the road at Dollymount† and as he passed on to the thin wooden bridge he felt the planks shaking with the tramp of heavily shod feet. A squad of Christian Brothers was on its way back from the Bull and had begun to pass, two by two, across the bridge. Soon the whole bridge was trembling and resounding. The uncouth faces passed him two by two, stained yellow or red or livid by the sea, and as he strove to look at them with ease and indifference, a faint stain of personal shame and commiseration rose to his own face. Angry with himself he tried to hide his face from their eyes by gazing down sideways into the shallow swirling water under the bridge but he still saw a reflection therein of their topheavy silk hats, and humble tapelike collars and loosely hanging clerical clothes.

—Brother Hickey.

Brother Quaid.

Brother MacArdle.

Brother Keogh.

Their piety would be like their names, like their faces, like their clothes; and it was idle for him to tell himself that their humble and contrite hearts, it might be, paid a far richer tribute of devotion than his

---

*From Newman's *The Idea of a University* (1873).
†Community northeast of Clontarf.

had ever been, a gift tenfold more acceptable than his elaborate adoration. It was idle for him to move himself to be generous towards them, to tell himself that if he ever came to their gates, stripped of his pride, beaten and in beggar's weeds, that they would be generous towards him, loving him as themselves. Idle and embittering, finally, to argue, against his own dispassionate certitude, that the commandment of love bade us not to love our neighbours as ourselves with the same amount and intensity of love but to love him as ourselves with the same kind of love.

He drew forth a phrase from his treasure and spoke it softly to himself:

—A day of dappled seaborne clouds.[*]

The phrase and the day and the scene harmonised in a chord. Words. Was it their colours? He allowed them to glow and fade, hue after hue: sunrise gold, the russet and green of apple orchards, azure of waves, the greyfringed fleece of clouds. No, it was not their colours: it was the poise and balance of the period itself. Did he then love the rhythmic rise and fall of words better than their associations of legend and colour? Or was it that, being as weak of sight as he was shy of mind, he drew less pleasure from the reflection of the glowing sensible world through the prism of a language manycoloured and richly storied than from the contemplation of an inner world of individual emotions mirrored perfectly in a lucid supple periodic prose.

He passed from the trembling bridge on to firm land again. At that instant, as it seemed to him, the air was chilled; and looking askance towards the water he saw a flying squall darkening and crisping suddenly the tide. A faint click at his heart, a faint throb in his throat told him once more of how his flesh dreaded the cold infrahuman odour of the sea: yet he did not strike across the downs on his left but held straight on along the spine of rocks that pointed against the river's mouth.

A veiled sunlight lit up faintly the grey sheet of water where the river was embayed. In the distance along the course of the slowflowing Liffey slender masts flecked the sky and, more distant still, the dim fabric of the city lay prone in haze. Like a scene on some vague arras,[†] old as man's weariness, the image of the seventh city of christendom was visible to him across the timeless air, no older nor more weary nor less patient of subjection than in the days of the thingmote.[‡]

---

[*]A near-quotation from Hugh Miller's *The Testimony of the Rocks; or, Geology in Its Bearings on the Two Theologies, Natural and Revealed* (1857).
[†]Tapestry.
[‡]Locale in Dublin that was the Scandinavian seat of law.

Disheartened, he raised his eyes towards the slow-drifting clouds, dappled and seaborne. They were voyaging across the deserts of the sky, a host of nomads on the march, voyaging high over Ireland, westward bound. The Europe they had come from lay out there beyond the Irish Sea, Europe of strange tongues and valleyed and woodbegirt and citadelled and of entrenched and marshalled races. He heard a confused music within him as of memories and names which he was almost conscious of but could not capture even for an instant; then the music seemed to recede, to recede, to recede: and from each receding trail of nebulous music there fell always one long-drawn calling note, piercing like a star the dusk of silence. Again! Again! Again! A voice from beyond the world was calling.

—Hello, Stephanos!*

—Here comes The Dedalus!

—Ao! Eh, give it over, Dwyer, I'm telling you or I'll give you a stuff in the kisser for yourself. . . . Ao!

—Good man, Towser! Duck him!

—Come along, Dedalus! Bous Stephanoumenos! Bous Stephaneforos!

—Duck him! Guzzle him now, Towser!

—Help! Help! . . . Ao!

He recognised their speech collectively before he distinguished their faces. The mere sight of that medley of wet nakedness chilled him to the bone. Their bodies, corpsewhite or suffused with a pallid golden light or rawly tanned by the suns, gleamed with the wet of the sea. Their divingstone, poised on its rude supports and rocking under their plunges, and the rough-hewn stones of the sloping breakwater over which they scrambled in their horseplay, gleamed with cold wet lustre. The towels with which they smacked their bodies were heavy with cold seawater: and drenched with cold brine was their matted hair.

He stood still in deference to their calls and parried their banter with easy words. How characterless they looked: Shuley without his deep unbuttoned collar, Ennis without his scarlet belt with the snaky clasp, and Connolly without his Norfolk coat † with the flapless sidepockets! It was a pain to see them and a swordlike pain to see the signs of adolescence that made repellent their pitiable nakedness. Perhaps they had taken refuge in number and noise from the secret dread in their souls.

---

*Crown or wreath (Greek).

†Loosely belted, single-breasted coat.

But he, apart from them and in silence, remembered in what dread he stood of the mystery of his own body.

—Stephanos Dedalos! Bous Stephanoumenos! Bous Stephaneforos!*

Their banter was not new to him and now it flattered his mild proud sovereignty. Now, as never before, his strange name seemed to him a prophecy.[16] So timeless seemed the grey warm air, so fluid and impersonal his own mood, that all ages were as one to him. A moment before the ghost of the ancient kingdom of the Danes[†] had looked forth through the vesture of the hazewrapped city. Now, at the name of the fabulous artificer,[‡] he seemed to hear the noise of dim waves and to see a winged form flying above the waves and slowly climbing the air. What did it mean? Was it a quaint device opening a page of some medieval book of prophecies and symbols, a hawklike man[§] flying sunward above the sea, a prophecy of the end he had been born to serve and had been following through the mists of childhood and boyhood, a symbol of the artist forging anew in his workshop out of the sluggish matter of the earth a new soaring impalpable imperishable being?

His heart trembled; his breath came faster and a wild spirit passed over his limbs as though he were soaring sunward. His heart trembled in an ecstasy of fear and his soul was in flight. His soul was soaring in an air beyond the world and the body he knew was purified in a breath and delivered of incertitude and made radiant and commingled with the element of the spirit. An ecstasy of flight made radiant his eyes and wild his breath and tremulous and wild and radiant his windswept limbs.

—One! Two! . . . Look out!

—O, Cripes, I'm drownded!

—One! Two! Three and away!

—The next! The next!

—One! . . . Uk!

—Stephaneforos!

His throat ached with a desire to cry aloud, the cry of a hawk or eagle on high, to cry piercingly of his deliverance to the winds. This was the call of life to his soul not the dull gross voice of the world of duties and despair, not the inhuman voice that had called him to the pale ser-

---

*Garland-bearing ox! Ox-souled! (Greek).
†Medieval Dublin was ruled by the Danes.
‡Epithet for Stephen's legendary Greek "father," Dædalus.
§Another epithet for Dædalus.

vice of the altar. An instant of wild flight had delivered him and the cry of triumph which his lips withheld cleft his brain.

—Stephaneforos!

What were they now but the cerements* shaken from the body of death—the fear he had walked in night and day, the incertitude that had ringed him round, the shame that had abased him within and without—cerements, the linens of the grave?

His soul had arisen from the grave of boyhood, spurning her grave-clothes. Yes! Yes! Yes! He would create proudly out of the freedom and power of his soul, as the great artificer whose name he bore, a living thing, new and soaring and beautiful, impalpable, imperishable.

He started up nervously from the stoneblock for he could no longer quench the flame in his blood. He felt his cheeks aflame and his throat throbbing with song. There was a lust of wandering in his feet that burned to set out for the ends of the earth. On! On! his heart seemed to cry. Evening would deepen above the sea, night fall upon the plains, dawn glimmer before the wanderer and show him strange fields and hills and faces. Where?

He looked northward towards Howth.† The sea had fallen below the line of seawrack on the shallow side of the breakwater and already the tide was running out fast along the foreshore. Already one long oval bank of sand lay warm and dry amid the wavelets. Here and there warm isles of sand gleamed above the shallow tide: and about the isles and around the long bank and amid the shallow currents of the beach were lightclad figures, wading and delving.

In a few moments he was barefoot, his stockings folded in his pockets, and his canvas shoes dangling by their knotted laces over his shoulders: and, picking a pointed salteaten stick out of the jetsam among the rocks, he clambered down the slope of the breakwater.

There was a long rivulet in the strand: and, as he waded slowly up its course, he wondered at the endless drift of seaweed. Emerald and black and russet and olive, it moved beneath the current, swaying and turning. The water of the rivulet was dark with endless drift and mirrored the highdrifting clouds. The clouds were drifting above him silently and silently the seatangle was drifting below him; and the grey warm air was still: and a new wild life was singing in his veins.

---

*Graveclothes.

†The Hill of Howth, the geographical landmark framing the north side of Dublin Bay.

Where was his boyhood now? Where was the soul that had hung back from her destiny, to brood alone upon the shame of her wounds and in her house of squalor and subterfuge to queen it in faded cerements and in wreaths that withered at the touch? Or, where was he.

He was alone. He was unheeded, happy, and near to the wild heart of life. He was alone and young and wilful and wildhearted, alone amid a waste of wild air and brackish waters and the seaharvest of shells and tangle and veiled grey sunlight and gayclad lightclad figures of children and girls and voices childish and girlish in the air.

A girl stood before him in midstream: alone and still, gazing out to sea. She seemed like one whom magic had changed into the likeness of a strange and beautiful seabird. Her long slender bare legs were delicate as a crane's and pure save where an emerald trail of seaweed had fashioned itself as a sign upon the flesh. Her thighs, fuller and softhued as ivory, were bared almost to the hips where the white fringes of her drawers were like feathering of soft white down. Her slate-blue skirts were kilted boldly about her waist and dovetailed behind her. Her bosom was as a bird's, soft and slight, slight and soft as the breast of some dark-plumaged dove. But her long fair hair was girlish: and girlish, and touched with the wonder of mortal beauty, her face.

She was alone and still, gazing out to sea; and when she felt his presence and the worship of his eyes her eyes turned to him in quiet sufferance of his gaze, without shame or wantonness. Long, long she suffered his gaze and then quietly withdrew her eyes from his and bent them towards the stream, gently stirring the water with her foot hither and thither. The first faint noise of gently moving water broke the silence, low and faint and whispering, faint as the bells of sleep; hither and thither, hither and thither: and a faint flame trembled on her cheek.

—Heavenly God! cried Stephen's soul, in an outburst of profane joy.

He turned away from her suddenly and set off across the strand. His cheeks were aflame; his body was aglow; his limbs were trembling. On and on and on and on he strode, far out over the sands, singing wildly to the sea, crying to greet the advent of the life that had cried to him.

Her image had passed into his soul for ever and no word had broken the holy silence of his ecstasy. Her eyes had called him and his soul had leaped at the call. To live, to err, to fall, to triumph, to recreate life out of life! A wild angel had appeared to him, the angel of mortal youth and beauty, an envoy from the fair courts of life, to throw open before him in an instant of ecstasy the gates of all the ways of error and glory. On and on and on and on!

He halted suddenly and heard his heart in the silence. How far had he walked? What hour was it?

There was no human figure near him nor any sound borne to him over the air. But the tide was near the turn and already the day was on the wane. He turned landward and ran towards the shore and, running up the sloping beach, reckless of the sharp shingle, found a sandy nook amid a ring of tufted sand knolls and lay down there that the peace and silence of the evening might still the riot of his blood.

He felt above him the vast indifferent dome and the calm processes of the heavenly bodies: and the earth beneath him, the earth that had borne him, had taken him to her breast.

He closed his eyes in the languor of sleep. His eyelids trembled as if they felt the vast cyclic movement of the earth and her watchers, trembled as if they felt the strange light of some new world. His soul was swooning into some new world, fantastic, dim, uncertain as under sea, traversed by cloudy shapes and beings. A world, a glimmer, or a flower? Glimmering and trembling, trembling and unfolding, a breaking light, an opening flower, it spread in endless succession to itself, breaking in full crimson and unfolding and fading to palest rose, leaf by leaf and wave of light by wave of light, flooding all the heavens with its soft flushes, every flush deeper than the other.

Evening had fallen when he woke and the sand and arid grasses of his bed glowed no longer. He rose slowly and, recalling the rapture of his sleep, sighed at its joy.

He climbed to the crest of the sandhill and gazed about him. Evening had fallen. A rim of the young moon cleft the pale waste of sky line, the rim of a silver hoop embedded in grey sand: and the tide was flowing in fast to the land with a low whisper of her waves, islanding a few last figures in distant pools.

CHAPTER V

HE DRAINED HIS THIRD cup of watery tea to the dregs and set to chewing the crusts of fried bread that were scattered near him, staring into the dark pool of the jar. The yellow dripping had been scooped out like a boghole, and the pool under it brought back to his memory the dark turfcoloured water of the bath in Clongowes. The bog of pawn tickets at his elbow had just been rifled and he took up idly one after another in his greasy fingers the blue and white dockets, scrawled and sanded and creased and bearing the name of the pledger as Daly or MacEvoy.

1 Pair Buskins.

1 D. Coat.

3 Articles and White.

1 Man's Pants.*

Then he put them aside and gazed thoughtfully at the lid of the box, speckled with louse marks, and asked vaguely:

—How much is the clock fast now?

His mother straightened the battered alarm clock that was lying on its side in the middle of the mantelpiece until its dial showed a quarter to twelve and then laid it once more on its side.

—An hour and twenty five minutes, she said. The right time now is twenty past ten. The dear† knows you might try to be in time for your lectures.

—Fill out the place for me to wash, said Stephen.

—Katey, fill out the place for Stephen to wash.

—Booty, fill out the place for Stephen to wash.

—I can't, I'm going for blue. Fill it out, you, Maggie.

When the enamelled basin had been fitted into the well of the sink and the old washing glove flung on the side of it, he allowed his mother

---

*Articles that the Dedalus family has pawned: "buskins" are boots; "articles and white" are undergarments.

†That is, God; an example of the Irish strategy of "dodging the curse," substituting an innocuous word for a profane or irreligious one.

to scrub his neck and root into the folds of his ears and into the interstices at the wings of his nose.

—Well, it's a poor case, she said, when a university student is so dirty that his mother has to wash him.

—But it gives you pleasure, said Stephen calmly.

An ear splitting whistle was heard from upstairs and his mother thrust a damp overall into his hands, saying:

—Dry yourself and hurry out for the love of goodness.

A second shrill whistle, prolonged angrily, brought one of the girls to the foot of the staircase.

—Yes, father?

—Is your lazy bitch of a brother gone out yet?

—Yes, father.

—Sure?

—Hm!

The girl came back, making signs to him to be quick and go out quietly by the back. Stephen laughed and said:

—He has a curious idea of genders if he thinks a bitch is masculine.

—Ah, it's a scandalous shame for you, Stephen, said his mother, and you'll live to rue the day you set your foot in that place. I know how it has changed you.

—Good morning, everybody, said Stephen, smiling and kissing the tips of his fingers in adieu.

The lane behind the terrace was waterlogged and as he went down it slowly, choosing his steps amid heaps of wet rubbish, he heard a mad nun screeching in the nun's madhouse beyond the wall.

—Jesus! O Jesus! Jesus!

He shook the sound out of his ears by an angry toss of his head and hurried on, stumbling through the mouldering offal, his heart already bitten by an ache of loathing and bitterness. His father's whistle, his mother's mutterings, the screech of an unseen maniac were to him now so many voices offending and threatening to humble the pride of his youth. He drove their echoes even out of his heart with an execration: but, as he walked down the avenue and felt the grey morning light falling about him through the dripping trees and smelt the strange wild smell of the wet leaves and bark, his soul was loosed of her miseries.

The rain laden trees of the avenue evoked in him as always, memories of the girls and women in the plays of Gerhart Hauptmann;* and

---

*(1862–1946); German dramatist, novelist, and poet.

Chapter V
— — — Stephen's Route

Saint Vincent's

Mud Island
(Sloblands of
Fairview)

Royal Canal

Baird's

Statue of Thomas Moore

Custom House

Liffey

Trinity College

Merrion
Square

Stephen's
Green

University College

the memory of their pale sorrows and the fragrance falling from the wet branches mingled in a mood of quiet joy. His morning walk across the city had begun; and he foreknew that as he passed the sloblands of Fairview* he would think of the cloistral silverveined prose of Newman; that as he walked along the North Strand Road, glancing idly at the windows of the provision shops, he would recall the dark humour of Guido Cavalcanti† and smile; that as he went by Baird's stone cutting works in Talbot Place the spirit of Ibsen‡ would blow through him like a keen wind, a spirit of wayward and boyish beauty; and that passing a grimy marine dealer's shop beyond the Liffey he would repeat the song by Ben Jonson which begins:

I was not wearier where I lay.§

His mind when wearied of its search for the essence of beauty amid the spectral words of Aristotle or Aquinas turned often for its pleasure to the dainty songs of the Elizabethans. His mind, in the venture of a doubting monk, stood often in shadow under the windows of that age, to hear the grave and mocking music of the lutenists or the frank laughter of waistcoateers until a laugh too low, a phrase, tarnished by time, of chambering and false honour, stung his monkish pride and drove him on from his lurking-place.

The lore which he was believed to pass his days brooding upon so that it had rapt him from the companionship of youth was only a garner of slender sentences from Aristotle's Poetics and Psychology‖ and a *Synopsis Philosophiæ Scholasticæ ad mentem divi Thomæ.*# His thinking was a dusk of doubt and selfmistrust, lit up at moments by the lightnings of intuition, but lightnings of so clear a splendour that in those moments the world perished about his feet as if it had been fire consumed: and thereafter his tongue grew heavy and he met the eyes of others with unanswering eyes for he felt that the spirit of beauty had folded him round like a mantle and that in reverie at least he had been

---

*Mudflats where the Tolka River empties into Dublin Bay.
†(c.1255–1300); Italian poet and friend of Dante.
‡Norwegian realist playwright Henrik Ibsen (1828–1906); Joyce's first published work was a review in 1900 of Ibsen's play *When We Dead Awaken*.
§From *The Vision of Delight* (1617), by English playwright Jonson (1572–1637).
‖Aristotle's texts *Poetics* and *De Anima*.
#*A Synopsis of the Scholastic Philosophy for the Understanding of Saint Thomas* (Latin).

acquainted with nobility. But, when this brief pride of silence upheld him no longer, he was glad to find himself still in the midst of common lives, passing on his way amid the squalor and noise and sloth of the city fearlessly and with a light heart.

Near the hoardings* on the canal he met the consumptive man with the doll's face and the brimless hat coming towards him down the slope of the bridge with little steps, tightly buttoned into his chocolate over-coat, and holding his furled umbrella a span or two from him like a di-vining rod. It must be eleven, he thought, and peered into a dairy to see the time. The clock in the dairy told him that it was five minutes to five but, as he turned away, he heard a clock somewhere near him, but un-seen, beating eleven strokes in swift precision. He laughed as he heard it for it made him think of McCann; and he saw him a squat figure in a shooting jacket and breeches and with a fair goatee, standing in the wind at Hopkins' corner,† and heard him say:

—Dedalus, you're an anti-social being, wrapped up in yourself. I'm not. I'm a democrat: and I'll work and act for social liberty and equal-ity among all classes and sexes in the United States of the Europe of the future.

Eleven! Then he was late for that lecture too. What day of the week was it? He stopped at a newsagent's to read the headline of a placard. Thursday. Ten to eleven, English; eleven to twelve, French; twelve to one, Physics. He fancied to himself the English lecture and felt, even at that distance, restless and helpless. He saw the heads of his classmates meekly bent as they wrote in their notebooks the points they were bid-den to note, nominal definitions, essential definitions and examples or dates of birth or death, chief works, a favourable and an unfavourable criticism side by side. His own head was unbent for his thoughts wan-dered abroad and whether he looked around the little class of students or out of the window across the desolate gardens of the Green‡ an odour assailed him of cheerless cellar damp and decay. Another head than his, right before him in the first benches, was poised squarely above its bending fellows like the head of a priest appealing without humility to the tabernacle for the humble worshippers about him. Why

---

*Billboards.
†The jeweler Hopkins & Hopkins was located at the corner of Sackville Street (now O'Connell Street) and Eden Quay.
‡St. Stephen's Green, a public park bordered by the Grafton Street shopping area on the north and University College Dublin on the south.

was it that when he thought of Cranly he could never raise before his mind the entire image of his body but only the image of the head and face? Even now against the grey curtain of the morning he saw it before him like the phantom of a dream, the face of a severed head or death-mask, crowned on the brows by its stiff black upright hair as by an iron crown. It was a priestlike face, priestlike in its pallor, in the wide winged nose, in the shadowings below the eyes and along the jaws, priestlike in the lips that were long and bloodless and faintly smiling: and Stephen, remembering swiftly how he had told Cranly of all the tumults and unrest and longings in his soul, day after day and night by night, only to be answered by his friend's listening silence, would have told himself that it was the face of a guilty priest who heard confessions of those whom he had not power to absolve but that he felt again in memory the gaze of its dark womanish eyes.

Through this image he had a glimpse of a strange dark cavern of speculation but at once turned away from it, feeling that it was not yet the hour to enter it. But the night shade of his friend's listlessness seemed to be diffusing in the air around him a tenuous and deadly exhalation; and he found himself glancing from one casual word to another on his right or left in stolid wonder that they had been so silently emptied of instantaneous sense until every mean shop legend bound his mind like the words of a spell and his soul shrivelled up sighing with age as he walked on in a lane among heaps of dead language. His own consciousness of language was ebbing from his brain and trickling into the very words themselves which set to band and disband themselves in wayward rhythms:

> *The ivy whines upon the wall,*
> *And whines and twines upon the wall,*
> *The yellow ivy upon the wall,*
> *Ivy, ivy up the wall.*

Did any one ever hear such drivel? Lord Almighty! Who ever heard of ivy whining on a wall? Yellow ivy: that was all right. Yellow ivory also. And what about ivory ivy?

The word now shone in his brain, clearer and brighter than any ivory sawn from the mottled tusks of elephants. *Ivory, ivoire, avorio, ebur.** One of the first examples that he had learnt in Latin had run:

---

*"Ivory" in French, Italian, and Latin.

*India mittit ebur;** and he recalled the shrewd northern face of the rector who had taught him to construe the Metamorphoses of Ovid in a courtly English, made whimsical by the mention of porkers and potsherds† and chines‡ of bacon. He had learnt what little he knew of the laws of Latin verse from a ragged book written by a Portuguese priest.

Contrahit orator, variant in carmine vates.§

The crises and victories and secessions in Roman history were handed on to him in the trite words *in tanto discrimine*‖ and he had tried to peer into the social life of the city of cities through the words *implere ollam denariorum* which the rector had rendered sonorously as the filling of a pot with denaries. The pages of his timeworn Horace# never felt cold to the touch even when his own fingers were cold: they were human pages: and fifty years before they had been turned by the human fingers of John Duncan Inverarity and by his brother, William Malcolm Inverarity. Yes, those were noble names on the dusky flyleaf and, even for so poor a Latinist as he, the dusky verses were as fragrant as though they had lain all those years in myrtle and lavender and vervain;** but yet it wounded him to think that he would never be but a shy guest at the feast of the world's culture and that the monkish learning, in terms of which he was striving to forge out an esthetic philosophy, was held no higher by the age he lived in than the subtle and curious jargons of heraldry and falconry.

The grey block of Trinity†† on his left, set heavily in the city's ignorance like a dull stone set in a cumbrous ring, pulled his mind downward; and while he was striving this way and that to free his feet from the fetters of the reformed conscience he came upon the droll statue of the national poet of Ireland.‡‡

---

*India sends ivory (Latin).
†Pieces of broken pottery.
‡Backbone of an animal, used in cooking.
§The orator summarizes, the poet-prophets transform in their verses (Latin); from Emmanuel Alvarez's book of Latin grammar.
‖With such great discrimination (Latin).
#Quintus Horatius Flaccus (65–8 B.C.), important Roman poet and satirist.
**Plant related to verbena, with elongated stalks of fragrant flowers.
††Trinity College, Dublin (also called the University of Dublin), the Protestant university founded in 1592 by Queen Elizabeth I.
‡‡Thomas Moore (1779–1852), author of the perennially popular *Irish Melodies*.

He looked at it without anger: for, though sloth of the body and of the soul crept over it like unseen vermin, over the shuffling feet and up the folds of the cloak and around the servile head, it seemed humbly conscious of its indignity. It was a Firbolg* in the borrowed cloak of Milesian;† and he thought of his friend Davin, the peasant student. It was a jesting name between them, but the young peasant bore with it lightly:

—Go on, Stevie, I have a hard head, you tell me. Call me what you will.

The homely version of his christian name on the lips of his friend had touched Stephen pleasantly when first heard for he was as formal in speech with others as they were with him. Often, as he sat in Davin's rooms in Grantham Street, wondering at his friend's well made boots that flanked the wall pair by pair and repeating for his friend's simple ear the verses and cadences of others which were the veils of his own longing and dejection, the rude Firbolg mind of his listener had drawn his mind towards it and flung it back again, drawing it by a quiet in-bred courtesy of attention or by a quaint, turn of old English speech or by the force of its delight in rude bodily skill—for Davin had sat at the feet of Michael Cusack, the Gael‡—repelling swiftly and suddenly by a grossness of intelligence or by a bluntness of feeling or by a dull stare of terror in the eyes, the terror of soul of a starving Irish village in which the curfew§ was still a nightly fear.

Side by side with his memory of the deeds of prowess of his uncle Mat Davin, the athlete, the young peasant worshipped the sorrowful legend of Ireland. The gossip of his fellow students which strove to render the flat life of the college significant at any cost loved to think of him as a young fenian.‖ His nurse had taught him Irish and shaped his rude imagination by the broken lights of Irish myth. He stood towards the myth upon which no individual mind had ever drawn out a line of

---

*In Irish legend, the Firbolgs were early inhabitants of Ireland, from around the fourth century B.C.

†Successors to the Firbolgs as rulers of Ireland.

‡Founder of the Gaelic Athletic Association (1884), dedicated to the revival of traditional Irish sport in Ireland.

§Reference to the nightly curfews imposed in rural Ireland by the British during periods of Irish nationalist unrest.

‖The Fenian Brotherhood, founded in 1858 by James Stephens; a revolutionary group dedicated to winning Irish independence; forerunner of the Irish Republican Army (I.R.A.).

beauty and to its unwieldy tales that divided themselves as they moved down the cycles in the same attitude as towards the Roman catholic religion, the attitude of dull witted loyal serf. Whatsoever of thought or of feeling came to him from England or by way of English culture his mind stood armed against in obedience to a password: and of the world that lay beyond England he knew only the foreign legion of France in which he spoke of serving.

Coupling this ambition with the young man's humour Stephen had often called him one of the tame geese:* and there was even a point of irritation in the name pointed against that very reluctance of speech and deed in his friend which seemed so often to stand between Stephen's mind, eager of speculation, and the hidden ways of Irish life.

One night the young peasant, his spirit stung by the violent or luxurious language in which Stephen escaped from the cold silence of intellectual revolt, had called up before Stephen's mind a strange vision. The two were walking slowly towards Davin's rooms through the dark narrow streets of the poorer jews.

—A thing happened to myself, Stevie, last autumn, coming on winter, and I never told it to a living soul and you are the first person now I ever told it to. I disremember if it was October or November. It was October because it was before I came up here to join the matriculation class.

Stephen had turned his smiling eyes towards his friend's face, flattered by his confidence and won over to sympathy by the speaker's simple accent.

—I was away all that day from my own place over in Buttevant—I don't know if you know where that is—at a hurling† match between the Croke's Own Boys and the Fearless Thurles‡ and by God, Stevie, that was the hard fight. My first cousin, Fonsy Davin, was stripped to his buff that day minding cool for the Limericks but he was up with the forwards half the time and shouting like mad. I never will forget that day. One of the Crokes made a woeful wipe§ at him one time with his caman‖ and I declare to God he was within an aim's ace of getting it at the side of his temple. Oh, honest to God, if the crook of it caught him that time he was done for.

---

*A play on the Irish "wild geese," expatriate Irish political figures.
†Irish game similar to field hockey and lacrosse.
‡Two local, semi-professional teams.
§Swing.
‖Or "hurley," the hurling equivalent of a hockey stick.

—I am glad he escaped, Stephen had said with a laugh, but surely that's not the strange thing that happened you?

—Well, I suppose that doesn't interest you but leastways there was such noise after the match that I missed the train home and I couldn't get any kind of a yoke* to give me a lift for, as luck would have it, there was a mass meeting that same day over in Castletownroche† and all the cars in the country were there. So there was nothing for it only to stay the night or to foot it out. Well, I started to walk and on I went and it was coming on night when I got into the Ballyhoura Hills, that's better than ten miles from Kilmallock‡ and there's a long lonely road after that. You wouldn't see the sign of a christian house along the road or hear a sound. It was pitch dark almost. Once or twice I stopped by the way under a bush to redden my pipe and only for the dew was thick I'd have stretched out there and slept. At last, after a bend of the road, I spied a little cottage with a light in the window. I went up and knocked at the door. A voice asked who was there and I answered I was over at the match in Buttevant and was walking back and that I'd be thankful for a glass of water. After a while a young woman opened the door and brought me out a big mug of milk. She was half undressed as if she was going to bed when I knocked and she had her hair hanging; and I thought by her figure and by something in the look of her eyes that she must be carrying a child. She kept me in talk a long while at the door and I thought it strange because her breast and her shoulders were bare. She asked me was I tired and would I like to stop the night there. She said she was all alone in the house and that her husband had gone that morning to Queenstown with his sister to see her off. And all the time she was talking, Stevie, she had her eyes fixed on my face and she stood so close to me I could hear her breathing. When I handed her back the mug at last she took my hand to draw me in over the threshold and said: *Come in and stay the night here. You've no call to be frightened. There's no one in but ourselves. . . . .* I didn't go in, Stevie. I thanked her and went on my way again, all in a fever. At the first bend of the road I looked back and she was standing at the door.

The last words of Davin's story sang in his memory and the figure of the woman in the story stood forth, reflected in other figures of the peasant women whom he had seen standing in the doorways at Clane

---

*Thing (Anglo-Irish).
†5 miles east-southeast from Buttevant.
‡Davin describes a route leading north from Buttevant.

as the college cars drove by, as a type of her race and of his own, a bat-like soul waking to the consciousness of itself in darkness and secrecy and loneliness and, through the eyes and voice and gesture of a woman without guile, calling the stranger to her bed.

A hand was laid on his arm and a young voice cried:

—Ah, gentleman, your own girl, sir! The first handsel* today, gentleman. Buy that lovely bunch. Will you, gentleman?

The blue flowers which she lifted towards him and her young blue eyes seemed to him at that instant images of guilelessness; and he halted till the image had vanished and he saw only her ragged dress and damp coarse hair and hoydenish† face.

—Do, gentleman! Don't forget your own girl, sir!

—I have no money, said Stephen.

—Buy them lovely ones, will you, sir? Only a penny.

—Did you hear what I said? asked Stephen, bending towards her. I told you I had no money. I tell you again now.

—Well, sure, you will some day, sir, please God, the girl answered after an instant.

—Possibly, said Stephen, but I don't think it likely.

He left her quickly, fearing that her intimacy might turn to gibing and wishing to be out of the way before she offered her ware to another, a tourist from England or a student of Trinity. Grafton Street, along which he walked, prolonged that moment of discouraged poverty. In the roadway at the head of the street a slab was set to the memory of Wolfe Tone‡ and he remembered having been present with his father at its laying. He remembered with bitterness that scene of tawdry tribute. There were four French delegates in a brake and one, a plump smiling young man, held, wedged on a stick, a card on which were printed the words: *Vive l'Irlande!*§

But the trees in Stephen's Green were fragrant of rain and the rain-sodden earth gave forth its mortal odour, a faint incense rising upward through the mould from many hearts. The soul of the gallant venal city which his elders had told him of had shrunk with time to a faint mor-

---

*First sale of the day.
†Boisterous.
‡(1763–1798); Irish revolutionary and a founder of the United Irishmen, an early republican group; he was instrumental in the failed rising (insurrection) of 1798, for which he was put to death.
§Long Live Ireland (French).

tal odour rising from the earth and he knew that in a moment when he entered the sombre college he would be conscious of a corruption other than that of Buck Egan and Burnchapel Whaley.*

It was too late to go upstairs to the French class. He crossed the hall and took the corridor to the left which led to the physics theatre. The corridor was dark and silent but not unwatchful. Why did he feel that it was not unwatchful? Was it because he had heard that in Buck Whaley's time there was a secret staircase there? Or was the jesuit house extra-territorial and was he walking among aliens? The Ireland of Tone and of Parnell seemed to have receded in space.

He opened the door of the theatre and halted in the chilly grey light that struggled through the dusty windows. A figure was crouching before the large grate and by its leanness and greyness he knew that it was the dean of studies lighting the fire. Stephen closed the door quietly and approached the fireplace.

Good morning, sir! Can I help you?

The priest looked up quickly and said:

—One moment now, Mr Dedalus, and you will see. There is an art in lighting a fire. We have the liberal arts and we have the useful arts. This is one of the useful arts.

—I will try to learn it, said Stephen.

—Not too much coal, said the dean, working briskly at his task, that is one of the secrets.

He produced four candle butts from the side pockets of his soutane and placed them deftly among the coals and twisted papers. Stephen watched him in silence. Kneeling thus on the flagstone to kindle the fire and busied with the disposition of his wisps of paper and candle butts he seemed more than ever a humble server making ready the place of sacrifice in an empty temple, a levite† of the Lord. Like a levite's robe of plain linen the faded worn soutane draped the kneeling figure of one whom the canonicals‡ or the bellybordered ephod§ would irk and trouble. His very body had waxed old in lowly service of the Lord—in tending the fire upon the altar, in bearing tidings secretly, in waiting upon worldlings, in striking swiftly when bidden—and yet had remained ungraced by aught of saintly or of prelatic beauty. Nay, his very soul had

---

*Two late-eighteenth-century characters associated with University College.
†Assistant in the Temple.
‡Clothing set by canon law for officiating at mass.
§Ornamental priestly garment.

waxed old in that service without growing towards light and beauty or spreading abroad a sweet odour of her sanctity—a mortified will no more responsive to the thrill of its obedience than was to the thrill of love or combat his ageing body, spare and sinewy, greyed with a silver-pointed down.

The dean rested back on his hunkers and watched the sticks catch. Stephen, to fill the silence, said:

—I am sure I could not light a fire.

—You are an artist, are you not, Mr Dedalus? said the dean, glancing up and blinking his pale eyes. The object of the artist is the creation of the beautiful. What the beautiful is is another question.

He rubbed his hands slowly and drily over the difficulty.

—Can you solve that question now? he asked.

—Aquinas, answered Stephen, says *pulcra sunt quœ visa placent.**

—This fire before us, said the dean, will be pleasing to the eye. Will it therefore be beautiful?

—In so far as it is apprehended by the sight, which I suppose means here esthetic intellection, it will be beautiful. But Aquinas also says *Bonum est in quod tendit appetitus.*† In so far as it satisfies the animal craving for warmth fire is a good. In hell, however, it is an evil.

—Quite so, said the dean, you have certainly hit the nail on the head.

He rose nimbly and went towards the door, set it ajar and said:

—A draught is said to be a help in these matters.

As he came back to the hearth, limping slightly but with a brisk step, Stephen saw the silent soul of a jesuit look out at him from the pale loveless eyes. Like Ignatius he was lame but in his eyes burned no spark of Ignatius' enthusiasm. Even the legendary craft of the company, a craft subtler and more secret than its fabled books of secret subtle wisdom, had not fired his soul with the energy of apostleship. It seemed as if he used the shifts and lore and cunning of the world, as bidden to do, for the greater glory of God, without joy in their handling or hatred of that in them which was evil but turning them, with a firm gesture of obedience, back upon themselves: and for all this silent service it seemed as if he loved not at all the master and little, if at all, the ends he served. *Similiter atque senis baculus,*‡ he was, as the founder would have had him, like a staff in an old man's hand, to be leaned on in the

---

*The beautiful are those things that, being seen, please (Latin).
†The good is that toward which the appetite tends (Latin).
‡Like an old man's walking stick (Latin).

road at nightfall or in stress of weather, to lie with a lady's nosegay on a garden seat, to be raised in menace.

The dean returned to the hearth and began to stroke his chin.

—When may we expect to have something from you on the esthetic question? he asked.

—From me! said Stephen in astonishment. I stumble on an idea once a fortnight* if I am lucky.

—These questions are very profound, Mr Dedalus, said the dean. It is like looking down from the cliffs of Moher† into the depths. Many go down into the depths and never come up. Only the trained diver can go down into those depths and explore them and come to the surface again.

—If you mean speculation, sir, said Stephen, I also am sure that there is no such thing as free thinking inasmuch as all thinking must be bound by its own laws.

—Ha!

—For my purpose I can work on at present by the light of one or two ideas of Aristotle and Aquinas.

—I see. I quite see your point.

—I need them only for my own use and guidance until I have done something for myself by their light. If the lamp smokes or smells I shall try to trim it. If it does not give light enough I shall sell it and buy another.

—Epictetus‡ also had a lamp, said the dean, which was sold for a fancy price after his death. It was the lamp he wrote his philosophical dissertations by. You know Epictetus?

—An old gentleman, said Stephen coarsely, who said that the soul is very like a bucketful of water.

—He tells us in his homely way, the dean went on, that he put an iron lamp before a statue of one of the gods and that a thief stole the lamp. What did the philosopher do? He reflected that it was in the character of a thief to steal and determined to buy an earthen lamp next day instead of the iron lamp.

A smell of molten tallow came up from the dean's candle butts and fused itself in Stephen's consciousness with the jingle of the words,

---

*Two-week period.
†On the western coast of Ireland, south of Galway.
‡(c. A.D. 55–c.135); Greek stoic philosopher; in his *Discourses*, he likened the soul to a bowl of water.

bucket and lamp and lamp and bucket. The priest's voice, too, had a hard jingling tone. Stephen's mind halted by instinct, checked by the strange tone and the imagery and by the priest's face which seemed like an unlit lamp or a reflector hung in a false focus. What lay behind it or within it? A dull torpor of the soul or the dullness of the thundercloud, charged with intellection and capable of the gloom of God?

—I meant a different kind of lamp, sir, said Stephen.

—Undoubtedly, said the dean.

—One difficulty, said Stephen, in esthetic discussion is to know whether words are being used according to the literary tradition or according to the tradition of the marketplace. I remember a sentence of Newman's,* in which he says of the Blessed Virgin that she was detained in the full company of the saints. The use of the word in the marketplace is quite different. *I hope I am not detaining you.*

—Not in the least, said the dean politely.

—No, no, said Stephen, smiling, I mean . . .

—Yes, yes: I see, said the dean quickly, I quite catch the point: *detain.*

He thrust forward his under jaw and uttered a dry short cough.

—To return to the lamp, he said, the feeding of it is also a nice problem. You must choose the pure oil and you must be careful when you pour it in not to overflow it, not to pour in more than the funnel can hold.

—What funnel? asked Stephen.

—The funnel through which you pour the oil into your lamp.

—That? said Stephen. Is that called a funnel? Is it not a tundish?

—What is a tundish?

—That. The . . . the funnel.

—Is that called a tundish in Ireland? asked the dean. I never heard the word in my life.

—It is called a tundish in Lower Drumcondra,† said Stephen, laughing, where they speak the best English.

—A tundish, said the dean reflectively. That is a most interesting word. I must look that word up. Upon my word I must.

His courtesy of manner rang a little false, and Stephen looked at the English convert with the same eyes as the elder brother in the parable may have turned on the prodigal.[17] A humble follower in the wake of

---

*From Newman's "The Glories of Mary."
†Working-class neighbourhood 2 miles from Dublin's city center.

clamorous conversions, a poor Englishman in Ireland, he seemed to have entered on the stage of jesuit history when that strange play of intrigue and suffering and envy and struggle and indignity had been all but given through—a late comer, a tardy spirit. From what had he set out? Perhaps he had been born and bred among serious dissenters, seeing salvation in Jesus only and abhoring the vain pomps of the establishment. Had he felt the need of an implicit faith amid the welter of sectarianism and the jargon of its turbulent schisms, six principal men, peculiar people, seed and snake baptists, supralapsarian dogmatists?* Had he found the true church all of a sudden in winding up to the end like a reel of cotton some finespun line of reasoning upon insufflation on the imposition of hands or the procession of the Holy Ghost?† Or had Lord Christ touched him and bidden him follow, like that disciple‡ who had sat at the receipt of custom, as he sat by the door of some zinc roofed chapel, yawning and telling over his church pence?

The dean repeated the word yet again.

—Tundish! Well now, that is interesting!

—The question you asked me a moment ago seems to me more interesting. What is that beauty which the artist struggles to express from lumps of earth, said Stephen coldly.

The little word seemed to have turned a rapier point of his sensitiveness against this courteous and vigilant foe. He felt with a smart of dejection that the man to whom he was speaking was a countryman of Ben Jonson. He thought:

—The language in which we are speaking is his before it is mine. How different are the words *home, Christ, ale, master,* on his lips and on mine! I cannot speak or write these words without unrest of spirit. His language, so familiar and so foreign, will always be for me an acquired speech. I have not made or accepted its words. My voice holds them at bay. My soul frets in the shadow of his language.

—And to distinguish between the beautiful and the sublime, the dean added, to distinguish between moral beauty and material beauty. And to inquire what kind of beauty is proper to each of the various arts. These are some interesting points we might take up.

Stephen, disheartened suddenly by the dean's firm dry tone, was

*Various sects that rebelled from the central control over dogma exercised by the Catholic Church.

†Practices and beliefs distinguishing various sects from the Church.

‡Matthew; see Matthew 9:9.

silent: and through the silence a distant noise of many boots and confused voices came up the staircase.

—In pursuing these speculations, said the dean conclusively, there is, however, the danger of perishing of inanition.* First you must take your degree. Set that before you as your first aim. Then, little by little, you will see your way. I mean in every sense, your way in life and in thinking. It may be uphill pedaling at first. Take Mr Moonan. He was a long time before he got to the top. But he got there.

—I may not have his talent, said Stephen quietly.

—You never know, said the dean brightly. We never can say what is in us. I most certainly should not be despondent. *Per aspera ad astra.*†

He left the hearth quickly and went towards the landing to oversee the arrival of the first arts' class.

Leaning against the fireplace Stephen heard him greet briskly and impartially every student of the class and could almost see the frank smiles of the coarser students. A desolating pity began to fall like dew upon his easily embittered heart for this faithful servingman of the knightly Loyola, for this half brother of the clergy, more venal than they in speech, more steadfast of soul than they, one whom he would never call his ghostly father: and he thought how this man and his companions had earned the name of worldlings at the hands not of the unworldly only but of the worldly also for having pleaded, during all their history, at the bar of God's justice for the souls of the lax and the lukewarm and the prudent.

The entry of the professor was signalled by a few rounds of Kentish fire‡ from the heavy boots of those students who sat on the highest tier of the gloomy theatre under the grey cobwebbed windows. The calling of the roll began, and the responses to the names were given out in all tones until the name of Peter Byrne was reached.

—Here!

A deep bass note in response came from the upper tier, followed by coughs of protest along the other benches.

The professor paused in his reading and called the next name:

—Cranly!

No answer.

—Mr Cranly!

---

*Lack of food and water.
†Through rough ways to the stars (Latin).
‡Loud volley of applause produced by hands or feet.

A smile flew across Stephen's face as he thought of his friend's studies.

—Try Leopardstown!* said a voice from the bench behind.

Stephen glanced up quickly but Moynihan's snoutish face, outlined on the grey light, was impassive. A formula was given out. Amid the rustling of the notebooks Stephen turned back again and said:

—Give me some paper for God's sake.

—Are you as bad as that? asked Moynihan with a broad grin.

He tore a sheet from his scribbler and passed it down, whispering:

—In case of necessity any layman or woman can do it.†

The formula which he wrote obediently on the sheet of paper, the coiling and uncoiling calculations of the professor, the spectrelike symbols of force and velocity fascinated and jaded Stephen's mind. He had heard some say that the old professor was an atheist freemason. Oh, the grey dull day! It seemed a limbo of painless patient consciousness through which souls of mathematicians might wander, projecting long slender fabrics from plane to plane of ever rarer and paler twilight, radiating swift eddies to the last verges of a universe ever vaster, farther and more impalpable.

—So we must distinguish between elliptical and ellipsoidal. Perhaps some of you gentlemen may be familiar with the works of Mr W. S. Gilbert. In one of his songs he speaks of the billiard sharp who is condemned to play:

> On a cloth untrue
> With a twisted cue
> And elliptical billiard balls.‡

—He means a ball having the form of the ellipsoid of the principal axes of which I spoke a moment ago.

Moynihan leaned down towards Stephen's ear and murmured:

—What price ellipsoidal balls! chase me, ladies, I'm in the cavalry!

His fellow student's rude humour ran like a gust through the cloister of Stephen's mind, shaking into gay life limp priestly vestments that hung upon the walls, setting them to sway and caper in a sabbath of misrule. The forms of the community emerged from the gust blown

---

*Horseracing track northwest of the city.
†Parody of language on baptism in the catechism.
‡From Gilbert and Sullivan's comic opera *The Mikado* (1885).

vestments, the dean of studies, the portly florid bursar with his cap of grey hair, the president, the little priest with feathery hair who wrote devout verses, the squat peasant form of the professor of economics, the tall form of the young professor of mental science discussing on the landing a case of conscience with his class like a giraffe cropping high leafage among a herd of antelopes, the grave troubled prefect of sodality, the plump round headed professor of Italian with his rogue's eyes. They came ambling and stumbling, tumbling and capering, kilting their gowns for leap frog, holding one another back, shaken with deep false laughter, smacking one another behind and laughing at their rude malice, calling to one another by familiar nicknames, protesting with sudden dignity at some rough usage, whispering two and two behind their hands.

The professor had gone to the glass cases on the sidewall, from a shelf of which he took down a set of coils, blew away the dust from many points and, bearing it carefully to the table, held a finger on it while he proceeded with his lecture. He explained that the wires in modern coils were of a compound called platinoid lately discovered by F. W. Martino.*

He spoke clearly the initials and surname of the discoverer. Moynihan whispered from behind:

—Good old Fresh Water Martin!

—Ask him, Stephen whispered back with weary humour, if he wants a subject for electrocution. He can have me.

Moynihan, seeing the professor bend over the coils, rose in his bench and, clacking noiselessly the fingers of his right hand, began to call with the voice of a slobbering urchin:—Please, teacher! This boy is after saying a bad word, teacher.

—Platinoid, the professor said solemnly, is preferred to German silver because it has a lower coefficient of resistance by changes of temperature. The platinoid wire is insulated and the covering of silk that insulates it is wound on the ebonite bobbins just where my finger is. If it were wound single an extra current would be induced in the coils. The bobbins are saturated in hot paraffin-wax . . .

A sharp Ulster voice said from the bench below Stephen:

—Are we likely to be asked questions on applied science?

The professor began to juggle gravely with the terms pure science

---

*American chemist.

and applied science. A heavybuilt student, wearing gold spectacles, stared with some wonder at the questioner. Moynihan murmured from behind in his natural voice:

—Isn't MacAlister a devil for his pound of flesh?

Stephen looked down coldly on the oblong skull beneath him overgrown with tangled twinecoloured hair. The voice, the accent, the mind of the questioner offended him and he allowed the offence to carry him towards wilful unkindness, bidding his mind think that the student's father would have done better had he sent his son to Belfast to study and have saved something on the train fare by so doing.

The oblong skull beneath did not turn to meet this shaft of thought and yet the shaft came back to its bowstring: for he saw in a moment the student's whey pale face.

—That thought is not mine, he said to himself quickly. It came from the comic Irishman in the bench behind. Patience. Can you say with certitude by whom the soul of your race was bartered and its elect betrayed—by the questioner or by the mocker? Patience. Remember Epictetus. It is probably in his character to ask such a question at such a moment in such a tone and to pronounce the word *science* as a monosyllable.

The droning voice of the professor continued to wind itself slowly round and round the coils it spoke of, doubling, trebling, quadrupling its somnolent energy as the coil multiplied its ohms of resistance.

Moynihan's voice called from behind in echo to a distant bell:

—Closing time, gents!*

The entrance hall was crowded and loud with talk. On a table near the door were two photographs in frames and between them a long roll of paper bearing an irregular tail of signatures. MacCann went briskly to and fro among the students, talking rapidly, answering rebuffs and leading one after another to the table. In the inner hall the dean of studies stood talking to a young professor, stroking his chin gravely and nodding his head.

Stephen, checked by the crowd at the door, halted irresolutely. From under the wide falling leaf of a soft hat Cranly's dark eyes were watching him.

—Have you signed? Stephen asked.

---

*Moynihan plays on the call of a pub owner at closing time.

Cranly closed his long thinlipped mouth, communed with himself an instant and answered:

—*Ego habeo.**

—What is it for?

—*Quod?*†

—What is it for?

Cranly turned his pale face to Stephen and said blandly and bitterly:

—*Per pax universalis.*‡

Stephen pointed to the Tsar's§ photograph and said:

—He has the face of a besotted‖ Christ.

The scorn and anger in his voice brought Cranly's eyes back from a calm survey of the walls of the hall.

—Are you annoyed? he asked.

—No, answered Stephen.

—Are you in bad humour?

—No.

—*Credo ut vos sanguinarius mendax estis,* said Cranly, *quia facies vostra monstrat ut vos in damno malo humore estis.*#

Moynihan, on his way to the table, said in Stephen's ear:

—MacCann is in tiptop form. Ready to shed the last drop. Brand new world. No stimulants and votes for the bitches.

Stephen smiled at the manner of this confidence and, when Moynihan had passed, turned again to meet Cranly's eyes.

—Perhaps you can tell me, he said, why he pours his soul so freely into my ear. Can you?

A dull scowl appeared on Cranly's forehead. He stared at the table where Moynihan had bent to write his name on the roll; and then said flatly:

—A sugar!

—*Quis est in malo humore,* said Stephen, *ego aut vos?***

---

*I have (dog Latin).
†What? (Latin).
‡For universal peace (Latin).
§Russian Tsar Nicholas II (1868–1918; ruled 1894–1917) initiated an international petition for peace that resulted in the Hague Peace Conference (1899).
‖Drunken.
#I believe you are a bloody liar because your face shows you are in a damned bad humour (dog Latin).
**Who is in a bad humour, you or me? (dog Latin).

Cranly did not take up the taunt: He brooded sourly on his judgment and repeated with the same flat force:

—A flaming bloody sugar, that's what he is!

It was his epitaph for all dead friendships and Stephen wondered whether it would ever be spoken in the same tone over his memory. The heavy lumpish phrase sank slowly out of hearing like a stone through a quagmire. Stephen saw it sink as he had seen many another, feeling its heaviness depress his heart. Cranly's speech, unlike that of Davin, had neither rare phrases of Elizabethan English nor quaintly turned versions of Irish idioms. Its drawl was an echo of the quays of Dublin given back by a bleak decaying seaport, its energy an echo of the sacred eloquence of Dublin given back flatly by a Wicklow pulpit.

The heavy scowl faded from Cranly's face as MacCann marched briskly towards them from the other side of the hall.

—Here you are! said MacCann cheerily.

—Here I am! said Stephen.

—Late as usual. Can you not combine the progressive tendency with a respect for punctuality?

—That question is out of order, said Stephen. Next business.

His smiling eyes were fixed on a silver wrapped tablet of milk chocolate which peeped out of the propagandist's breast-pocket. A little ring of listeners closed round to hear the war of wits. A lean student with olive skin and lank black hair thrust his face between the two, glancing from one to the other at each phrase and seeming to try to catch each flying phrase in his open moist mouth. Cranly took a small grey handball from his pocket and began to examine it closely, turning it over and over.

—Next business? said MacCann. Hom!

He gave a loud cough of laughter, smiled broadly, and tugged twice at the strawcoloured goatee which hung from his blunt chin.

—The next business is to sign the testimonial.

—Will you pay me anything if I sign? asked Stephen.

—I thought you were an idealist, said MacCann.

The gipsylike student looked about him and addressed the onlookers in an indistinct bleating voice.

—By hell, that's a queer notion. I consider that notion to be a mercenary notion.

His voice faded into silence. No heed was paid to his words. He turned his olive face, equine in expression, towards Stephen, inviting him to speak again.

MacCann began to speak with fluent energy of the Tsar's rescript, of Stead,* of general disarmament, arbitration in cases of international disputes, of the signs of the times, of the new humanity and the new gospel of life which would make it the business of the community to secure as cheaply as possible the greatest possible happiness of the greatest possible number.

The gipsy student responded to the close of the period by crying:

—Three cheers for universal brotherhood!

—Go on, Temple, said a stout ruddy student near him. I'll stand you a pint after.

—I'm a believer in universal brotherhood, said Temple, glancing about him out of his dark, oval eyes. Marx† is only a bloody cod.‡

Cranly gripped his arm tightly to check his tongue, smiling uneasily, and repeated:

—Easy, easy, easy!

Temple struggled to free his arm but continued, his mouth flecked by a thin foam:

—Socialism was founded by an Irishman and the first man in Europe who preached the freedom of thought was Collins.§ Two hundred years ago. He denounced priestcraft, the philosopher of Middlesex. Three cheers for John Anthony Collins!

A thin voice from the verge of the ring replied:

—Pip! pip!

Moynihan murmured beside Stephen's ear:

—And what about John Anthony's poor little sister:

> *Lottie Collins lost her drawers;*
> *Won't you kindly lend her yours?* ||

Stephen laughed and Moynihan, pleased with the result, murmured again:

—We'll have five bob each way# on John Anthony Collins.

---

*William Thomas Stead (1849–1912), English journalist.

†Karl Marx (1818–1883) maintained that class conflict was inevitable.

‡Practical joke.

§Anthony Collins (1676–1729), English theologian.

||Lottie Collins was a late-nineteenth-century music-hall performer, whose best-known number was "Tra-Ra-Ra-Boom-De-Ay."

#That is, they are betting 5 shillings on each possible outcome.

—I am waiting for your answer, said MacCann briefly.

—The affair doesn't interest me in the least, said Stephen wearily. You know that well. Why do you make a scene about it?

—Good! said MacCann, smacking his lips. You are a reactionary, then?

—Do you think you impress me, Stephen asked, when you flourish your wooden sword?

—Metaphors! said MacCann bluntly. Come to facts.

Stephen blushed and turned aside. MacCann stood his ground and said with hostile humour:

—Minor poets, I suppose, are above such trivial questions as the question of universal peace.

Cranly raised his head and held the handball between the two students by way of a peaceoffering, saying:

—*Pax super totum sanguinarium globum.**

Stephen, moving away the bystanders, jerked his shoulder angrily in the direction of the Tsar's image, saying:

—Keep your icon. If you must have a Jesus, let us have a legitimate Jesus.

—By hell, that's a good one! said the gipsy student to those about him, that's a fine expression. I like that expression immensely.

He gulped down the spittle in his throat as if he were gulping down the phrase and, fumbling at the peak of his tweed cap, turned to Stephen, saying:

—Excuse me, sir, what do you mean by that expression you uttered just now?

Feeling himself jostled by the students near him, he said to them:

—I am curious to know now what he meant by that expression.

He turned again to Stephen and said in a whisper:

—Do you believe in Jesus? I believe in man. Of course, I don't know if you believe in man. I admire you, sir. I admire the mind of man independent of all religions. Is that your opinion about the mind of Jesus?

—Go on, Temple, said the stout ruddy student, returning, as was his wont, to his first idea, that pint is waiting for you.

—He thinks I'm an imbecile, Temple explained to Stephen, because I'm a believer in the power of mind.

Cranly linked his arms into those of Stephen and his admirer and said:

---

*Peace all over this bloody globe (dog Latin).

—*Nos ad manum ballum jocabimus.**

Stephen, in the act of being led away, caught sight of MacCann's flushed bluntfeatured face.

—My signature is of no account, he said politely. You are right to go your way. Leave me to go mine.

—Dedalus, said MacCann crisply, I believe you're a good fellow but you have yet to learn the dignity of altruism and the responsibility of the human individual.

A voice said:

—Intellectual crankery is better out of this movement than in it.

Stephen, recognizing the harsh tone of MacAlister's voice, did not turn in the direction of the voice. Cranly pushed solemnly through the throng of students, linking Stephen and Temple like a celebrant attended by his ministers on his way to the altar.

Temple bent eagerly across Cranly's breast and said:

—Did you hear MacAlister what he said? That youth is jealous of you. Did you see that? I bet Cranly didn't see that. By hell, I saw that at once.

As they crossed the inner hall the dean of studies was in the act of escaping from the student with whom he had been conversing. He stood at the foot of the staircase, a foot on the lowest step, his threadbare soutane gathered about him for the ascent with womanish care, nodding his head often and repeating:

—Not a doubt of it, Mr Hackett! Very fine! Not a doubt of it!

In the middle of the hall the prefect of the college sodality was speaking earnestly, in a soft querulous voice, with a boarder. As he spoke he wrinkled a little his freckled brow, and bit, between his phrases, at a tiny bone pencil.

—I hope the matric† men will all come. The first arts men are pretty sure. Second arts, too. We must make sure of the newcomers.

Temple bent again across Cranly, as they were passing through the doorway, and said in a swift whisper:

—Do you know that he is a married man? He was a married man before they converted him. He has a wife and children somewhere. By hell, I think that's the queerest notion I ever heard! Eh?

His whisper trailed off into sly cackling laughter. The moment they were through the doorway Cranly seized him rudely by the neck and shook him, saying:

---

*Let's go play handball (dog Latin).
†Abbreviation for "matriculation," or first-year, class.

—You flaming floundering fool! I'll take my dying bible there isn't a bigger bloody ape, do you know, than you in the whole flaming bloody world!

Temple wriggled in his grip, laughing still with sly content, while Cranly repeated flatly at every rude shake:

—A flaming flaring bloody idiot!

They crossed the weedy garden together. The president, wrapped in a heavy loose cloak, was coming towards them along one of the walks, reading his office.* At the end of the walk he halted before turning and raised his eyes. The students saluted, Temple fumbling as before at the peak of his cap. They walked forward in silence. As they neared the alley Stephen could hear the thuds of the players' hands and the wet smacks of the ball and Davin's voice crying out excitedly at each stroke.

The three students halted round the box on which Davin sat to follow the game. Temple, after a few moments, sidled across to Stephen and said:

—Excuse me, I wanted to ask you do you believe that Jean Jacques Rousseau† was a sincere man?

Stephen laughed outright. Cranly, picking up the broken stave of a cask from the grass at his feet, turned swiftly and said sternly:

—Temple, I declare to the living God if you say another word, do you know, to anybody on any subject I'll kill you *super spottum.*‡

—He was like you, I fancy, said Stephen, an emotional man.

—Blast him, curse him! said Cranly broadly. Don't talk to him at all. Sure, you might as well be talking, do you know, to a flaming chamberpot as talking to Temple. Go home, Temple. For God's sake, go home.

—I don't care a damn about you, Cranly, answered Temple, moving out of reach of the uplifted stave and pointing at Stephen. He's the only man I see in this institution that has an individual mind.

—Institution! Individual! cried Cranly. Go home, blast you, for you're a hopeless bloody man.

—I'm an emotional man, said Temple. That's quite rightly expressed. And I'm proud that I'm an emotionalist.

He sidled out of the alley, smiling slyly. Cranly watched him with a blank expressionless face.

---

*Reading through a daily selection of prayers and devotions.
†(1712–1778); French philosopher and writer who influenced the Romantics.
‡On the spot (dog Latin).

—Look at him! he said. Did you ever see such a go-by-the-wall?*

His phrase was greeted by a strange laugh from a student who lounged against the wall, his peaked cap down on his eyes. The laugh, pitched in a high key and coming from a so muscular frame, seemed like the whinny of an elephant. The student's body shook all over and, to ease his mirth, he rubbed both his hands delightedly, over his groins.

—Lynch is awake, said Cranly.

Lynch, for answer, straightened himself and thrust forward his chest.

—Lynch puts out his chest, said Stephen, as a criticism of life.

Lynch smote himself sonorously on the chest and said:

—Who has anything to say about my girth?

Cranly took him at the word and the two began to tussle. When their faces had flushed with the struggle they drew apart, panting. Stephen bent down towards Davin who, intent on the game, had paid no heed to the talk of the others.

—And how is my little tame goose? he asked. Did he sign, too?

Davin nodded and said:—And you, Stevie?

Stephen shook his head.—You're a terrible man, Stevie, said Davin, taking the short pipe from his mouth—always alone.

—Now that you have signed the petition for universal peace, said Stephen, I suppose you will burn that little copybook I saw in your room.

As Davin did not answer Stephen began to quote:

—Long pace, fianna!† Right incline, fianna! Fianna, by numbers, salute, one, two!

—That's a different question, said Davin. I'm an Irish nationalist, first and foremost. But that's you all out. You're a born sneerer, Stevie.

—When you make the next rebellion with hurleysticks, said Stephen, and want the indispensable informer, tell me. I can find you a few in this college.

—I can't understand you, said Davin. One time I hear you talk against English literature. Now you talk against the Irish informers. What with your name and your ideas . . . are you Irish at all?

—Come with me now to the office of arms and I will show you the tree of my family, said Stephen.

—Then be one of us, said Davin. Why don't you learn Irish? Why did you drop out of the league class after the first lesson?

---

*Insignificant person.

†The Irish name for the Fenians (see note on p. 159).

—You know one reason why, answered Stephen.

Davin tossed his head and laughed.

—Oh, come now, he said. Is it on account of that certain young lady and Father Moran? But that's all in your own mind, Stevie. They were only talking and laughing.

Stephen paused and laid a friendly hand upon Davin's shoulder.

—Do you remember, he said, when we knew each other first? The first morning we met you asked me to show you the way to the matriculation class, putting a very strong stress on the first syllable. You remember? Then you used to address the jesuits as father,* you remember? I ask myself about you: *Is he as innocent as his speech?*

—I'm a simple person, said Davin. You know that. When you told me that night in Harcourt Street those things about your private life, honest to God, Stevie, I was not able to eat my dinner. I was quite bad. I was awake a long time that night. Why did you tell me those things?

—Thanks, said Stephen. You mean I am a monster.

—No, said Davin, but I wish you had not told me.

A tide began to surge beneath the calm surface of Stephen's friendliness.

—This race and this country and this life produced me, he said. I shall express myself as I am.

—Try to be one of us, repeated Davin. In your heart you are an Irishman but your pride is too powerful.

—My ancestors threw off their language and took another, Stephen said. They allowed a handful of foreigners to subject them. Do you fancy I am going to pay in my own life and person debts they made? What for?

—For our freedom, said Davin.

—No honourable and sincere man, said Stephen, has given up to you his life and his youth and his affections from the days of Tone to those of Parnell but you sold him to the enemy or failed him in need or reviled him and left him for another. And you invite me to be one of you. I'd see you damned first.

—They died for their ideals, Stevie, said Davin. Our day will come yet, believe me.

Stephen, following his own thought, was silent for an instant.

—The soul is born, he said vaguely, first in those moments I told you

---

*Only those Jesuits who are ordained priests are properly addressed as "father"; others are called simply "mister."

of. It has a slow and dark birth, more mysterious than the birth of the body. When the soul of a man is born in this country there are nets flung at it to hold it back from flight. You talk to me of nationality, language, religion. I shall try to fly by those nets.

Davin knocked the ashes from his pipe.

—Too deep for me, Stevie, he said. But a man's country comes first. Ireland first, Stevie. You can be a poet or mystic after.

—Do you know what Ireland is? asked Stephen with cold violence. Ireland is the old sow that eats her farrow.*

Davin rose from his box and went towards the players, shaking his head sadly. But in a moment his sadness left him and he was hotly disputing with Cranly and the two players who had finished their game. A match of four was arranged, Cranly insisting, however, that his ball should be used. He let it rebound twice or thrice to his hand and struck it strongly and swiftly towards the base of the alley, exclaiming in answer to its thud:

—Your soul!

Stephen stood with Lynch till the score began to rise. Then he plucked him by the sleeve to come away. Lynch obeyed, saying:

—Let us eke go, as Cranly has it.

Stephen smiled at this sidethrust.

They passed back through the garden and out through the hall where the doddering porter was pinning up a notice in the frame. At the foot of the steps they halted and Stephen took a packet of cigarettes from his pocket and offered it to his companion.

—I know you are poor, he said.

—Damn your yellow insolence, answered Lynch.

This second proof of Lynch's culture made Stephen smile again.

—It was a great day for European culture, he said, when you made up your mind to swear in yellow.

They lit their cigarettes and turned to the right. After a pause Stephen began:

—Aristotle has not defined pity and terror.† I have. I say . . .

Lynch halted and said bluntly:

—Stop! I won't listen! I am sick. I was out last night on a yellow drunk with Horan and Goggins.

---

*Litter of pigs.
†According to Aristotle in the *Poetics*, pity and terror are proper concerns of tragedy; through the spectators' vicarious participation in the story, they are purged of these emotions.

Chapter V

········· (Stephen's walk with Lynch)

▬▬▬▬ (Stephen's walk with Cranly)

Stephen went on:

—Pity is the feeling which arrests the mind in the presence of whatsoever is grave and constant in human sufferings and unites it with the human sufferer. Terror is the feeling which arrests the mind in the presence of whatsoever is grave and constant in human sufferings and unites it with the secret cause.

—Repeat, said Lynch.

Stephen repeated the definitions slowly.

—A girl got into a hansom* a few days ago, he went on, in London. She was on her way to meet her mother whom she had not seen for many years. At the corner of a street the shaft of a lorry shivered the window of the hansom in the shape of a star. A long fine needle of the shivered glass pierced her heart. She died on the instant. The reporter called it a tragic death. It is not. It is remote from terror and pity according to the terms of my definitions.

—The tragic emotion, in fact, is a face looking two ways, towards terror and towards pity, both of which are phases of it. You see I use the word *arrest*. I mean that the tragic emotion is static. Or rather the dramatic emotion is. The feelings excited by improper art are kinetic, desire or loathing. Desire urges us to possess, to go to something; loathing urges us to abandon, to go from something. The arts which excite them, pornographical or didactic, are therefore improper arts. The esthetic emotion (I used the general term) is therefore static. The mind is arrested and raised above desire and loathing.

—You say that art must not excite desire, said Lynch, I told you that one day I wrote my name in pencil on the backside of the Venus of Praxiteles† in the Museum. Was that not desire?

—I speak of normal natures, said Stephen. You also told me that when you were a boy in that charming carmelite‡ school you ate pieces of dried cowdung.

Lynch broke again into a whinny of laughter and again rubbed both his hands over his groins but without taking them from his pockets.

—O, I did! I did! he cried.

Stephen turned towards his companion and looked at him for a moment boldly in the eyes. Lynch, recovering from his laughter, answered

---

*Horse-drawn carriage.

†A plaster copy of this statue was, at the time, on display in the National Museum, adjacent to the National Library.

‡Order founded in the twelfth century at Mount Carmel, Palestine.

his look from his humbled eyes. The long slender flattened skull beneath the long pointed cap brought before Stephen's mind the image of a hooded reptile. The eyes, too, were reptilelike in glint and gaze. Yet at that instant, humbled and alert in their look, they were lit by one tiny human point, the window of a shrivelled soul, poignant and self-embittered.

—As for that, Stephen said in polite parenthesis, we are all animals. I also am an animal.

—You are, said Lynch.

—But we are just now in a mental world, Stephen continued. The desire and loathing excited by improper esthetic means are really not esthetic emotions not only because they are kinetic in character but also because they are not more than physical. Our flesh shrinks from what it dreads and responds to the stimulus of what it desires by a purely reflex action of the nervous system. Our eyelid closes before we are aware that the fly is about to enter our eye.

—Not always, said Lynch critically.

—In the same way, said Stephen, your flesh responded to the stimulus of a naked statue but it was, I say, simply a reflex action of the nerves. Beauty expressed by the artist cannot awaken in us an emotion which is kinetic or a sensation which is purely physical. It awakens, or ought to awaken, or induces, or ought to induce, an esthetic stasis, an ideal pity or an ideal terror, a stasis called forth, prolonged and at last dissolved by what I call the rhythm of beauty.

—What is that exactly? asked Lynch.

—Rhythm, said Stephen, is the first formal esthetic relation of part to art in any esthetic whole or of an esthetic whole to its part or parts or of any part to the esthetic whole of which it is a part.

—If that is rhythm, said Lynch, let me hear what you call beauty: and, please remember, though I did eat a cake of cowdung once, that I admire only beauty.

Stephen raised his cap as if in greeting. Then, blushing slightly, he laid his hand on Lynch's thick tweed sleeve.

—We are right, he said, and the others are wrong. To speak of these things and to try to understand their nature and, having understood it, to try slowly and humbly and constantly to express, to press out again, from the gross earth or what it brings forth, from sound and shape and colour which are the prison gates of our soul, an image of the beauty we have come to understand—that is art.

They had reached the canal bridge and, turning from their course, went on by the trees. A crude grey light, mirrored in the sluggish water, and a smell of wet branches over their heads seemed to war against the course of Stephen's thought.

—But you have not answered my question, said Lynch. What is art? What is the beauty it expresses?

—That was the first definition I gave you, you sleepyheaded wretch, said Stephen, when I began to try to think out the matter for myself. Do you remember the night? Cranly lost his temper and began to talk about Wicklow bacon.

—I remember, said Lynch. He told us about them flaming fat devils of pigs.

—Art, said Stephen, is the human disposition of sensible or intelligible matter for an esthetic end. You remember the pigs and forgot that. You are a distressing pair, you and Cranly.

Lynch made a grimace at the raw grey sky and said:

—If I am to listen to your esthetic philosophy give me at least another cigarette. I don't care about it. I don't even care about women. Damn you and damn everything. I want a job of five hundred a year. You can't get me one.

Stephen handed him the packet of cigarettes. Lynch took the last one that remained, saying simply:

—Proceed!

—Aquinas, said Stephen, says that is beautiful the apprehension of which pleases.

Lynch nodded.

—I remember that, he said. *Pulcra sunt quæ visa placent.*

—He uses the word *visa*, said Stephen, to cover esthetic apprehensions of all kinds, whether through sight or hearing or through any other avenue of apprehension. This word, though it is vague, is clear enough to keep away good and evil, which excite desire and loathing. It means certainly a stasis and not a kinesis. How about the true? It produces also a stasis of the mind. You would not write your name in pencil across the hypothenuse of a rightangled triangle.

—No, said Lynch, give me the hypothenuse of the Venus of Praxiteles.

—Static therefore, said Stephen. Plato, I believe, said that beauty is the splendour of truth.* I don't think that it has a meaning but the true and the beautiful are akin. Truth is beheld by the intellect which is ap-

---

*Although Plato makes assertions similar to this in both *Phaedrus* and *Symposium*, Joyce came upon the remark in one of Gustave Flaubert's letters.

peased by the most satisfying relations of the intelligible: beauty is beheld by the imagination which is appeased by the most satisfying relations of the sensible. The first step in the direction of truth is to understand the frame and scope of the intellect itself, to comprehend the act itself of intellection. Aristotle's entire system of philosophy rests upon his book of psychology and that, I think, rests on his statement that the same attribute cannot at the same time and in the same connexion belong to and not belong to the same subject. The first step in the direction of beauty is to understand the frame and scope of the imagination, to comprehend the act itself of esthetic apprehension. Is that clear?—

—But what is beauty? asked Lynch impatiently. Out with another definition. Something we see and like! Is that the best you and Aquinas can do?

—Let us take woman, said Stephen.

—Let us take her! said Lynch fervently.

—The Greek, the Turk, the Chinese, the Copt, the Hottentot, said Stephen, all admire a different type of female beauty. That seems to be a maze out of which we cannot escape. I see, however, two ways out. One is this hypothesis: that every physical quality admired by men in women is in direct connexion with the manifold functions of women for the propagation of the species. It may be so. The world, it seems, is drearier than even you, Lynch, imagined. For my part I dislike that way out. It leads to eugenics rather than to esthetic. It leads you out of the maze into a new gaudy lecture room were MacCann, with one hand on *The Origin of Species** and the other hand on the new testament, tells you that you admired the great flanks of Venus because you felt that she would bear you burly offspring and admired her great breasts because you felt that she would give good milk to her children and yours.

—Then MacCann is a sulphuryellow liar, said Lynch energetically.

—There remains another way out, said Stephen laughing.

—To wit? said Lynch.

—This hypothesis, Stephen began.

A long dray† laden with old iron came round the corner of sir Patrick Dun's hospital covering the end of Stephen's speech with the harsh roar of jangled and rattling metal. Lynch closed his ears and gave out oath after oath till the dray had passed. Then he turned on his heel

---

*Published in 1859 by Charles Darwin (1809–1882), the book establishes the concept of natural selection as the guiding factor in human evolution.

†Horse-drawn cart for hauling goods.

rudely. Stephen turned also and waited for a few moments till his companion's ill-humour had had its vent.

—This hypothesis, Stephen repeated, is the other way out: that, though the same object may not seem beautiful to all people, all people who admire a beautiful object find in it certain relations which satisfy and coincide with the stages themselves of all esthetic apprehension. These relations of the sensible, visible to you through one form and to me through another, must be therefore the necessary qualities of beauty. Now, we can return to our old friend saint Thomas for another pennyworth of wisdom.

Lynch laughed.

—It amuses me vastly, he said, to hear you quoting him time after time like a jolly round friar. Are you laughing in your sleeve?

—MacAlister, answered Stephen, would call my esthetic theory applied Aquinas. So far as this side of esthetic philosophy extends Aquinas will carry me all along the line. When we come to the phenomena of artistic conception, artistic gestation and artistic reproduction, I require a new terminology and a new personal experience.

—Of course, said Lynch. After all Aquinas, in spite of his intellect, was exactly a good round friar. But you will tell me about the new personal experience and new terminology some other day. Hurry up and finish the first part.

—Who knows? said Stephen, smiling. Perhaps Aquinas would understand me better than you. He was a poet himself. He wrote a hymn for Maundy Thursday. It begins with the words *Pange lingua gloriosi.** They say it is the highest glory of the hymnal. It is an intricate and soothing hymn. I like it: but there is no hymn that can be put beside that mournful and majestic processional song, the *Vexilla Regis*† of Venantius Fortunatus.

Lynch began to sing softly and solemnly in a deep bass voice:

> *Inpleta sunt quœ concinit*
> *David fideli carmine*
> *Dicendo nationibus*
> *Regnavit a lingo Deus.*‡

---

*Tell, my tongue, of the glory . . . (Latin).

†"The Banners of the King Advance" (Latin), by Italian poet Venantius Fortunatus (c.540–c.600).

‡Fulfilled is all that David told / In true prophetic song of old / Amidst the nations, God, saith he, / Hath reigned and triumphed from the Tree (Latin); this is the second stanza of "Vexilla Regis."

—That's great! he said, well pleased. Great music!

They turned into Lower Mount Street. A few steps from the corner a fat young man, wearing a silk neckcloth, saluted them and stopped.

—Did you hear the results of the exams? he asked. Griffin was plucked. Halpin and O'Flynn are through the home civil. Moonan got fifth place in the Indian. O'Shaughnessy got fourteenth. The Irish fellows in Clark's gave them a feed last night. They all ate curry.

His pallid bloated face expressed benevolent malice and, as he had advanced through his tidings of success, his small fat encircled eyes vanished out of sight and his weak wheezing voice out of hearing.

In reply to a question of Stephen's his eyes and his voice came forth again from their lurking places.

—Yes, MacCullagh and I, he said. He's taking pure mathematics and I'm taking constitutional history. There are twenty subjects. I'm taking botany too. You know I'm a member of the field club.

He drew back from the other two in a stately fashion and placed a plump woollen gloved hand on his breast, from which muttered wheezing laughter at once broke forth.

—Bring us a few turnips and onions the next time you go out, said Stephen drily, to make a stew.

The fat student laughed indulgently and said:

—We are all highly respectable people in the field club. Last Saturday we went out to Glenmalure,* seven of us.

—With women, Donovan? said Lynch.

Donovan again laid his hand on his chest and said:

—Our end is the acquisition of knowledge.

Then he said quickly:

—I hear you are writing some essay about esthetics.

Stephen made a vague gesture of denial.

—Goethe and Lessing,[18] said Donovan, have written a lot on that subject, the classical school and the romantic school and all that. The Laocoon interested me very much when I read it. Of course it is idealistic, German, ultra profound.

Neither of the others spoke. Donovan took leave of them urbanely.

—I must go, he said softly and benevolently. I have a strong suspicion, amounting almost to a conviction, that my sister intended to make pancakes today for the dinner of the Donovan family.

---

*Park south of Dublin.

—Goodbye, Stephen said in his wake. Don't forget the turnips for me and my mate.

Lynch gazed after him, his lip curling in slow scorn till his face resembled a devil's mask:

—To think that that yellow pancake eating excrement can get a good job, he said at length, and I have to smoke cheap cigarettes!

They turned their faces towards Merrion Square and went on for a little in silence.

—To finish what I was saying about beauty, said Stephen, the most satisfying relations of the sensible must therefore correspond to the necessary phases of artistic apprehension. Find these and you find the qualities of universal beauty. Aquinas says: *Ad pulcritudinem tria requiruntur integritas, consonantia, claritas*. I translate it so: *Three things are needed for beauty, wholeness, harmony and radiance*. Do these correspond to the phases of apprehension? Are you following?

—Of course, I am, said Lynch. If you think I have an excrementatious intelligence run after Donovan and ask him to listen to you.

Stephen pointed to a basket which a butcher's boy had slung inverted on his head.

—Look at that basket, he said.

—I see it, said Lynch.

—In order to see that basket, said Stephen, your mind first of all separates the basket from the rest of the visible universe which is not the basket. The first phase of apprehension is a bounding line drawn about the object to be apprehended. An esthetic image is presented to us either in space or in time. What is audible is presented in time, what is visible is presented in space. But temporal or spatial, the esthetic image is first luminously apprehended as selfbounded and selfcontained upon the immeasurable background of space or time which is not it. You apprehended it as *one* thing. You see it as one whole. You apprehend its wholeness. That is *integritas*.

—Bull's eye! said Lynch, laughing. Go on.

—Then, said Stephen, you pass from point to point, led by its formal lines; you apprehend it as balanced part against part within its limits; you feel the rhythm of its structure. In other words, the synthesis of immediate perception is followed by the analysis of apprehension. Having first felt that it is *one* thing you feel now that it is a *thing*. You apprehend it as complex, multiple, divisible, separable, made up of its parts, the result of its parts and their sum, harmonious. That is *consonantia*.

—Bull's eye again! said Lynch wittily. Tell me now what is *claritas* and you win the cigar.

—The connotation of the word, Stephen said, is rather vague. Aquinas uses a term which seems to be inexact. It baffled me for a long time. It would lead you to believe that he had in mind symbolism or idealism, the supreme quality of beauty being a light from some other world, the idea of which the matter was but the shadow, the reality of which it was but the symbol. I thought he might mean that *claritas* was the artistic discovery and representation of the divine purpose in anything or a force of generalization which would make the esthetic image a universal one, make it outshine its proper conditions. But that is literary talk. I understand it so. When you have apprehended that basket as one thing and have then analysed it according to its form and apprehended it as a thing you make the only synthesis which is logically and esthetically permissible. You see that it is that thing which it is and no other thing. The radiance of which he speaks is the scholastic *quidditas*, the *whatness* of a thing. This supreme quality is felt by the artist when the esthetic image is first conceived in his imagination. The mind in that mysterious instant Shelley likened beautifully to a fading coal.* The instant wherein that supreme quality of beauty, the clear radiance of the esthetic image, is apprehended luminously by the mind which has been arrested by its wholeness and fascinated by its harmony is the luminous silent stasis of esthetic pleasure, a spiritual state very like to that cardiac condition which the Italian physiologist Luigi Galvani, using a phrase almost as beautiful as Shelley's, called the enchantment of the heart.†

Stephen paused and, though his companion did not speak, felt that his words had called up around them a thought enchanted silence.

—What I have said, he began again, refers to beauty in the wider sense of the word, in the sense which the word has in the literary tradition. In the market place it has another sense. When we speak of beauty in the second sense of the term our judgment is influenced in the first place by the art itself and by the form of that art. The image, it is clear, must be set between the mind or senses of the artist himself and the mind or senses of others. If you bear this in memory you will see that art necessarily divides itself into three forms progressing from

---

*Allusion to Shelley's "A Defence of Poetry" (1821).
†Galvani (1737–1798) used the phrase to describe a physiological process witnessed during experimentation on frogs.

one to the next. These forms are: the lyrical form, the form wherein the artist presents his image in immediate relation to himself; the epical form, the form wherein he presents his image in mediate relation to himself and to others; the dramatic form, the form wherein he presents his image in immediate relation to others.

—That you told me a few nights ago, said Lynch, and we began the famous discussion.

—I have a book at home, said Stephen, in which I have written down questions which are more amusing than yours were. In finding the answers to them I found the theory of the esthetic which I am try-ing to explain. Here are some questions I set myself: *Is a chair finely made tragic or comic? Is the portrait of Mona Lisa good if I desire to see it? Is the bust of Sir Philip Crampton* lyrical, epical or dramatic? If not, why not?*

—Why not, indeed? said Lynch, laughing.

—*If a man hacking in fury at a block of wood,* Stephen continued, *make there an image of a cow, is that image a work of art? If not, why not?*

—That's a lovely one, said Lynch, laughing again. That has the true scholastic stink.

—Lessing, said Stephen, should not have taken a group of statues to write of. The art, being inferior, does not present the forms I spoke of distinguished clearly one from another. Even in literature, the highest and most spiritual art, the forms are often confused. The lyrical form is in fact the simplest verbal vesture of an instant of emotion, a rhythmi-cal cry such as ages ago cheered on the man who pulled at the oar or dragged stones up a slope. He who utters it is more conscious of the in-stant of emotion than of himself as feeling emotion. The simplest epi-cal form is seen emerging out of lyrical literature when the artist prolongs and broods upon himself as the centre of an epical event and this form progresses till the centre of emotional gravity is equidistant from the artist himself and from others. The narrative is no longer purely personal. The personality of the artist passes into the narration itself, flowing round and round the persons and the action like a vital sea. This progress you will see easily in that old English ballad *Turpin Hero,*† which begins in the first person and ends in the third person. The dramatic form is reached when the vitality which has flowed and

---

*(1777–1858); the notoriously ugly bust of this Dublin surgeon has since been re-moved.
†Street ballad from the early eighteenth century.

eddied round each person fills every person with such vital force that he or she assumes a proper and intangible esthetic life. The personality of the artist, at first a cry or a cadence or a mood and then a fluid and lambent narrative, finally refines itself out of existence, impersonalizes itself, so to speak. The esthetic image in the dramatic form is life purified in and reprojected from the human imagination. The mystery of esthetic like that of material creation is accomplished. The artist, like the God of the creation, remains within or behind or beyond or above his handiwork, invisible, refined out of existence, indifferent, paring his fingernails.

—Trying to refine them also out of existence, said Lynch.

A fine rain began to fall from the high veiled sky and they turned into the duke's lawn,* to reach the national library before the shower came.

—What do you mean, Lynch asked surlily, by prating about beauty and the imagination in this miserable God forsaken island? No wonder the artist retired within or behind his handiwork after having perpetrated this country.

The rain fell faster. When they passed through the passage beside the royal Irish academy† they found many students sheltering under the arcade of the library. Cranly, leaning against a pillar, was picking his teeth with a sharpened match, listening to some companions. Some girls stood near the entrance door. Lynch whispered to Stephen:

—Your beloved is here.

Stephen took his place silently on the step below the group of students, heedless of the rain which fell fast, turning his eyes towards her from time to time. She too stood silently among her companions. She has no priest to flirt with, he thought with conscious bitterness, remembering how he had seen her last. Lynch was right. His mind, emptied of theory and courage, lapsed back into a listless peace.

He heard the students talking among themselves. They spoke of two friends who had passed the final medical examination, of the chances of getting places on ocean liners, of poor and rich practices.

—That's all a bubble. An Irish country practice is better.

—Hynes was two years in Liverpool and he says the same. A frightful hole he said it was. Nothing but midwifery cases.

---

*Lawn beside the Duke of Leinster's house, in the same block as the National Library and the National Museum.
†Founded in 1785 to promote the study of letters and sciences.

—Do you mean to say it is better to have a job here in the country than in a rich city like that? I know a fellow . . .

—Hynes has no brains. He got through by stewing,* pure stewing.

—Don't mind him. There's plenty of money to be made in a big commercial city.

—Depends on the practice.

—*Ego credo ut vita pauperum est simpliciter atrox, simpliciter sanguinarius atrox, in Liverpoolio.*†

Their voices reached his ears as if from a distance in interrupted pulsation. She was preparing to go away with her companions.

The quick light shower had drawn off, tarrying in clusters of diamonds among the shrubs of the quadrangle where an exhalation was breathed forth by the blackened earth. Their trim boots prattled as they stood on the steps of the colonnade, talking quietly and gaily, glancing at the clouds, holding their umbrellas at cunning angles against the few last raindrops, closing them again, holding their skirts demurely.

And if he had judged her harshly? If her life were a simple rosary of hours, her life simple and strange as a bird's life, gay in the morning, restless all day, tired at sundown? Her heart simple and wilful as a bird's heart?

*   *   *   *

Towards dawn he awoke. O what sweet music! His soul was all dewy wet. Over his limbs in sleep pale cool waves of light had passed. He lay still, as if his soul lay amid cool waters, conscious of faint sweet music. His mind was waking slowly to a tremulous morning knowledge, a morning inspiration. A spirit filled him, pure as the purest water, sweet as dew, moving as music. But how faintly it was inbreathed, how passionlessly, as if the seraphim themselves were breathing upon him! His soul was waking slowly, fearing to awake wholly. It was that windless hour of dawn when madness wakes and strange plants open to the light and the moth flies forth silently.

An enchantment of the heart! The night had been enchanted. In a dream or vision he had known the ecstasy of seraphic life. Was it an instant of enchantment only or long hours and years and ages?

The instant of inspiration seemed now to be reflected from all sides

---

*Mindless labor; "cramming."

†I believe that the life of the poor is simply awful, simply bloody awful, in Liverpool (dog Latin).

at once from a multitude of cloudy circumstances of what had happened or of what might have happened. The instant flashed forth like a point of light and now from cloud on cloud of vague circumstance confused form was veiling softly its afterglow. O! In the virgin womb of the imagination the word was made flesh. Gabriel* the seraph† had come to the virgin's chamber. An afterglow deepened within his spirit, whence the white flame had passed, deepening to a rose and ardent light. That rose and ardent light was her strange wilful heart, strange that no man had known or would know, wilful from before the beginning of the world: and lured by that ardent roselike glow the choirs of the seraphim were falling from heaven.

> *Are you not weary of ardent ways,*
> *Lure of the fallen seraphim?*
> *Tell no more of enchanted days.*

The verses passed from his mind to his lips and, murmuring them over, he felt the rhythmic movement of a villanelle‡ pass through them. The roselike glow sent forth its rays of rhyme; ways, days, blaze, praise, raise. Its rays burned up the world, consumed the hearts of men and angels: the rays from the rose that was her wilful heart.

> *Your eyes have set man's heart ablaze*
> *And you have had your will of him.*
> *Are you not weary of ardent ways?*

And then? The rhythm died away, ceased, began again to move and beat. And then? Smoke, incense ascending from the altar of the world.

> *Above the flame the smoke of praise*
> *Goes up from ocean rim to rim*
> *Tell no more of enchanted days.*

Smoke went up from the whole earth, from the vapoury oceans, smoke of her praise. The earth was like a swinging swaying censer, a

---

*The archangel who will herald the Last Judgment; he announced to the Virgin Mary that she was pregnant with Jesus, conceived by the Holy Spirit (Luke 1:26–38).
†Member of the seraphim, the highest order of angels.
‡Poem usually comprising five tercets followed by a quatrain, based on two rhymes.

ball of incense, an ellipsoidal ball. The rhythm died out at once; the cry of his heart was broken. His lips began to murmur the first verses over and over; then went on stumbling through half verses, stammering and baffled; then stopped. The heart's cry was broken.

The veiled windless hour had passed and behind the panes of the naked window the morning light was gathering. A bell beat faintly very far away. A bird twittered; two birds, three. The bell and the bird ceased: and the dull white light spread itself east and west, covering the world, covering the roselight in his heart.

Fearing to lose all, he raised himself suddenly on his elbow to look for paper and pencil. There was neither on the table; only the soup plate he had eaten the rice from for supper and the candlestick with its tendrils of tallow and its paper socket, singed by the last flame. He stretched his arm wearily towards the foot of the bed, groping with his hand in the pockets of the coat that hung there. His fingers found a pencil and then a cigarette packet. He lay back and, tearing open the packet, placed the last cigarette on the window ledge and began to write out the stanzas of the villanelle in small neat letters on the rough cardboard surface.

Having written them out he lay back on the lumpy pillow, murmuring them again. The lumps of knotted flock under his head reminded him of the lumps of knotted horsehair in the sofa of her parlour on which he used to sit, smiling or serious, asking himself why he had come, displeased with her and with himself, confounded by the print of the Sacred Heart* above the untenanted sideboard. He saw her approach him in a lull of the talk and beg him to sing one of his curious songs. Then he saw himself sitting at the old piano, striking chords softly from its speckled keys and singing, amid the talk which had risen again in the room, to her who leaned beside the mantelpiece a dainty song of the Elizabethans, a sad and sweet loth to depart, the victory chant of Agincourt,† the happy air of Greensleeves. While he sang and she listened, or feigned to listen, his heart was at rest but when the quaint old songs had ended and he heard again the voices in the room he remembered his own sarcasm: the house where young men are called by their christian names a little too soon.

At certain instants her eyes seemed about to trust him but he had waited in vain. She passed now dancing lightly across his memory as

---

*Color illustration of Jesus, heart exposed, in token of His love for humankind.
†"Ballad of Agincourt" (1605), a poem by Michael Drayton that recalls English King Henry V's victory over the French in 1415.

she had been that night at the carnival ball, her white dress a little lifted, a white spray nodding in her hair. She danced lightly in the round. She was dancing towards him and, as she came, her eyes were a little averted and a faint glow was on her cheek. At the pause in the chain of hands her hand had lain in his an instant, a soft merchandise.

—You are a great stranger now.

—Yes. I was born to be a monk.

—I am afraid you are a heretic.

—Are you much afraid?

For answer she had danced away from him along the chain of hands, dancing lightly and discreetly, giving herself to none. The white spray nodded to her dancing and when she was in shadow the glow was deeper on her cheek.

A monk! His own image started forth a profaner of the cloister, a heretic Franciscan, willing and willing not to serve, spinning like Gherardino da Borgo San Donnino,* a lithe web of sophistry and whispering in her ear.

No, it was not his image. It was like the image of the young priest in whose company he had seen her last, looking at him out of dove's eyes, toying with the pages of her Irish phrasebook.

—Yes, yes, the ladies are coming round to us. I can see it every day. The ladies are with us. The best helpers the language has.

—And the church, Father Moran?

—The church too. Coming round too. The work is going ahead there too. Don't fret about the church.

Bah! he had done well to leave the room in disdain. He had done well not to salute her on the steps of the library. He had done well to leave her to flirt with her priest, to toy with a church which was the scullery-maid of christendom.

Rude brutal anger routed the last lingering instant of ecstasy from his soul. It broke up violently her fair image and flung the fragments on all sides. On all sides distorted reflections of her image started from his memory: the flower girl in the ragged dress with damp coarse hair and a hoyden's face who had called herself his own girl and begged his handsel, the kitchen-girl in the next house who sang over the clatter of her plates, with the drawl of a country singer, the first bars of *By Killarney's Lakes and Fells,*† a girl who had laughed gaily to see him stum-

---

*Imprisoned in the thirteenth century for heresy.
†Ballad by the popular Michael William Balfe (1808–1870).

ble when the iron grating in the footpath near Cork Hill had caught the broken sole of his shoe, a girl he had glanced at, attracted by her small ripe mouth as she passed out of Jacob's biscuit factory, who had cried to him over her shoulder:

—Do you like what you seen of me, straight hair and curly eyebrows?

And yet he felt that, however he might revile and mock her image, his anger was also a form of homage. He had left the classroom in disdain that was not wholly sincere, feeling that perhaps the secret of her race lay behind those dark eyes upon which her long lashes flung a quick shadow. He had told himself bitterly as he walked through the streets that she was a figure of the womanhood of her country, a batlike soul waking to the consciousness of itself in darkness and secrecy and loneliness, tarrying awhile, loveless and sinless, with her mild lover and leaving him to whisper of innocent transgressions in the latticed ear of a priest. His anger against her found vent in coarse railing at her paramour, whose name and voice and features offended his baffled pride: a priested peasant, with a brother a policeman in Dublin and a brother a potboy in Moycullen.* To him she would unveil her soul's shy nakedness, to one who was but schooled in the discharging of a formal rite rather than to him, a priest of the eternal imagination, transmuting the daily bread of experience into the radiant body of everliving life.

The radiant image of the eucharist united again in an instant his bitter and despairing thoughts, their cries arising unbroken in a hymn of thanksgiving.

> Our broken cries and mournful lays†
> Rise in one eucharistic hymn.
> Are you not weary of ardent ways?
> While sacrificing hands upraise
> The chalice flowing to the brim,
> Tell no more of enchanted days.

He spoke the verses aloud from the first lines till the music and rhythm suffused his mind, turning it to quiet indulgence; then copied them painfully to feel them the better by seeing them; then lay back on his bolster.

The full morning light had come. No sound was to be heard: but he

---

*Small village in County Galway.

†A lay is a simple narrative poem or song.

knew that all around him life was about to awaken in common noises, hoarse voices, sleepy prayers. Shrinking from that life he turned towards the wall, making a cowl of the blanket and staring at the great overblown scarlet flowers of the tattered wallpaper. He tried to warm his perishing joy in their scarlet glow, imaging a roseway from where he lay upwards to heaven all strewn with scarlet flowers. Weary! Weary! He too was weary of ardent ways.

A gradual warmth, a languorous weariness passed over him, descending along his spine from his closely cowled head. He felt it descend and, seeing himself as he lay, smiled. Soon he would sleep.

He had written verses for her again after ten years. Ten years before she had worn her shawl cowlwise about her head, sending sprays of her warm breath into the night air, tapping her foot upon the glassy road. It was the last tram; the lank brown horses knew it and shook their bells to the clear night in admonition. The conductor talked with the driver, both nodding often in the green light of the lamp. They stood on the steps of the tram, he on the upper, she on the lower. She came up to his step many times between their phrases and went down again and once or twice remained beside him forgetting to go down and then went down. Let be! Let be!

Ten years from that wisdom of children to his folly. If he sent her the verses? They would be read out at breakfast amid the tapping of eggshells. Folly indeed! Her brothers would laugh and try to wrest the page from each other with their strong hard fingers. The suave priest, her uncle, seated in his armchair would hold the page at arm's length, read it smiling and approve of the literary form.

No, no: that was folly. Even if he sent her the verses she would not show them to others. No, no: she could not.

He began to feel that he had wronged her. A sense of her innocence moved him almost to pity her, an innocence he had never understood till he had come to the knowledge of it through sin, an innocence which she too had not understood while she was innocent or before the strange humiliation of her nature had first come upon her. Then first her soul had begun to live as his soul had when he had first sinned: and a tender compassion filled his heart as he remembered her frail pallor and her eyes, humbled and saddened by the dark shame of womanhood.

While his soul had passed from ecstasy to languor where had she been? Might it be, in the mysterious ways of spiritual life, that her soul at those same moments had been conscious of his homage? It might be.

A glow of desire kindled again his soul and fired and fulfilled all his body. Conscious of his desire she was waking from odorous sleep, the temptress of his villanelle. Her eyes, dark and with a look of languor, were opening to his eyes. Her nakedness yielded to him, radiant, warm, odorous and lavish limbed, enfolded him like a shining cloud, enfolded him like water with a liquid life: and like a cloud of vapour or like waters circumfluent in space the liquid letters of speech, symbols of the element of mystery, flowed forth over his brain.

Are you not weary of ardent ways?
Lure of the fallen seraphim?
Tell no more of enchanted days.

Your eyes have set man's heart ablaze
And you have had your will of him.
Are you not weary of ardent ways?

Above the flame the smoke of praise
Goes up from ocean rim to rim.
Tell no more of enchanted days.

Our broken cries and mournful lays
Rise in one eucharistic hymn.
Are you not weary of ardent ways?

While sacrificing hands upraise
The chalice flowing to the brim.
Tell no more of enchanted days.

And still you hold our longing gaze
With languorous look and lavish limb!
Are you not weary of ardent ways?
Tell no more of enchanted days.

*   *   *   *

What birds were they? He stood on the steps of the library to look at them, leaning wearily on his ashplant.* They flew round and round the jutting shoulder of a house in Molesworth Street. The air of the late

---

*Walking stick.

March evening made clear their flight, their dark darting quivering bodies flying clearly against the sky as against a limp hung cloth of smoky tenuous blue.

He watched their flight; bird after bird: a dark flash, a swerve, a flutter of wings. He tried to count them before all their darting quivering bodies passed: Six, ten, eleven: and wondered were they odd or even in number. Twelve, thirteen: for two came wheeling down from the upper sky. They were flying high and low but ever round and round in straight and curving lines and ever flying from left to right, circling about a temple of air.

He listened to the cries: like the squeak of mice behind the wainscot: a shrill twofold note. But the notes were long and shrill and whirring, unlike the cry of vermin, falling a third or a fourth and trilled as the flying beaks clove the air. Their cry was shrill and clear and fine and falling like threads of silken light unwound from whirring spools.

The inhuman clamour soothed his ears in which his mother's sobs and reproaches murmured insistently and the dark frail quivering bodies wheeling and fluttering and swerving round an airy temple of the tenuous sky soothed his eyes which still saw the image of his mother's face.

Why was he gazing upwards from the steps of the porch, hearing their shrill twofold cry, watching their flight? For an augury* of good or evil? A phrase of Cornelius Agrippa† flew through his mind and then there flew hither an thither shapeless thoughts from Swedenborg‡ on the correspondence of birds to things of the intellect and of how the creatures of the air have their knowledge and know their times and seasons because they, unlike man, are in the order of their life and have not perverted that order by reason.

And for ages men had gazed upward as he was gazing at birds in flight. The colonnade above him made him think vaguely of an ancient temple and the ashplant on which he leaned wearily of the curved stick of an augur. A sense of fear of the unknown moved in the heart of his weariness, a fear of symbols and portents, of the hawklike man whose name he bore soaring out of his captivity on osier§ woven wings, of

---

*Omen.

†Heinrich Cornelius Agrippa von Nettesheim (1486–1535), German physician, philosopher, and occultist.

‡Emanuel Swedenborg (1688–1772), Swedish scientist and mystic.

§Flexible twigs used for wicker work.

Thoth,* the god of writers, writing with a reed upon a tablet and bearing on his narrow ibis head the cusped moon.

He smiled as he thought of the god's image, for it made him think of a bottle-nosed judge in a wig, putting commas into a document which he held at arm's length and he knew that he would not have remembered the god's name but that it was like an Irish oath. It was folly. But was it for this folly that he was about to leave for ever the house of prayer and prudence into which he had been born and the order of life out of which he had come?

They came back with shrill cries over the jutting shoulder of the house, flying darkly against the fading air. What birds were they? He thought that they must be swallows who had come back from the south. Then he was to go away? for they were birds ever going and coming, building ever an unlasting home under the eaves of men's houses and ever leaving the homes they had built to wander.

> *Bend down your faces, Oona and Aleel,*
> *I gaze upon them as the swallow gazes*
> *Upon the nest under the eave before*
> *He wander the loud waters.*†

A soft liquid joy like the noise of many waters flowed over his memory and he felt in his heart the soft peace of silent spaces of fading tenuous sky above the waters, of oceanic silence, of swallows flying through the seadusk over the flowing waters.

A soft liquid joy flowed through the words where the soft long vowels hurtled noiselessly and fell away, lapping and flowing back and ever shaking the white bells of their waves in mute chime and mute peal and soft low swooning cry; and he felt that the augury he had sought in the wheeling darting birds and in the pale space of sky above him had come forth from his heart like a bird from a turret quietly and swiftly.

Symbol of departure or of loneliness? The verses crooned in the ear of his memory composed slowly before his remembering eyes the scene of the hall on the night of the opening of the national theatre. He was

---

*Scribe of the Egyptian gods; depicted with the head of an ibis.

†From Irish writer W. B. Yeats's play *The Countess Cathleen,* which on May 8, 1899, opened the new national theater, the Irish Literary Theatre (which in 1904 became the Abbey Theatre); many in the audience thought the play was "anti-Irish," and a loud protest ensued.

alone at the side of the balcony, looking out of jaded eyes at the culture of Dublin in the stalls and at the tawdry scenecloths and human dolls framed by the garish lamps of the stage. A burly policeman sweated behind him and seemed at every moment about to act. The catcalls and hisses and mocking cries ran in rude gusts round the hall from his scattered fellow students.

—A libel on Ireland!

—Made in Germany!

—Blasphemy!

—We never sold our faith!

—No Irish woman ever did it!

—We want no amateur atheist.

—We want no budding buddhists.

A sudden swift hiss fell from the windows above him and he knew that the electric lamps had been switched on in the reader's room. He turned into the pillared hall, now calmly lit, went up the staircase and passed in through the clicking turnstile.

Cranly was sitting over near the dictionaries. A thick book, opened at the frontispiece, lay before him on the wooden rest. He leaned back in his chair, inclining his ear like that of a confessor to the face of the medical student who was reading to him a problem from the chess page of a journal. Stephen sat down at his right and the priest at the other side of the table closed his copy of *The Tablet** with an angry snap and stood up.

Cranly gazed after him blandly and vaguely. The medical student went on in a softer voice:

—Pawn to king's fourth.

—We had better go, Dixon, said Stephen in warning. He has gone to complain.

Dixon folded the journal and rose with dignity, saying:

—Our men retired in good order.

—With guns and cattle, added Stephen, pointing to the titlepage of Cranly's book on which was written *Diseases of the Ox.*

As they passed through a lane of the tables Stephen said:

—Cranly, I want to speak to you.

Cranly did not answer or turn. He laid his book on the counter and passed out, his well shod feet sounding flatly on the floor. On the staircase he paused and gazing absently at Dixon repeated:

---

*Conservative Catholic paper.

—Pawn to king's bloody fourth.

—Put it that way if you like, Dixon said.

He had a quiet toneless voice and urbane manners and on a finger of his plump clean hand he displayed at moments a signet ring.

As they crossed the hall a man of dwarfish stature came towards them. Under the dome of his tiny hat his unshaven face began to smile with pleasure and he was heard to murmur. The eyes were melancholy as those of a monkey.

—Good evening, gentlemen, said the stubble grown monkeyish face.

—Warm weather for March, said Cranly. They have the windows open upstairs.

Dixon smiled and turned his ring. The blackish monkey puckered face pursed its human mouth with gentle pleasure and its voice purred:

—Delightful weather for March. Simply delightful.

—There are two nice young ladies upstairs, captain, tired of waiting, Dixon said.

Cranly smiled and said kindly:

—The captain has only one love: sir Walter Scott. Isn't that so, captain?

—What are you reading now, captain? Dixon asked. *The Bride of Lammermoor?**

—I love old Scott, the flexible lips said. I think he writes something lovely. There is no writer can touch sir Walter Scott.

He moved a thin shrunken brown hand gently in the air in time to his praise and his thin quick eyelids beat often over his sad eyes.

Sadder to Stephen's ear was his speech: a genteel accent, low and moist, marred by errors: and, listening to it, he wondered was the story true and was the thin blood that flowed in his shrunken frame noble and come of an incestuous love?

The park trees were heavy with rain and rain fell still and ever in the lake, lying grey like a shield. A game of swans flew there and the water and the shore beneath were fouled with their greenwhite slime. They embraced softly, impelled by the grey rainy light, the wet silent trees, the shieldlike witnessing lake, the swans. They embraced without joy or passion, his arm about his sister's neck. A grey woollen cloak was wrapped athwart her from her shoulder to her waist: and her fair head

---

*1819; one of Sir Walter Scott's immensely popular novels.

was bent in willing shame. He had loose redbrown hair and tender shapely strong freckled hands. Face? There was no face seen. The brother's face was bent upon her fair rain fragrant hair. The hand freckled and strong and shapely and caressing was Davin's hand.

He frowned angrily upon his thought and on the shrivelled mannikin* who had called it forth. His father's gibes at the Bantry gang† leaped out of his memory. He held them at a distance and brooded uneasily on his own thought again. Why were they not Cranly's hands? Had Davin's simplicity and innocence stung him more secretly?

He walked on across the hall with Dixon, leaving Cranly to take leave elaborately of the dwarf.

Under the colonnade Temple was standing in the midst of a little group of students. One of them cried:

—Dixon, come over till you hear. Temple is in grand form.

Temple turned on him his dark gipsy eyes.

—You're a hypocrite, O'Keeffe, he said. And Dixon is a smiler. By hell, I think that's a good literary expression.

He laughed slily, looking in Stephen's face, repeating:

—By hell, I'm delighted with that name. A smiler.

A stout student who stood below them on the steps said:

—Come back to the mistress, Temple. We want to hear about that.

—He had, faith, Temple said. And he was a married man too. And all the priests used to be dining there. By hell, I think they all had a touch.‡

—We shall call it riding a hack§ to spare the hunter, said Dixon.

—Tell us, Temple, O'Keeffe said, how many quarts of porter have you in you?

—All your intellectual soul is in that phrase, O'Keeffe, said Temple with open scorn.

He moved with a shambling gait round the group and spoke to Stephen.

—Did you know that the Forsters are the kings of Belgium?‖ he asked.

---

*Little man.
†Anti-Parnellite politicians from Bantry, in the southwest of Ireland.
‡That is, sexual intercourse.
§Common, working horse.
‖King Leopold I of Belgium (1790–1865) was not descended from the House of Flanders.

Cranly came out through the door of the entrance hall, his hat thrust back on the nape of his neck and picking his teeth with care.

—And here's the wiseacre, said Temple. Do you know that about the Forsters?

He paused for an answer. Cranly dislodged a fig seed from his teeth on the point of his rude toothpick and gazed at it intently.

—The Forster family, Temple said, is descended from Baldwin the First, king of Flanders. He was called the Forester. Forester and Forster are the same name. A descendant of Baldwin the First, captain Francis Forster, settled in Ireland and married the daughter of the last chieftain of Clanbrassil. Then there are the Blake Forsters.[19] That's a different branch.

—From Baldhead, king of Flanders, Cranly repeated, rooting again deliberately at his gleaming uncovered teeth.

—Where did you pick up all that history? O'Keeffe asked.

—I know all the history of your family too, Temple said, turning to Stephen. Do you know what Giraldus Cambrensis* says about your family?

—Is he descended from Baldwin too? asked a tall consumptive student with dark eyes.

—Baldhead, Cranly repeated, sucking at a crevice in his teeth.

—*Pernobilis et pervetusta familia,*[†] Temple said to Stephen.

The stout student who stood below them on the steps farted briefly. Dixon turned towards him saying in a soft voice:

—Did an angel speak?

Cranly turned also and said vehemently but without anger:

—Goggins, you're the flamingest dirty devil I ever met, do you know.

—I had it on my mind to say that, Goggins answered firmly. It did no one any harm, did it?

—We hope, Dixon said suavely, that it was not of the kind known to science as a *paulo post futurum.*[‡]

—Didn't I tell you he was a smiler? said Temple, turning right and left. Didn't I give him that name?

—You did. We're not deaf, said the tall consumptive.

---

*Gerald of Wales (c.1146–c.1223); Norman-Welsh author of the earliest accounts of Ireland by a foreigner.

†A noble and distinguished family (Latin).

‡State resulting from a future act (Latin)

Cranly still frowned at the stout student below him. Then, with a snort of disgust, he shoved him violently down the steps.

—Go away from here, he said rudely. Go away you stinkpot. And you are a stinkpot.

Goggins skipped down on to the gravel and at once returned to his place with good humour. Temple turned back to Stephen and asked:

—Do you believe in the law of heredity?

—Are you drunk or what are you or what are you trying to say? asked Cranly, facing round on him with an expression of wonder.

—The most profound sentence ever written, Temple said with enthusiasm, is the sentence at the end of the zoology. Reproduction is the beginning of death.

He touched Stephen timidly at the elbow and said eagerly:

—Do you feel how profound that is because you are a poet?

Cranly pointed his long forefinger.

—Look at him! he said with scorn to the other. Look at Ireland's hope!

They laughed at his words and gesture. Temple turned on him bravely, saying:

—Cranly, you're always sneering at me. I can see that. But I am as good as you any day. Do you know what I think about you now as compared with myself?

—My dear man, said Cranly urbanely, you are incapable, do you know, absolutely incapable of thinking.

—But do you know, Temple went on, what I think of you and of myself compared together?

—Out with it, Temple! the stout student cried from the steps. Get it out in bits!

Temple turned right and left, making sudden feeble gestures as he spoke.

—I'm a ballocks,* he said, shaking his head in despair. I am and I know I am. And I admit it that I am.

Dixon patted him lightly on the shoulder and said mildly:

—And it does you every credit, Temple.

—But he, Temple said, pointing to Cranly, he is a ballocks, too, like me. Only he doesn't know it. And that's the only difference, I see.

A burst of laughter covered his words. But he turned again to Stephen and said with a sudden eagerness:

---

*Testicle.

—That word is a most interesting word. That's the only English dual number.* Did you know?

—Is it? Stephen said vaguely.

He was watching Cranly's firm featured suffering face, lit up now by a smile of false patience. The gross name had passed over it like foul water poured over an old stone image, patient of injuries: and, as he watched him, he saw him raise his hat in salute and uncover the black hair that stood up stiffly from his forehead like an iron crown.

She passed out from the porch of the library and bowed across Stephen in reply to Cranly's greeting. He also? Was there not a slight flush on Cranly's cheek? Or had it come forth at Temple's words? The light had waned. He could not see.

Did that explain his friend's listless silence, his harsh comments, the sudden intrusions of rude speech with which he had shattered so often Stephen's ardent wayward confessions? Stephen had forgiven freely for he had found this rudeness also in himself. And he remembered an evening when he had dismounted from a borrowed creaking bicycle to pray to God in a wood near Malahide. He had lifted up his arms and spoken in ecstasy to the sombre nave of the trees, knowing that he stood on holy ground and in a holy hour. And when two constabulary men had come into sight round a bend in the gloomy road he had broken off his prayer to whistle loudly an air from the last pantomime.

He began to beat the frayed end of his ashplant against the base of a pillar. Had Cranly not heard him? Yet he could wait. The talk about him ceased for a moment: and a soft hiss fell again from a window above. But no other sound was in the air and the swallows whose flight had followed with idle eyes were sleeping.

She had passed through the dusk. And therefore the air was silent save for one soft hiss that fell. And therefore the tongues about him had ceased their babble. Darkness was falling.

Darkness falls from the air.†

A trembling joy, lambent as a faint light, played like a fairy host around him. But why? Her passage through the darkening air or the verse with its black vowels and its opening sound, rich and lutelike?

---

*Special grammatical form of the plural, denoting just two or a pair.
†As Stephen later realizes, the line is actually "Brightness falls from the air"; it is from a song from Thomas Nashe's *Summer's Last Will and Testament* (1600).

He walked away slowly towards the deeper shadows at the end of the colonnade, beating the stone softly with his stick to hide his revery from the students whom he had left: and allowed his mind to summon back to itself the age of Dowland and Byrd and Nash.*

Eyes, opening from the darkness of desire, eyes that dimmed the breaking east. What was their languid grace but the softness of chambering? And what was their shimmer but the shimmer of the scum that mantled the cesspool of the court of a slobbering Stuart.† And he tasted in the language of memory ambered wines, dying fallings of sweet airs, the proud pavan:‡ and saw with the eyes of memory kind gentlewomen in Covent Garden wooing from their balconies with sucking mouths and the pox fouled§ wenches of the taverns and young wives that, gaily yielding to their ravishers, clipped and clipped again.

The images he had summoned gave him no pleasure. They were secret and enflaming but her image was not entangled by them. That was not the way to think of her. It was not even the way in which he thought of her. Could his mind then not trust itself? Old phrases, sweet only with a disinterred sweetness like the fig seeds Cranly rooted out of his gleaming teeth.

It was not thought nor vision, though he knew vaguely that her figure was passing homeward through the city. Vaguely first and then more sharply he smelt her body. A conscious unrest seethed in his blood. Yes, it was her body he smelt: a wild and languid smell: the tepid limbs over which his music had flowed desirously and the secret soft linen upon which her flesh distilled odour and a dew.

A louse crawled over the nape of his neck and, putting his thumb and forefinger deftly beneath his loose collar, he caught it. He rolled its body, tender yet brittle as a grain of rice, between thumb and finger for an instant before he let it fall from him and wondered would it live or die. There came to his mind a curious phrase from Cornelius a Lapide‖ which said that the lice born of human sweat were not created by God with the other animals on the sixth day. But the tickling of the skin of

---

*John Dowland (1563?–1626) was an English lutist; William Byrd (1543–1623), a composer of church music and madrigals; Thomas Nashe (1567–1601), an English poet.

†The reference is probably to James I, who took the throne in 1603.

‡Stately dance music.

§Infected with venereal disease.

‖(1567–1637); Jesuit author who maintained that some "creeping things"—like flies, maggots, and lice—were not created by God.

his neck made his mind raw and red. The life of his body, ill clad, ill fed, louse eaten, made him close his eyelids in a sudden spasm of despair: and in the darkness he saw the brittle bright bodies of lice falling from the air and turning often as they fell. Yes; and it was not darkness that fell from the air. It was brightness.

Brightness falls from the air.

He had not even remembered rightly Nash's line. All the images it had awakened were false. His mind bred vermin. His thoughts were lice born of the sweat of sloth.

He came back quickly along the colonnade towards the group of students. Well then let her go and be damned to her! She could love some clean athlete who washed himself every morning to the waist and had black hair on his chest. Let her.

Cranly had taken another dried fig from the supply in his pocket and was eating it slowly and noisily. Temple sat on the pediment of a pillar, leaning back, his cap pulled down on his sleepy eyes. A squat young man came out of the porch, a leather portfolio tucked under his armpit. He marched towards the group, striking the flags* with the ferrule† of his heavy umbrella. Then, raising the umbrella in salute, he said to all:

—Good evening, sirs.

He struck the flags again and tittered while his head trembled with a slight nervous movement. The tall consumptive student and Dixon and O'Keeffe were speaking in Irish and did not answer him. Then, turning to Cranly, he said:

—Good evening, particularly to you.

He moved the umbrella in indication and tittered again. Cranly, who was still chewing the fig, answered with loud movements of his jaws.

—Good? Yes. It is a good evening.

The squat student looked at him seriously and shook his umbrella gently and reprovingly.

—I can see, he said, that you are about to make obvious remarks.

—Um, Cranly answered, holding out what remained of the half chewed fig and jerking it towards the squat student's mouth in sign that he should eat.

---

*Flagstones.
†Metal tip.

The squat student did not eat it but, indulging his special humour, said gravely, still tittering and prodding his phrase with his umbrella:

—Do you intend that . . .

He broke off, pointed bluntly to the munched pulp of the fig and said loudly:

—I allude to that.

—Um, Cranly said as before.

—Do you intend that now, the squat student said, as *ipso facto* or, let us say, as so to speak?

Dixon turned aside from his group, saying:

—Goggins was waiting for you, Glynn. He has gone round to the Adelphi* to look for you and Moynihan. What have you there? he asked, tapping the portfolio under Glynn's arm.

—Examination papers, Glynn answered. I give them monthly examinations to see that they are profiting by my tuition.

He also tapped the portfolio and coughed gently and smiled.

—Tuition! said Cranly rudely. I suppose you mean the barefooted children that are taught by a bloody ape like you. God help them!

He bit off the rest of the fig and flung away the butt.

—I suffer little children to come unto me,[†] Glynn said amiably.

—A bloody ape, Cranly repeated with emphasis, and a blasphemous bloody ape!

Temple stood up and, pushing past Cranly addressed Glynn:

—That phrase you said now, he said, is from the new testament about suffer the children to come to me.

—Go to sleep again, Temple, said O'Keeffe.

—Very well, then, Temple continued, still addressing Glynn, and if Jesus suffered the children to come why does the church send them all to hell if they die unbaptised?[‡] Why is that?

—Were you baptised yourself, Temple? the consumptive student asked.

—But why are they sent to hell if Jesus said they were all to come? Temple said, his eyes searching Glynn's eyes.

Glynn coughed and said gently, holding back with difficulty the nervous titter in his voice and moving his umbrella at every word:

---

*Hotel near St. Stephen's Green.
†Allusion to Mark 10:14.
‡In Catholic teaching, unbaptized children go to limbo, not hell.

—And, as you remark, if it is thus I ask emphatically whence comes this thusness.

—Because the church is cruel like all old sinners, Temple said.

—Are you quite orthodox on that point, Temple? Dixon said suavely.

—Saint Augustine says that about unbaptised children going to hell, Temple answered, because he was a cruel old sinner too.

—I bow to you, Dixon said, but I had the impression that limbo* existed for such cases.

—Don't argue with him, Dixon, Cranly said brutally. Don't talk to him or look at him. Lead him home with a sugan† the way you'd lead a bleating goat.

—Limbo! Temple cried. That's a fine invention too. Like hell.

—But with the unpleasantness left out, Dixon said.

He turned smiling to the others and said:

—I think I am voicing the opinions of all present in saying so much.

—You are, Glynn said in a firm tone. On that point Ireland is united.

He struck the ferrule of his umbrella on the stone floor of the colonnade.

—Hell, Temple said. I can respect that invention of the grey spouse of Satan.‡ Hell is Roman, like the walls of the Romans, strong and ugly. But what is limbo?

—Put him back into the perambulator,§ Cranly, O'Keeffe called out.

Cranly made a swift step towards Temple, halted, stamping his foot, crying as if to a fowl:

—Hoosh!

Temple moved away nimbly.

—Do you know what limbo is? he cried. Do you know what we call a notion like that in Roscommon?‖

—Hoosh! Blast you! Cranly cried, clapping his hands.

—Neither my arse nor my elbow! Temple cried out scornfully. And that's what I call limbo.

---

*Region bordering on hell set aside for unbaptized children and the righteous who died before the coming of Christ.
†Straw rope.
‡That is, Sin.
§Baby stroller.
‖County in central Ireland.

—Give us that stick here, Cranly said.

He snatched the ashplant roughly from Stephen's hand and sprang down the steps: but Temple, hearing him move in pursuit, fled through the dusk like a wild creature, nimble and fleet footed. Cranly's heavy boots were heard loudly charging across the quadrangle and then returning heavily, foiled and spurning the gravel at each step.

His step was angry and with an angry abrupt gesture he thrust the stick back into Stephen's hand. Stephen felt that his anger had another cause, but feigning patience, touched his arm slightly and said quietly:

—Cranly, I told you I wanted to speak to you. Come away.

Cranly looked at him for a few moments and asked:

—Now?

—Yes, now, Stephen said. We can't speak here. Come away.

They crossed the quadrangle together without speaking. The bird call from Siegfried* whistled softly followed them from the steps of the porch. Cranly turned: and Dixon, who had whistled, called out:

—Where are you fellows off to? What about that game, Cranly?

They parleyed in shouts across the still air about a game of billiards to be played in the Adelphi hotel. Stephen walked on alone and out into the quiet of Kildare Street opposite Maple's hotel he stood to wait, patient again. The name of the hotel, a colourless polished wood, and its colourless front stung him like a glance of polite disdain. He stared angrily back at the softly lit drawingroom of the hotel in which he imagined the sleek lives of the patricians of Ireland housed in calm. They thought of army commissions and land agents:† peasants greeted them along the roads in the country: they knew the names of certain French dishes and gave orders to jarvies‡ in highpitched provincial voices which pierced through their skintight accents.

How could he hit their conscience or how cast his shadow over the imaginations of their daughters, before their squires begat upon them, that they might breed a race less ignoble than their own? And under the deepened dusk he felt the thoughts and desires of the race to which he belonged flitting like bats, across the dark country lanes, under trees by the edges of streams and near the pool mottled bogs. A woman had waited in the doorway as Davin had passed by at night and, offering him a cup of milk, had all but wooed him to her bed: for Davin had the

---

*Opening motif in Richard Wagner's opera *Siegfried* (1871).
†Those who manage rental properties for absentee landlords.
‡Hackney cab drivers.

mild eyes of one who could be secret. But him no woman's eyes had wooed.

His arm was taken in a strong grip and Cranly's voice said:

—Let us eke go.

They walked southward in silence. Then Cranly said:

—That blithering idiot, Temple! I swear to Moses, do you know, that I'll be the death of that fellow one time.

But his voice was no longer angry and Stephen wondered was he thinking of her greeting to him under the porch.

They turned to the left and walked on as before. When they had gone on so far for some time Stephen said:

—Cranly, I had an unpleasant quarrel this evening.

—With your people? Cranly asked.

—With my mother.

—About religion?

—Yes, Stephen answered.

After a pause Cranly asked:

—What age is your mother?

—Not old, Stephen said. She wishes me to make my easter duty.*

—And will you?

—I will not, Stephen said.

—Why not? Cranly said.

—I will not serve, answered Stephen.

—That remark was made before, Cranly said calmly.

—It is made behind now, said Stephen hotly.

Cranly pressed Stephen's arm, saying:

—Go easy, my dear man. You're an excitable bloody man, do you know.

He laughed nervously as he spoke and, looking up into Stephen's face with moved and friendly eyes, said:

—Do you know that you are an excitable man?

—I daresay I am, said Stephen, laughing also.

Their minds, lately estranged, seemed suddenly to have been drawn closer, one to the other.

—Do you believe in the eucharist? Cranly asked.

—I do not, Stephen said.

—Do you disbelieve then?

—I neither believe in it nor disbelieve in it, Stephen answered.

---

*To make one's confession and receive communion during the Easter season.

—Many persons have doubts, even religious persons, yet they overcome them or put them aside, Cranly said. Are your doubts on that point too strong?

—I do not wish to overcome them, Stephen answered.

Cranly, embarrassed for a moment, took another fig from his pocket and was about to eat it when Stephen said:

—Don't, please. You cannot discuss this question with your mouth full of chewed fig.

Cranly examined the fig by the light of a lamp under which he halted. Then he smelt it with both nostrils, bit a tiny piece, spat it out and threw the fig rudely into the gutter. Addressing it as it lay, he said:

—Depart from me, ye cursed, into everlasting fire!*

Taking Stephen's arm, he went on again and said:

—Do you not fear that those words may be spoken to you on the day of judgment?

—What is offered me on the other hand? Stephen asked. An eternity of bliss in the company of the dean of studies?

—Remember, Cranly said, that he would be glorified.

—Ay, Stephen said somewhat bitterly, bright agile, impassible and, above all, subtle.

—It is a curious thing, do you know, Cranly said dispassionately, how your mind is supersaturated with the religion in which you say you disbelieve. Did you believe in it when you were at school? I bet you did.

—I did, Stephen answered.

— And were you happier then? Cranly asked softly. Happier than you are now, for instance!

—Often happy, Stephen said, and often unhappy. I was someone else then.

—How someone else? What do you mean by that statement?

—I mean, said Stephen, that I was not myself as I am now, as I had to become.

—Not as you are now, not as you had to become, Cranly repeated. Let me ask you a question. Do you love your mother?

Stephen shook his head slowly.

—I don't know what your words mean, he said simply.

—Have you never loved anyone? Cranly asked.

—Do you mean women?

---

*Matthew 25:41 (Douay version).

—I am not speaking of that, Cranly said in a colder tone. I ask you if you ever felt love towards anyone or anything.

Stephen walked on beside his friend, staring gloomily at the footpath.

—I tried to love God, he said at length. It seems now I failed. It is very difficult. I tried to unite my will with the will of God instant by instant. In that I did not always fail. I could perhaps do that still . . .

Cranly cut him short by asking:

—Has your mother had a happy life?

—How do I know? Stephen said.

—How many children had she?

—Nine or ten, Stephen answered. Some died.

—Was your father. . . . Cranly interrupted himself for an instant: and then said: I don't want to pry into your family affairs. But was your father what is called well-to-do? I mean when you were growing up?

—Yes, Stephen said.

—What was he? Cranly asked after a pause.

Stephen began to enumerate glibly his father's attributes.

—A medical student, an oarsman, a tenor, an amateur actor, a shouting politician, a small landlord, a small investor, a drinker, a good fellow, a storyteller, somebody's secretary, something in a distillery, a taxgatherer, a bankrupt and at present a praiser of his own past.

Cranly laughed, tightening his grip on Stephen's arm, and said:

—The distillery is damn good.

—Is there anything else you want to know? Stephen asked.

—Are you in good circumstances at present?

—Do I look it? Stephen asked bluntly.

—So then, Cranly went on musingly, you were born in the lap of luxury.

He used the phrase broadly and loudly as he often used technical expressions as if he wished his hearer to understand that they were used by him without conviction.

—Your mother must have gone through a good deal of suffering, he said then. Would you not try to save her from suffering more even if . . . or would you?

—If I could, Stephen said, that would cost me very little.

—Then do so, Cranly said. Do as she wishes you to do. What is it for you? You disbelieve in it. It is a form: nothing else. And you will set her mind at rest.

He ceased and, as Stephen did not reply, remained silent. Then, as if giving utterance to the process of his own thought, he said:

—Whatever else is unsure in this stinking dunghill of a world a mother's love is not. Your mother brings you into the world, carries you first in her body. What do we know about what she feels? But whatever she feels, it, at least, must be real. It must be. What are our ideas or ambitions? Play. Ideas! Why, that bloody bleating goat Temple has ideas. MacCann has ideas too. Every jackass going the roads thinks he has ideas.

Stephen, who had been listening to the unspoken speech behind the words, said with assumed carelessness:

—Pascal,* if I remember rightly, would not suffer his mother to kiss him as he feared the contact of her sex.

—Pascal was a pig, said Cranly.

—Aloysius Gonzaga,† I think, was of the same mind, Stephen said.

—And he was another pig then, said Cranly.

—The church calls him a saint, Stephen objected.

—I don't care a flaming damn what anyone calls him, Cranly said rudely and flatly. I call him a pig.

Stephen, preparing the words neatly in his mind, continued:

—Jesus, too, seems to have treated his mother with scant courtesy in public but Suarez,20 a jesuit theologian and Spanish gentleman, has apologised for him.

—Did the idea ever occur to you, Cranly asked, that Jesus was not what he pretended to be?

—The first person to whom that idea occurred, Stephen answered, was Jesus himself.

—I mean, Cranly said, hardening in his speech, did the idea ever occur to you that he was himself a conscious hypocrite, what he called the jews of his time, a white sepulchre?‡ Or, to put it more plainly, that he was a blackguard?§

—That idea never occurred to me, Stephen answered. But I am curious to know are you trying to make a convert of me or a pervert of yourself?

---

*Blaise Pascal (1623–1662), French mathematician and philosopher.
†(1568–1591); Italian Jesuit.
‡Jesus said (Matthew 23:27): "Woe to you, scribes and Pharisees, hypocrites; because you are like to whited sepulchres, which outwardly appear to men beautiful but within are full of dead men's bones and of all filthiness" (Douay version).
§Scoundrel.

He turned towards his friend's face and saw there a raw smile which some force of will strove to make finely significant.

Cranly asked suddenly in a plain sensible tone:—Tell me the truth. Were you at all shocked by what I said?

—Somewhat, Stephen said.

—And why were you shocked, Cranly pressed on in the same tone, if you feel sure that our religion is false and that Jesus was not the son of God?

—I am not at all sure of it, Stephen said. He is more like a son of God than a son of Mary.

—And is that why you will not communicate,* Cranly asked, because you are not sure of that too, because you feel that the host, too, may be the body and blood of the son of God and not a wafer of bread. And because you fear that it may be?

—Yes, Stephen said quietly, I feel that and I also fear it.

—I see, Cranly said.

Stephen, struck by his tone of closure, reopened the discussion at once by saying:

—I fear many things: dogs, horses, firearms, the sea, thunderstorms, machinery, the country roads at night.

—But why do you fear a bit of bread?

—I imagine, Stephen said, that there is a malevolent reality behind those things I say I fear.

—Do you fear then, Cranly asked, that the God of the Roman catholics would strike you dead and damn you if you made a sacrilegious communion?

—The God of the Roman catholics could do that now, Stephen said. I fear more than that the chemical action which would be set up in my soul by a false homage to a symbol behind which are massed twenty centuries of authority and veneration.

—Would you, Cranly asked, in extreme danger commit that particular sacrilege? For instance, if you lived in the penal days?†

—I cannot answer for the past, Stephen replied. Possibly not.

—Then, said Cranly, you do not intend to become a protestant?

—I said that I had lost the faith, Stephen answered, but not that I had lost selfrespect. What kind of liberation would that be to forsake

---

*Partake of the Eucharist.

†Late-sixteenth- and seventeenth-century period when the practice of Roman Catholicism was strictly proscribed in Ireland.

an absurdity which is logical and coherent and to embrace one which is illogical and incoherent?

They had walked on towards the township of Pembroke* and now, as they went on slowly along the avenues, the trees and the scattered lights in the villas soothed their minds. The air of wealth and repose diffused about them seemed to comfort their neediness. Behind a hedge of laurel a light glimmered in the window of a kitchen and the voice of a servant was heard singing as she sharpened knives. She sang, in short broken bars,

> *Rosie O'Grady.*†

Cranly stopped to listen, saying:

—*Mulier cantat.*‡

The soft beauty of the Latin word touched with an enchanting touch the dark of the evening, with a touch fainter and more persuading than the touch of music or of a woman's hand. The strife of their minds was quelled. The figure of woman as she appears in the liturgy of the church passed silently through the darkness: a white robed figure, small and slender as a boy, and with a falling girdle. Her voice, frail and high as a boy's, was heard intoning from a distant choir the first words of a woman which pierce the gloom and clamour of the first chanting of the passion:§

—*Et tu cum Jesu Galilæo eras.*[21]

And all hearts were touched and turned to her voice, shining like a young star, shining clearer as the voice intoned the proparoxyton‖ and more faintly as the cadence died.

The singing ceased. They went on together, Cranly repeating in strongly stressed rhythm the end of the refrain:

> *And when we are married,*
> *O, how happy we'll be*
> *For I love sweet Rosie O'Grady*
> *And Rosie O'Grady loves me.*

—There's real poetry for you, he said. There's real love.

---

*District in southeast Dublin.
†Popular song.
‡A woman is singing (Latin).
§The sufferings of Jesus, culminating in His crucifixion.
‖Word accented on the second from last syllable.

He glanced sideways at Stephen with a strange smile and said:

—Do you consider that poetry? Or do you know what the words mean?

—I want to see Rosie first, said Stephen.

—She's easy to find, Cranly said.

His hat had come down on his forehead. He shoved it back: and in the shadow of the trees Stephen saw his pale face, framed by the dark, and his large dark eyes. Yes. His face was handsome: and his body was strong and hard. He had spoken of a mother's love. He felt then the sufferings of women, the weaknesses of their bodies and souls: and would shield them with a strong and resolute arm and bow his mind to them.

Away then: it is time to go. A voice spoke softly to Stephen's lonely heart, bidding him go and telling him that his friendship was coming to an end. Yes; he would go. He could not strive against another. He knew his part.

—Probably I shall go away, he said.

—Where? Cranly asked.

—Where I can, Stephen said.

—Yes, Cranly said. It might be difficult for you to live here now. But is it that makes you go?

—I have to go, Stephen answered.

—Because, Cranly continued, you need not look upon yourself as driven away if you do not wish to go or as a heretic or an outlaw. There are many good believers who think as you do. Would that surprise you? The church is not the stone building nor even the clergy and their dogmas. It is the whole mass of those born into it. I don't know what you wish to do in life. Is it what you told me the night we were standing outside Harcourt Street station?

—Yes, Stephen said, smiling in spite of himself at Cranly's way of remembering thoughts in connexion with places. The night you spent half an hour wrangling with Doherty about the shortest way from Sallygap to Larras.*

—Pothead! Cranly said with calm contempt. What does he know about the way from Sallygap to Larras? Or what does he know about anything for that matter? And the big slobbering washingpot head of him!

He broke out into a loud long laugh.

---

*A distance of 9 miles through the Dublin mountains, south of the city.

—Well? Stephen said. Do you remember the rest?

—What you said, is it? Cranly asked. Yes, I remember it. To discover the mode of life or of art whereby your spirit could express itself in unfettered freedom.

Stephen raised his hat in acknowledgment.

—Freedom! Cranly repeated. But you are not free enough yet to commit a sacrilege. Tell me would you rob?

—I would beg first, Stephen said.

—And if you got nothing, would you rob?

—You wish me to say, Stephen answered, that the rights of property are provisional and that in certain circumstances it is not unlawful to rob. Everyone would act in that belief. So I will not make you that unswer. Apply to the jesuit theologian Juan Mariana de Talavera* who will also explain to you in what circumstances you may lawfully kill your king and whether you had better hand him his poison in a goblet or smear it for him upon his robe or his saddlebow.† Ask me rather would I suffer others to rob me or, if they did, would I call down upon them what I believe is called the chastisement of the secular arm?

—And would you?

—I think, Stephen said, it would pain me much to do as to be robbed.

—I see, Cranly said.

He produced his match and began to clean the crevice between two teeth. Then he said carelessly:

—Tell me, for example, would you deflower a virgin?

—Excuse me, Stephen said politely, is that not the ambition of most young gentlemen?

—What then is your point of view? Cranly asked.

His last phrase, sour smelling as the smoke of charcoal and disheartening, excited Stephen's brain, over which its fumes seemed to brood.

—Look here, Cranly, he said. You have asked me what I would do and what I would not do. I will tell you what I will do and what I will not do. I will not serve that in which I no longer believe, whether it call itself my home, my fatherland or my church: and I will try to express myself in some mode of life or art as freely as I can and as wholly as I can, using for my defence the only arms I allow myself to use, silence, exile and cunning.

---

*(1536–1624); Spanish Jesuit scholar.
†Arched front of a saddle.

Cranly seized his arm and steered him round so as to lead back towards Leeson Park. He laughed almost slyly and pressed Stephen's arm with an elder's affection.

—Cunning indeed! he said. Is it you? You poor poet, you!

—And you made me confess to you, Stephen said, thrilled by his touch, as I have confessed to you so many other things, have I not?

—Yes, my child, Cranly said, still gaily.

—You made me confess the fears that I have. But I will tell you also what I do not fear. I do not fear to be alone or to be spurned for another or to leave whatever I have to leave. And I am not afraid to make a mistake, even a great mistake, a lifelong mistake and perhaps as long as eternity too.

Cranly, now grave again, slowed his pace and said:

—Alone, quite alone. You have no fear of that. And you know what that word means? Not only to be separate from all others but to have not even one friend.

—I will take the risk, said Stephen.

—And not to have any one person, Cranly said, who would be more than a friend, more even than the noblest and truest friend a man ever had.

His words seemed to have struck some deep chord in his own nature. Had he spoken of himself, of himself as he was or wished to be? Stephen watched his face for some moments in silence. A cold sadness was there. He had spoken of himself, of his own loneliness which he feared.

—Of whom are you speaking? Stephen asked at length.

Cranly did not answer.

*   *   *

20 March. Long talk with Cranly on the subject of my revolt.

He had his grand manner on. I supple and suave. Attacked me on the score of love for one's mother. Tried to imagine his mother: cannot. Told me once, in a moment of thoughtlessness, his father was sixty-one when he was born. Can see him. Strong farmer type. Pepper and salt suit. Square feet. Unkempt grizzled beard. Probably attends coursing matches.* Pays his dues regularly but not plentifully to Father Dwyer of Larras. Sometimes talks to girls after nightfall. But his mother? Very young or very old? Hardly the first. If so, Cranly would not have spo-

---

*Contests between hunting dogs.

ken as he did. Old then. Probably, and neglected. Hence Cranly's despair of soul: the child of exhausted loins.

21 March, morning. Thought this in bed last night but was too lazy and free to add it. Free, yes. The exhausted loins are those of Elizabeth and Zachary.* Then he is the precursor. Item: he eats chiefly belly bacon and dried figs. Read locusts and wild honey.† Also, when thinking of him, saw always a stern severed head or death mask as if outlined on a grey curtain or veronica.‡ Decollation§ they call it in the fold. Puzzled for the moment by saint John at the Latin gate.²² What do I see? A decollated precursor trying to pick the lock.

21 March, night. Free. Soul free and fancy free. Let the dead bury the dead.|| Ay. And let the dead marry the dead.

22 March. In company with Lynch followed a sizable hospital nurse. Lynch's idea. Dislike it. Two lean hungry greyhounds walking after a heifer.

23 March. Have not seen her since that night. Unwell? Sits at the fire perhaps with mamma's shawl on her shoulders. But not peevish. A nice bowl of gruel? Won't you now?

24 March. Began with a discussion with my mother. Subject: B.V.M.# Handicapped by my sex and youth. To escape held up relations between Jesus and Papa against those between Mary and her son. Said religion was not a lying-in hospital.** Mother indulgent. Said I have a queer mind and have read too much. Not true. Have read little and understood less. Then she said I would come back to faith because I had a restless mind. This means to leave church by backdoor of sin and reenter through the skylight of repentance. Cannot repent. Told her so and asked for sixpence. Got threepence.

Then went to college. Other wrangle with little roundhead rogue's eye Ghezzi. This time about Bruno the Nolan.†† Began in Italian and ended in pidgin English. He said Bruno was a terrible heretic. I said he

---

*Elderly parents of John the Baptist; see Luke 1:5–25.
†John the Baptist's diet while living in the wilderness.
‡Cloth similar to the one, given to Christ by Saint Veronica on his way to Calvary, on which the image of his face was imprinted.
§Beheading.
||Reference to Luke 9:59–60.
#Blessed Virgin Mary.
**Maternity hospital.
††Giordano Bruno (1548–1600), a heretic burned at the stake for his unorthodox views.

was terribly burned. He agreed to this with some sorrow. Then gave me recipe for what he calls *risotto alla bergamasca.** When he pronounces a soft *o* he protrudes his full carnal lips as if he kissed the vowel. Has he? And could he repent? Yes, he could: and cry two round rogue's tears, one from each eye.

Crossing Stephen's, that is, my Green, remembered that his countrymen and not mine had invented what Cranly the other night called our religion. A quartet of them, soldiers of the ninetyseventh infantry regiment, sat at the foot of the cross and tossed up dice for the overcoat of the crucified.[†]

Went to library. Tried to read three reviews. Useless. She is not out yet. Am I alarmed? About what? That she will never be out again.

Blake wrote:

> *I wonder if William Bond will die,*
> *For assuredly he is very ill.*[‡]

Alas, poor William!

I was once at a diorama in Rotunda.[§] At the end were pictures of big nobs. Among them William Ewart Gladstone,[||] just then dead. Orchestra played *O, Willie, we have missed you.*[#]

A race of clodhoppers!**

25 March, morning. Troubled night of dreams. Want to get them off my chest.

A long curving gallery. From the floor ascend pillars of dark vapours. It is peopled by the images of fabulous kings, set in stone. Their hands are folded upon their knees in token of weariness and their eyes are darkened for the errors of men go up before them for ever as dark vapours.

Strange figures advance as from a cave. They are not as tall as men. One does not seem to stand quite apart from another. Their faces are phosphorescent, with darker streaks. They peer at me and their eyes seem to ask me something. They do not speak.

---

*Rice dish.

†The casting of lots for Christ's garments is narrated in Matthew 27:35, Mark 15:24, Luke 23:34, and John 19:24; it is prefigured, as well, in Psalms 21:19.

‡From the poem "William Bond," by William Blake (1757–1827).

§Performing arts venue at the north end of Sackville (now O'Connell) Street.

||British prime minister; he died in May 1898.

#From a popular song by American songwriter Stephen Foster (1826–1864).

**Dumplings.

30 March. This evening Cranly was in the porch of the library, proposing a problem to Dixon and her brother. A mother let her child fall into the Nile. Still harping on the mother. A crocodile seized the child. Mother asked it back. Crocodile said all right if she told him what he was going to do with the child, eat it or not eat it.

This mentality, Lepidus* would say, is indeed bred out of your mud by the operation of your sun.

And mine? Is it not too? Then into Nile mud with it.

1 April. Disapprove of this last phrase.

2 April. Saw her drinking tea and eating cakes in Johnston's, Mooney and O'Brien's.† Rather, lynxeyed Lynch saw her as we passed. He tells me Cranly was invited there by brother. Did he bring his crocodile? Is he the shining light now? Well, I discovered him. I protest I did. Shining quietly behind a bushel of Wicklow bran.

3 April. Met Davin at the cigar shop opposite Findlater's church. He was in a black sweater and had a hurleystick. Asked me was it true I was going away and why. Told him the shortest way to Tara was *via* Holyhead.‡ Just then my father came up. Introduction. Father, polite and observant. Asked Davin if he might offer him some refreshment. Davin could not, was going to a meeting. When we came away father told me he had a good honest eye. Asked me why I did not join a rowing club. I pretended to think it over. Told me then how he broke Pennyfeather's heart. Wants me to read law.§ Says I was cut out for that. More mud, more crocodiles.

5 April. Wild spring. Scudding clouds. O life! Dark stream of swirling bogwater on which apple trees have cast down their delicate flowers. Eyes of girls among the leaves. Girls demure and romping. All fair or auburn: no dark ones. They blush better. Houp-la!

6 April. Certainly she remembers the past. Lynch says all women do. Then she remembers the time of her childhood—and mine if I was ever a child. The past is consumed in the present and the present is living only because it brings forth the future. Statues of women, if Lynch

---

*In Shakespeare's *Anthony and Cleopatra* (act 2, scene 7), Lepidus says, "Your serpent of Egypt is bred now of your mud by the operation of your sun; so is your crocodile."

†Chain of Dublin cafés.

‡Tara is a mythological name for Ireland. Holyhead is the Welsh port city across the Irish Sea from Dublin—a common destination for those leaving Ireland.

§Study to become an attorney.

be right, should always be fully draped, one hand of the woman feeling regretfully her own hinder parts.

6 April, later. Michael Robartes remembers forgotten beauty and, when his arms wrap her round, he presses in his arms the loveliness which has long faded from the world.* Not this. Not at all. I desire to press in my arms the loveliness which has not yet come into the world.

10 April. Faintly, under the heavy night, through the silence of the city which has turned from dreams to dreamless sleep as a weary lover whom no caresses move, the sound of hoofs upon the road. Not so faintly now as they come near the bridge: and in a moment as they pass the darkened windows the silence is cloven by alarm as by an arrow. They are heard now far away, hoofs that shine amid the heavy night as gems, hurrying beyond the sleeping fields to what journey's end—what heart?—bearing what tidings?

11 April. Read what I wrote last night. Vague words for a vague emotion. Would she like it? I think so. Then I should have to like it also.

13 April. That tundish has been on my mind for a long time. I looked it up and find it English† and good old blunt English too. Damn the dean of studies and his funnel! What did he come here for to teach us his own language or to learn it from us. Damn him one way or the other!

14 April. John Alphonsus Mulrennan has just returned from the west of Ireland. European and Asiatic papers please copy. He told us he met an old man there in a mountain cabin. Old man had red eyes and short pipe. Old man spoke Irish. Mulrennan spoke Irish. Then old man and Mulrennan spoke English. Mulrennan spoke to him about universe and stars. Old man sat, listened, smoked, spat. Then said:

—Ah, there must be terrible queer creatures at the latter end of the world.

I fear him. I fear his redrimmed horny eyes. It is with him I must struggle all through this night till day come, till he or I lie dead, gripping him by the sinewy throat till . . . Till what? Till he yield to me? No. I mean him no harm.

15 April. Met her today point blank in Grafton Street. The crowd brought us together. We both stopped. She asked me why I never came,

---

*From "He remembers forgotten beauty," a poem by William Butler Yeats (1865–1939).

†Indeed, the word appears in Shakespeare's *Measure for Measure* (act 3, scene 2).

said she had heard all sorts of stories about me. This was only to gain time. Asked me, was I writing poems? About whom? I asked her. This confused her more and I felt sorry and mean. Turned off that valve at once and opened the spiritual-heroic refrigerating apparatus, invented and patented in all countries by Dante Alighieri.* Talked rapidly of myself and my plans. In the midst of it unluckily I made a sudden gesture of a revolutionary nature. I must have looked like a fellow throwing a handful of peas up into the air. People began to look at us. She shook hands a moment after and, in going away, said she hoped I would do what I said.

Now I call that friendly, don't you?

Yes, I liked her today. A little or much? Don't know. I liked her and it seems a new feeling to me. Then, in that case, all the rest, all that I thought I thought and all that I felt I felt, all the rest before now, in fact . . . O, give it up, old chap! Sleep it off!

16 April. Away! Away!

The spell of arms and voices: the white arms of roads, their promise of close embraces and the black arms of tall ships that stand against the moon, their tale of distant nations. They are held out to say: We are alone—come. And the voices say with them: We are your kinsmen. And the air is thick with their company as they call to me, their kinsman, making ready to go, shaking the wings of their exultant and terrible youth.

26 April. Mother is putting my new secondhand clothes in order. She prays now, she says, that I may learn in my own life and away from home and friends what the heart is and what it feels. Amen. So be it. Welcome, O life! I go to encounter for the millionth time the reality of experience and to forge in the smithy of my soul the uncreated conscience of my race.

27 April. Old father, old artificer,† stand me now and ever in good stead.

THE END

Dublin, 1904.
Trieste, 1914.

---

*Throughout *La Vita Nuova* (c.1293), Dante seems to have kept his strong feelings for Beatrice in check.
†That is, Dædalus.

DUBLINERS

CONTENTS

THE SISTERS

THERE WAS NO HOPE for him this time: it was the third stroke. Night after night I had passed the house (it was vacation time) and studied the lighted square of window: and night after night I had found it lighted in the same way, faintly and evenly. If he was dead, I thought, I would see the reflection of candles on the darkened blind for I knew that two candles must be set at the head of a corpse. He had often said to me: *I am not long for this world,* and I had thought his words idle. Now I knew they were true. Every night as I gazed up at the window I said softly to myself the word paralysis. It had always sounded strangely in my ears, like the word gnomon* in the Euclid[†] and the word simony[‡] in the Catechism. But now it sounded to me like the name of some maleficent and sinful being. It filled me with fear, and yet I longed to be nearer to it and to look upon its deadly work.

Old Cotter was sitting at the fire, smoking, when I came downstairs to supper. While my aunt was ladling out my stirabout[§] he said, as if returning to some former remark of his:

—No, I wouldn't say he was exactly . . . but there was something queer . . . there was something uncanny about him. I'll tell you my opinion. . . .

He began to puff at his pipe, no doubt arranging his opinion in his mind. Tiresome old fool! When we knew him first he used to be rather interesting, talking of faints and worms;[||] but I soon grew tired of him and his endless stories about the distillery.

—I have my own theory about it, he said. I think it was one of those . . . peculiar cases. . . . But it's hard to say. . . .

---

*Geometrical form created when a parallelogram is removed from the corner of a larger parallelogram.
†Geometry textbook based on the work of Euclid (c.300 B.C.).
‡The sin of selling spiritual blessings or pardons.
§Hot cereal.
||Technical terms from the distilling trade.

He began to puff again at his pipe without giving us his theory. My uncle saw me staring and said to me:

—Well, so your old friend is gone, you'll be sorry to hear.

—Who? said I.

—Father Flynn.

—Is he dead?

—Mr Cotter here has just told us. He was passing by the house.

I knew that I was under observation so I continued eating as if the news had not interested me. My uncle explained to old Cotter.

—The youngster and he were great friends. The old chap taught him a great deal, mind you; and they say he had a great wish for him.

—God have mercy on his soul, said my aunt piously.

Old Cotter looked at me for a while. I felt that his little beady black eyes were examining me but I would not satisfy him by looking up from my plate. He returned to his pipe and finally spat rudely into the grate.

—I wouldn't like children of mine, he said, to have too much to say to a man like that.

—How do you mean, Mr Cotter? asked my aunt.

—What I mean is, said old Cotter, it's bad for children. My idea is: let a young lad run about and play with young lads of his own age and not be . . . Am I right, Jack?

—That's my principle, too, said my uncle. Let him learn to box his corner. That's what I'm always saying to that Rosicrucian* there: take exercise. Why, when I was a nipper every morning of my life I had a cold bath, winter and summer. And that's what stands to me now. Education is all very fine and large. . . . Mr Cotter might take a pick of that leg of mutton, he added to my aunt.

—No, no, not for me, said old Cotter.

My aunt brought the dish from the safe and put it on the table.

—But why do you think it's not good for children, Mr Cotter? she asked.

—It's bad for children, said old Cotter, because their minds are so impressionable. When children see things like that, you know, it has an effect. . . .

I crammed my mouth with stirabout for fear I might give utterance to my anger. Tiresome old red-nosed imbecile!

It was late when I fell asleep. Though I was angry with old Cotter for alluding to me as a child, I puzzled my head to extract meaning

---

*Member of an esoteric, mystical order.

from his unfinished sentences. In the dark of my room I imagined that I saw again the heavy grey face of the paralytic. I drew the blankets over my head and tried to think of Christmas. But the grey face still followed me. It murmured; and I understood that it desired to confess something. I felt my soul receding into some pleasant and vicious region; and there again I found it waiting for me. It began to confess to me in a murmuring voice and I wondered why it smiled continually and why the lips were so moist with spittle. But then I remembered that it had died of paralysis and I felt that I too was smiling feebly as if to absolve the simoniac of his sin.

The next morning after breakfast I went down to look at the little house in Great Britain Street. It was an unassuming shop, registered under the vague name of *Drapery*.* The drapery consisted mainly of children's bootees and umbrellas; and on ordinary days a notice used to hang in the window, saying: *Umbrellas Re-covered* No notice was visible now for the shutters were up. A crape bouquet was tied to the door-knocker with ribbon. Two poor women and a telegram boy were reading the card pinned on the crape. I also approached and read:

JULY 1ST, 1895
THE REV. JAMES FLYNN (FORMERLY OF S. CATHERINE'S CHURCH,
MEATH STREET), AGED SIXTY-FIVE YEARS.
R. I. P.†

The reading of the card persuaded me that he was dead and I was disturbed to find myself at check. Had he not been dead I would have gone into the little dark room behind the shop to find him sitting in his arm-chair by the fire, nearly smothered in his greatcoat. Perhaps my aunt would have given me a packet of High Toast‡ for him and this present would have roused him from his stupefied doze. It was always I who emptied the packet into his black snuffbox for his hands trembled too much to allow him to do this without spilling half the snuff about the floor. Even as he raised his large trembling hand to his nose little clouds of smoke dribbled through his fingers over the front of his coat. It may have been these constant showers of snuff which gave his ancient priestly garments their green faded look for the red hand-

---

*Dry goods: material, clothing, notions (small useful articles).
†*Requiescat in Pace*, Latin for "rest in peace."
‡Brand of snuff, a pulverized form of tobacco for inhaling.

kerchief, blackened, as it always was, with the snuff-stains of a week, with which he tried to brush away the fallen grains, was quite inefficacious.*

I wished to go in and look at him but I had not the courage to knock. I walked away slowly along the sunny side of the street, reading all the theatrical advertisements in the shop-windows as I went. I found it strange that neither I nor the day seemed in a mourning mood and I felt even annoyed at discovering in myself a sensation of freedom as if I had been freed from something by his death. I wondered at this for, as my uncle had said the night before, he had taught me a great deal. He had studied in the Irish college in Rome† and he had taught me to pronounce Latin properly. He had told me stories about the catacombs and about Napoleon Bonaparte, and he had explained to me the meaning of the different ceremonies of the Mass and of the different vestments‡ worn by the priest. Sometimes he had amused himself by putting difficult questions to me, asking me what one should do in certain circumstances or whether such and such sins were mortal or venial or only imperfections. His questions showed me how complex and mysterious were certain institutions of the Church which I had always regarded as the simplest acts. The duties of the priest towards the Eucharist§ and towards the secrecy of the confessional seemed so grave to me that I wondered how anybody had ever found in himself the courage to undertake them; and I was not surprised when he told me that the fathers of the Church had written books as thick as the *Post Office Directory* and as closely printed as the law notices in the newspaper, elucidating all these intricate questions. Often when I thought of this I could make no answer or only a very foolish and halting one upon which he used to smile and nod his head twice or thrice. Sometimes he used to put me through the responses of the Mass which he had made me learn by heart; and, as I pattered, he used to smile pensively and nod his head, now and then pushing huge pinches of snuff up each nostril alternately. When he smiled he used to uncover his big discoloured teeth and let his tongue lie upon his lower lip—a habit which had made me feel uneasy in the beginning of our acquaintance before I knew him well.

As I walked along in the sun I remembered old Cotter's words and tried to remember what had happened afterwards in the dream. I re-

---

*Without effect.
†Institution for the training of Irish priests.
‡Priestly garments.
§The sacrament of Holy Communion.

membered that I had noticed long velvet curtains and a swinging lamp of antique fashion. I felt that I had been very far away, in some land where the customs were strange—in Persia,* I thought. . . . But I could not remember the end of the dream.

In the evening my aunt took me with her to visit the house of mourning. It was after sunset; but the window-panes of the houses that looked to the west reflected the tawny gold of a great bank of clouds. Nannie received us in the hall; and, as it would have been unseemly to have shouted at her, my aunt shook hands with her for all. The old woman pointed upwards interrogatively and, on my aunt's nodding, proceeded to toil up the narrow staircase before us, her bowed head being scarcely above the level of the banister-rail. At the first landing she stopped and beckoned us forward encouragingly towards the open door of the dead-room. My aunt went in and the old woman, seeing that I hesitated to enter, began to beckon to me again repeatedly with her hand.

I went in on tiptoe. The room through the lace end of the blind was suffused with dusky golden light amid which the candles looked like pale thin flames. He had been coffined. Nannie gave the lead and we three knelt down at the foot of the bed. I pretended to pray but I could not gather my thoughts because the old woman's mutterings distracted me. I noticed how clumsily her skirt was hooked at the back and how the heels of her cloth boots were trodden down all to one side. The fancy came to me that the old priest was smiling as he lay there in his coffin.

But no. When we rose and went up to the head of the bed I saw that he was not smiling. There he lay, solemn and copious, vested as for the altar, his large hands loosely retaining a chalice.† His face was very truculent, grey and massive, with black cavernous nostrils and circled by a scanty white fur. There was a heavy odour in the room—the flowers.

We crossed ourselves and came away. In the little room downstairs we found Eliza seated in his arm-chair in state. I groped my way towards my usual chair in the corner while Nannie went to the sideboard and brought out a decanter of sherry and some wine-glasses. She set these on the table and invited us to take a little glass of wine. Then, at her sister's bidding, she filled out the sherry into the glasses and passed them to us. She pressed me to take some cream crackers also but I declined because I thought I would make too much noise eating them.

---

*Modern-day Iran.
†Cup in which the communion wine is held.

She seemed to be somewhat disappointed at my refusal and went over quietly to the sofa where she sat down behind her sister. No one spoke: we all gazed at the empty fireplace.

My aunt waited until Eliza sighed and then said:

—Ah, well, he's gone to a better world.

Eliza sighed again and bowed her head in assent. My aunt fingered the stem of her wine-glass before sipping a little.

—Did he . . . peacefully? she asked.

—Oh, quite peacefully, ma'am, said Eliza. You couldn't tell when the breath went out of him. He had a beautiful death, God be praised.

—And everything . . . ?

—Father O'Rourke was in with him a Tuesday and anointed him and prepared him and all.*

—He knew then?

—He was quite resigned.

—He looks quite resigned, said my aunt.

—That's what the woman we had in to wash him said. She said he just looked as if he was asleep, he looked that peaceful and resigned. No one would think he'd make such a beautiful corpse.

—Yes, indeed, said my aunt.

She sipped a little more from her glass and said:

—Well, Miss Flynn, at any rate it must be a great comfort for you to know that you did all you could for him. You were both very kind to him, I must say.

Eliza smoothed her dress over her knees.

—Ah, poor James! she said. God knows we done all we could, as poor as we are—we wouldn't see him want anything while he was in it.

Nannie had leaned her head against the sofa-pillow and seemed about to fall asleep.

—There's poor Nannie, said Eliza, looking at her, she's wore out. All the work we had, she and me, getting in the woman to wash him and then laying him out and then the coffin and then arranging about the Mass in the chapel. Only for Father O'Rourke I don't know what we'd done at all. It was him brought us all them flowers and them two candlesticks out of the chapel and wrote out the notice for the *Freeman's General*† and took charge of all the papers for the cemetery and poor James's insurance.

---

*Prepared his body for burial according to traditional procedures.
†Obituary notice that will appear in the Dublin *Freeman's Journal* (not "General").

—Wasn't that good of him? said my aunt.

Eliza closed her eyes and shook her head slowly.

—Ah, there's no friends like the old friends, she said, when all is said and done, no friends that a body can trust.

—Indeed, that's true, said my aunt. And I'm sure now that he's gone to his eternal reward he won't forget you and all your kindness to him.

—Ah, poor James! said Eliza. He was no great trouble to us. You wouldn't hear him in the house any more than now. Still, I know he's gone and all to that. . . .

—It's when it's all over that you'll miss him, said my aunt.

—I know that, said Eliza. I won't be bringing him in his cup of beef-tea* any more, nor you, ma'am, sending him his snuff. Ah, poor James!

She stopped, as if she were communing with the past and then said shrewdly:

—Mind you, I noticed there was something queer† coming over him latterly. Whenever I'd bring in his soup to him there I'd find him with his breviary‡ fallen to the floor, lying back in the chair and his mouth open.

She laid a finger against her nose and frowned: then she continued:

—But still and all he kept on saying that before the summer was over he'd go out for a drive one fine day just to see the old house again where we were all born down in Irishtown§ and take me and Nannie with him. If we could only get one of them new-fangled carriages that makes no noise that Father O'Rourke told him about, them with the rheumatic‖ wheels, for the day cheap—he said, at Johnny Rush's over the way there and drive out the three of us together of a Sunday evening. He had his mind set on that. . . . Poor James!

—The Lord have mercy on his soul! said my aunt.

Eliza took out her handkerchief and wiped her eyes with it. Then she put it back again in her pocket and gazed into the empty grate for some time without speaking.

—He was too scrupulous always, she said. The duties of the priest-hood was too much for him. And then his life was, you might say, crossed.

---

*Beef bouillon.

†Strange.

‡Prayer book.

§Working-class seaside Dublin neighborhood south of the River Liffey.

‖That is, pneumatic; a malapropism.

—Yes, said my aunt. He was a disappointed man. You could see that.

A silence took possession of the little room and, under cover of it, I approached the table and tasted my sherry and then returned quietly to my chair in the corner. Eliza seemed to have fallen into a deep revery. We waited respectfully for her to break the silence: and after a long pause she said slowly:

—It was that chalice he broke. . . . That was the beginning of it. Of course, they say it was all right, that it contained nothing, I mean. But still. . . . They say it was the boy's fault. But poor James was so nervous, God be merciful to him!

—And was that it? said my aunt. I heard something. . . .

Eliza nodded.

—That affected his mind, she said. After that he began to mope by himself, talking to no one and wandering about by himself. So one night he was wanted for to go on a call and they couldn't find him anywhere. They looked high up and low down; and still they couldn't see a sight of him anywhere. So then the clerk suggested to try the chapel. So then they got the keys and opened the chapel and the clerk and Father O'Rourke and another priest that was there brought in a light for to look for him. . . . And what do you think but there he was, sitting up by himself in the dark in his confession-box, wide-awake and laughing-like softly to himself?

She stopped suddenly as if to listen. I too listened; but there was no sound in the house; and I knew that the old priest was lying still in his coffin as we had seen him, solemn and truculent in death, an idle chalice on his breast.

Eliza resumed:

—Wide-awake and laughing-like to himself. . . . So then, of course, when they saw that, that made them think that there was something gone wrong with him. . . .

AN ENCOUNTER

IT WAS JOE DILLON who introduced the Wild West to us. He had a little library made up of old numbers of *The Union Jack, Pluck* and *The Halfpenny Marvel.** Every evening after school we met in his back garden and arranged Indian battles. He and his fat young brother Leo, the idler, held the loft of the stable while we tried to carry it by storm; or we fought a pitched battle on the grass. But, however well we fought, we never won siege or battle and all our bouts ended with Joe Dillon's war dance of victory. His parents went to eight-o'clock mass every morning in Gardiner Street and the peaceful odour of Mrs Dillon was prevalent in the hall of the house. But he played too fiercely for us who were younger and more timid. He looked like some kind of an Indian when he capered round the garden, an old tea-cosy† on his head, beating a tin with his fist and yelling:

—Ya! yaka, yaka, yaka!

Everyone was incredulous when it was reported that he had a vocation for the priesthood. Nevertheless it was true.

A spirit of unruliness diffused itself among us and, under its influence, differences of culture and constitution were waived. We banded ourselves together, some boldly, some in jest and some almost in fear: and of the number of these latter, the reluctant Indians who were afraid to seem studious or lacking in robustness, I was one. The adventures related in the literature of the Wild West were remote from my nature but, at least, they opened doors of escape. I liked better some American detective stories which were traversed from time to time by unkempt fierce and beautiful girls. Though there was nothing wrong in these stories and though their intention was sometimes literary they were circulated secretly at school. One day when Father Butler was hearing the four pages of Roman History clumsy Leo Dillon was discovered with a copy of *The Halfpenny Marvel.*

---

*Inexpensive boys' magazines.
†Fabric cover to keep a teapot warm.

"An Encounter"

- - - Route the boys take

—This page or this page? This page? Now, Dillon, up! *Hardly had the day* . . . Go on! What day? *Hardly had the day dawned* . . . Have you studied it? What have you there in your pocket?

Everyone's heart palpitated as Leo Dillon handed up the paper and everyone assumed an innocent face. Father Butler turned over the pages, frowning.

—What is this rubbish? he said. *The Apache Chief!* Is this what you read instead of studying your Roman History? Let me not find any more of this wretched stuff in this college.* The man who wrote it, I suppose, was some wretched fellow who writes these things for a drink. I'm surprised at boys like you, educated, reading such stuff. I could understand it if you were . . . National School† boys. Now, Dillon, I advise you strongly, get at your work or . . .

This rebuke during the sober hours of school paled much of the glory of the Wild West for me and the confused puffy face of Leo Dillon awakened one of my consciences. But when the restraining influence of the school was at a distance I began to hunger again for wild sensations, for the escape which those chronicles of disorder alone seemed to offer me. The mimic warfare of the evening became at last as wearisome to me as the routine of school in the morning because I wanted real adventures to happen to myself. But real adventures, I reflected, do not happen to people who remain at home: they must be sought abroad.

The summer holidays were near at hand when I made up my mind to break out of the weariness of school life for one day at least. With Leo Dillon and a boy named Mahony I planned a day's miching.‡ Each of us saved up sixpence. We were to meet at ten in the morning on the Canal Bridge. Mahony's big sister was to write an excuse for him and Leo Dillon was to tell his brother to say he was sick. We arranged to go along the Wharf Road until we came to the ships, then to cross in the ferryboat and walk out to see the Pigeon House.§ Leo Dillon was afraid we might meet Father Butler or someone out of the college; but Mahony asked, very sensibly, what would Father Butler be doing out at the Pigeon House. We were reassured: and I brought the first stage of the plot to an end by collecting sixpence from the other two, at the same time showing them my own sixpence. When we were making the last arrangements on the eve we were all vaguely excited. We shook hands, laughing, and Mahony said:

—Till to-morrow, mates!

That night I slept badly. In the morning I was first-comer to the bridge as I lived nearest. I hid my books in the long grass near the ash-pit at the end of the garden where nobody ever came and hurried along the canal bank. It was a mild sunny morning in the first week of June. I sat up on the coping of the bridge admiring my frail canvas shoes which I had diligently pipeclayed* overnight and watching the docile horses pulling a tramload of business people up the hill. All the branches of the tall trees which lined the mall were gay with little light green leaves and the sunlight slanted through them on to the water. The granite stone of the bridge was beginning to be warm and I began to pat it with my hands in time to an air† in my head. I was very happy.

When I had been sitting there for five or ten minutes I saw Mahony's grey suit approaching. He came up the hill, smiling, and clambered up beside me on the bridge. While we were waiting he brought out the catapult which bulged from his inner pocket and explained some improvements which he had made in it. I asked him why he had brought it and he told me he had brought it to have some gas‡ with the birds. Mahony used slang freely, and spoke of Father Butler as Old Bunser. We waited on for a quarter of an hour more but still there was no sign of Leo Dillon. Mahony, at last, jumped down and said:

—Come along. I knew Fatty'd funk it.§

—And his sixpence . . . ? I said.

—That's forfeit, said Mahony. And so much the better for us—a bob and a tanner instead of a bob.

We walked along the North Strand Road till we came to the Vitriol Works and then turned to the right along the Wharf Road. Mahony began to play the Indian as soon as we were out of public sight. He chased a crowd of ragged girls, brandishing his unloaded catapult and, when two ragged boys began, out of chivalry, to fling stones at us, he proposed that we should charge them. I objected that the boys were too small, and so we walked on, the ragged troop screaming after us: *Swad-*

---

*Whitened with fine white clay.
†Tune, melody.
‡Fun.
§Lose his courage.

dlers! Swaddlers! thinking that we were Protestants because Mahony, who was dark-complexioned, wore the silver badge of a cricket club in his cap. When we came to the Smoothing Iron we arranged a siege; but it was a failure because you must have at least three. We revenged ourselves on Leo Dillon by saying what a funk he was and guessing how many he would get* at three o-clock from Mr Ryan.

We came then near the river. We spent a long time walking about the noisy streets flanked by high stone walls, watching the working of cranes and engines and often being shouted at for our immobility by the drivers of groaning carts. It was noon when we reached the quays and, as all the labourers seemed to be eating their lunches, we bought two big currant buns and sat down to eat them on some metal piping beside the river. We pleased ourselves with the spectacle of Dublin's commerce—the barges signalled from far away by their curls of woolly smoke, the brown fishing fleet beyond Ringsend, the big white sailing-vessel which was being discharged on the opposite quay. Mahony said it would be right skit† to run away to sea on one of those big ships and even I, looking at the high masts, saw, or imagined, the geography which had been scantily dosed to me at school gradually taking substance under my eyes. School and home seemed to recede from us and their influences upon us seemed to wane.

We crossed the Liffey‡ in the ferryboat, paying our toll to be transported in the company of two labourers and a little Jew with a bag. We were serious to the point of solemnity, but once during the short voyage our eyes met and we laughed. When we landed we watched the discharging of the graceful three-master which we had observed from the other quay. Some bystander said that she was a Norwegian vessel. I went to the stern and tried to decipher the legend upon it but, failing to do so, I came back and examined the foreign sailors to see had any of them green eyes for I had some confused notion. . . . The sailors' eyes were blue and grey and even black. The only sailor whose eyes could have been called green was a tall man who amused the crowd on the quay§ by calling out cheerfully every time the planks fell:

---

*That is, how many times would his hands be beaten with the pandybat, a small club, similar to a blackjack, in which a hard core of whalebone is covered in leather.
†Fun.
‡The river running west to east through downtown Dublin, dividing it into south and north.
§Commercial stretch of road alongside the river.

—All right! All right!

When we were tired of this sight we wandered slowly into Ringsend. The day had grown sultry, and in the windows of the grocers' shops musty biscuits lay bleaching. We bought some biscuits and chocolate which we ate sedulously as we wandered through the squalid streets where the families of the fishermen live. We could find no dairy and so we went into a huckster's shop and bought a bottle of raspberry lemonade each. Refreshed by this, Mahony chased a cat down a lane, but the cat escaped into a wide field. We both felt rather tired and when we reached the field we made at once for a sloping bank over the ridge of which we could see the Dodder.*

It was too late and we were too tired to carry out our project of visiting the Pigeon House. We had to be home before four o'clock lest our adventure should be discovered. Mahony looked regretfully at his catapult and I had to suggest going home by train before he regained any cheerfulness. The sun went in behind some clouds and left us to our jaded thoughts and the crumbs of our provisions.

There was nobody but ourselves in the field. When we had lain on the bank for some time without speaking I saw a man approaching from the far end of the field. I watched him lazily as I chewed one of those green stems on which girls tell fortunes. He came along by the bank slowly. He walked with one hand upon his hip and in the other hand he held a stick with which he tapped the turf lightly. He was shabbily dressed in a suit of greenish-black and wore what we used to call a jerry hat† with a high crown. He seemed to be fairly old for his moustache was ashen-grey. When he passed at our feet he glanced up at us quickly and then continued his way. We followed him with our eyes and saw that when he had gone on for perhaps fifty paces he turned about and began to retrace his steps. He walked towards us very slowly, always tapping the ground with his stick, so slowly that I thought he was looking for something in the grass.

He stopped when he came level with us and bade us good-day. We answered him and he sat down beside us on the slope slowly and with great care. He began to talk of the weather, saying that it would be a very hot summer and adding that the seasons had changed greatly since he was a boy—a long time ago. He said that the happiest time of one's life was undoubtedly one's schoolboy days and that he would give any-

---

*Another of Dublin's four rivers.
†Soft felt hat.

thing to be young again. While he expressed these sentiments which bored us a little we kept silent. Then he began to talk of school and of books. He asked us whether we had read the poetry of Thomas Moore or the works of Sir Walter Scott and Lord Lytton.[1] I pretended that I had read every book he mentioned so that in the end he said:

—Ah, I can see you are a bookworm like myself. Now, he added, pointing to Mahony who was regarding us with open eyes, he is different; he goes in for games.

He said he had all Sir Walter Scott's works and all Lord Lytton's works at home and never tired of reading them. Of course, he said, there were some of Lord Lytton's works which boys couldn't read. Mahony asked why couldn't boys read them—a question which agitated and pained me because I was afraid the man would think I was as stupid as Mahony. The man, however, only smiled. I saw that he had great gaps in his mouth between his yellow teeth. Then he asked us which of us had the most sweethearts. Mahony mentioned lightly that he had three totties.* The man asked me how many I had. I answered that I had none. He did not believe me and said he was sure I must have one. I was silent.

—Tell us, said Mahony pertly to the man, how many have you yourself?

The man smiled as before and said that when he was our age he had lots of sweethearts.

—Every boy, he said, has a little sweetheart.

His attitude on this point struck me as strangely liberal in a man of his age. In my heart I thought that what he said about boys and sweethearts was reasonable. But I disliked the words in his mouth and I wondered why he shivered once or twice as if he feared something or felt a sudden chill. As he proceeded I noticed that his accent was good. He began to speak to us about girls, saying what nice soft hair they had and how soft their hands were and how all girls were not so good as they seemed to be if one only knew. There was nothing he liked, he said, so much as looking at a nice young girl, at her nice white hands and her beautiful soft hair. He gave me the impression that he was repeating something which he had learned by heart or that, magnetised by some words of his own speech, his mind was slowly circling round and round in the same orbit. At times he spoke as if he were simply alluding to some fact that everybody knew, and at times he lowered his voice and

---

*Sweethearts, girlfriends.

spoke mysteriously as if he were telling us something secret which he did not wish others to overhear. He repeated his phrases over and over again, varying them and surrounding them with his monotonous voice. I continued to gaze towards the foot of the slope, listening to him.

After a long while his monologue paused. He stood up slowly, saying that he had to leave us for a minute or so, a few minutes, and, without changing the direction of my gaze, I saw him walking slowly away from us towards the near end of the field. We remained silent when he had gone. After a silence of a few minutes I heard Mahony exclaim:

—I say! Look what he's doing!

As I neither answered nor raised my eyes Mahony exclaimed again:

—I say . . . He's a queer* old josser!†

—In case he asks us for our names, I said, let you be Murphy and I'll be Smith.

We said nothing further to each other. I was still considering whether I would go away or not when the man came back and sat down beside us again. Hardly had he sat down when Mahony, catching sight of the cat which had escaped him, sprang up and pursued her across the field. The man and I watched the chase. The cat escaped once more and Mahony began to throw stones at the wall she had escaladed.‡ Desisting from this, he began to wander about the far end of the field, aimlessly.

After an interval the man spoke to me. He said that my friend was a very rough boy and asked did he get whipped often at school. I was going to reply indignantly that we were not National School boys to be whipped, as he called it; but I remained silent. He began to speak on the subject of chastising boys. His mind, as if magnetised again by his speech, seemed to circle slowly round and round its new centre. He said that when boys were that kind they ought to be whipped and well whipped. When a boy was rough and unruly there was nothing would do him any good but a good sound whipping. A slap on the hand or a box on the ear was no good: what he wanted was to get a nice warm whipping. I was surprised at this sentiment and involuntarily glanced up at his face. As I did so I met the gaze of a pair of bottle-green eyes peering at me from under a twitching forehead. I turned my eyes away again.

---

*Joyce plays on both the conventional and underground meanings this word carried in turn-of-the-century Ireland: "strange" but also, increasingly, "homosexual."
†Simpleton.
‡Mounted or scaled.

The man continued his monologue. He seemed to have forgotten his recent liberalism. He said that if ever he found a boy talking to girls or having a girl for a sweetheart he would whip him and whip him; and that would teach him not to be talking to girls. And if a boy had a girl for a sweetheart and told lies about it then he would give him such a whipping as no boy ever got in this world. He said that there was nothing in this world he would like so well as that. He described to me how he would whip such a boy as if he were unfolding some elaborate mystery. He would love that, he said, better than anything in this world; and his voice, as he led me monotonously through the mystery, grew almost affectionate and seemed to plead with me that I should understand him.

I waited till his monologue paused again. Then I stood up abruptly. Lest I should betray my agitation I delayed a few moments pretending to fix my shoe properly and then, saying that I was obliged to go, I bade him good-day. I went up the slope calmly but my heart was beating quickly with fear that he would seize me by the ankles. When I reached the top of the slope I turned round and, without looking at him, called loudly across the field:

—Murphy!

My voice had an accent of forced bravery in it and I was ashamed of my paltry stratagem. I had to call the name again before Mahony saw me and hallooed in answer. How my heart beat as he came running across the field to me! He ran as if to bring me aid. And I was penitent; for in my heart I had always despised him a little.

Christian Brothers' School

N. Circular Rd.

◄ North Richmond Street

Sea

Amiens Street Station

River Liffey

Grand Canal

Trinity College

Merrion Square

Stephen's Green

Dublin—Kingstown Railway

Araby

"Araby"

The Boy's Route:

on foot ----

by rail +++

ARABY

North Richmond Street, being blind,* was a quiet street except at the hour when the Christian Brothers' School[†] set the boys free. An uninhabited house of two storeys stood at the blind end, detached from its neighbours in a square ground. The other houses of the street, conscious of decent lives within them, gazed at one another with brown imperturbable faces.

The former tenant of our house, a priest, had died in the back drawing-room. Air, musty from having been long enclosed, hung in all the rooms, and the waste room behind the kitchen was littered with old useless papers. Among these I found a few paper-covered books, the pages of which were curled and damp: *The Abbot*, by Walter Scott, *The Devout Communicant* and *The Memoirs of Vidocq*.[‡] I liked the last best because its leaves were yellow. The wild garden behind the house contained a central apple-tree and a few straggling bushes under one of which I found the late tenant's rusty bicycle-pump. He had been a very charitable priest; in his will he had left all his money to institutions and the furniture of his house to his sister.

When the short days of winter came dusk fell before we had well eaten our dinners. When we met in the street the houses had grown sombre. The space of sky above us was the colour of ever-changing violet and towards it the lamps of the street lifted their feeble lanterns. The cold air stung us and we played till our bodies glowed. Our shouts echoed in the silent street. The career[§] of our play brought us through the dark muddy lanes behind the houses where we ran the gauntlet of the rough tribes from the cottages, to the back doors of the dark drip-

---

*That is, a dead-end street.

†Inexpensive day schools, run by the volunteers of the Christian Brothers, that emphasized practical learning.

‡Three popular nineteenth-century texts emphasizing, respectively, romance (*The Abbott* is a novel by Sir Walter Scott), religious devotion, and crime and detection.

§Reckless running.

ping gardens where odours arose from the ashpits, to the dark odorous stables where a coachman smoothed and combed the horse or shook music from the buckled harness. When we returned to the street light from the kitchen windows had filled the areas. If my uncle was seen turning the corner we hid in the shadow until we had seen him safely housed. Or if Mangan's sister came out on the doorstep to call her brother in to his tea* we watched her from our shadow peer up and down the street. We waited to see whether she would remain or go in and, if she remained, we left our shadow and walked up to Mangan's steps resignedly. She was waiting for us, her figure defined by the light from the half-opened door. Her brother always teased her before he obeyed and I stood by the railings looking at her. Her dress swung as she moved her body and the soft rope of her hair tossed from side to side.

Every morning I lay on the floor in the front parlour watching her door. The blind was pulled down to within an inch of the sash so that I could not be seen. When she came out on the doorstep my heart leaped. I ran to the hall, seized my books and followed her. I kept her brown figure always in my eye and, when we came near the point at which our ways diverged, I quickened my pace and passed her. This happened morning after morning. I had never spoken to her, except for a few casual words, and yet her name was like a summons to all my foolish blood.

Her image accompanied me even in places the most hostile to romance. On Saturday evenings when my aunt went marketing I had to go to carry some of the parcels. We walked through the flaring streets, jostled by drunken men and bargaining women, amid the curses of labourers, the shrill litanies of shop-boys who stood on guard by the barrels of pigs' cheeks, the nasal chanting of street-singers, who sang a *come-all-you*† about O'Donovan Rossa,‡ or a ballad about the troubles in our native land. These noises converged in a single sensation of life for me: I imagined that I bore my chalice§ safely through a throng of foes. Her name sprang to my lips at moments in strange prayers and praises which I myself did not understand. My eyes were often full of tears (I could not tell why) and at times a flood from my heart seemed

---

*The evening meal.
†A popular ballad, often beginning with the phrase "Come all you [Irish men]," etc.
‡Jeremiah O'Donovan Rossa (1831–1915), Irish nationalist leader.
§Cup in which the communion wine is held.

to pour itself out into my bosom. I thought little of the future. I did not know whether I would ever speak to her or not or, if I spoke to her, how I could tell her of my confused adoration. But my body was like a harp and her words and gestures were like fingers running upon the wires.

One evening I went into the back drawing-room in which the priest had died. It was a dark rainy evening and there was no sound in the house. Through one of the broken panes I heard the rain impinge upon the earth, the fine incessant needles of water playing in the sodden beds. Some distant lamp or lighted window gleamed below me. I was thankful that I could see so little. All my senses seemed to desire to veil themselves and, feeling that I was about to slip from them, I pressed the palms of my hands together until they trembled, murmuring: *O love! O love!* many times.

At last she spoke to me. When she addressed the first words to me I was so confused that I did not know what to answer. She asked me was I going to *Araby*.* I forgot whether I answered yes or no. It would be a splendid bazaar, she said she would love to go.

—And why can't you? I asked.

While she spoke she turned a silver bracelet round and round her wrist. She could not go, she said, because there would be a retreat† that week in her convent.‡ Her brother and two other boys were fighting for their caps and I was alone at the railings. She held one of the spikes, bowing her head towards me. The light from the lamp opposite our door caught the white curve of her neck, lit up her hair that rested there and, falling, lit up the hand upon the railing. It fell over one side of her dress and caught the white border of a petticoat, just visible as she stood at ease.

—It's well for you, she said.

—If I go, I said, I will bring you something.

What innumerable follies laid waste my waking and sleeping thoughts after that evening! I wished to annihilate the tedious intervening days. I chafed against the work of school. At night in my bedroom and by day in the classroom her image came between me and the page I strove to read. The syllables of the word *Araby* were called to me through the silence in which my soul luxuriated and cast an Eastern enchantment over me. I asked for leave to go to the bazaar on Saturday

---

*Bazaar held to support the Jervis Street Hospital, Dublin, held May 14–19, 1894.
†Period of withdrawal for the purpose of spiritual reflection and teaching.
‡That is, a convent school.

night. My aunt was surprised and hoped it was not some Freemason*
affair. I answered few questions in class. I watched my master's face pass
from amiability to sternness; he hoped I was not beginning to idle. I
could not call my wandering thoughts together. I had hardly any patience with the serious work of life which, now that it stood between
me and my desire, seemed to me child's play, ugly monotonous child's
play.

On Saturday morning I reminded my uncle that I wished to go to
the bazaar in the evening. He was fussing at the hallstand, looking for
the hat-brush, and answered me curtly:

—Yes, boy, I know.

As he was in the hall I could not go into the front parlour and lie at
the window. I left the house in bad humour and walked slowly towards
the school. The air was pitilessly raw and already my heart misgave me.

When I came home to dinner my uncle had not yet been home. Still
it was early. I sat staring at the clock for some time and, when its ticking began to irritate me, I left the room. I mounted the staircase and
gained the upper part of the house. The high cold empty gloomy rooms
liberated me and I went from room to room singing. From the front
window I saw my companions playing below in the street. Their cries
reached me weakened and indistinct and, leaning my forehead against
the cool glass, I looked over at the dark house where she lived. I may
have stood there for an hour, seeing nothing but the brown-clad figure
cast by my imagination, touched discreetly by the lamplight at the
curved neck, at the hand upon the railings and at the border below the
dress.

When I came downstairs again I found Mrs Mercer sitting at the
fire. She was an old garrulous woman, a pawnbroker's widow, who collected used stamps for some pious purpose. I had to endure the gossip
of the tea-table. The meal was prolonged beyond an hour and still my
uncle did not come. Mrs Mercer stood up to go: she was sorry she
couldn't wait any longer, but it was after eight o'clock and she did not
like to be out late, as the night air was bad for her. When she had gone
I began to walk up and down the room, clenching my fists. My aunt
said:

—I'm afraid you may put off your bazaar for this night of Our Lord.

At nine o'clock I heard my uncle's latchkey in the halldoor. I heard

---

*Relating to the secret fraternal order of Free and Accepted Masons, regarded by
Catholics as a Protestant sect.

him talking to himself and heard the hallstand rocking when it had received the weight of his overcoat. I could interpret these signs. When he was midway through his dinner I asked him to give me the money to go to the bazaar. He had forgotten.

—The people are in bed and after their first sleep now, he said.

I did not smile. My aunt said to him energetically:

—Can't you give him the money and let him go? You've kept him late enough as it is.

My uncle said he was very sorry he had forgotten. He said he believed in the old saying: *All work and no play makes Jack a dull boy.* He asked me where I was going and, when I had told him a second time he asked me did I know *The Arab's Farewell to his Steed.** When I left the kitchen he was about to recite the opening lines of the piece to my aunt.

I held a florin tightly in my hand as I strode down Buckingham Street towards the station. The sight of the streets thronged with buyers and glaring with gas recalled to me the purpose of my journey. I took my seat in a third-class carriage of a deserted train. After an intolerable delay the train moved out of the station slowly. It crept onward among ruinous houses and over the twinkling river. At Westland Row Station a crowd of people pressed to the carriage doors; but the porters moved them back, saying that it was a special train for the bazaar. I remained alone in the bare carriage. In a few minutes the train drew up beside an improvised wooden platform. I passed out on to the road and saw by the lighted dial of a clock that it was ten minutes to ten. In front of me was a large building which displayed the magical name.

I could not find any sixpenny entrance and, fearing that the bazaar would be closed, I passed in quickly through a turnstile, handing a shilling to a weary-looking man. I found myself in a big hall girdled at half its height by a gallery. Nearly all the stalls were closed and the greater part of the hall was in darkness. I recognised a silence like that which pervades a church after a service. I walked into the centre of the bazaar timidly. A few people were gathered about the stalls which were still open. Before a curtain, over which the words *Café Chantant*† were written in coloured lamps, two men were counting money on a salver.‡ I listened to the fall of the coins.

---

*Poem by English writer Caroline Sheridan Norton (1808–1877).

†Café with musical entertainment.

‡Serving tray.

Remembering with difficulty why I had come I went over to one of the stalls and examined porcelain vases and flowered tea-sets. At the door of the stall a young lady was talking and laughing with two young gentlemen. I remarked their English accents and listened vaguely to their conversation.

—O, I never said such a thing!

—O, but you did!

—O, but I didn't!

—Didn't she say that?

—Yes, I heard her.

—O, there's a . . . fib!

Observing me the young lady came over and asked me did I wish to buy anything. The tone of her voice was not encouraging; she seemed to have spoken to me out of a sense of duty. I looked humbly at the great jars that stood like eastern guards at either side of the dark entrance to the stall and murmured:

—No, thank you.

The young lady changed the position of one of the vases and went back to the two young men. They began to talk of the same subject. Once or twice the young lady glanced at me over her shoulder.

I lingered before her stall, though I knew my stay was useless, to make my interest in her wares seem the more real. Then I turned away slowly and walked down the middle of the bazaar. I allowed the two pennies to fall against the sixpence in my pocket. I heard a voice call from one end of the gallery that the light was out. The upper part of the hall was now completely dark.

Gazing up into the darkness I saw myself as a creature driven and derided by vanity; and my eyes burned with anguish and anger.

EVELINE

S̲H̲E̲ S̲A̲T̲ A̲T̲ T̲H̲E̲ window watching the evening invade the avenue. Her head was leaned against the window curtains and in her nostrils was the odour of dusty cretonne.* She was tired.

Few people passed. The man out of the last house passed on his way home; she heard his footsteps clacking along the concrete pavement and afterwards crunching on the cinder path before the new red houses. One time there used to be a field there in which they used to play every evening with other people's children. Then a man from Belfast bought the field and built houses in it— not like their little brown houses but bright brick houses with shining roofs. The children of the avenue used to play together in that field—the Devines, the Waters, the Dunns, little Keogh the cripple, she and her brothers and sisters. Ernest, however, never played: he was too grown up. Her father used often to hunt them in out of the field with his blackthorn stick;† but usually little Keogh used to keep *nix* ‡ and call out when he saw her father coming. Still they seemed to have been rather happy then. Her father was not so bad then; and besides, her mother was alive. That was a long time ago; she and her brothers and sisters were all grown up; her mother was dead. Tizzie Dunn was dead, too, and the Waters had gone back to England. Everything changes. Now she was going to go away like the others, to leave her home.

Home! She looked round the room, reviewing all its familiar objects which she had dusted once a week for so many years, wondering where on earth all the dust came from. Perhaps she would never see again those familiar objects from which she had never dreamed of being divided. And yet during all those years she had never found out the name of the priest whose yellowing photograph hung on the wall above the broken harmonium beside the coloured print of the promises made to

---

*Heavy cotton fabric.
†Walking stick.
‡Lookout.

Blessed Margaret Mary Alacoque.* He had been a school friend of her father. Whenever he showed the photograph to a visitor her father used to pass it with a casual word:

—He is in Melbourne now.

She had consented to go away, to leave her home. Was that wise? She tried to weigh each side of the question. In her home anyway she had shelter and food; she had those whom she had known all her life about her. Of course she had to work hard, both in the house and at business. What would they say of her in the Stores when they found out that she had run away with a fellow? Say she was a fool, perhaps; and her place would be filled up by advertisement. Miss Gavan would be glad. She had always had an edge on her, especially whenever there were people listening.

—Miss Hill, don't you see these ladies are waiting.

—Look lively, Miss Hill, please.

She would not cry many tears at leaving the Stores.

But in her new home, in a distant unknown country, it would not be like that. Then she would be married—she, Eveline. People would treat her with respect then. She would not be treated as her mother had been. Even now, though she was over nineteen, she sometimes felt herself in danger of her father's violence. She knew it was that that had given her the palpitations. When they were growing up he had never gone for her, like he used to go for Harry and Ernest, because she was a girl; but latterly he had begun to threaten her and say what he would do to her only for her dead mother's sake. And now she had nobody to protect her. Ernest was dead and Harry, who was in the church decorating business, was nearly always down somewhere in the country. Besides, the invariable squabble for money on Saturday nights had begun to weary her unspeakably. She always gave her entire wages—seven shillings—and Harry always sent up what he could but the trouble was to get any money from her father. He said she used to squander the money, that she had no head, that he wasn't going to give her his hard-earned money to throw about the streets, and much more, for he was usually fairly bad on Saturday night. In the end he would give her the money and ask her had she any intention of buying Sunday's dinner. Then she had to rush out as quickly as she could and do her marketing, holding her black leather purse tightly in her hand as she elbowed

---

*(1647–1690); French nun who was made a saint in 1920; she was instrumental in the establishment of the devotion to the Sacred Heart of Jesus.

her way through the crowds and returning home late under her load of provisions. She had hard work to keep the house together and to see that the two young children who had been left to her charge went to school regularly and got their meals regularly. It was hard work—a hard life—but now that she was about to leave it she did not find it a wholly undesirable life.

She was about to explore another life with Frank. Frank was very kind, manly, open-hearted. She was to go away with him by the night-boat to be his wife and to live with him in Buenos Ayres where he had a home waiting for her. How well she remembered the first time she had seen him; he was lodging in a house on the main road where she used to visit. It seemed a few weeks ago. He was standing at the gate, his peaked cap pushed back on his head and his hair tumbled forward over a face of bronze. Then they had come to know each other. He used to meet her outside the Stores every evening and see her home. He took her to see *The Bohemian Girl** and she felt elated as she sat in an unaccustomed part of the theatre with him. He was awfully fond of music and sang a little. People knew that they were courting and, when he sang about the lass that loves a sailor, she always felt pleasantly confused. He used to call her Poppens out of fun. First of all it had been an excitement for her to have a fellow and then she had begun to like him. He had tales of distant countries. He had started as a deck boy at a pound a month on a ship of the Allan Line† going out to Canada. He told her the names of the ships he had been on and the names of the different services. He had sailed through the Straits of Magellan and he told her stories of the terrible Patagonians. He had fallen on his feet in Buenos Ayres, he said, and had come over to the old country just for a holiday. Of course, her father had found out the affair and had forbidden her to have anything to say to him.

—I know these sailor chaps, he said.

One day he had quarrelled with Frank and after that she had to meet her lover secretly.

The evening deepened in the avenue. The white of two letters in her lap grew indistinct. One was to Harry; the other was to her father. Ernest had been her favourite but she liked Harry too. Her father was becoming old lately, she noticed; he would miss her. Sometimes he

---

*1843 opera with music by Irish composer Michael William Balfe (1808–1870), libretto by Alfred Bunn.

†Steamships serving England and America.

could be very nice. Not long before, when she had been laid up for a day, he had read her out a ghost story and made toast for her at the fire. Another day, when their mother was alive, they had all gone for a picnic to the Hill of Howth.* She remembered her father putting on her mother's bonnet to make the children laugh.

Her time was running out but she continued to sit by the window, leaning her head against the window curtain, inhaling the odour of dusty cretonne. Down far in the avenue she could hear a street organ playing. She knew the air.† Strange that it should come that very night to remind her of the promise to her mother, her promise to keep the home together as long as she could. She remembered the last night of her mother's illness; she was again in the close dark room at the other side of the hall and outside she heard a melancholy air of Italy. The organ-player had been ordered to go away and given sixpence. She remembered her father strutting back into the sickroom saying:

—Damned Italians! coming over here!

As she mused the pitiful vision of her mother's life laid its spell on the very quick of her being—that life of commonplace sacrifices closing in final craziness. She trembled as she heard again her mother's voice saying constantly with foolish insistence:

—Derevaun Seraun!‡ Derevaun Seraun!

She stood up in a sudden impulse of terror. Escape! She must escape! Frank would save her. He would give her life, perhaps love, too. But she wanted to live. Why should she be unhappy? She had a right to happiness. Frank would take her in his arms, fold her in his arms. He would save her.

*   *   *   *   *   *   *   *   *   *

She stood among the swaying crowd in the station at the North Wall.§ He held her hand and she knew that he was speaking to her, saying something about the passage over and over again. The station was full of soldiers with brown baggages. Through the wide doors of the sheds she caught a glimpse of the black mass of the boat, lying in beside the quay wall, with illumined portholes. She answered nothing.

---

*Geographical landmark framing the north side of Dublin Bay.
†Tune, melody.
‡Though some have claimed that this phrase sounds similar to something in Irish, it is probably meant simply as gibberish.
§North Liffey quayside for eastern departures

She felt her cheek pale and cold and, out of a maze of distress, she prayed to God to direct her, to show her what was her duty. The boat blew a long mournful whistle into the mist. If she went, tomorrow she would be on the sea with Frank, steaming toward Buenos Ayres. Their passage had been booked. Could she still draw back after all he had done for her? Her distress awoke a nausea in her body and she kept moving her lips in silent fervent prayer.

A bell clanged upon her heart. She felt him seize her hand:

—Come!

All the seas of the world tumbled about her heart. He was drawing her into them: he would drown her. She gripped with both hands at the iron railing.

—Come!

No! No! No! It was impossible. Her hands clutched the iron in frenzy. Amid the seas she sent a cry of anguish!

—Eveline! Evvy!

He rushed beyond the barrier and called to her to follow. He was shouted at to go on but he still called to her. She set her white face to him, passive, like a helpless animal. Her eyes gave him no sign of love or farewell or recognition.

AFTER THE RACE

THE CARS CAME SCUDDING in towards Dublin, running evenly like pellets in the groove of the Naas* Road. At the crest of the hill at Inchicore† sightseers had gathered in clumps to watch the cars careering homeward and through this channel of poverty and inaction the Continent sped its wealth and industry. Now and again the clumps of people raised the cheer of the gratefully oppressed. Their sympathy, however, was for the blue cars—the cars of their friends, the French.‡

The French, moreover, were virtual victors. Their team had finished solidly; they had been placed second and third and the driver of the winning German car was reported a Belgian. Each blue car, therefore, received a double measure of welcome as it topped the crest of the hill and each cheer of welcome was acknowledged with smiles and nods by those in the car. In one of these trimly built cars was a party of four young men whose spirits seemed to be at present well above the level of successful Gallicism: in fact, these four young men were almost hilarious. They were Charles Ségouin, the owner of the car; Andreé Rivière, a young electrician of Canadian birth; a huge Hungarian named Villona and a neatly groomed young man named Doyle. Ségouin was in good humour because he had unexpectedly received some orders in advance (he was about to start a motor establishment in Paris) and Rivière was in good humour because he was to be appointed manager of the establishment; these two young men (who were cousins) were also in good humour because of the success of the French cars. Villona was in good humour because he had had a very satisfactory luncheon; and besides he was an optimist by nature. The fourth member of the party, however, was too excited to be genuinely happy.

He was about twenty-six years of age, with a soft, light brown mous-

---

*County Kildare town southeast of Dublin.
†Village on the south bank of the Liffey.
‡The relationship between the Irish and the French is longstanding; the aid of the French In the unsuccessful 1798 rebellion, led by Wolfe Tone, is but one example.

tache and rather innocent-looking grey eyes. His father, who had begun life as an advanced Nationalist,* had modified his views early. He had made his money as a butcher in Kingstown† and by opening shops in Dublin and in the suburbs he had made his money many times over. He had also been fortunate enough to secure some of the police contracts and in the end he had become rich enough to be alluded to in the Dublin newspapers as a merchant prince. He had sent his son to England to be educated in a big Catholic college and had afterwards sent him to Dublin University‡ to study law. Jimmy did not study very earnestly and took to bad courses for a while. He had money and he was popular; and he divided his time curiously between musical and motoring circles. Then he had been sent for a term to Cambridge to see a little life. His father, remonstrative, but covertly proud of the excess, had paid his bills and brought him home. It was at Cambridge that he had met Ségouin. They were not much more than acquaintances as yet but Jimmy found great pleasure in the society of one who had seen so much of the world and was reputed to own some of the biggest hotels in France. Such a person (as his father agreed) was well worth knowing, even if he had not been the charming companion he was. Villona was entertaining also—a brilliant pianist—but, unfortunately, very poor.

The car ran on merrily with its cargo of hilarious youth. The two cousins sat on the front seat; Jimmy and his Hungarian friend sat behind. Decidedly Villona was in excellent spirits; he kept up a deep bass hum of melody for miles of the road. The Frenchmen flung their laughter and light words over their shoulders and often Jimmy had to strain forward to catch the quick phrase. This was not altogether pleasant for him, as he had nearly always to make a deft guess at the meaning and shout back a suitable answer in the face of a high wind. Besides Villona's humming would confuse anybody; the noise of the car, too.

Rapid motion through space elates one; so does notoriety; so does the possession of money. These were three good reasons for Jimmy's excitement. He had been seen by many of his friends that day in the company of these Continentals. At the control Ségouin had presented him to one of the French competitors and, in answer to his confused mur-

---

*Supporter of Home Rule for Ireland, and of Charles Stewart Parnell.
†Port city south of Dublin; now known once again by its Irish name, Dun Laoghaire.
‡That is, Trinity College, Dublin (also called the University of Dublin), the Protestant university founded in 1592 by Queen Elizabeth I.

mur of compliment, the swarthy face of the driver had disclosed a line of shining white teeth. It was pleasant after that honour to return to the profane world of spectators amid nudges and significant looks. Then as to money—he really had a great sum under his control. Ségouin, perhaps, would not think it a great sum but Jimmy who, in spite of temporary errors, was at heart the inheritor of solid instincts knew well with what difficulty it had been got together. This knowledge had previously kept his bills within the limits of reasonable recklessness and, if he had been so conscious of the labour latent in money when there had been question merely of some freak of the higher intelligence, how much more so now when he was about to stake the greater part of his substance! It was a serious thing for him.

Of course, the investment was a good one and Ségouin had managed to give the impression that it was by a favour of friendship the mite* of Irish money was to be included in the capital of the concern. Jimmy had a respect for his father's shrewdness in business matters and in this case it had been his father who had first suggested the investment; money to be made in the motor business, pots of money. Moreover Ségouin had the unmistakable air of wealth. Jimmy set out to translate into days' work that lordly car in which he sat. How smoothly it ran. In what style they had come careering along the country roads! The journey laid a magical finger on the genuine pulse of life and gallantly the machinery of human nerves strove to answer the bounding courses of the swift blue animal.

They drove down Dame Street. The street was busy with unusual traffic, loud with the horns of motorists and the gongs of impatient tram-drivers. Near the Bank† Ségouin drew up and Jimmy and his friend alighted. A little knot of people collected on the footpath to pay homage to the snorting motor. The party was to dine together that evening in Ségouin's hotel and, meanwhile, Jimmy and his friend, who was staying with him, were to go home to dress. The car steered out slowly for Grafton Street while the two young men pushed their way through the knot of gazers. They walked northward with a curious feeling of disappointment in the exercise, while the city hung its pale globes of light above them in a haze of summer evening.

In Jimmy's house this dinner had been pronounced an occasion. A

---

*Tiny amount.

†The Bank of Ireland building, across the street from Trinity College; the home of the Irish Parliament before the Act of Union in 1800.

certain pride mingled with his parents' trepidation, a certain eagerness, also, to play fast and loose for the names of great foreign cities have at least this virtue. Jimmy, too, looked very well when he was dressed and, as he stood in the hall giving a last equation to the bows of his dress tie, his father may have felt even commercially satisfied at having secured for his son qualities often unpurchaseable. His father, therefore, was unusually friendly with Villona and his manner expressed a real respect for foreign accomplishments; but this subtlety of his host was probably lost upon the Hungarian, who was beginning to have a sharp desire for his dinner.

The dinner was excellent, exquisite. Ségouin, Jimmy decided, had a very refined taste. The party was increased by a young Englishman named Routh whom Jimmy had seen with Ségouin at Cambridge. The young men supped in a snug room lit by electric candle lamps. They talked volubly and with little reserve. Jimmy, whose imagination was kindling, conceived the lively youth of the Frenchmen twined elegantly upon the firm framework of the Englishman's manner. A graceful image of his, he thought, and a just one. He admired the dexterity with which their host directed the conversation. The five young men had various tastes and their tongues had been loosened. Villona, with immense respect, began to discover to the mildly surprised Englishman the beauties of the English madrigal, deploring the loss of old instruments. Rivière, not wholly ingenuously, undertook to explain to Jimmy the triumph of the French mechanicians. The resonant voice of the Hungarian was about to prevail in ridicule of the spurious lutes of the romantic painters when Ségouin shepherded his party into politics. Here was congenial ground for all. Jimmy, under generous influences, felt the buried zeal of his father wake to life within him: he aroused the torpid Routh at last. The room grew doubly hot and Ségouin's task grew harder each moment: there was even danger of personal spite. The alert host at an opportunity lifted his glass to Humanity and, when the toast had been drunk, he threw open a window significantly.

That night the city wore the mask of a capital. The five young men strolled along Stephen's Green* in a faint cloud of aromatic smoke. They talked loudly and gaily and their cloaks dangled from their shoulders. The people made way for them. At the corner of Grafton Street a short fat man was putting two handsome ladies on a car in charge of

---

*St. Stephen's Green, a public park bordered by the Grafton Street shopping area on the north and University College Dublin on the south.

another fat man. The car drove off and the short fat man caught sight of the party.

—André.

—It's Farley!

A torrent of talk followed. Farley was an American. No one knew very well what the talk was about. Villona and Rivière were the noisiest, but all the men were excited. They got up on a car, squeezing themselves together amid much laughter. They drove by the crowd, blended now into soft colours, to a music of merry bells. They took the train at Westland Row and in a few seconds, as it seemed to Jimmy, they were walking out of Kingstown Station. The ticket-collector saluted Jimmy; he was an old man:

—Fine night, sir!

It was a serene summer night; the harbour lay like a darkened mirror at their feet. They proceeded towards it with linked arms, singing *Cadet Roussel** in chorus, stamping their feet at every:

—Ho! Ho! Hohé, vraiment!

They got into a rowboat at the slip and made out for the American's yacht. There was to be supper, music, cards. Villona said with conviction:

—It is delightful!

There was a yacht piano in the cabin. Villona played a waltz for Farley and Rivière, Farley acting as cavalier and Rivière as lady. Then an impromptu square dance, the men devising original figures. What merriment! Jimmy took his part with a will; this was seeing life, at least. Then Farley got out of breath and cried *Stop!* A man brought in a light supper, and the young men sat down to it for form's sake. They drank, however: it was Bohemian. They drank Ireland, England, France, Hungary, the United States of America. Jimmy made a speech, a long speech, Villona saying: *Hear! hear!* whenever there was a pause. There was a great clapping of hands when he sat down. It must have been a good speech. Farley clapped him on the back and laughed loudly. What jovial fellows! What good company they were!

Cards! cards! The table was cleared. Villona returned quietly to his piano and played voluntaries for them. The other men played game after game, flinging themselves boldly into the adventure. They drank the health of the Queen of Hearts and of the Queen of Diamonds.

---

*French regimental song dating from the 1790s.

Jimmy felt obscurely the lack of an audience: the wit was flashing. Play ran very high and paper began to pass.* Jimmy did not know exactly who was winning but he knew that he was losing. But it was his own fault for he frequently mistook his cards and the other men had to calculate his I.O.U.'s for him. They were devils of fellows but he wished they would stop: it was getting late. Someone gave the toast of the yacht *The Belle of Newport* and then someone proposed one great game for a finish.

The piano had stopped; Villona must have gone up on deck. It was a terrible game. They stopped just before the end of it to drink for luck. Jimmy understood that the game lay between Routh and Ségouin. What excitement! Jimmy was excited too; he would lose, of course. How much had he written away? The men rose to their feet to play the last tricks, talking and gesticulating. Routh won. The cabin shook with the young men's cheering and the cards were bundled together. They began then to gather in what they had won. Farley and Jimmy were the heaviest losers.

He knew that he would regret in the morning but at present he was glad of the rest, glad of the dark stupor that would cover up his folly. He leaned his elbows on the table and rested his head between his hands, counting the beats of his temples. The cabin door opened and he saw the Hungarian standing in a shaft of grey light:

—Daybreak, gentlemen!

---

*That is, IOUs are being used in place of money.

"Two Gallants"

— — — Corley's Route (with and without Lenehan)
• • • • • Lenehan's Route (solus)

Refreshment Bar (?)

Gt. Britain (Parnell) Street

O'Connell Street

Earl Street

Red Light District

Capel Street

River Liffey

City Hall

Castle

Trinity College

Grafton Street

Duke's Lawn

Tram to Donnybrook

Merrion Square

Stephen's Green

University College

TWO GALLANTS

THE GREY WARM EVENING of August had descended upon the city and a mild warm air, a memory of summer, circulated in the streets. The streets, shuttered for the repose of Sunday, swarmed with a gaily coloured crowd. Like illumined pearls the lamps shone from the summits of their tall poles upon the living texture below which, changing shape and hue unceasingly, sent up into the warm grey evening air an unchanging, unceasing murmur.

Two young men came down the hill of Rutland Square.* One of them was just bringing a long monologue to a close. The other, who walked on the verge of the path and was at times obliged to step on to the road, owing to his companion's rudeness, wore an amused listening face. He was squat and ruddy. A yachting cap was shoved far back from his forehead and the narrative to which he listened made constant waves of expression break forth over his face from the corners of his nose and eyes and mouth. Little jets of wheezing laughter followed one another out of his convulsed body. His eyes, twinkling with cunning enjoyment, glanced at every moment towards his companion's face. Once or twice he rearranged the light waterproof† which he had slung over one shoulder in toreador fashion. His breeches, his white rubber shoes and his jauntily slung waterproof expressed youth. But his figure fell into rotundity at the waist, his hair was scant and grey and his face, when the waves of expression had passed over it, had a ravaged look.

When he was quite sure that the narrative had ended he laughed noiselessly for fully half a minute. Then he said:

—Well! . . . That takes the biscuit!

His voice seemed winnowed of vigour; and to enforce his words he added with humour:

---

*Now known as Parnell Square; at the northern end of Sackville (now O'Connell) Street.
†Raincoat.

—That takes the solitary, unique, and, if I may so call it, *recherché**
biscuit!

He became serious and silent when he had said this. His tongue was
tired for he had been talking all the afternoon in a public-house† in
Dorset Street. Most people considered Lenehan a leech but, in spite of
this reputation, his adroitness and eloquence had always prevented his
friends from forming any general policy against him. He had a brave
manner of coming up to a party of them in a bar and of holding himself nimbly at the borders of the company until he was included in a
round. He was a sporting vagrant armed with a vast stock of stories,
limericks and riddles. He was insensitive to all kinds of discourtesy. No
one knew how he achieved the stern task of living, but his name was
vaguely associated with racing tissues.‡

—And where did you pick her up, Corley? he asked.

Corley ran his tongue swiftly along his upper lip.

—One night, man, he said, I was going along Dame Street and I
spotted a fine tart under Waterhouse's clock§ and said good-night, you
know. So we went for a walk round by the canal and she told me she
was a slavey‖ in a house in Baggot Street. I put my arm round her and
squeezed her a bit that night. Then next Sunday, man, I met her by appointment. We went out to Donnybrook# and I brought her into a field
there. She told me she used to go with a dairyman. . . . It was fine, man.
Cigarettes every night she'd bring me and paying the tram out and
back. And one night she brought me two bloody fine cigars—O, the
real cheese, you know, that the old fellow used to smoke. . . . I was
afraid, man, she'd get in the family way. But she's up to the dodge.**

—Maybe she thinks you'll marry her, said Lenehan.

—I told her I was out of a job, said Corley. I told her I was in
Pim's.†† She doesn't know my name. I was too hairy‡‡ to tell her that.
But she thinks I'm a bit of class, you know.

Lenehan laughed again, noiselessly.

---

*Exquisite, over-refined.
†Pub; a licensed premises open to the public, as opposed to a private bar or club.
‡Newspapers with information about the day's horse racing.
§Formerly, a familiar landmark and rendezvous point in downtown Dublin.
‖Working-class woman or one of questionable virtue.
#Rural area southeast of Dublin.
**Deceit.
††Large downtown department store.
‡‡Careful.

—Of all the good ones ever I heard, he said, that emphatically takes the biscuit.

Corley's stride acknowledged the compliment. The swing of his burly body made his friend execute a few light skips from the path to the roadway and back again. Corley was the son of an inspector of police and he had inherited his father's frame and gait. He walked with his hands by his sides, holding himself erect and swaying his head from side to side. His head was large, globular and oily; it sweated in all weathers; and his large round hat, set upon it sideways, looked like a bulb which had grown out of another. He always stared straight before him as if he were on parade and, when he wished to gaze after someone in the street, it was necessary for him to move his body from the hips. At present he was about town. Whenever any job was vacant a friend was always ready to give him the hard word.* He was often to be seen walking with policemen in plain clothes, talking earnestly. He knew the inner side of all affairs and was fond of delivering final judgments. He spoke without listening to the speech of his companions. His conversation was mainly about himself: what he had said to such a person and what such a person had said to him and what he had said to settle the matter. When he reported these dialogues he aspirated the first letter of his name after the manner of Florentines.

Lenehan offered his friend a cigarette. As the two young men walked on through the crowd Corley occasionally turned to smile at some of the passing girls but Lenehan's gaze was fixed on the large faint moon circled with a double halo. He watched earnestly the passing of the grey web of twilight across its face. At length he said:

—Well . . . tell me, Corley, I suppose you'll be able to pull it off all right, eh?

Corley closed one eye expressively as an answer.

—Is she game for that? asked Lenehan dubiously. You can never know women.

—She's all right, said Corley. I know the way to get around her, man. She's a bit gone on me.

—You're what I call a gay Lothario,† said Lenehan. And the proper kind of a Lothario, too!

A shade of mockery relieved the servility of his manner. To save

---

*An insider tip.
†Seductive young man; similar to a "Don Juan."

himself he had the habit of leaving his flattery open to the interpretation of raillery. But Corley had not a subtle mind.

—There's nothing to touch a good slavey, he affirmed. Take my tip for it.

—By one who has tried them all, said Lenehan.

—First I used to go with girls, you know, said Corley, unbosoming; girls off the South Circular. I used to take them out, man, on the tram somewhere and pay the tram or take them to a band or a play at the theatre or buy them chocolate and sweets or something that way. I used to spend money on them right enough, he added, in a convincing tone, as if he was conscious of being disbelieved.

But Lenehan could well believe it, he nodded gravely.

—I know that game, he said, and it's a mug's game.*

—And damn the thing I ever got out of it, said Corley.

—Ditto here, said Lenehan.

—Only off of one of them, said Corley.

He moistened his upper lip by running his tongue along it. The recollection brightened his eyes. He too gazed at the pale disc of the moon, now nearly veiled, and seemed to meditate.

—She was . . . a bit of all right, he said regretfully.

He was silent again. Then he added:

—She's on the turf† now. I saw her driving down Earl Street one night with two fellows with her on a car.‡

—I suppose that's your doing, said Lenehan.

—There was others at her before me, said Corley philosophically.

This time Lenehan was inclined to disbelieve. He shook his head to and fro and smiled.

—You know you can't kid me, Corley, he said.

—Honest to God! said Corley. Didn't she tell me herself?

Lenehan made a tragic gesture.

—Base betrayer! he said.

As they passed along the railings of Trinity College,§ Lenehan skipped out into the road and peered up at the clock.

—Twenty after, he said.

---

*Fool's game; futile.
†Working as a prostitute.
‡Horse-drawn hackney coach, or "hack."
§The Protestant university founded in 1592 by Queen Elizabeth I; also called the University of Dublin.

—Time enough, said Corley. She'll be there all right. I always let her wait a bit.

Lenehan laughed quietly.

—Ecod! Corley, you know how to take them, he said.

—I'm up to all their little tricks, Corley confessed.

—But tell me, said Lenehan again, are you sure you can bring it off all right? You know it's a ticklish job. They're damn close on that point. Eh? . . . What?

His bright, small eyes searched his companion's face for reassurance. Corley swung his head to and fro as if to toss aside an insistent insect, and his brows gathered.

—I'll pull it off, he said. Leave it to me, can't you?

Lenehan said no more. He did not wish to ruffle his friend's temper, to be sent to the devil and told that his advice was not wanted. A little tact was necessary. But Corley's brow was soon smooth again. His thoughts were running another way.

—She's a fine decent tart, he said, with appreciation; that's what she is.

They walked along Nassau Street and then turned into Kildare Street. Not far from the porch of the club* a harpist stood in the roadway, playing to a little ring of listeners. He plucked at the wires heedlessly, glancing quickly from time to time at the face of each new-comer and from time to time, wearily also, at the sky. His harp, too, heedless that her coverings had fallen about her knees, seemed weary alike of the eyes of strangers and of her master's hands. One hand played in the bass the melody of *Silent, O Moyle,*† while the other hand careered in the treble after each group of notes. The notes of the air sounded deep and full.

The two young men walked up the street without speaking, the mournful music following them. When they reached Stephen's Green‡ they crossed the road. Here the noise of trams, the lights and the crowd released them from their silence.

—There she is! said Corley.

At the corner of Hume Street a young woman was standing. She wore a blue dress and a white sailor hat. She stood on the curbstone, swinging a sunshade in one hand. Lenehan grew lively.

—Let's have a look at her, Corley, he said.

---

*The Kildare Street Club, an exclusive gentleman's club.
†From Thomas Moore's *Irish Melodies*.
‡St. Stephen's Green, a public park bordered by the Grafton Street shopping area on the north and University College Dublin on the south.

Corley glanced sideways at his friend and an unpleasant grin appeared on his face.

—Are you trying to get inside me?* he asked.

—Damn it! said Lenehan boldly, I don't want an introduction. All I want is to have a look at her. I'm not going to eat her.

—O . . . A look at her? said Corley, more amiably. Well . . . I'll tell you what. I'll go over and talk to her and you can pass by.

—Right! said Lenehan.

Corley had already thrown one leg over the chains when Lenehan called out:

—And after? Where will we meet?

—Half ten,† answered Corley, bringing over his other leg.

—Where?

—Corner of Merrion Street. We'll be coming back.

—Work it all right now, said Lenehan in farewell.

Corley did not answer. He sauntered across the road swaying his head from side to side. His bulk, his easy pace, and the solid sound of his boots had something of the conqueror in them. He approached the young woman and, without saluting, began at once to converse with her. She swung her umbrella more quickly and executed half turns on her heels. Once or twice when he spoke to her at close quarters she laughed and bent her head.

Lenehan observed them for a few minutes. Then he walked rapidly along beside the chains at some distance and crossed the road obliquely. As he approached Hume Street corner he found the air heavily scented and his eyes made a swift anxious scrutiny of the young woman's appearance. She had her Sunday finery on. Her blue serge skirt was held at the waist by a belt of black leather. The great silver buckle of her belt seemed to depress the centre of her body, catching the light stuff of her white blouse like a clip. She wore a short black jacket with mother-of-pearl buttons and a ragged black boa. The ends of her tulle‡ collarette had been carefully disordered and a big bunch of red flowers was pinned in her bosom stems upwards. Lenehan's eyes noted approvingly her stout short muscular body. Frank rude health glowed in her face, on her fat red cheeks and in her unabashed blue eyes. Her features were blunt. She had broad nostrils, a straggling mouth which lay open in a

---

*Steal the advantage from me.
†Half-past ten.
‡Sheer, often starched, silk netting.

contented leer, and two projecting front teeth. As he passed Lenehan took off his cap and, after about ten seconds, Corley returned a salute to the air. This he did by raising his hand vaguely and pensively changing the angle of position of his hat.

Lenehan walked as far as the Shelbourne Hotel* where he halted and waited. After waiting for a little time he saw them coming towards him and, when they turned to the right, he followed them, stepping lightly in his white shoes, down one side of Merrion Square.† As he walked on slowly, timing his pace to theirs, he watched Corley's head which turned at every moment towards the young woman's face like a big ball revolving on a pivot. He kept the pair in view until he had seen them climbing the stairs of the Donnybrook tram; then he turned about and went back the way he had come.

Now that he was alone his face looked older. His gaiety seemed to forsake him and, as he came by the railings of the Duke's Lawn,‡ he allowed his hand to run along them. The air which the harpist had played began to control his movements. His softly padded feet played the melody while his fingers swept a scale of variations idly along the railings after each group of notes.

He walked listlessly round Stephen's Green and then down Grafton Street. Though his eyes took note of many elements of the crowd through which he passed they did so morosely. He found trivial all that was meant to charm him and did not answer the glances which invited him to be bold. He knew that he would have to speak a great deal, to invent and to amuse, and his brain and throat were too dry for such a task. The problem of how he could pass the hours till he met Corley again troubled him a little. He could think of no way of passing them but to keep on walking. He turned to the left when he came to the corner of Rutland Square and felt more at ease in the dark quiet street, the sombre look of which suited his mood. He paused at last before the window of a poor-looking shop over which the words *Refreshment Bar* were printed in white letters. On the glass of the window were two flying inscriptions: *Ginger Beer* and *Ginger Ale.*§ A cut ham was exposed on a

---

*At the time, Dublin's most fashionable hotel, at the north end of St. Stephen's Green.

†Fashionable neighborhood to the east of St. Stephen's Green.

‡The lawn beside the Duke of Leinster's house, in the same block as the National Library and the National Museum.

§Temperance (that is, nonalcoholic) beverages.

great blue dish while near it on a plate lay a segment of very light plum-pudding. He eyed this food earnestly for some time and then, after glancing warily up and down the street, went into the shop quickly.

He was hungry for, except some biscuits which he had asked two grudging curates* to bring him, he had eaten nothing since breakfast-time. He sat down at an uncovered wooden table opposite two work-girls and a mechanic. A slatternly† girl waited on him.

—How much is a plate of peas? he asked.

—Three halfpence,‡ sir, said the girl.

—Bring me a plate of peas, he said, and a bottle of ginger beer.

He spoke roughly in order to belie his air of gentility for his entry had been followed by a pause of talk. His face was heated. To appear natural he pushed his cap back on his head and planted his elbows on the table. The mechanic and the two work-girls examined him point by point before resuming their conversation in a subdued voice. The girl brought him a plate of grocer's hot peas, seasoned with pepper and vinegar, a fork and his ginger beer. He ate his food greedily and found it so good that he made a note of the shop mentally. When he had eaten all the peas he sipped his ginger beer and sat for some time thinking of Corley's adventure. In his imagination he beheld the pair of lovers walking along some dark road; he heard Corley's voice in deep energetic gallantries and saw again the leer of the young woman's mouth. This vision made him feel keenly his own poverty of purse and spirit. He was tired of knocking about, of pulling the devil by the tail, of shifts and intrigues. He would be thirty-one in November. Would he never get a good job? Would he never have a home of his own? He thought how pleasant it would be to have a warm fire to sit by and a good dinner to sit down to. He had walked the streets long enough with friends and with girls. He knew what those friends were worth: he knew the girls too. Experience had embittered his heart against the world. But all hope had not left him. He felt better after having eaten than he had felt before, less weary of his life, less vanquished in spirit. He might yet be able to settle down in some snug corner and live happily if he could only come across some good simple-minded girl with a little of the ready.

He paid twopence halfpenny to the slatternly girl and went out of the shop to begin his wandering again. He went into Capel Street and

---

*Dublin lingo for "bartenders."

†Untidy.

‡That is, 3½ pence.

walked along towards the City Hall. Then he turned into Dame Street. At the corner of George's Street he met two friends of his and stopped to converse with them. He was glad that he could rest from all his walking. His friends asked him had he seen Corley and what was the latest. He replied that he had spent the day with Corley. His friends talked very little. They looked vacantly after some figures in the crowd and sometimes made a critical remark. One said that he had seen Mac an hour before in Westmoreland Street. At this Lenehan said that he had been with Mac the night before in Egan's.* The young man who had seen Mac in Westmoreland Street asked was it true that Mac had won a bit over a billiard match. Lenehan did not know: he said that Holohan had stood them drinks in Egan's.

He left his friends at a quarter to ten and went up George's Street. He turned to the left at the City Markets† and walked on into Grafton Street. The crowd of girls and young men had thinned and on his way up the street he heard many groups and couples bidding one another goodnight. He went as far as the clock of the College of Surgeons:‡ it was on the stroke of ten. He set off briskly along the northern side of the Green hurrying for fear Corley should return too soon. When he reached the corner of Merrion Street he took his stand in the shadow of a lamp and brought out one of the cigarettes which he had reserved and lit it. He leaned against the lamp post and kept his gaze fixed on the part from which he expected to see Corley and the young woman return.

His mind became active again. He wondered had Corley managed it successfully. He wondered if he had asked her yet or if he would leave it to the last. He suffered all the pangs and thrills of his friend's situation as well as those of his own. But the memory of Corley's slowly revolving head calmed him somewhat: he was sure Corley would pull it off all right. All at once the idea struck him that perhaps Corley had seen her home by another way and given him the slip. His eyes searched the street: there was no sign of them. Yet it was surely half-an-hour since he had seen the clock of the College of Surgeons. Would Corley do a thing like that? He lit his last cigarette and began to smoke it nervously. He strained his eyes as each tram stopped at the far corner of the square. They must have gone home by another way. The paper of his cigarette broke and he flung it into the road with a curse.

---

*A pub.
†The South City Market Arcade.
‡On the west side of St. Stephen's Green.

Suddenly he saw them coming towards him. He started with delight and keeping close to his lamp-post tried to read the result in their walk. They were walking quickly, the young woman taking quick short steps, while Corley kept beside her with his long stride. They did not seem to be speaking. An intimation of the result pricked him like the point of a sharp instrument. He knew Corley would fail; he knew it was no go.

They turned down Baggot Street and he followed them at once, taking the other footpath. When they stopped he stopped too. They talked for a few moments and then the young woman went down the steps into the area of a house. Corley remained standing at the edge of the path, a little distance from the front steps. Some minutes passed. Then the hall-door was opened slowly and cautiously. A woman came running down the front steps and coughed. Corley turned and went towards her. His broad figure hid hers from view for a few seconds and then she reappeared running up the steps. The door closed on her and Corley began to walk swiftly towards Stephen's Green.

Lenehan hurried on in the same direction. Some drops of light rain fell. He took them as a warning and, glancing back towards the house which the young woman had entered to see that he was not observed, he ran eagerly across the road. Anxiety and his swift run made him pant. He called out:

—Hallo, Corley!

Corley turned his head to see who had called him, and then continued walking as before. Lenehan ran after him, settling the waterproof on his shoulders with one hand.

—Hallo, Corley! he cried again.

He came level with his friend and looked keenly in his face. He could see nothing there.

—Well? he said. Did it come off?

They had reached the corner of Ely Place. Still without answering Corley swerved to the left and went up the side street. His features were composed in stern calm. Lenehan kept up with his friend, breathing uneasily. He was baffled and a note of menace pierced through his voice.

—Can't you tell us? he said. Did you try her?

Corley halted at the first lamp and stared grimly before him. Then with a grave gesture he extended a hand towards the light and, smiling, opened it slowly to the gaze of his disciple. A small gold coin* shone in the palm.

---

*Either a sovereign or half-sovereign.

THE BOARDING HOUSE

MRS MOONEY WAS A butcher's daughter. She was a woman who was quite able to keep things to herself: a determined woman. She had married her father's foreman and opened a butcher's shop near Spring Gardens.* But as soon as his father-in-law was dead Mr Mooney began to go to the devil. He drank, plundered the till, ran headlong into debt. It was no use making him take the pledge:† he was sure to break out again a few days after. By fighting his wife in the presence of customers and by buying bad meat he ruined his business. One night he went for his wife with the cleaver and she had to sleep in a neighbour's house.

After that they lived apart. She went to the priest and got a separation‡ from him with care of the children. She would give him neither money nor food nor house-room; and so he was obliged to enlist himself as a sheriff's man. He was a shabby stooped little drunkard with a white face and a white moustache and white eyebrows, pencilled above his little eyes, which were pink-veined and raw; and all day long he sat in the bailiff's room, waiting to be put on a job. Mrs Mooney, who had taken what remained of her money out of the butcher business and set up a boarding house in Hardwicke Street, was a big imposing woman. Her house had a floating population made up of tourists from Liverpool and the Isle of Man§ and, occasionally, *artistes* from the music halls. Its resident population was made up of clerks from the city. She governed the house cunningly and firmly, knew when to give credit, when to be stern and when to let things pass. All the resident young men spoke of her as *The Madam*.||

Mrs Mooney's young men paid fifteen shillings a week for board

---

*Neighborhood on the northeast side of Dublin.
†The temperance pledge—that is, to not drink alcohol.
‡Divorce would have been impossible for a Catholic couple in Ireland at this time.
§Popular seaside holiday destinations.
||The implication is that Mrs Mooney runs not just a boarding house but a house with some features of a brothel.

and lodgings (beer or stout at dinner excluded). They shared in common tastes and occupations and for this reason they were very chummy with one another. They discussed with one another the chances of favourites and outsiders.* Jack Mooney, the Madam's son, who was clerk to a commission agent in Fleet Street, had the reputation of being a hard case. He was fond of using soldiers' obscenities: usually he came home in the small hours. When he met his friends he had always a good one to tell them and he was always sure to be on to a good thing—that is to say, a likely horse or a likely *artiste*. He was also handy with the mits† and sang comic songs. On Sunday nights there would often be a reunion in Mrs Mooney's front drawing-room. The music-hall *artistes* would oblige; and Sheridan played waltzes and polkas and vamped accompaniments. Polly Mooney, the Madam's daughter, would also sing. She sang:

> *I'm a . . . naughty girl.*
> *You needn't sham:*
> *You know I am.*‡

Polly was a slim girl of nineteen; she had light soft hair and a small full mouth. Her eyes, which were grey with a shade of green through them, had a habit of glancing upwards when she spoke with anyone, which made her look like a little perverse madonna. Mrs Mooney had first sent her daughter to be a typist in a corn-factor's§ office but, as a disreputable sheriff's man used to come every other day to the office, asking to be allowed to say a word to his daughter, she had taken her daughter home again and set her to do housework. As Polly was very lively the intention was to give her the run of the young men. Besides, young men like to feel that there is a young woman not very far away. Polly, of course, flirted with the young men but Mrs Mooney, who was a shrewd judge, knew that the young men were only passing the time away: none of them meant business. Things went on so for a long time and Mrs Mooney began to think of sending Polly back to typewriting when she noticed that something was going on between Polly and one of the young men. She watched the pair and kept her own counsel.

---

*Terms from horse racing.
†That is, he is something of a boxer.
‡Risqué music-hall song.
§Broker between grower and wholesaler.

Polly knew that she was being watched, but still her mother's persistent silence could not be misunderstood. There had been no open complicity between mother and daughter, no open understanding but, though people in the house began to talk of the affair, still Mrs Mooney did not intervene. Polly began to grow a little strange in her manner and the young man was evidently perturbed. At last, when she judged it to be the right moment, Mrs Mooney intervened. She dealt with moral problems as a cleaver deals with meat: and in this case she had made up her mind.

It was a bright Sunday morning of early summer, promising heat, but with a fresh breeze blowing. All the windows of the boarding house were open and the lace curtains ballooned gently towards the street be neath the raised sashes. The belfry of George's Church sent out constant peals and worshippers, singly or in groups, traversed the little circus before the church, revealing their purpose by their self-contained demeanour no less than by the little volumes in their gloved hands. Breakfast was over in the boarding house and the table of the breakfast-room was covered with plates on which lay yellow streaks of eggs with morsels of bacon-fat and bacon-rind. Mrs Mooney sat in the straw arm-chair and watched the servant Mary remove the breakfast things. She made Mary collect the crusts and pieces of broken bread to help to make Tuesday's breadpudding. When the table was cleared, the broken bread collected, the sugar and butter safe under lock and key, she began to reconstruct the interview which she had had the night before with Polly. Things were as she had suspected: she had been frank in her questions and Polly had been frank in her answers. Both had been somewhat awkward, of course. She had been made awkward by her not wishing to receive the news in too cavalier a fashion or to seem to have connived and Polly had been made awkward not merely because allusions of that kind always made her awkward but also because she did not wish it to be thought that in her wise innocence she had divined the intention behind her mother's tolerance.

Mrs Mooney glanced instinctively at the little gilt clock on the mantelpiece as soon as she had become aware through her revery that the bells of George's Church had stopped ringing. It was seventeen minutes past eleven: she would have lots of time to have the matter out with Mr Doran and then catch short twelve at Marlborough Street.* She was sure she would win. To begin with she had all the weight of social

---

*The last, abbreviated Mass at noon on Sunday.

opinion on her side: she was an outraged mother. She had allowed him to live beneath her roof, assuming that he was a man of honour, and he had simply abused her hospitality. He was thirty-four or thirty-five years of age, so that youth could not be pleaded as his excuse; nor could ignorance be his excuse since he was a man who had seen something of the world. He had simply taken advantage of Polly's youth and inexperience: that was evident. The question was: What reparation would he make?

There must be reparation made in such case. It is all very well for the man: he can go his ways as if nothing had happened, having had his moment of pleasure, but the girl has to bear the brunt. Some mothers would be content to patch up such an affair for a sum of money; she had known cases of it. But she would not do so. For her only one reparation could make up for the loss of her daughter's honour: marriage.

She counted all her cards again before sending Mary up to Mr Doran's room to say that she wished to speak with him. She felt sure she would win. He was a serious young man, not rakish or loud-voiced like the others. If it had been Mr Sheridan or Mr Meade or Bantam Lyons her task would have been much harder. She did not think he would face publicity. All the lodgers in the house knew something of the affair; details had been invented by some. Besides, he had been employed for thirteen years in a great Catholic wine-merchant's office and publicity would mean for him, perhaps, the loss of his sit.* Whereas if he agreed all might be well. She knew he had a good screw† for one thing and she suspected he had a bit of stuff put by.‡

Nearly the half-hour! She stood up and surveyed herself in the pier-glass.§ The decisive expression of her great florid face satisfied her and she thought of some mothers she knew who could not get their daughters off their hands.

Mr Doran was very anxious indeed this Sunday morning. He had made two attempts to shave but his hand had been so unsteady that he had been obliged to desist. Three days' reddish beard fringed his jaws and every two or three minutes a mist gathered on his glasses so that he had to take them off and polish them with his pocket-handkerchief. The recollection of his confession of the night before was a cause of

---

*"Situation"; job.
†A good salary.
‡Money in savings.
§Long, narrow mirror.

acute pain to him; the priest had drawn out every ridiculous detail of the affair and in the end had so magnified his sin that he was almost thankful at being afforded a loophole of reparation. The harm was done. What could he do now but marry her or run away? He could not brazen it out.* The affair would be sure to be talked of and his employer certain to hear of it. Dublin is such a small city: everyone knows everyone else's business. He felt his heart leap warmly in his throat as he heard in his excited imagination old Mr Leonard calling out in his rasping voice: *Send Mr Doran here, please.*

All his long years of service gone for nothing! All his industry and diligence thrown away! As a young man he had sown his wild oats, of course; he had boasted of his free-thinking and denied the existence of God to his companions in public-houses. But that was all passed and done with . . . nearly. He still bought a copy of *Reynold's Newspaper*† every week but he attended to his religious duties and for nine-tenths of the year lived a regular life. He had money enough to settle down on; it was not that. But the family would look down on her. First of all there was her disreputable father and then her mother's boarding house was beginning to get a certain fame. He had a notion that he was being had. He could imagine his friends talking of the affair and laughing. She *was* a little vulgar; some times she said *I seen* and *If I had've known.* But what would grammar matter if he really loved her? He could not make up his mind whether to like her or despise her for what she had done. Of course he had done it too. His instinct urged him to remain free, not to marry. Once you are married you are done for, it said.

While he was sitting helplessly on the side of the bed in shirt and trousers she tapped lightly at his door and entered. She told him all, that she had made a clean breast of it to her mother and that her mother would speak with him that morning. She cried and threw her arms round his neck, saying:

—O Bob! Bob! What am I to do? What am I to do at all?

She would put an end to herself, she said.

He comforted her feebly, telling her not to cry, that it would be all right, never fear. He felt against his shirt the agitation of her bosom.

It was not altogether his fault that it had happened. He remembered well, with the curious patient memory of the celibate, the first casual caresses her dress, her breath, her fingers had given him. Then late one night

---

*Weather the criticism.
†Radical London newspaper.

as he was undressing for bed she had tapped at his door, timidly. She wanted to relight her candle at his for hers had been blown out by a gust. It was her bath night. She wore a loose open combing jacket* of printed flannel. Her white instep shone in the opening of her furry slippers and the blood glowed warmly behind her perfumed skin. From her hands and wrists too as she lit and steadied her candle a faint perfume arose.

On nights when he came in very late it was she who warmed up his dinner. He scarcely knew what he was eating feeling her beside him alone, at night, in the sleeping house. And her thoughtfulness! If the night was anyway cold or wet or windy there was sure to be a little tumbler of punch† ready for him. Perhaps they could be happy together. . . .

They used to go upstairs together on tiptoe, each with a candle, and on the third landing exchange reluctant good-nights. They used to kiss. He remembered well her eyes, the touch of her hand and his delirium. . . .

But delirium passes. He echoed her phrase, applying it to himself: *What am I to do?* The instinct of the celibate warned him to hold back. But the sin was there; even his sense of honour told him that reparation must be made for such a sin.

While he was sitting with her on the side of the bed Mary came to the door and said that the missus wanted to see him in the parlour. He stood up to put on his coat and waistcoat, more helpless than ever. When he was dressed he went over to her to comfort her. It would be all right, never fear. He left her crying on the bed and moaning softly: *O my God!*

Going down the stairs his glasses became so dimmed with moisture that he had to take them off and polish them. He longed to ascend through the roof and fly away to another country where he would never hear again of his trouble, and yet a force pushed him downstairs step by step. The implacable faces of his employer and of the Madam stared upon his discomfiture. On the last flight of stairs he passed Jack Mooney who was coming up from the pantry nursing two bottles of *Bass*.‡ They saluted coldly; and the lover's eyes rested for a second or two on a thick bulldog face and a pair of thick short arms. When he reached the foot of the staircase he glanced up and saw Jack regarding him from the door of the return-room.§

---

*Type of robe.
†Hot whiskey drink.
‡A British ale.
§Room for returning empty bottles.

Suddenly he remembered the night when one of the music-hall *artistes*, a little blond Londoner, had made a rather free allusion to Polly. The reunion had been almost broken up on account of Jack's violence. Everyone tried to quiet him. The music-hall *artiste*, a little paler than usual, kept smiling and saying that there was no harm meant: but Jack kept shouting at him that if any fellow tried that sort of a game on with his sister he'd bloody* well put his teeth down his throat, so he would.

    *   *   *   *   *   *   *   *   *   *

Polly sat for a little time on the side of the bed, crying. Then she dried her eyes and went over to the looking-glass. She dipped the end of the towel in the water-jug and refreshed her eyes with the cool water. She looked at herself in profile and readjusted a hairpin above her ear. Then she went back to the bed again and sat at the foot. She regarded the pillows for a long time and the sight of them awakened in her mind secret, amiable memories. She rested the nape of her neck against the cool iron bed-rail and fell into a revery. There was no longer any perturbation visible on her face.

She waited on patiently, almost cheerfully, without alarm, her memories gradually giving place to hopes and visions of the future. Her hopes and visions were so intricate that she no longer saw the white pillows on which her gaze was fixed or remembered that she was waiting for anything.

At last she heard her mother calling. She started to her feet and ran to the banisters.

—Polly! Polly!

—Yes, mamma?

—Come down, dear. Mr Doran wants to speak to you.

Then she remembered what she had been waiting for.

---

*An oath strong enough, during this period, that it almost prevented the publication of *Dubliners*.

A LITTLE CLOUD

EIGHT YEARS BEFORE HE had seen his friend off at the North Wall* and wished him godspeed. Gallaher had got on. You could tell that at once by his travelled air, his well-cut tweed suit, and fearless accent. Few fellows had talents like his and fewer still could remain unspoiled by such success. Gallaher's heart was in the right place and he had deserved to win. It was something to have a friend like that.

Little Chandler's thoughts ever since lunchtime had been of his meeting with Gallaher, of Gallaher's invitation and of the great city London where Gallaher lived. He was called Little Chandler because, though he was but slightly under the average stature, he gave one the idea of being a little man. His hands were white and small, his frame was fragile, his voice was quiet and his manners were refined. He took the greatest care of his fair silken hair and moustache and used perfume discreetly on his handkerchief. The half-moons of his nails were perfect and when he smiled you caught a glimpse of a row of childish white teeth.

As he sat at his desk in the King's Inns† he thought what changes those eight years had brought. The friend whom he had known under a shabby and necessitous guise had become a brilliant figure on the London Press. He turned often from his tiresome writing to gaze out of the office window. The glow of a late autumn sunset covered the grass plots and walks. It cast a shower of kindly golden dust on the untidy nurses and decrepit old men who drowsed on the benches; it flickered upon all the moving figures—on the children who ran screaming along the gravel paths and on everyone who passed through the gardens. He watched the scene and thought of life; and (as always happened when he thought of life) he became sad. A gentle melancholy took possession of him. He felt how useless it was to struggle against fortune, this being the burden of wisdom which the ages had bequeathed to him.

He remembered the books of poetry upon his shelves at home. He

---

*North Liffey quayside for eastern departures.
†Imposing building housing legal offices on the north side of the Liffey.

had bought them in his bachelor days and many an evening, as he sat
in the little room off the hall, he had been tempted to take one down
from the bookshelf and read out something to his wife. But shyness had
always held him back; and so the books had remained on their shelves.
At times he repeated lines to himself and this consoled him.

When his hour had struck he stood up and took leave of his desk
and of his fellow-clerks punctiliously. He emerged from under the feu-
dal arch of the King's Inns, a neat modest figure, and walked swiftly
down Henrietta Street. The golden sunset was waning and the air had
grown sharp. A horde of grimy children populated the street. They
stood or ran in the roadway or crawled up the steps before the gaping
doors or squatted like mice upon the thresholds. Little Chandler gave
them no thought. He picked his way deftly through all that minute
vermin-like life and under the shadow of the gaunt spectral mansions
in which the old nobility of Dublin had roystered.* No memory of the
past touched him, for his mind was full of a present joy.

He had never been in Corless's† but he knew the value of the name.
He knew that people went there after the theatre to eat oysters and
drink liqueurs; and he had heard that the waiters there spoke French
and German. Walking swiftly by at night he had seen cabs drawn up
before the door and richly dressed ladies, escorted by cavaliers, alight
and enter quickly. They wore noisy dresses and many wraps. Their faces
were powdered and they caught up their dresses, when they touched
earth, like alarmed Atalantas.‡ He had always passed without turning
his head to look. It was his habit to walk swiftly in the street even by
day and whenever he found himself in the city late at night he hurried
on his way apprehensively and excitedly. Sometimes, however, he
courted the causes of his fear. He chose the darkest and narrowest
streets and, as he walked boldly forward, the silence that was spread
about his footsteps troubled him, the wandering, silent figures troubled
him; and at times a sound of low fugitive laughter made him tremble
like a leaf.

He turned to the right towards Capel Street. Ignatius Gallaher on
the London Press! Who would have thought it possible eight years before? Still, now that he reviewed the past, Little Chandler could re-

---

*Reveled.
†That is, in the Burlington Hotel and Restaurant, previously owned by Thomas
Corless.
‡In Ovid's *Metamorphoses*, Atalanta is a virginal Greek princess.

member many signs of future greatness in his friend. People used to say that Ignatius Gallaher was wild. Of course, he did mix with a rakish set of fellows at that time, drank freely and borrowed money on all sides. In the end he had got mixed up in some shady affair, some money transaction: at least, that was one version of his flight. But nobody denied him talent. There was always a certain . . . something in Ignatius Gallaher that impressed you in spite of yourself. Even when he was out at elbows and at his wits' end for money he kept up a bold face. Little Chandler remembered (and the remembrance brought a slight flush of pride to his cheek) one of Ignatius Gallaher's sayings when he was in a tight corner:

—Half time now, boys, he used to say lightheartedly. Where's my considering cup?

That was Ignatius Gallaher all out; and, damn it, you couldn't but admire him for it.

Little Chandler quickened his pace. For the first time in his life he felt himself superior to the people he passed. For the first time his soul revolted against the dull inelegance of Capel Street. There was no doubt about it: if you wanted to succeed you had to go away. You could do nothing in Dublin. As he crossed Grattan Bridge he looked down the river towards the lower quays and pitied the poor stunted houses. They seemed to him a band of tramps, huddled together along the river-banks, their old coats covered with dust and soot, stupefied by the panorama of sunset and waiting for the first chill of night to bid them arise, shake themselves and begone. He wondered whether he could write a poem to express his idea. Perhaps Gallaher might be able to get it into some London paper for him. Could he write something original? He was not sure what idea he wished to express but the thought that a poetic moment had touched him took life within him like an infant hope. He stepped onward bravely.

Every step brought him nearer to London, farther from his own sober inartistic life. A light began to tremble on the horizon of his mind. He was not so old—thirty-two. His temperament might be said to be just at the point of maturity. There were so many different moods and impressions that he wished to express in verse. He felt them within him. He tried to weigh his soul to see if it was a poet's soul. Melancholy was the dominant note of his temperament, he thought, but it was a melancholy tempered by recurrences of faith and resignation and simple joy. If he could give expression to it in a book of poems perhaps men would listen. He would never be popular: he saw that. He could not sway the crowd but he might appeal to a little circle of kindred minds. The English critics, perhaps, would recognise him as one of the Celtic school* by reason of the melancholy tone of his poems; besides that, he would put in allusions. He began to invent sentences and phrases from the notice which his book would get. *Mr Chandler has the gift of easy and graceful verse. . . . A wistful sadness pervades these poems. . . . The Celtic note.* It was a pity his name was not more Irish-looking. Perhaps it would be better to insert his mother's name before the surname: Thomas Malone Chandler, or better still: T. Malone Chandler. He would speak to Gallaher about it.

He pursued his revery so ardently that he passed his street and had to turn back. As he came near Corless's his former agitation began to overmaster him and he halted before the door in indecision. Finally he opened the door and entered.

The light and noise of the bar held him at the doorways for a few moments. He looked about him, but his sight was confused by the shining of many red and green wine-glasses. The bar seemed to him to be full of people and he felt that the people were observing him curiously. He glanced quickly to right and left (frowning slightly to make his errand appear serious), but when his sight cleared a little he saw that nobody had turned to look at him: and there, sure enough, was Ignatius Gallaher leaning with his back against the counter and his feet planted far apart.

—Hallo, Tommy, old hero, here you are! What is it to be? What will you have? I'm taking whisky: better stuff than we get across the water. Soda? Lithia?[†] No mineral? I'm the same. Spoils the flavour. . . . Here, *garçon*, bring us two halves of malt whisky, like a good fellow. . . . Well, and how have you been pulling along since I saw you last? Dear God, how old we're getting! Do you see any signs of aging in me—eh, what? A little grey and thin on the top—what?

Ignatius Gallaher took off his hat and displayed a large closely cropped head. His face was heavy, pale and clean-shaven. His eyes, which were of bluish slate-colour, relieved his unhealthy pallor and shone out plainly above the vivid orange tie he wore. Between these rival features the lips appeared very long and shapeless and colourless. He bent his head and felt with two sympathetic fingers the thin hair at

---

*Member of a movement that attempted to revive traditional Irish language, arts, and culture; Joyce liked to refer to it with the derisive pun "cultic."
†Mineral water.

the crown. Little Chandler shook his head as a denial. Ignatius Gallaher put on his hat again.

—It pulls you down, he said, Press life. Always hurry and scurry, looking for copy and sometimes not finding it: and then, always to have something new in your stuff. Damn proofs and printers, I say, for a few days. I'm deuced glad, I can tell you, to get back to the old country. Does a fellow good, a bit of a holiday. I feel a ton better since I landed again in dear dirty Dublin. . . . Here you are, Tommy. Water? Say when.

Little Chandler allowed his whisky to be very much diluted.

—You don't know what's good for you, my boy, said Ignatius Gallaher. I drink mine neat.*

—I drink very little as a rule, said Little Chandler modestly. An odd half-one or so when I meet any of the old crowd: that's all.

—Ah, well, said Ignatius Gallaher, cheerfully, here's to us and to old times and old acquaintance.

They clinked glasses and drank the toast.

—I met some of the old gang to-day, said Ignatius Gallaher. O'Hara seems to be in a bad way. What's he doing?

—Nothing, said Little Chandler. He's gone to the dogs.

—But Hogan has a good sit,† hasn't he?

—Yes; he's in the Land Commission.‡

—I met him one night in London and he seemed to be very flush. . . . Poor O'Hara! Boose, I suppose?

—Other things, too, said Little Chandler shortly.

Ignatius Gallaher laughed.

—Tommy, he said, I see you haven't changed an atom. You're the very same serious person that used to lecture me on Sunday mornings when I had a sore head and a fur on my tongue. You'd want to knock about a bit in the world. Have you never been anywhere even for a trip?

—I've been to the Isle of Man,§ said Little Chandler.

Ignatius Gallaher laughed.

—The Isle of Man! he said. Go to London or Paris: Paris, for choice. That's do you good.

—Have you seen Paris?

---

*Without ice or water.
†A good situation (job).
‡It oversaw the process of transferring Irish land from former landlords to tenants.
§Popular seaside holiday destination.

—I should think I have! I've knocked about there a little.

—And is it really so beautiful as they say? asked Little Chandler.

He sipped a little of his drink while Ignatius Gallaher finished his boldly.

—Beautiful? said Ignatius Gallaher, pausing on the word and on the flavour of his drink. It's not so beautiful, you know. Of course, it is beautiful. . . . But it's the life of Paris; that's the thing. Ah, there's no city like Paris for gaiety, movement, excitement. . . .

Little Chandler finished his whisky and, after some trouble, succeeded in catching the barman's eye. He ordered the same again.

—I've been to the Moulin Rouge,* Ignatius Gallaher continued when the barman had removed their glasses, and I've been to all the Bohemian cafés. Hot stuff! Not for a pious chap like you, Tommy.

Little Chandler said nothing until the barman returned with two glasses: then he touched his friend's glass lightly and reciprocated the former toast. He was beginning to feel somewhat disillusioned. Gallaher's accent and way of expressing himself did not please him. There was something vulgar in his friend which he had not observed before. But perhaps it was only the result of living in London amid the bustle and competition of the Press. The old personal charm was still there under this new gaudy manner. And, after all, Gallaher had lived, he had seen the world. Little Chandler looked at his friend enviously.

—Everything in Paris is gay, said Ignatius Gallaher. They believe in enjoying life—and don't you think they're right? If you want to enjoy yourself properly you must go to Paris. And, mind you, they've a great feeling for the Irish there. When they heard I was from Ireland they were ready to eat me, man.

Little Chandler took four or five sips from his glass.

—Tell me, he said, is it true that Paris is so . . . immoral as they say.

Ignatius Gallaher made a catholic gesture with his right arm.

—Every place is immoral, he said. Of course you do find spicy bits in Paris. Go to one of the students' balls, for instance. That's lively, if you like, when the *cocottes*† begin to let themselves loose. You know what they are, I suppose?

—I've heard of them, said Little Chandler.

Ignatius Gallaher drank off his whisky and shook his head.

---

*Parisian nightclub renowned for its cancan dancers.
†Prostitutes.

—Ah, he said, you may say what you like. There's no woman like the Parisienne—for style, for go.

—Then it is an immoral city, said Little Chandler, with timid insistence—I mean, compared with London or Dublin?

—London! said Ignatius Gallaher. It's six of one and half-a-dozen of the other. You ask Hogan, my boy. I showed him a bit about London when he was over there. He'd open your eye. . . . I say, Tommy, don't make punch of that whisky: liquor up.

—No, really. . . .

—O, come on, another one won't do you any harm. What is it? The same again, I suppose?

—Well . . . all right.

—*François*, the same again. . . . Will you smoke, Tommy?

Ignatius Gallaher produced his cigar-case. The two friends lit their cigars and puffed at them in silence until their drinks were served.

—I'll tell you my opinion, said Ignatius Gallaher, emerging after some time from the clouds of smoke in which he had taken refuge, it's a rum* world. Talk of immorality! I've heard of cases—what am I saying?—I've known them: cases of . . . immorality. . . .

Ignatius Gallaher puffed thoughtfully at his cigar and then, in a calm historian's tone, he proceeded to sketch for his friend some pictures of the corruption which was rife abroad. He summarised the vices of many capitals and seemed inclined to award the palm to Berlin. Some things he could not vouch for (his friends had told him), but of others he had had personal experience. He spared neither rank nor caste. He revealed many of the secrets of religious houses on the Continent and described some of the practices which were fashionable in high society and ended by telling, with details, a story about an English duchess—a story which he knew to be true. Little Chandler was astonished.

—Ah, well, said Ignatius Gallaher, here we are in old jog-along Dublin where nothing is known of such things.

—How dull you must find it, said Little Chandler, after all the other places you've seen!

—Well, said Ignatius Gallaher, it's a relaxation to come over here, you know. And, after all, it's the old country, as they say, isn't it? You can't help having a certain feeling for it. That's human nature. . . . But tell me something about yourself. Hogan told me you had . . . tasted the joys of connubial bliss. Two years ago, wasn't it?

---

*Odd.

Little Chandler blushed and smiled.

—Yes, he said. I was married last May twelve months.

—I hope it's not too late in the day to offer my best wishes, said Ignatius Gallaher. I didn't know your address or I'd have done so at the time.

He extended his hand, which Little Chandler took.

—Well, Tommy, he said, I wish you and yours every joy in life, old chap, and tons of money, and may you never die till I shoot you. And that's the wish of a sincere friend, an old friend. You know that?

—I know that, said Little Chandler.

—Any youngsters? said Ignatius Gallaher.

Little Chandler blushed again.

—We have one child, he said.

—Son or daughter?

—A little boy.

Ignatius Gallaher slapped his friend sonorously on the back.

—Bravo, he said, I wouldn't doubt you, Tommy.

Little Chandler smiled, looked confusedly at his glass and bit his lower lip with three childishly white front teeth.

—I hope you'll spend an evening with us, he said, before you go back. My wife will be delighted to meet you. We can have a little music and—

—Thanks awfully, old chap, said Ignatius Gallaher, I'm sorry we didn't meet earlier. But I must leave to-morrow night.

—To-night, perhaps . . . ?

—I'm awfully sorry, old man. You see I'm over here with another fellow, clever young chap he is too, and we arranged to go to a little card-party. Only for that . . .

—O, in that case. . . .

—But who knows? said Ignatius Gallaher considerately. Next year I may take a little skip over here now that I've broken the ice. It's only a pleasure deferred.

—Very well, said Little Chandler, the next time you come we must have an evening together. That's agreed now, isn't it?

—Yes, that's agreed, said Ignatius Gallaher. Next year if I come, *parole d' honneur.**

—And to clinch the bargain, said Little Chandler, we'll just have one more now.

---

*Word of honor (French).

Ignatius Gallaher took out a large gold watch and looked at it.

—Is it to be the last? he said. Because you know, I have an a.p.*

—O, yes, positively, said Little Chandler.

—Very well, then, said Ignatius Gallaher, let us have another one as a *deoc an doruis*†—that's good vernacular for a small whisky, I believe.

Little Chandler ordered the drinks. The blush which had risen to his face a few moments before was establishing itself. A trifle made him blush at any time: and now he felt warm and excited. Three small whiskies had gone to his head and Gallaher's strong cigar had confused his mind, for he was a delicate and abstinent person. The adventure of meeting Gallaher after eight years, of finding himself with Gallaher in Corless's surrounded by lights and noise, of listening to Gallaher's stories and of sharing for a brief space Gallaher's vagrant and triumphant life, upset the equipoise of his sensitive nature. He felt acutely the contrast between his own life and his friend's, and it seemed to him unjust. Gallaher was his inferior in birth and education. He was sure that he could do something better than his friend had ever done, or could ever do, something higher than mere tawdry journalism if he only got the chance. What was it that stood in his way? His unfortunate timidity! He wished to vindicate himself in some way, to assert his manhood. He saw behind Gallaher's refusal of his invitation. Gallaher was only patronising him by his friendliness just as he was patronising Ireland by his visit.

The barman brought their drinks. Little Chandler pushed one glass towards his friend and took up the other boldly.

—Who knows? he said, as they lifted their glasses. When you come next year I may have the pleasure of wishing long life and happiness to Mr and Mrs Ignatius Gallaher.

Ignatius Gallaher in the act of drinking closed one eye expressively over the rim of his glass. When he had drunk he smacked his lips decisively, set down his glass and said:

—No blooming fear of that, my boy. I'm going to have my fling first and see a bit of life and the world before I put my head in the sack—if I ever do.

—Some day you will, said Little Chandler calmly.

Ignatius Gallaher turned his orange tie and slate-blue eyes full upon his friend.

—You think so? he said.

---

*Appointment.
†Irish for "drink of the door"; that is, one for the road.

—You'll put your head in the sack, repeated Little Chandler stoutly, like everyone else if you can find the girl.

He had slightly emphasised his tone and he was aware that he had betrayed himself; but, though the colour had heightened in his cheek, he did not flinch from his friend's gaze. Ignatius Gallaher watched him for a few moments and then said:

—If ever it occurs, you may bet your bottom dollar there'll be no mooning and spooning about it. I mean to marry money. She'll have a good fat account at the bank or she won't do for me.

Little Chandler shook his head.

—Why, man alive, said Ignatius Gallaher, vehemently, do you know what it is? I've only to say the word and to-morrow I can have the woman and the cash. You don't believe it? Well, I know it. There are hundreds—what am I saying?—thousands of rich Germans and Jews, rotten with money, that'd only be too glad. . . . You wait a while, my boy. See if I don't play my cards properly. When I go about a thing I mean business, I tell you. You just wait.

He tossed his glass to his mouth, finished his drink and laughed loudly. Then he looked thoughtfully before him and said in a calmer tone:

—But I'm in no hurry. They can wait. I don't fancy tying myself up to one woman, you know.

He imitated with his mouth the act of tasting and made a wry face.

—Must get a bit stale, I should think, he said.

*   *   *   *   *   *   *   *   *   *

Little Chandler sat in the room off the hall, holding a child in his arms. To save money they kept no servant but Annie's young sister Monica came for an hour or so in the morning and an hour or so in the evening to help. But Monica had gone home long ago. It was a quarter to nine. Little Chandler had come home late for tea* and, moreover, he had forgotten to bring Annie home the parcel of coffee from Bewley's.†
Of course she was in a bad humour and gave him short answers. She said she would do without any tea but when it came near the time at which the shop at the corner closed she decided to go out herself for a quarter of a pound of tea and two pounds of sugar. She put the sleeping child deftly in his arms and said:

---

*The evening meal.
†Bewley's Oriental Café, a downtown Dublin institution.

—Here. Don't waken him.

A little lamp with a white china shade stood upon the table and its light fell over a photograph which was enclosed in a frame of crumpled horn.* It was Annie's photograph. Little Chandler looked at it, pausing at the thin tight lips. She wore the pale blue summer blouse which he had brought her home as a present one Saturday. It had cost him ten and elevenpence; but what an agony of nervousness it had cost him! How he had suffered that day, waiting at the shop door until the shop was empty, standing at the counter and trying to appear at his ease while the girl piled ladies' blouses before him, paying at the desk and forgetting to take up the odd penny of his change, being called back by the cashier, and finally, striving to hide his blushes as he left the shop by examining the parcel to see if it was securely tied. When he brought the blouse home Annie kissed him and said it was very pretty and stylish; but when she heard the price she threw the blouse on the table and said it was a regular swindle to charge ten and elevenpence for it. At first she wanted to take it back but when she tried it on she was delighted with it, especially with the make of the sleeves, and kissed him and said he was very good to think of her.

Hm! . . .

He looked coldly into the eyes of the photograph and they answered coldly. Certainly they were pretty and the face itself was pretty. But he found something mean in it. Why was it so unconscious and ladylike? The composure of the eyes irritated him. They repelled him and defied him: there was no passion in them, no rapture. He thought of what Gallaher had said about rich Jewesses. Those dark Oriental eyes, he thought, how full they are of passion, of voluptuous longing! . . . Why had he married the eyes in the photograph?

He caught himself up at the question and glanced nervously round the room. He found something mean in the pretty furniture which he had bought for his house on the hire system.† Annie had chosen it herself and it reminded him of her. It too was prim and pretty. A dull resentment against his life awoke within him. Could he not escape from his little house? Was it too late for him to try to live bravely like Gallaher? Could he go to London? There was the furniture still to be paid for. If he could only write a book and get it published, that might open the way for him.

---

*Possibly tortoise shell.
†Rental, or rent-to-own.

A volume of Byron's poems lay before him on the table. He opened it cautiously with his left hand lest he should waken the child and began to read the first poem in the book:

> *Hushed are the winds and still the evening gloom,*
> *Not e'en a Zephyr wanders through the grove,*
> *Whilst I return to view my Margaret's tomb*
> *And scatter flowers on the dust I love.**

He paused. He felt the rhythm of the verse about him in the room. How melancholy it was! Could he, too, write like that, express the melancholy of his soul in verse? There were so many things he wanted to describe: his sensation of a few hours before on Grattan Bridge, for example. If he could get back again into that mood. . . .

The child awoke and began to cry. He turned from the page and tried to hush it: but it would not be hushed. He began to rock it to and fro in his arms but its wailing cry grew keener. He rocked it faster while his eyes began to read the second stanza:

> *Within this narrow cell reclines her clay,*
> *That clay where once . . .*

It was useless. He couldn't read. He couldn't do anything. The wailing of the child pierced the drum of his ear. It was useless, useless! He was a prisoner for life. His arms trembled with anger and suddenly bending to the child's face he shouted:

—Stop!

The child stopped for an instant, had a spasm of fright and began to scream. He jumped up from his chair and walked hastily up and down the room with the child in his arms. It began to sob piteously, losing its breath for four or five seconds, and then bursting out anew. The thin walls of the room echoed the sound. He tried to soothe it but it sobbed more convulsively. He looked at the contracted and quivering face of the child and began to be alarmed. He counted seven sobs without a break between them and caught the child to his breast in fright. If it died! . . .

The door was burst open and a young woman ran in, panting.

—What is it? What is it? she cried.

---

*From Byron's "On the Death of a Young Lady" (1802).

The child, hearing its mother's voice, broke out into a paroxysm of sobbing.

—It's nothing, Annie . . . it's nothing. . . . He began to cry . . .

She flung her parcels on the floor and snatched the child from him.

What have you done to him? she cried, glaring into his face.

Little Chandler sustained for one moment the gaze of her eyes and his heart closed together as he met the hatred in them. He began to stammer:

—It's nothing. . . . He . . . he began to cry. . . . I couldn't . . . I didn't do anything. . . . What?

Giving no heed to him she began to walk up and down the room, clasping the child tightly in her arms and murmuring:

—My little man! My little mannie! Was 'ou frightened, love? . . . There now, love! There now! . . . Lambabaun!* Mamma's little lamb of the world! . . . There now!

Little Chandler felt his cheeks suffused with shame and he stood back out of the lamplight. He listened while the paroxysm of the child's sobbing grew less and less; and tears of remorse started to his eyes.

---

*From the Irish *leanbhán* ("small child").

"Counterparts"

■■■ Farrington's route to tram after work

River Liffey

Grand Canal

Merrion Square

Trinity College

Stephen's Green

Ballast Office

Terry Kelly's

O'Neill's Shop

tram

Mulligan's

The Scotch House

Crosbie & Alleyne

Davy Byrne's

COUNTERPARTS

THE BELL RANG FURIOUSLY and, when Miss Parker went to the tube,* a furious voice called out in a piercing North of Ireland accent:

—Send Farrington here!

Miss Parker returned to her machine, saying to a man who was writing at a desk:

—Mr Alleyne wants you upstairs.

The man muttered *Blast him!* under his breath and pushed back his chair to stand up. When he stood up he was tall and of great bulk. He had a hanging face, dark wine-coloured, with fair eyebrows and moustache: his eyes bulged forward slightly and the whites of them were dirty. He lifted up the counter and, passing by the clients, went out of the office with a heavy step.

He went heavily upstairs until he came to the second landing, where a door bore a brass plate with the inscription *Mr Alleyne*. Here he halted, puffing with labour and vexation, and knocked. The shrill voice cried:

—Come in!

The man entered Mr Alleyne's room. Simultaneously Mr Alleyne, a little man wearing gold-rimmed glasses on a clean-shaven face, shot his head up over a pile of documents. The head itself was so pink and hairless it seemed like a large egg reposing on the papers. Mr Alleyne did not lose a moment:

—Farrington? What is the meaning of this? Why have I always to complain of you? May I ask you why you haven't made a copy of that contract between Bodley and Kirwan? I told you it must be ready by four o'clock.

—But Mr Shelley said, sir—

—*Mr Shelley said, sir.* . . . Kindly attend to what I say and not to what *Mr Shelley says, sir.* You have always some excuse or another for shirking

---

*Voice tube, an early forerunner of the intercom.

work. Let me tell you that if the contract is not copied before this evening
I'll lay the matter before Mr Crosbie. . . . Do you hear me now?

—Yes, sir.

—Do you hear me now? . . . Ay and another little matter! I might as
well be talking to the wall as talking to you. Understand once for all that
you get a half an hour for your lunch and not an hour and a half. How
many courses do you want, I'd like to know. . . . Do you mind me now?

—Yes, sir.

Mr Alleyne bent his head again upon his pile of papers. The man
stared fixedly at the polished skull which directed the affairs of Crosbie
& Alleyne, gauging its fragility. A spasm of rage gripped his throat for
a few moments and then passed, leaving after it a sharp sensation of
thirst. The man recognised the sensation and felt that he must have a
good night's drinking. The middle of the month was passed and, if he
could get the copy done in time, Mr Alleyne might give him an order
on the cashier. He stood still, gazing fixedly at the head upon the pile
of papers. Suddenly Mr Alleyne began to upset all the papers, searching for something. Then, as if he had been unaware of the man's presence till that moment, he shot up his head again, saying:

—Eh? Are you going to stand there all day? Upon my word, Farrington, you take things easy!

—I was waiting to see . . .

—Very good, you needn't wait to see. Go downstairs and do your work.

The man walked heavily towards the door and, as he went out of the
room, he heard Mr Alleyne cry after him that if the contract was not
copied by evening Mr Crosbie would hear of the matter.

He returned to his desk in the lower office and counted the sheets
which remained to be copied. He took up his pen and dipped it in the
ink but he continued to stare stupidly at the last words he had written:
In no case shall the said Bernard Bodley be . . . The evening was falling
and in a few minutes they would be lighting the gas: then he could
write. He felt that he must slake the thirst in his throat. He stood up
from his desk and, lifting the counter as before, passed out of the office. As he was passing out the chief clerk looked at him inquiringly.

—It's all right, Mr Shelley, said the man, pointing with his finger to
indicate the objective of his journey.

The chief clerk glanced at the hat-rack, but, seeing the row complete, offered no remark. As soon as he was on the landing the man
pulled a shepherd's plaid cap out of his pocket, put it on his head and
ran quickly down the rickety stairs. From the street door he walked on

furtively on the inner side of the path towards the corner and all at once dived into a doorway. He was now safe in the dark snug of O'Neill's shop,* and, filling up the little window that looked into the bar with his inflamed face, the colour of dark wine or dark meat, he called out:

—Here, Pat, give us a g.p.,† like a good fellow.

The curate‡ brought him a glass of plain porter. The man drank it at a gulp and asked for a caraway§ seed. He put his penny on the counter and, leaving the curate to grope for it in the gloom, retreated out of the snug as furtively as he had entered it.

Darkness, accompanied by a thick fog, was gaining upon the dusk of February and the lamps in Eustace Street had been lit. The man went up by the houses until he reached the door of the office, wondering whether he could finish his copy in time. On the stairs a moist pungent odour of perfumes saluted his nose: evidently Miss Delacour had come while he was out in O'Neill's. He crammed his cap back again into his pocket and re-entered the office, assuming an air of absent mindedness.

—Mr Alleyne has been calling for you, said the chief clerk severely. Where were you?

The man glanced at the two clients who were standing at the counter as if to intimate that their presence prevented him from answering. As the clients were both male the chief clerk allowed himself a laugh.

—I know that game, he said. Five times in one day is a little bit. . . . Well, you better look sharp and get a copy of our correspondence in the Delacour case for Mr Alleyne.

This address in the presence of the public, his run upstairs and the porter he had gulped down so hastily confused the man and, as he sat down at his desk to get what was required, he realised how hopeless was the task of finishing his copy of the contract before half past five. The dark damp night was coming and he longed to spend it in the bars, drinking with his friends amid the glare of gas and the clatter of glasses. He got out the Delacour correspondence and passed out of the office. He hoped Mr Alleyne would not discover that the last two letters were missing.

The moist pungent perfume lay all the way up to Mr Alleyne's room. Miss Delacour was a middle-aged woman of Jewish appearance. Mr Alleyne was said to be sweet on her or on her money. She came to the of-

---

*O'Neill's shop is a pub; the snug is a partitioned portion of the counter.
†Glass of porter, a dark ale.
‡Dublin lingo for a bartender.
§To disguise the smell of alcohol on his breath.

fice often and stayed a long time when she came. She was sitting beside his desk now in an aroma of perfumes, smoothing the handle of her umbrella and nodding the great black feather in her hat. Mr Alleyne had swivelled his chair round to face her and thrown his right foot jauntily upon his left knee. The man put the correspondence on the desk and bowed respectfully but neither Mr Alleyne nor Miss Delacour took any notice of his bow. Mr Alleyne tapped a finger on the correspondence and then flicked it towards him as if to say: *That's all right: you can go.*

The man returned to the lower office and sat down again at his desk. He stared intently at the incomplete phrase: *In no case shall the said Bernard Bodley be . . .* and thought how strange it was that the last three words began with the same letter. The chief clerk began to hurry Miss Parker, saying she would never have the letters typed in time for post. The man listened to the clicking of the machine for a few minutes and then set to work to finish his copy. But his head was not clear and his mind wandered away to the glare and rattle of the public-house. It was a night for hot punches.* He struggled on with his copy, but when the clock struck five he had still fourteen pages to write. Blast it! He couldn't finish it in time. He longed to execrate aloud, to bring his fist down on something violently. He was so enraged that he wrote *Bernard Bernard* instead of *Bernard Bodley* and had to begin again on a clean sheet.

He felt strong enough to clear out the whole office single-handed. His body ached to do something, to rush out and revel in violence. All the indignities of his life enraged him. . . . Could he ask the cashier privately for an advance? No, the cashier was no good, no damn good: he wouldn't give an advance. . . . He knew where he would meet the boys: Leonard and O'Halloran and Nosey Flynn. The barometer of his emotional nature was set for a spell of riot.

His imagination had so abstracted him that his name was called twice before he answered. Mr Alleyne and Miss Delacour were standing outside the counter and all the clerks had turned round in anticipation of something. The man got up from his desk. Mr Alleyne began a tirade of abuse, saying that two letters were missing. The man answered that he knew nothing about them, that he had made a faithful copy. The tirade continued: it was so bitter and violent that the man could hardly restrain his fist from descending upon the head of the manikin† before him:

—I know nothing about any other two letters, he said stupidly.

---

*Hot whiskey drinks.
†Little man.

—*You—know—nothing.* Of course you know nothing, said Mr Alleyne. Tell me, he added, glancing first for approval to the lady beside him, do you take me for a fool? Do you think me an utter fool?

The man glanced from the lady's face to the little egg-shaped head and back again; and, almost before he was aware of it, his tongue had found a felicitous moment:

—I don't think, sir, he said, that that's a fair question to put to me.

There was a pause in the very breathing of the clerks. Everyone was astounded (the author of the witticism no less than his neighbours) and Miss Delacour, who was a stout amiable person, began to smile broadly. Mr Alleyne flushed to the hue of a wild rose and his mouth twitched with a dwarf's passion. He shook his fist in the man's face till it seemed to vibrate like the knob of some electric machine:

—You impertinent ruffian! You impertinent ruffian! I'll make short work of you! Wait till you see! You'll apologise to me for your impertinence or you'll quit the office instanter!* You'll quit this, I'm telling you, or you'll apologise to me!

            *   *   *   *   *   *   *   *   *   *

He stood in a doorway opposite the office watching to see if the cashier would come out alone. All the clerks passed out and finally the cashier came out with the chief clerk. It was no use trying to say a word to him when he was with the chief clerk. The man felt that his position was bad enough. He had been obliged to offer an abject apology to Mr Alleyne for his impertinence but he knew what a hornet's nest the office would be for him. He could remember the way in which Mr Alleyne had hounded little Peake out of the office in order to make room for his own nephew. He felt savage and thirsty and revengeful, annoyed with himself and with everyone else. Mr Alleyne would never give him an hour's rest; his life would be a hell to him. He had made a proper fool of himself this time. Could he not keep his tongue in his cheek? But they had never pulled together from the first, he and Mr Alleyne, ever since the day Mr Alleyne had overheard him mimicking his North of Ireland accent to amuse Higgins and Miss Parker: that had been the beginning of it. He might have tried Higgins for the money, but sure Higgins never had anything for himself. A man with two establishments to keep up, of course he couldn't. . . .

---

*Instantly.

He felt his great body again aching for the comfort of the public-house.* The fog had begun to chill him and he wondered could he touch† Pat in O'Neill's. He could not touch him for more than a bob—and a bob was no use. Yet he must get money somewhere or other: he had spent his last penny for the g.p. and soon it would be too late for getting money anywhere. Suddenly, as he was fingering his watch-chain, he thought of Terry Kelly's pawn-office in Fleet Street. That was the dart!‡ Why didn't he think of it sooner?

He went through the narrow alley of Temple Bar§ quickly, mutter-ing to himself that they could all go to hell because he was going to have a good night of it. The clerk in Terry Kelly's said *A crown!* but the consignor held out for six shillings; and in the end the six shillings was allowed him literally. He came out of the pawn-office joyfully, making a little cylinder of the coins between his thumb and fingers. In West-moreland Street the footpaths were crowded with young men and women returning from business and ragged urchins ran here and there yelling out the names of the evening editions. The man passed through the crowd, looking on the spectacle generally with proud satisfaction and staring masterfully at the office-girls. His head was full of the noises of tram-gongs and swishing trolleys and his nose already sniffed the curling fumes of punch. As he walked on he preconsidered the terms in which he would narrate the incident to the boys:

—So, I just looked at him—coolly, you know, and looked at her. Then I looked back at him again—taking my time, you know. *I don't think that that's a fair question to put to me,* says I.

Nosey Flynn was sitting up in his usual corner of Davy Byrne's‖ and, when he heard the story, he stood Farrington a half-one,# saying it was as smart a thing as ever he heard. Farrington stood a drink in his turn. After a while O'Halloran and Paddy Leonard came in and the story was repeated to them. O'Halloran stood tailors** of malt, hot, all round and told the story of the retort he had made to the chief clerk when he was in Callan's of Fownes's Street; but, as the retort was after the man-

---

*Pub; a licensed premises open to the public, as opposed to a private bar or club.
†Ask for a loan.
‡Answer.
§Commercial area south of the Liffey and west of the Bank of Ireland.
‖Pub off Grafton Street, between St. Stephen's Green and Trinity College; made famous in *Ulysses* as the spot where Leopold Bloom eats his lunch.
#A glass (half-pint) of beer or ale.
**Large glasses.

ner of the liberal shepherds in the eclogues, he had to admit that it was not as clever as Farrington's retort. At this Farrington told the boys to polish off that and have another.

Just as they were naming their poisons who should come in but Higgins! Of course he had to join in with the others. The men asked him to give his version of it, and he did so with great vivacity for the sight of five small hot whiskies was very exhilarating. Everyone roared laughing when he showed the way in which Mr Alleyne shook his fist in Farrington's face. Then he imitated Farrington, saying, *And here was my nabs,* * as cool as you please*, while Farrington looked at the company out of his heavy dirty eyes, smiling and at times drawing forth stray drops of liquor from his moustache with the aid of his lower lip.

When that round was over there was a pause. O'Halloran had money but neither of the other two seemed to have any; so the whole party left the shop somewhat regretfully. At the corner of Duke Street Higgins and Nosey Flynn bevelled off to the left while the other three turned back towards the city. Rain was drizzling down on the cold streets and, when they reached the Ballast Office,[†] Farrington suggested the Scotch House.[‡] The bar was full of men and loud with the noise of tongues and glasses. The three men pushed past the whining match-sellers at the door and formed a little party at the corner of the counter. They began to exchange stories. Leonard introduced them to a young fellow named Weathers who was performing at the Tivoli[§] as an acrobat and knockabout *artiste*. Farrington stood a drink all round. Weathers said he would take a small Irish and Apollinaris.[||] Farrington, who had definite notions of what was what, asked the boys would they have an Apollinaris too; but the boys told Tim to make theirs hot. The talk became theatrical. O'Halloran stood a round and then Farrington stood another round, Weathers protesting that the hospitality was too Irish. He promised to get them in behind the scenes and introduce them to some nice girls. O'Halloran said that he and Leonard would go, but that Farrington wouldn't go because he was a married man; and Farrington's heavy dirty eyes leered at the company in token that he understood he was being chaffed. Weathers made them all have just one little tincture at his

---

*Gentleman.
†Headquarters of the Dublin Port and Docks Board.
‡A pub.
§A music hall.
||Irish whiskey and mineral water.

expense and promised to meet them later on at Mulligan's in Poolbeg Street.

When the Scotch House closed they went round to Mulligan's. They went into the parlour at the back and O'Halloran ordered small hot specials* all round. They were all beginning to feel mellow. Farrington was just standing another round when Weathers came back. Much to Farrington's relief he drank a glass of bitter† this time. Funds were getting low but they had enough to keep them going. Presently two young women with big hats and a young man in a check suit came in and sat at a table close by. Weathers saluted them and told the company that they were out of the Tivoli. Farrington's eyes wandered at every moment in the direction of one of the young women. There was something striking in her appearance. An immense scarf of peacock-blue muslin was wound round her hat and knotted in a great bow under her chin; and she wore bright yellow gloves, reaching to the elbow. Farrington gazed admiringly at the plump arm which she moved very often and with much grace; and when, after a little time, she answered his gaze he admired still more her large dark brown eyes. The oblique staring expression in them fascinated him. She glanced at him once or twice and, when the party was leaving the room, she brushed against his chair and said *O, pardon!* in a London accent. He watched her leave the room in the hope that she would look back at him, but he was disappointed. He cursed his want of money and cursed all the rounds he had stood, particularly all the whiskies and Apollinaris which he had stood to Weathers. If there was one thing that he hated it was a sponge.‡ He was so angry that he lost count of the conversation of his friends.

When Paddy Leonard called him he found that they were talking about feats of strength. Weathers was showing his biceps muscle to the company and boasting so much that the other two had called on Farrington to uphold the national honour. Farrington pulled up his sleeve accordingly and showed his biceps muscle to the company. The two arms were examined and compared and finally it was agreed to have a trial of strength. The table was cleared and the two men rested their elbows on it, clasping hands. When Paddy Leonard said *Go!* each was to try to bring down the other's hand on to the table. Farrington looked very serious and determined.

---

*Hot whiskey punch.
†Dry ale.
‡Freeloader.

The trial began. After about thirty seconds Weathers brought his opponent's hand slowly down on to the table. Farrington's dark wine-coloured face flushed darker still with anger and humiliation at having been defeated by such a stripling.

—You're not to put the weight of your body behind it. Play fair, he said.

—Who's not playing fair? said the other.

—Come on again. The two best out of three.

The trial began again. The veins stood out on Farrington's forehead, and the pallor of Weathers' complexion changed to peony. Their hands and arms trembled under the stress. After a long struggle Weathers again brought his opponent's hand slowly on to the table. There was a murmur of applause from the spectators. The curate, who was standing beside the table, nodded his red head towards the victor and said with stupid familiarity:

—Ah! that's the knack!

—What the hell do you know about it? said Farrington fiercely, turning on the man. What do you put in your gab* for?

—Sh, sh! said O'Halloran, observing the violent expression of Farrington's face. Pony up, boys. We'll have just one little smahan† more and then we'll be off.

A very sullen-faced man stood at the corner of O'Connell Bridge waiting for the little Sandymount tram to take him home. He was full of smouldering anger and revengefulness. He felt humiliated and discontented; he did not even feel drunk; and he had only twopence in his pocket. He cursed everything. He had done for himself in the office, pawned his watch, spent all his money; and he had not even got drunk. He began to feel thirsty again and he longed to be back again in the hot reeking public-house. He had lost his reputation as a strong man, having been defeated twice by a mere boy. His heart swelled with fury and, when he thought of the woman in the big hat who had brushed against him and said *Pardon!* his fury nearly choked him.

His tram let him down at Shelbourne Road and he steered his great body along in the shadow of the wall of the barracks.‡ He loathed returning to his home. When he went in by the side-door he found the kitchen empty and the kitchen fire nearly out. He bawled upstairs:

---

*Mouth or speech.

†From the Irish *smeachán* ("little taste").

‡The Beggar's Bush Infantry Barracks.

—Ada! Ada!

His wife was a little sharp-faced woman who bullied her husband when he was sober and was bullied by him when he was drunk. They had five children. A little boy came running down the stairs.

—Who is that? said the man, peering through the darkness.

—Me, pa.

—Who are you? Charlie?

—No, pa. Tom.

—Where's your mother?

—She's out at the chapel.

—That's right. . . . Did she think of leaving any dinner for me?

—Yes, pa. I—

—Light the lamp. What do you mean by having the place in darkness? Are the other children in bed?

The man sat down heavily on one of the chairs while the little boy lit the lamp. He began to mimic his son's flat accent, saying half to himself: *At the chapel. At the chapel, if you please!* When the lamp was lit he banged his fist on the table and shouted:

—What's for my dinner?

—I'm going . . . to cook it, pa, said the little boy.

The man jumped up furiously and pointed to the fire.

—On that fire! You let the fire out! By God, I'll teach you to do that again!

He took a step to the door and seized the walking-stick which was standing behind it.

—I'll teach you to let the fire out! he said, rolling up his sleeve in order to give his arm free play.

The little boy cried *O, pa!* and ran whimpering round the table, but the man followed him and caught him by the coat. The little boy looked about him wildly but, seeing no way of escape, fell upon his knees.

—Now, you'll let the fire out the next time! said the man, striking at him vigorously with the stick. Take that, you little whelp!

The boy uttered a squeal of pain as the stick cut his thigh. He clasped his hands together in the air and his voice shook with fright.

—O, pa! he cried. Don't beat me, pa! And I'll . . . I'll say a *Hail Mary** for you. . . . I'll say a *Hail Mary* for you, pa, if you don't beat me. . . . I'll say a *Hail Mary.* . . .

---

*Catholic devotional prayer beginning: "Hail Mary, full of grace, the Lord is with thee."

CLAY

THE MATRON HAD GIVEN her leave to go out as soon as the women's tea* was over and Maria looked forward to her evening out. The kitchen was spick and span: the cook said you could see yourself in the big copper boilers. The fire was nice and bright and on one of the side-tables were four very big barmbracks.† These barmbracks seemed uncut; but if you went closer you would see that they had been cut into long thick even slices and were ready to be handed round at tea. Maria had cut them herself.

Maria was a very, very small person indeed but she had a very long nose and a very long chin. She talked a little through her nose, always soothingly: *Yes, my dear,* and *No, my dear.* She was always sent for when the women quarrelled over their tubs and always succeeded in making peace. One day the matron had said to her:

—Maria, you are a veritable peace-maker!

And the sub-matron and two of the Board ladies had heard the compliment. And Ginger Mooney was always saying what she wouldn't do to the dummy‡ who had charge of the irons if it wasn't for Maria. Everyone was so fond of Maria.

The women would have their tea at six o'clock and she would be able to get away before seven. From Ballsbridge§ to the Pillar,|| twenty minutes; from the Pillar to Drumcondra,# twenty minutes; and twenty minutes to buy the things. She would be there before eight. She took out her purse with the silver clasps and read again the words *A Present from Belfast.* She was very fond of that purse because Joe had brought it to her five years before when he and Alphy had gone to Belfast on a Whit-

---

*The evening meal.
†From the Irish *báirín breac*; a brown cake similar to fruitcake.
‡Mute.
§Fashionable southeast Dublin neighborhood.
||Nelson's Pillar, honoring Admiral Lord Nelson; it stood at the center of Sackville (now O'Connell) Street until 1966, when the I.R.A. demolished it.
#Working-class neighborhood 2 miles north of Dublin's city center.

Monday* trip. In the purse were two half-crowns and some coppers. She would have five shillings clear after paying tram fare. What a nice evening they would have, all the children singing! Only she hoped that Joe wouldn't come in drunk. He was so different when he took any drink.

Often he had wanted her to go and live with them; but she would have felt herself in the way (though Joe's wife was ever so nice with her) and she had become accustomed to the life of the laundry. Joe was a good fellow. She had nursed him and Alphy too; and Joe used often say:

—Mamma is mamma but Maria is my proper mother.

After the break-up at home the boys had got her that position in the *Dublin by Lamplight* laundry,[†] and she liked it. She used to have such a bad opinion of Protestants but now she thought they were very nice people, a little quiet and serious, but still very nice people to live with. Then she had her plants in the conservatory and she liked looking after them. She had lovely ferns and wax-plants and, whenever anyone came to visit her, she always gave the visitor one or two slips[‡] from her conservatory. There was one thing she didn't like and that was the tracts on the walks; but the matron was such a nice person to deal with, so genteel.

When the cook told her everything was ready she went into the women's room and began to pull the big bell. In a few minutes the women began to come in by twos and threes, wiping their steaming hands in their petticoats and pulling down the sleeves of their blouses over their red steaming arms. They settled down before their huge mugs which the cook and the dummy filled up with hot tea, already mixed with milk and sugar in huge tin cans. Maria superintended the distribution of the barmbrack and saw that every woman got her four slices. There was a great deal of laughing and joking during the meal. Lizzie Fleming said Maria was sure to get the ring[§] and, though Fleming had said that for so many Hallow Eves,[||] Maria had to laugh and say she didn't want any ring or man either; and when she laughed her grey-green eyes sparkled with disappointed shyness and the tip of her nose nearly met the tip of her chin. Then Ginger Mooney lifted up her mug of tea and proposed Maria's health while all the other women

---

*The Monday following Pentecost, the seventh Sunday after Easter.
†Founded in the 1850s with a mission to reform prostitutes.
‡Cuttings.
§The one discovering the ring in her piece of barmbrack was supposed to marry within the year.
||Halloweens.

clattered with their mugs on the table, and said she was sorry she hadn't a sup of porter* to drink it in. And Maria laughed again till the tip of her nose nearly met the tip of her chin and till her minute body nearly shook itself asunder because she knew that Mooney meant well though, of course, she had the notions of a common woman.

But wasn't Maria glad when the women had finished their tea and the cook and the dummy had begun to clear away the tea-things! She went into her little bedroom and, remembering that the next morning was a mass morning, changed the hand of the alarm from seven to six. Then she took off her working skirt and her house-boots and laid her best skirt out on the bed and her tiny dress-boots beside the foot of the bed. She changed her blouse too and, as she stood before the mirror, she thought of how she used to dress for mass on Sunday morning when she was a young girl; and she looked with quaint affection at the diminutive body which she had so often adorned. In spite of its years she found it a nice tidy little body.

When she got outside the streets were shining with rain and she was glad of her old brown waterproof.† The tram was full and she had to sit on the little stool at the end of the car, facing all the people, with her toes barely touching the floor. She arranged in her mind all she was going to do and thought how much better it was to be independent and to have your own money in your pocket. She hoped they would have a nice evening. She was sure they would but she could not help thinking what a pity it was Alphy and Joe were not speaking. They were always falling out now but when they were boys together they used to be the best of friends: but such was life.

She got out of her tram at the Pillar and ferreted her way quickly among the crowds. She went into Downes's cake-shop but the shop was so full of people that it was a long time before she could get herself attended to. She bought a dozen of mixed penny cakes, and at last came out of the shop laden with a big bag. Then she thought what else would she buy: she wanted to buy something really nice. They would be sure to have plenty of apples and nuts. It was hard to know what to buy and all she could think of was cake. She decided to buy some plum-cake but Downes's plumcake had not enough almond icing on top of it so she went over to a shop in Henry Street. Here she was a long time in suiting herself and the stylish young lady behind the counter, who

---

*Dark ale.
†Raincoat.

was evidently a little annoyed by her, asked her was it wedding-cake she wanted to buy. That made Maria blush and smile at the young lady; but the young lady took it all very seriously and finally cut a thick slice of plumcake, parcelled it up and said:

—Two-and-four, please.

She thought she would have to stand in the Drumcondra tram because none of the young men seemed to notice her but an elderly gentleman made room for her. He was a stout gentleman and he wore a brown hard hat; he had a square red face and a greyish moustache. Maria thought he was a colonel-looking gentleman and she reflected how much more polite he was than the young men who simply stared straight before them. The gentleman began to chat with her about Hallow Eve and the rainy weather. He supposed the bag was full of good things for the little ones and said it was only right that the youngsters should enjoy themselves while they were young. Maria agreed with him and favoured him with demure nods and hems. He was very nice with her, and when she was getting out at the Canal Bridge she thanked him and bowed, and he bowed to her and raised his hat and smiled agreeably; and while she was going up along the terrace, bending her tiny head under the rain, she thought how easy it was to know a gentleman even when he has a drop taken.

Everybody said: *O, here's Maria!* when she came to Joe's house. Joe was there, having come home from business, and all the children had their Sunday dresses on. There were two big girls in from next door and games were going on. Maria gave the bag of cakes to the eldest boy, Alphy, to divide and Mrs Donnelly said it was too good of her to bring such a big bag of cakes and made all the children say:

—Thanks, Maria.

But Maria said she had brought something special for papa and mamma, something they would be sure to like, and she began to look for her plumcake. She tried in Downes's bag and then in the pockets of her waterproof and then on the hallstand but nowhere could she find it. Then she asked all the children had any of them eaten it—by mistake, of course—but the children all said no and looked as if they did not like to eat cakes if they were to be accused of stealing. Everybody had a solution for the mystery and Mrs Donnelly said it was plain that Maria had left it behind her in the tram. Maria, remembering how confused the gentleman with the greyish moustache had made her, coloured with shame and vexation and disappointment. At the thought of the failure of her little surprise and of the two and four-pence she had thrown away for nothing she nearly cried outright.

But Joe said it didn't matter and made her sit down by the fire. He was very nice with her. He told her all that went on in his office, repeating for her a smart answer which he had made to the manager. Maria did not understand why Joe laughed so much over the answer he had made but she said that the manager must have been a very overbearing person to deal with. Joe said he wasn't so bad when you knew how to take him, that he was a decent sort so long as you didn't rub him the wrong way. Mrs Donnelly played the piano for the children and they danced and sang. Then the two next-door girls handed round the nuts. Nobody could find the nutcrackers and Joe was nearly getting cross over it and asked how did they expect Maria to crack nuts without a nutcracker. But Maria said she didn't like nuts and that they weren't to bother about her. Then Joe asked would she take a bottle of stout and Mrs Donnelly said there was port wine* too in the house if she would prefer that. Maria said she would rather they didn't ask her to take anything: but Joe insisted.

So Maria let him have his way and they sat by the fire talking over old times and Maria thought she would put in a good word for Alphy. But Joe cried that God might strike him stone dead if ever he spoke a word to his brother again and Maria said she was sorry she had mentioned the matter. Mrs Donnelly told her husband it was a great shame for him to speak that way of his own flesh and blood but Joe said that Alphy was no brother of his and there was nearly being a row on the head of it. But Joe said he would not lose his temper on account of the night it was and asked his wife to open some more stout. The two next-door girls had arranged some Hallow Eve games and soon everything was merry again. Maria was delighted to see the children so merry and Joe and his wife in such good spirits. The next-door girls put some saucers on the table and then led the children up to the table, blindfold.[2] One got the prayer-book and the other three got the water; and when one of the next-door girls got the ring Mrs Donnelly shook her finger at the blushing girl as much as to say: *O, I know all about it!* They insisted then on blindfolding Maria and leading her up to the table to see what she would get; and, while they were putting on the bandage, Maria laughed and laughed again till the tip of her nose nearly met the tip of her chin.

They led her up to the table amid laughing and joking and she put her hand out in the air as she was told to do. She moved her hand about here and there in the air and descended on one of the saucers. She felt a soft wet substance with her fingers and was surprised that nobody

---

*Dark, fortified wine.

spoke or took off her bandage. There was a pause for a few seconds; and then a great deal of scuffling and whispering. Somebody said something about the garden, and at last Mrs Donnelly said something very cross to one of the next-door girls and told her to throw it out at once: that was no play. Maria understood that it was wrong that time and so she had to do it over again: and this time she got the prayer-book.

After that Mrs Donnelly played Miss McCloud's Reel* for the children and Joe made Maria take a glass of wine. Soon they were all quite merry again and Mrs Donnelly said Maria would enter a convent before the year was out because she had got the prayer-book. Maria had never seen Joe so nice to her as he was that night, so full of pleasant talk and reminiscences. She said they were all very good to her.

At last the children grew tired and sleepy and Joe asked Maria would she not sing some little song before she went, one of the old songs. Mrs Donnelly said *Do, please, Maria!* and so Maria had to get up and stand beside the piano. Mrs Donnelly bade the children be quiet and listen to Maria's song. Then she played the prelude and said *Now, Maria!* and Maria, blushing very much, began to sing in a tiny quavering voice. She sang *I Dreamt that I Dwelt,*[†] and when she came to the second verse she sang again:

> *I dreamt that I dwelt in marble halls*
> *With vassals and serfs at my side*
> *And of all who assembled within those walls*
> *That I was the hope and the pride.*
> *I had riches too great to count, could boast*
> *Of a high ancestral name,*
> *But I also dreamt, which pleased me most,*
> *That you loved me still the same.*

But no one tried to show her her mistake;[‡] and when she had ended her song Joe was very much moved. He said that there was no time like the long ago and no music for him like poor old Balfe, whatever other people might say; and his eyes filled up so much with tears that he could not find what he was looking for and in the end he had to ask his wife to tell him where the corkscrew was.

---

*A traditional Irish dance tune.

†From the opera *The Bohemian Girl* (1843), with music by Irish composer Michael William Balfe, libretto by Alfred Bunn.

‡Maria, whether through inadvertence or avoidance, sings the first verse twice.

"A Painful Case"

A PAINFUL CASE

MR JAMES DUFFY LIVED in Chapelizod* because he wished to live as far as possible from the city of which he was a citizen and because he found all the other suburbs of Dublin mean, modern and pretentious. He lived in an old sombre house and from his windows he could look into the disused distillery or upwards along the shallow river on which Dublin is built. The lofty walls of his uncarpeted room were free from pictures. He had himself bought every article of furniture in the room: a black iron bedstead, an iron washstand, four cane chairs, a clothes-rack, a coalscuttle, a fender and irons and a square table on which lay a double desk. A bookcase had been made in an alcove by means of shelves of white wood. The bed was clothed with white bedclothes and a black and scarlet rug covered the foot. A little hand-mirror hung above the washstand and during the day a white-shaded lamp stood as the sole ornament of the mantelpiece. The books on the white wooden shelves were arranged from below upwards according to bulk. A complete Wordsworth stood at one end of the lowest shelf and a copy of the *Maynooth Catechism,*† sewn into the cloth cover of a notebook, stood at one end of the top shelf. Writing materials were always on the desk. In the desk lay a manuscript translation of Hauptmann's *Michael Kramer,*‡ the stage directions of which were written in purple ink, and a little sheaf of papers held together by a brass pin. In these sheets a sentence was inscribed from time to time and, in an ironical moment, the headline of an advertisement for *Bile Beans*§ had been pasted on to the first sheet. On lifting the lid of the desk a faint fragrance escaped—the fragrance of new cedarwood pencils or of a bottle of gum or of an over-ripe apple which might have been left there and forgotten.

    Mr Duffy abhorred anything which betokened physical or mental

---

*Western suburb of Dublin, not far from the large Phoenix Park.
†The standard Irish catechism.
‡1900 German drama, which Joyce translated the following summer.
§Medicine sold to relieve gas.

disorder. A mediaeval doctor would have called him saturnine.* His face, which carried the entire tale of his years, was of the brown tint of Dublin streets. On his long and rather large head grew dry black hair and a tawny moustache did not quite cover an unamiable mouth. His cheekbones also gave his face a harsh character; but there was no harshness in the eyes which, looking at the world from under their tawny eyebrows, gave the impression of a man ever alert to greet a redeeming instinct in others but often disappointed. He lived at a little distance from his body, regarding his own acts with doubtful side-glances. He had an odd autobiographical habit which led him to compose in his mind from time to time a short sentence about himself containing a subject in the third person and a predicate in the past tense. He never gave alms to beggars and walked firmly, carrying a stout hazel.

He had been for many years cashier of a private bank in Baggot Street. Every morning he came in from Chapelizod by tram. At midday he went to Dan Burke's† and took his lunch—a bottle of lager beer and a small trayful of arrowroot biscuits.‡ At four o'clock he was set free. He dined in an eating-house in George's Street where he felt himself safe from the society of Dublin's gilded youth and where there was a certain plain honesty in the bill of fare. His evenings were spent either before his landlady's piano or roaming about the outskirts of the city. His liking for Mozart's music brought him sometimes to an opera or a concert: these were the only dissipations of his life.

He had neither companions nor friends, church nor creed. He lived his spiritual life without any communion with others, visiting his relatives at Christmas and escorting them to the cemetery when they died. He performed these two social duties for old dignity' sake but conceded nothing further to the conventions which regulate the civic life. He allowed himself to think that in certain circumstances he would rob his bank but, as these circumstances never arose, his life rolled out evenly—an adventureless tale.

One evening he found himself sitting beside two ladies in the Rotunda.§ The house, thinly peopled and silent, gave distressing prophecy of failure. The lady who sat next him looked round at the deserted house once or twice and then said:

---

*Gloomy.
†A grocery.
‡Bland cookies.
§Performing arts venue at the north end of Sackville (now O'Connell) Street.

—What a pity there is such a poor house* tonight! It's so hard on people to have to sing to empty benches.

He took the remark as an invitation to talk. He was surprised that she seemed so little awkward. While they talked he tried to fix her permanently in his memory. When he learned that the young girl beside her was her daughter he judged her to be a year or so younger than himself. Her face, which must have been handsome, had remained intelligent. It was an oval face with strongly marked features. The eyes were very dark blue and steady. Their gaze began with a defiant note but was confused by what seemed a deliberate swoon of the pupil into the iris, revealing for an instant a temperament of great sensibility. The pupil reasserted itself quickly, this half-disclosed nature fell again under the reign of prudence, and her astrakhan jacket,[1] moulding a bosom of a certain fulness, struck the note of defiance more definitely.

He met her again a few weeks afterwards at a concert in Earlsfort Terrace and seized the moments when her daughter's attention was diverted to become intimate. She alluded once or twice to her husband but her tone was not such as to make the allusion a warning. Her name was Mrs Sinico. Her husband's great-great-grandfather had come from Leghorn.[‡] Her husband was captain of a mercantile boat plying between Dublin and Holland; and they had one child.

Meeting her a third time by accident he found courage to make an appointment. She came. This was the first of many meetings; they met always in the evening and chose the most quiet quarters for their walks together. Mr Duffy, however, had a distaste for underhand ways and, finding that they were compelled to meet stealthily, he forced her to ask him to her house. Captain Sinico encouraged his visits, thinking that his daughter's hand was in question. He had dismissed his wife so sincerely from his gallery of pleasures that he did not suspect that anyone else would take an interest in her. As the husband was often away and the daughter out giving music lessons Mr Duffy had many opportunities of enjoying the lady's society. Neither he nor she had had any such adventure before and neither was conscious of any incongruity. Little by little he entangled his thoughts with hers. He lent her books, provided her with ideas, shared his intellectual life with her. She listened to all.

Sometimes in return for his theories she gave out some fact of her

---

*Small audience.

†Short jacket made from the wool of young lambs.

‡British name for the Italian seaport of Livorno.

own life. With almost maternal solicitude she urged him to let his nature open to the full: she became his confessor. He told her that for
some time he had assisted at the meetings of an Irish Socialist Party
where he had felt himself a unique figure amidst a score of sober workmen in a garret lit by an inefficient oil-lamp. When the party had divided into three sections, each under its own leader and in its own
garret, he had discontinued his attendances. The workmen's discus-
sions, he said, were too timorous; the interest they took in the question
of wages was inordinate. He felt that they were hard-featured realists
and that they resented an exactitude which was the produce of a leisure
not within their reach. No social revolution, he told her, would be likely
to strike Dublin for some centuries.

She asked him why did he not write out his thoughts. For what, he
asked her, with careful scorn. To compete with phrasemongers, incapable of thinking consecutively for sixty seconds? To submit himself to
the criticisms of an obtuse middle class which entrusted its morality to
policemen and its fine arts to impresarios?

He went often to her little cottage outside Dublin; often they spent
their evenings alone. Little by little, as their thoughts entangled, they
spoke of subjects less remote. Her companionship was like a warm soil
about an exotic. Many times she allowed the dark to fall upon them, re-
fraining from lighting the lamp. The dark discreet room, their isolation,
the music that still vibrated in their ears united them. This union exalted him, wore away the rough edges of his character, emotionalised
his mental life. Sometimes he caught himself listening to the sound of
his own voice. He thought that in her eyes he would ascend to an angelical stature; and, as he attached the fervent nature of his companion
more and more closely to him, he heard the strange impersonal voice
which he recognised as his own, insisting on the soul's incurable loneliness. We cannot give ourselves, it said: we are our own. The end of
these discourses was that one night during which she had shown every
sign of unusual excitement, Mrs Sinico caught up his hand passionately
and pressed it to her cheek.

Mr Duffy was very much surprised. Her interpretation of his words
disillusioned him. He did not visit her for a week; then he wrote to her
asking her to meet him. As he did not wish their last interview to be
troubled by the influence of their ruined confessional they met in a little cakeshop near the Parkgate.* It was cold autumn weather but in

---

*Near the main entrance to Phoenix Park, on the western boundary of Dublin.

spite of the cold they wandered up and down the roads of the Park for nearly three hours. They agreed to break off their intercourse: every bond, he said, is a bond to sorrow. When they came out of the Park they walked in silence towards the tram; but here she began to tremble so violently that, fearing another collapse on her part, he bade her good-bye quickly and left her. A few days later he received a parcel containing his books and music.

Four years passed. Mr Duffy returned to his even way of life. His room still bore witness of the orderliness of his mind. Some new pieces of music encumbered the music-stand in the lower room and on his shelves stood two volumes by Nietzsche: *Thus Spake Zarathustra* and *The Gay Science.** He wrote seldom in the sheaf of papers which lay in his desk. One of his sentences, written two months after his last interview with Mrs Sinico, read: Love between man and man is impossible because there must not be sexual intercourse and friendship between man and woman is impossible because there must be sexual intercourse. He kept away from concerts lest he should meet her. His father died; the junior partner of the bank retired. And still every morning he went into the city by tram and every evening walked home from the city after having dined moderately in George's Street and read the evening paper for dessert.

One evening as he was about to put a morsel of corned beef and cabbage into his mouth his hand stopped. His eyes fixed themselves on a paragraph in the evening paper which he had propped against the water-carafe. He replaced the morsel of food on his plate and read the paragraph attentively. Then he drank a glass of water, pushed his plate to one side, doubled the paper down before him between his elbows and read the paragraph over and over again. The cabbage began to deposit a cold white grease on his plate. The girl came over to him to ask was his dinner not properly cooked. He said it was very good and ate a few mouthfuls of it with difficulty. Then he paid his bill and went out.

He walked along quickly through the November twilight, his stout hazel stick striking the ground regularly, the fringe of the buff *Mail*[†] peeping out of a side-pocket of his tight reefer over-coat. On the lonely

---

*Two texts (1883–1892 and 1882, respectively) in which Friedrich Nietzsche elaborated his philosophy of the "will to power" and the eternal return, and described the figure of the *Übermensch* (superman).

†The conservative-leaning *Dublin Evening Mail*, which was published on light brown paper.

road which leads from the Parkgate to Chapelizod he slackened his pace. His stick struck the ground less emphatically and his breath, issuing irregularly, almost with a sighing sound, condensed in the wintry air. When he reached his house he went up at once to his bedroom and, taking the paper from his pocket, read the paragraph again by the failing light of the window. He read it not aloud, but moving his lips as a priest does when he reads the prayers *Secreto*.* This was the paragraph:

DEATH OF A LADY AT SYDNEY PARADE†
A PAINFUL CASE

To-day at the City of Dublin Hospital the Deputy Coroner (in the absence of Mr Leverett) held an inquest on the body of Mrs Emily Sinico, aged forty-three years, who was killed at Sydney Parade Station yesterday evening. The evidence showed that the deceased lady, while attempting to cross the line, was knocked down by the engine of the ten o'clock slow train from Kingstown,‡ thereby sustaining injuries of the head and right side which led to her death.

James Lennon, driver of the engine, stated that he had been in the employment of the railway company for fifteen years. On hearing the guard's whistle he set the train in motion and a second or two afterwards brought it to rest in response to loud cries. The train was going slowly.

P. Dunne, railway porter, stated that as the train was about to start he observed a woman attempting to cross the lines. He ran towards her and shouted, but, before he could reach her, she was caught by the buffer of the engine and fell to the ground.

A juror.—You saw the lady fall?

Witness.—Yes.

Police Sergeant Croly deposed that when he arrived he found the deceased lying on the platform apparently dead. He had the body taken to the waiting-room pending the arrival of the ambulance.

Constable 57E corroborated.

Dr Halpin, assistant house surgeon of the City of Dublin Hospital, stated that the deceased had two lower ribs fractured and had sustained severe contusions of the right shoulder. The right side of the head had

---

*Latin for "in secret"; that is, read silently, to oneself.

†Suburb southwest of the city center.

‡Port city south of Dublin; now known once again by its Irish name, Dun Laoghaire.

been injured in the fall. The injuries were not sufficient to have caused death in a normal person. Death, in his opinion, had been probably due to shock and sudden failure of the heart's action.

Mr H. B. Patterson Finlay, on behalf of the railway company, expressed his deep regret at the accident. The company had always taken every precaution to prevent people crossing the lines except by the bridges, both by placing notices in every station and by the use of patent spring gates at level crossings. The deceased had been in the habit of crossing the lines late at night from platform to platform and, in view of certain other circumstances of the case, he did not think the railway officials were to blame.

Captain Sinico, of Leoville,* Sydney Parade, husband of the deceased, also gave evidence. He stated that the deceased was his wife. He was not in Dublin at the time of the accident as he had arrived only that morning from Rotterdam.† They had been married for twenty two years and had lived happily until about two years ago when his wife began to be rather intemperate in her habits.

Miss Mary Sinico said that of late her mother had been in the habit of going out at night to buy spirits. She, witness, had often tried to reason with her mother and had induced her to join a League.‡ She was not at home until an hour after the accident.

The jury returned a verdict in accordance with the medical evidence and exonerated Lennon from all blame.

The Deputy Coroner said it was a most painful case, and expressed great sympathy with Captain Sinico and his daughter. He urged on the railway company to take strong measures to prevent the possibility of similar accidents in the future. No blame attached to anyone.

Mr Duffy raised his eyes from the paper and gazed out of his window on the cheerless evening landscape. The river lay quiet beside the empty distillery and from time to time a light appeared in some house on the Lucan§ road. What an end! The whole narrative of her death revolted him and it revolted him to think that he had ever spoken to her of what he held sacred. The threadbare phrases, the inane expressions of sympathy, the cautious words of a reporter won over to conceal the

---

*After the English fashion, the name of the Sinicos' home.
†Seaport in the Netherlands.
‡A temperance league (one that advocates not drinking alcohol).
§Village 4 miles west of Chapelizod.

details of a commonplace vulgar death attacked his stomach. Not merely had she degraded herself; she had degraded him. He saw the squalid tract of her vice, miserable and malodorous. His soul's companion! He thought of the hobbling wretches whom he had seen carrying cans and bottles to be filled by the barman. Just God, what an end! Evidently she had been unfit to live, without any strength of purpose, an easy prey to habits, one of the wrecks on which civilisation has been reared. But that she could have sunk so low! Was it possible he had deceived himself so utterly about her? He remembered her outburst of that night and interpreted it in a harsher sense than he had ever done. He had no difficulty now in approving of the course he had taken.

As the light failed and his memory began to wander he thought her hand touched his. The shock which had first attacked his stomach was now attacking his nerves. He put on his over-coat and hat quickly and went out. The cold air met him on the threshold; it crept into the sleeves of his coat. When he came to the public-house at Chapelizod Bridge he went in and ordered a hot punch.*

The proprietor served him obsequiously but did not venture to talk. There were five or six workingmen in the shop discussing the value of a gentleman's estate in County Kildare. They drank at intervals from their huge pint tumblers and smoked, spitting often on the floor and sometimes dragging the sawdust over their spits with their heavy boots. Mr Duffy sat on his stool and gazed at them, without seeing or hearing them. After a while they went out and he called for another punch. He sat a long time over it. The shop was very quiet. The proprietor sprawled on the counter reading the *Herald*† and yawning. Now and again a tram was heard swishing along the lonely road outside.

As he sat there, living over his life with her and evoking alternately the two images in which he now conceived her, he realised that she was dead, that she had ceased to exist, that she had become a memory. He began to feel ill at ease. He asked himself what else could he have done. He could not have carried on a comedy of deception with her; he could not have lived with her openly. He had done what seemed to him best. How was he to blame? Now that she was gone he understood how lonely her life must have been, sitting night after night alone in that room. His life would be lonely too until he, too, died, ceased to exist, became a memory—if anyone remembered him.

---

*Whiskey punch.

†The Dublin *Evening Herald*, more nationalist than the *Evening Mail*.

It was after nine o'clock when he left the shop. The night was cold and gloomy. He entered the Park* by the first gate and walked along under the gaunt trees. He walked through the bleak alleys where they had walked four years before. She seemed to be near him in the darkness. At moments he seemed to feel her voice touch his ear, her hand touch his. He stood still to listen. Why had he withheld life from her? Why had he sentenced her to death? He felt his moral nature falling to pieces.

When he gained the crest of the Magazine Hill[†] he halted and looked along the river towards Dublin, the lights of which burned redly and hospitably in the cold night. He looked down the slope and, at the base, in the shadow of the wall of the Park, he saw some human figures lying. Those venal and furtive loves filled him with despair. He gnawed the rectitude of his life; he felt that he had been outcast from life's feast. One human being had seemed to love him and he had denied her life and happiness: he had sentenced her to ignominy, a death of shame. He knew that the prostrate creatures down by the wall were watching him and wished him gone. No one wanted him; he was outcast from life's feast. He turned his eyes to the grey gleaming river, winding along towards Dublin. Beyond the river he saw a goods train winding out of Kingsbridge Station, like a worm with a fiery head winding through the darkness, obstinately and laboriously. It passed slowly out of sight; but still he heard in his ears the laborious drone of the engine reiterating the syllables of her name.

He turned back the way he had come, the rhythm of the engine pounding in his ears. He began to doubt the reality of what memory told him. He halted under a tree and allowed the rhythm to die away. He could not feel her near him in the darkness nor her voice touch his ear. He waited for some minutes listening. He could hear nothing: the night was perfectly silent. He listened again: perfectly silent. He felt that he was alone.

---

*Phoenix Park, on the western outskirts of the city, the largest enclosed urban park in the world.
†Landmark in Phoenix Park.

OLD JACK RAKED THE cinders together with a piece of cardboard and spread them judiciously over the whitening dome of coals. When the dome was thinly covered his face lapsed into darkness but, as he set himself to fan the fire again, his crouching shadow ascended the opposite wall and his face slowly re-emerged into light. It was an old man's face, very bony and hairy. The moist blue eyes blinked at the fire and the moist mouth fell open at times, munching once or twice mechanically when it closed. When the cinders had caught he laid the piece of cardboard against the wall, sighed and said:

—That's better now, Mr O'Connor.

Mr O'Connor, a grey-haired young man, whose face was disfigured by many blotches and pimples, had just brought the tobacco for a cigarette into a shapely cylinder but when spoken to he undid his handiwork meditatively. Then he began to roll the tobacco again meditatively and after a moment's thought decided to lick the paper.

—Did Mr Tierney say when he'd be back? he asked in a husky falsetto.

—He didn't say.

Mr O'Connor put his cigarette into his mouth and began to search his pockets. He took out a pack of thin pasteboard cards.

—I'll get you a match, said the old man.

—Never mind, this'll do, said Mr O'Connor.

He selected one of the cards and read what was printed on it:

MUNICIPAL ELECTIONS
ROYAL EXCHANGE WARD*

Mr Richard J. Tierney, P.L.G.,† respectfully solicits the favour of
your vote and influence at the coming election in
the Royal Exchange Ward.

---

*One of twenty administrative units in Dublin.
†Poor Law Guardian, elected to oversee public relief.

Mr O'Connor had been engaged by Tierney's agent to canvass one part of the ward but, as the weather was inclement and his boots let in the wet, he spent a great part of the day sitting by the fire in the Committee Room* in Wicklow Street with Jack, the old caretaker. They had been sitting thus since the short day had grown dark. It was the sixth of October,[†] dismal and cold out of doors.

Mr O'Connor tore a strip off the card and, lighting it, lit his cigarette. As he did so the flame lit up a leaf of dark glossy ivy in the lapel of his coat.[‡] The old man watched him attentively and then, taking up the piece of cardboard again, began to fan the fire slowly while his companion smoked.

—Ah, yes, he said, continuing, it's hard to know what way to bring up children. Now who'd think he'd turn out like that! I sent him to the Christian Brothers[§] and I done what I could for him, and there he goes boosing about. I tried to make him someway decent.

He replaced the cardboard wearily.

—Only I'm an old man now I'd change his tune for him. I'd take the stick to his back and beat him while I could stand over him—as I done many a time before. The mother, you know, she cocks him up with this and that. . . .

—That's what ruins children, said Mr O'Connor.

—To be sure it is, said the old man. And little thanks you get for it, only impudence. He takes th'upper hand of me whenever he sees I've a sup taken. What's the world coming to when sons speaks that way to their fathers?

—What age is he? said Mr O'Connor.

—Nineteen, said the old man.

—Why don't you put him to something?

—Sure, amn't I never done at the drunken bowsy[||] ever since he left school? *I won't keep you,* I says. *You must get a job for yourself.* But, sure, it's worse whenever he gets a job; he drinks it all."

---

*The room in which the action of the story takes place, but also an allusion to Committee Room 15 in Westminster, where Charles Stewart Parnell was deposed in December 1890.

†The anniversary of Parnell's death in 1891.

‡Associated with the memory of Parnell.

§Brotherhood of Catholic laymen, founded in Waterford, County Munster, in 1802 by Edmund Ignatius Rice.

||Layabout.

Mr O'Connor shook his head in sympathy, and the old man fell silent, gazing into the fire. Someone opened the door of the room and called out:

—Hello! Is this a Freemason's meeting?*

—Who's that? said the old man.

—What are you doing in the dark? asked a voice.

—Is that you, Hynes? asked Mr O'Connor.

—Yes. What are you doing in the dark? said Mr Hynes, advancing into the light of the fire.

He was a tall, slender young man with a light brown moustache. Imminent little drops of rain hung at the brim of his hat and the collar of his jacket-coat was turned up.

—Well, Mat, he said to Mr O'Connor, how goes it?

Mr O'Connor shook his head. The old man left the hearth, and after stumbling about the room returned with two candlesticks which he thrust one after the other into the fire and carried to the table. A denuded room came into view and the fire lost all its cheerful colour. The walls of the room were bare except for a copy of an election address. In the middle of the room was a small table on which papers were heaped.

Mr Hynes leaned against the mantelpiece and asked:

—Has he paid you yet?

—Not yet, said Mr O'Connor. I hope to God he'll not leave us in the lurch to-night.

Mr Hynes laughed.

—O, he'll pay you. Never fear, he said.

—I hope he'll look smart about it if he means business, said Mr O'Connor.

—What do you think, Jack? said Mr Hynes satirically to the old man.

The old man returned to his seat by the fire, saying:

—It isn't but he has it, anyway. Not like the other tinker.†

—What other tinker? said Mr Hynes.

—Colgan, said the old man scornfully.

—It is because Colgan's a working-man you say that? What's the difference between a good honest bricklayer and a publican‡—eh? Hasn't the working-man as good a right to be in the Corporation§ as anyone

---

*Meeting of the secret fraternal order of Free and Accepted Masons, regarded by Catholics as a Protestant sect.

†Gypsy.

‡Pub owner.

§The Dublin Corporation, the city's governing body.

else—ay, and a better right than those shoneens* that are always hat in hand before any fellow with a handle to his name?† Isn't that so, Mat? said Mr Hynes, addressing Mr O'Connor.

—I think you're right, said Mr O'Connor.

—One man is a plain honest man with no hunker-sliding‡ about him. He goes in to represent the labour classes. This fellow you're working for only wants to get some job or other.

—Of course, the working-classes should be represented, said the old man.

—The working-man, said Mr Hynes, gets all kicks and no halfpence. But it's labour produces everything. The working-man is not looking for fat jobs for his sons and nephews and cousins. The working-man is not going to drag the honour of Dublin in the mud to please a German monarch.§

—How's that? said the old man.

—Don't you know they want to present an address of welcome to Edward Rex if he comes here next year? What do we want kowtowing to a foreign king?

—Our man won't vote for the address, said Mr O'Connor. He goes in on the Nationalist ticket.||

—Won't he? said Mr Hynes. Wait till you see whether he will or not. I know him. Is it Tricky Dicky Tierney?

—By God! perhaps you're right, Joe, said Mr O'Connor. Anyway, I wish he'd turn up with the spondulics.#

The three men fell silent. The old man began to rake more cinders together. Mr Hynes took off his hat, shook it and then turned down the collar of his coat, displaying, as he did so, an ivy leaf in the lapel.

—If this man was alive, he said, pointing to the leaf, we'd have no talk of an address of welcome.

—That's true, said Mr O'Connor.

—Musha, God be with them times! said the old man. There was some life in it then.

The room was silent again. Then a bustling little man with a snuffling nose and very cold ears pushed in the door. He walked over

*Worthless men.
†Title.
‡Laziness.
§That is, English King Edward VII, who was related to German royalty.
||That of the Irish Parliamentary Party, opposed to English rule in Ireland.
#Money.

quickly to the fire, rubbing his hands as if he intended to produce a spark from them.

—No money, boys, he said.

—Sit down here, Mr Henchy, said the old man, offering him his chair.

—O, don't stir, Jack, don't stir, said Mr Henchy.

He nodded curtly to Mr Hynes and sat down on the chair which the old man vacated.

—Did you serve Aungier Street? he asked Mr O'Connor.

—Yes, said Mr O'Connor, beginning to search his pockets for memoranda.

—Did you call on Grimes?

—I did.

—Well? How does he stand?

—He wouldn't promise. He said: *I won't tell anyone what way I'm going to vote.* But I think he'll be all right.

—Why so?

—He asked me who the nominators were; and I told him. I mentioned Father Burke's name. I think it'll be all right.

Mr Henchy began to snuffle and to rub his hands over the fire at a terrific speed. Then he said:

—For the love of God, Jack, bring us a bit of coal. There must be some left.

The old man went out of the room.

—It's no go, said Mr Henchy, shaking his head. I asked the little shoeboy, but he said: O, now, Mr Henchy, when I see the work going on properly I won't forget you, you may be sure. Mean little tinker! 'Usha, how could he be anything else?

—What did I tell you, Mat? said Mr Hynes. Tricky Dicky Tierney.

—O, he's as tricky as they make 'em, said Mr Henchy. He hasn't got those little pigs' eyes for nothing. Blast his soul! Couldn't he pay up like a man instead of: *O, now, Mr Henchy, I must speak to Mr Fanning. . . . I've spent a lot of money*? Mean little schoolboy of hell! I suppose he forgets the time his little old father kept the hand-me-down shop in Mary's Lane.

—But is that a fact? asked Mr O'Connor.

—God, yes, said Mr Henchy. Did you never hear that? And the men used to go in on Sunday morning before the houses were open to buy a waistcoat or a trousers—moya! But Tricky Dicky's little old father always had a tricky little black bottle up in a corner. Do you mind now? That's that. That's where he first saw the light.

The old man returned with a few lumps of coal which he placed here and there on the fire.

—That's a nice how-do-you-do, said Mr O'Connor. How does he expect us to work for him if he won't stump up?

—I can't help it, said Mr Henchy. I expect to find the bailiffs in the hall when I go home.

Mr Hynes laughed and, shoving himself away from the mantelpiece with the aid of his shoulders, made ready to leave.

—It'll be all right when King Eddie comes, he said. Well, boys, I'm off for the present. See you later. 'Bye, 'bye.

He went out of the room slowly. Neither Mr Henchy nor the old man said anything, but, just as the door was closing, Mr O'Connor, who had been staring moodily into the fire, called out suddenly:

—'Bye, Joe.

Mr Henchy waited a few moments and then nodded in the direction of the door.

—Tell me, he said across the fire, what brings our friend in here? What does he want?

—'Usha, poor Joe! said Mr O'Connor, throwing the end of his cigarette into the fire, he's hard up, like the rest of us.

Mr Henchy snuffled vigorously and spat so copiously that he nearly put out the fire, which uttered a hissing protest.

—To tell you my private and candid opinion, he said, I think he's a man from the other camp. He's a spy of Colgan's, if you ask me. Just go round and try and find out how they're getting on. They won't suspect you. Do you twig?*

—Ah, poor Joe is a decent skin, said Mr O'Connor.

—His father was a decent, respectable man, Mr Henchy admitted. Poor old Larry Hynes! Many a good turn he did in his day! But I'm greatly afraid our friend is not nineteen carat. Damn it, I can understand a fellow being hard up, but what I can't understand is a fellow sponging.† Couldn't he have some spark of manhood about him?

—He doesn't get a warm welcome from me when he comes, said the old man. Let him work for his own side and not come spying around here.

—I don't know, said Mr O'Connor dubiously, as he took out cigarette-papers and tobacco. I think Joe Hynes is a straight man. He's a clever chap, too, with the pen. Do you remember that thing he wrote . . . ?

---

*From the Irish word *tuig* ("understand").
†Freeloading.

—Some of these hillsiders and fenians[3] are a bit too clever if you ask me, said Mr Henchy. Do you know what my private and candid opinion is about some of those little jokers? I believe half of them are in the pay of the Castle.*

—There's no knowing, said the old man.

—O, but I know it for a fact, said Mr Henchy. They're Castle hacks. . . . I don't say Hynes. . . . No, damn it, I think he's a stroke above that. . . . But there's a certain little nobleman with a cock-eye— you know the patriot I'm alluding to?

Mr O'Connor nodded.

—There's a lineal descendant of Major Sirr[†] for you if you like! O, the heart's blood of a patriot! That's a fellow now that'd sell his country for fourpence—ay—and go down on his bended knees and thank the Almighty Christ he had a country to sell.

There was a knock at the door.

—Come in! said Mr Henchy.

A person resembling a poor clergyman or a poor actor appeared in the doorway. His black clothes were tightly buttoned on his short body and it was impossible to say whether he wore a clergyman's collar or a layman's, because the collar of his shabby frock-coat, the uncovered buttons of which reflected the candlelight, was turned up about his neck. He wore a round hat of hard black felt. His face, shining with raindrops, had the appearance of damp yellow cheese save where two rosy spots indicated the cheekbones. He opened his very long mouth suddenly to express disappointment and at the same time opened wide his very bright blue eyes to express pleasure and surprise.

—O Father Keon! said Mr Henchy, jumping up from his chair. Is that you? Come in!

—O, no, no, no! said Father Keon quickly, pursuing his lips as if he were addressing a child.

—Won't you come in and sit down?

—No, no, no! said Father Keon, speaking in a discreet, indulgent, velvety voice. Don't let me disturb you now! I'm just looking for Mr Fanning. . . .

---

*Dublin Castle, home of the Dublin Corporation and the city's municipal government.

†Head of the Dublin police who was instrumental in putting down the 1798 rebellion.

—He's round at the *Black Eagle*,* said Mr Henchy. But won't you come in and sit down a minute?

—No, no, thank you. It was just a little business matter, said Father Keon. Thank you, indeed.

He retreated from the doorway and Mr Henchy, seizing one of the candlesticks, went to the door to light him downstairs.

—O, don't trouble, I beg!

—No, but the stairs is so dark.

—No, no, I can see. . . . Thank you, indeed.

—Are you right now?

—All right, thanks. . . . Thanks.

Mr Henchy returned with the candlestick and put it on the table. He sat down again at the fire. There was silence for a few moments.

—Tell me, John, said Mr O'Connor, lighting his cigarette with another pasteboard card.

—Hm?

—What he is exactly?

—Ask me an easier one, said Mr Henchy.

—Fanning and himself seem to me very thick. They're often in Kavanagh's together. Is he a priest at all?

—Mmmyes, I believe so. . . . I think he's what you call a black sheep. We haven't many of them, thank God! but we have a few. . . . He's an unfortunate man of some kind. . . .

—And how does he knock it out? asked Mr O'Connor.

—That's another mystery.

—Is he attached to any chapel or church or institution or—

—No, said Mr Henchy, I think he's travelling on his own account. . . . God forgive me, he added, I thought he was the dozen of stout.

—Is there any chance of a drink itself? asked Mr O'Connor.

—I'm dry too, said the old man.

—I asked that little shoeboy three times, said Mr Henchy, would he send up a dozen of stout. I asked him again now, but he was leaning on the counter in his shirt-sleeves having a deep goster† with Alderman Cowley.

—Why didn't you remind him? said Mr O'Connor.

—Well, I couldn't go over while he was talking to Alderman Cowley. I just waited till I caught his eye, and said: *About that little matter I was*

---

*A pub.

†From the Irish *gasrán* ("conversation").

speaking to you about. . . . That'll be all right, Mr H., he said. Yerra, sure
the little hop-o'-my-thumb* has forgotten all about it.

—There's some deal on in that quarter, said Mr O'Connor thoughtfully. I saw the three of them hard at it yesterday at Suffolk Street corner.

—I think I know the little game they're at, said Mr Henchy. You
must owe the City Fathers money nowadays if you want to be made
Lord Mayor. Then they'll make you Lord Mayor. By God! I'm thinking seriously of becoming a City Father myself. What do you think?
Would I do for the job?

Mr O'Connor laughed.

—So far as owing money goes. . . .

—Driving out of the Mansion House,† said Mr Henchy, in all my
vermin,‡ with Jack here standing up behind me in a powdered wig—eh?

—And make me your private secretary, John.

—Yes. And I'll make Father Keon my private chaplain. We'll have a
family party.

—Faith, Mr Henchy, said the old man, you'd keep up better style
than some of them. I was talking one day to old Keegan, the porter. *And
how do you like your new master, Pat?* says I to him. *You haven't much entertaining now,* says I. *Entertaining!* says he. *He'd live on the smell of an
oil-rag.* And do you know what he told me? Now, I declare to God, I
didn't believe him.

—What? said Mr Henchy and Mr O'Connor.

—He told me: *What do you think of a Lord Mayor of Dublin sending
out for a pound of chops for his dinner? How's that for high living?* says he.
Wisha! wisha, says I. *A pound of chops,* says he, *coming into the Mansion
House. Wisha!* says I, *what kind of people is going at all now?*

At this point there was a knock at the door, and a boy put in his head.

—What is it? said the old man.

—From the *Black Eagle,* said the boy, walking in sideways and de-
positing a basket on the floor with a noise of shaken bottles.

The old man helped the boy to transfer the bottles from the basket
to the table and counted the full tally. After the transfer the boy put his
basket on his arm and asked:

—Any bottles?

—What bottles? said the old man.

—Won't you let us drink them first? said Mr Henchy.

---

*Dwarf.
†Official residence of the Lord Mayor.
‡A pun on "ermine," the fur trimming of the Mayor's robes.

—I was told to ask for bottles.

—Come back to-morrow, said the old man.

—Here, boy! said Mr Henchy, will you run over to O'Farrell's and ask him to lend us a corkscrew—for Mr Henchy, say. Tell him we won't keep it a minute. Leave the basket there.

The boy went out and Mr Henchy began to rub his hands cheerfully, saying:

—Ah, well, he's not so bad after all. He's as good as his word, anyhow.

—There's no tumblers, said the old man.

—O, don't let that trouble you, Jack, said Mr Henchy. Many's the good man before now drank out of the bottle.

—Anyway, it's better than nothing, said Mr O'Connor.

—He's not a bad sort, said Mr Henchy, only Fanning has such a loan of him. He means well, you know, in his own tinpot way.

The boy came back with the corkscrew. The old man opened three bottles and was handing back the corkscrew when Mr Henchy said to the boy,

—Would you like a drink, boy?

—If you please, sir, said the boy.

The old man opened another bottle grudgingly, and handed it to the boy.

—What age are you? he asked.

—Seventeen, said the boy.

As the old man said nothing further, the boy took the bottle, said:—Here's my best respects, sir, to Mr Henchy, drank the contents, put the bottle back on the table and wiped his mouth with his sleeve. Then he took up the corkscrew and went out of the door sideways, muttering some form of salutation.

—That's the way it begins, said the old man.

—The thin edge of the wedge, said Mr Henchy.

The old man distributed the three bottles which he had opened and the men drank from them simultaneously. After having drunk each placed his bottle on the mantelpiece within hand's reach and drew in a long breath of satisfaction

—Well, I did a good day's work to-day, said Mr Henchy, after a pause.

—That so, John?

—Yes. I got him one or two sure things in Dawson Street, Crofton and myself. Between ourselves, you know, Crofton (he's a decent chap, of course), but he's not worth a damn as a canvasser. He hasn't a word to throw to a dog. He stands and looks at the people while I do the talking.

Here two men entered the room. One of them was a very fat man, whose blue serge clothes seemed to be in danger of falling from his sloping figure. He had a big face which resembled a young ox's face in expression, staring blue eyes and a grizzled moustache. The other man, who was much younger and frailer, had a thin, clean-shaven face. He wore a very high double collar and a wide-brimmed bowler hat.

—Hello, Crofton! said Mr Henchy to the fat man. Talk of the devil . . .

—Where did the boose come from? asked the young man. Did the cow calve?

—O, of course, Lyons spots the drink first thing! said Mr O'Connor, laughing.

—Is that the way you chaps canvass, said Mr Lyons, and Crofton and I out in the cold and rain looking for votes?

—Why, blast your soul, said Mr Henchy, I'd get more votes in five minutes than you two'd get in a week.

—Open two bottles of stout, Jack, said Mr O'Connor.

—How can I? said the old man, when there's no corkscrew?

—Wait now, wait now! said Mr Henchy, getting up quickly. Did you ever see this little trick?

He took two bottles from the table and, carrying them to the fire, put them on the hob.* Then he sat down again by the fire and took another drink from his bottle. Mr Lyons sat on the edge of the table, pushed his hat towards the nape of his neck and began to swing his legs.

—Which is my bottle? he asked.

—This, lad, said Mr Henchy.

Mr Crofton sat down on a box and looked fixedly at the other bottle on the hob. He was silent for two reasons. The first reason, sufficient in itself, was that he had nothing to say; the second reason was that he considered his companions beneath him. He had been a canvasser for Wilkins, the Conservative, but when the Conservatives had withdrawn their man and, choosing the lesser of two evils, given their support to the Nationalist candidate, he had been engaged to work for Mr Tierney.

In a few minutes an apologetic *Pok!* was heard as the cork flew out of Mr Lyons' bottle. Mr Lyons jumped off the table, went to the fire, took his bottle and carried it back to the table.

—I was just telling them, Crofton, said Mr Henchy, that we got a good few votes to-day.

—Who did you get? asked Mr Lyons.

—Well, I got Parkes for one, and I got Atkinson for two, and I got

---

*Shelf within a fireplace.

Ward of Dawson Street. Fine old chap he is, too—regular old toff,* old Conservative! *But isn't your candidate a Nationalist?* said he. *He's a respectable man,* said I. *He's in favour of whatever will benefit this country. He's a big ratepayer,*[†] I said. *He has extensive house property in the city and three places of business and isn't it to his own advantage to keep down the rates? He's a prominent and respected citizen,* said I, *and a Poor Law Guardian, and he doesn't belong to any party, good, bad, or indifferent.* That's the way to talk to 'em.

—And what about the address to the King? said Mr Lyons, after drinking and smacking his lips.

—Listen to me, said Mr Henchy. What we want in this country, as I said to old Ward, is capital. The King's coming here will mean an influx of money into this country. The citizens of Dublin will benefit by it. Look at all the factories down by the quays there, idle! Look at all the money there is in the country if we only worked the old industries, the mills, the shipbuilding yards and factories. It's capital we want.

—But look here, John, said Mr O'Connor. Why should we welcome the King of England? Didn't Parnell himself . . .[‡]

—Parnell, said Mr Henchy, is dead. Now, here's the way I look at it. Here's this chap come to the throne after his old mother keeping him out of it till the man was grey. He's a man of the world, and he means well by us. He's a jolly fine decent fellow, if you ask me, and no damn nonsense about him. He just says to himself: *The old one never went to see these wild Irish. By Christ, I'll go myself and see what they're like.* And are we going to insult the man when he comes over here on a friendly visit? Eh? Isn't that right, Crofton?

Mr Crofton nodded his head.

—But after all now, said Mr Lyons argumentatively, King Edward's life, you know, is not the very . . .[§]

—Let bygones be bygones, said Mr Henchy. I admire the man personally. He's just an ordinary knockabout like you and me. He's fond of his glass of grog[||] and he's a bit of a rake,[#] perhaps, and he's a good sportsman. Damn it, can't we Irish play fair?

---

*Gentleman.

†Taxpayer.

‡Parnell had opposed a welcome for the Prince of Wales, later Edward VII, back in 1885.

§Before his ascension to the throne, Edward's life was the subject of public scandal and gossip.

||Hard liquor.

#Libertine.

—That's all very fine, said Mr Lyons. But look at the case of Parnell now.

—In the name of God, said Mr Henchy, where's the analogy between the two cases?

—What I mean, said Mr Lyons, is we have our ideals. Why, now, would we welcome a man like that? Do you think now after what he did Parnell was a fit man to lead us? And why, then, would we do it for Edward the Seventh?

—This is Parnell's anniversary, said Mr O'Connor, and don't let us stir up any bad blood. We all respect him now that he's dead and gone—even the Conservatives, he added, turning to Mr Crofton.

Pok! The tardy cork flew out of Mr Crofton's bottle. Mr Crofton got up from his box and went to the fire. As he returned with his capture he said in a deep voice:

—Our side of the house respects him, because he was a gentleman.

—Right you are, Crofton! said Mr Henchy fiercely. He was the only man that could keep that bag of cats in order. *Down, ye dogs! Lie down, ye curs!* That's the way he treated them. Come in Joe! Come in! he called out, catching sight of Mr Hynes in the doorway.

Mr Hynes came in slowly.

—Open another bottle of stout, Jack, said Mr Henchy. O, I forgot there's no corkscrew! Here, show me one here and I'll put it at the fire.

The old man handed him another bottle and he placed it on the hob.

—Sit down, Joe, said Mr O'Connor, we're just talking about the Chief.*

—Ay, ay! said Mr Henchy.

Mr Hynes sat on the side of the table near Mr Lyons but said nothing.

—There's one of them, anyhow, said Mr Henchy, that didn't renege him. By God, I'll say for you, Joe! No, by God, you stuck to him like a man!

—O, Joe, said Mr O'Connor suddenly. Give us that thing you wrote—do you remember? Have you got it on you?

—O, ay! said Mr Henchy. Give us that. Did you ever hear that, Crofton? Listen to this now: splendid thing.

—Go on, said Mr O'Connor. Fire away, Joe.

Mr Hynes did not seem to remember at once the piece to which they were alluding, but, after reflecting a while, he said:

—O, that thing is it. . . . Sure, that's old now.

---

*Parnell.

—Out with it, man! said Mr O'Connor.

—'Sh, 'sh, said Mr Henchy. Now, Joe!

Mr Hynes hesitated a little longer. Then amid the silence he took off his hat, laid it on the table and stood up. He seemed to be rehearsing the piece in his mind. After a rather long pause he announced:

THE DEATH OF PARNELL

6th October, 1891

He cleared his throat once or twice and then began to recite:

> *He is dead. Our Uncrowned King is dead.*
> *O, Erin, mourn with grief and woe*
> *For he lies dead whom the fell gang*
> *Of modern hypocrites laid low.*
>
> *He lies slain by the coward hounds*
> *He raised to glory from the mire;*
> *And Erin's hopes and Erin's dreams*
> *Perish upon her monarch's pyre.*
>
> *In palace, cabin or in cot*
> *The Irish heart where'er it be*
> *Is bowed with woe—for he is gone*
> *Who would have wrought her destiny.*
>
> *He would have had his Erin famed,*
> *The green flag gloriously unfurled,*
> *Her statesmen, bards and warriors raised*
> *Before the nations of the World.*
>
> *He dreamed (alas, 'twas but a dream!)*
> *Of Liberty: but as he strove*
> *To clutch that idol, treachery*
> *Sundered him from the thing he loved.*
>
> *Shame on the coward, caitiff* hands*
> *That smote their Lord or with a kiss*
> *Betrayed him to the rabble-rout*
> *Of fawning priests—no friends of his.*

---

*Cowardly.

May everlasting shame consume
  The memory of those who tried
To befoul and smear the exalted name
  Of one who spurned them in his pride.

He fell as fall the mighty ones,
  Nobly undaunted to the last,
And death has now united him
  With Erin's heroes of the past.

No sound of strife disturb his sleep!
  Calmly he rests: no human pain
Or high ambition spurs him now
  The peaks of glory to attain.

They had their way: they laid him low.
  But Erin, list, his spirit may
Rise, like the Phoenix from the flames,
  When breaks the dawning of the day,

The day that brings us Freedom's reign.
  And on that day may Erin well
Pledge in the cup she lifts to Joy
  One grief—the memory of Parnell.

Mr Hynes sat down again on the table. When he had finished his recitation there was a silence and then a burst of clapping: even Mr Lyons clapped. The applause continued for a little time. When it had ceased all the auditors drank from their bottles in silence.

Pok! The cork flew out of Mr Hynes' bottle, but Mr Hynes remained sitting flushed and bareheaded on the table. He did not seem to have heard the invitation.

—Good man, Joe! said Mr O'Connor, taking out his cigarette papers and pouch the better to hide his emotion.

—What do you think of that, Crofton? cried Mr Henchy. Isn't that fine? What?

Mr Crofton said that it was a very fine piece of writing.

A MOTHER

MR HOLOHAN, ASSISTANT SECRETARY of the *Eire Abu** Society, had been walking up and down Dublin for nearly a month, with his hands and pockets full of dirty pieces of paper, arranging about the series of concerts. He had a game leg and for this his friends called him Hoppy Holohan. He walked up and down constantly, stood by the hour at street corners arguing the point and made notes; but in the end it was Mrs Kearney who arranged everything.

Miss Devlin had become Mrs Kearney out of spite. She had been educated in a high-class convent,[†] where she had learned French and music. As she was naturally pale and unbending in manner she made few friends at school. When she came to the age of marriage she was sent out to many houses, where her playing and ivory manners were much admired. She sat amid the chilly circle of her accomplishments, waiting for some suitor to brave it and offer her a brilliant life. But the young men whom she met were ordinary and she gave them no encouragement, trying to console her romantic desires by eating a great deal of Turkish Delight[‡] in secret. However, when she drew near the limit and her friends began to loosen their tongues about her, she silenced them by marrying Mr Kearney, who was a bootmaker on Ormond Quay.

He was much older than she. His conversation, which was serious, took place at intervals in his great brown beard. After the first year of married life, Mrs Kearney perceived that such a man would wear better than a romantic person, but she never put her own romantic ideas away. He was sober, thrifty and pious; he went to the altar every first Friday, sometimes with her, oftener by himself. But she never weakened in her religion and was a good wife to him. At some party in a strange house when she lifted her eyebrow ever so slightly he stood up to take his leave and, when his cough troubled him, she put the eider-down

---

*Ireland to Victory (Irish); a nationalist slogan.
†That is, a convent school.
‡Candy made of fruit juice and gelatin.

341

quilt over his feet and made a strong rum punch. For his part, he was a model father. By paying a small sum every week into a society, he ensured for both his daughters a dowry of one hundred pounds each when they came to the age of twenty-four. He sent the older daughter, Kathleen, to a good convent, where she learned French and music, and afterward paid her fees at the Academy.* Every year in the month of July Mrs Kearney found occasion to say to some friend:

—My good man is packing us off to Skerries for a few weeks.

If it was not Skerries it was Howth or Greystones.†

When the Irish Revival‡ began to be appreciable Mrs Kearney determined to take advantage of her daughter's name and brought an Irish teacher to the house. Kathleen and her sister sent Irish picture postcards to their friends and these friends sent back other Irish picture postcards. On special Sundays, when Mr Kearney went with his family to the pro-cathedral,§ a little crowd of people would assemble after mass at the corner of Cathedral Street. They were all friends of the Kearneys—musical friends or Nationalist‖ friends; and, when they had played every little counter of gossip, they shook hands with one another all together, laughing at the crossing of so many hands, and said good-bye to one another in Irish. Soon the name of Miss Kathleen Kearney began to be heard often on people's lips. People said that she was very clever at music and a very nice girl and, moreover, that she was a believer in the language movement. Mrs Kearney was well content at this. Therefore she was not surprised when one day Mr Holohan came to her and proposed that her daughter should be the accompanist at a series of four grand concerts which his Society was going to give in the Antient Concert Rooms. She brought him into the drawing-room, made him sit down and brought out the decanter and the silver biscuit-barrel. She entered heart and soul into the details of the enterprise, advised and dissuaded: and finally a contract was drawn up by which Kathleen was to receive eight guineas for her services as accompanist at the four grand concerts.

---

*The Royal Irish Academy of Music.

†Skerries, Howth, Greystones were well-to-do seaside communities near Dublin.

‡An attempt to revive traditional Irish language, arts, and culture.

§A pro-cathedral is a parish church used as a cathedral (seat of a diocese); the reference here is to the Catholic St. Mary's Pro-Cathedral, on the corner of Marlborough and Cathedral Streets; the city's other two cathedrals (St. Patrick's and Christ Church) are both Protestant.

‖One who desires Irish independence from Britain; also, frequently, one who subscribes to the program of the Irish (or Celtic) Revival.

As Mr Holohan was a novice in such delicate matters as the wording of bills and the disposing of items for a programme, Mrs Kearney helped him. She had tact. She knew what *artistes* should go into capitals and what *artistes* should go into small type. She knew that the first tenor would not like to come on after Mr Meade's comic turn. To keep the audience continually diverted she slipped the doubtful items in between the old favourites. Mr Holohan called to see her every day to have her advice on some point. She was invariably friendly and advising—homely, in fact. She pushed the decanter towards him, saying:

—Now, help yourself, Mr Holohan!

And while he was helping himself she said:

—Don't be afraid! Don't be afraid of it!

Everything went on smoothly. Mrs Kearney bought some lovely blush-pink charmeuse* in Brown Thomas's† to let into the front of Kathleen's dress. It cost a pretty penny; but there are occasions when a little expense is justifiable. She took a dozen of two-shilling tickets for the final concert and sent them to those friends who could not be trusted to come otherwise. She forgot nothing, and, thanks to her, everything that was to be done was done.

The concerts were to be on Wednesday, Thursday, Friday and Saturday. When Mrs Kearney arrived with her daughter at the Antient Concert Rooms on Wednesday night she did not like the look of things. A few young men, wearing bright blue badges in their coats, stood idle in the vestibule; none of them wore evening dress. She passed by with her daughter and a quick glance through the open door of the hall showed her the cause of the stewards' idleness. At first she wondered had she mistaken the hour. No, it was twenty minutes to eight.

In the dressing-room behind the stage she was introduced to the secretary of the Society, Mr Fitzpatrick. She smiled and shook his hand. He was a little man, with a white, vacant face. She noticed that he wore his soft brown hat carelessly on the side of his head and that his accent was flat. He held a programme in his hand, and, while he was talking to her, he chewed one end of it into a moist pulp. He seemed to bear disappointments lightly. Mr Holohan came into the dressing-room every few minutes with reports from the box-office. The *artistes* talked among themselves nervously, glanced from time to time at the mirror and rolled and unrolled their music. When it was nearly half-past eight, the few

---

*Soft satin.

†Fashionable downtown department store.

people in the hall began to express their desire to be entertained. Mr Fitzpatrick came in, smiled vacantly at the room, and said:

—Well now, ladies and gentlemen. I suppose we'd better open the ball.

Mrs Kearney rewarded his very flat final syllable with a quick stare of contempt, and then said to her daughter encouragingly:

—Are you ready, dear?

When she had an opportunity, she called Mr Holohan aside and asked him to tell her what it meant. Mr Holohan did not know what it meant. He said that the committee had made a mistake in arranging for four concerts: four was too many.

—And the *artistes!* said Mrs Kearney. Of course they are doing their best, but really they are not good.

Mr Holohan admitted that the *artistes* were no good but the committee, he said, had decided to let the first three concerts go as they pleased and reserve all the talent for Saturday night. Mrs Kearney said nothing, but, as the mediocre items followed one another on the platform and the few people in the hall grew fewer and fewer, she began to regret that she had put herself to any expense for such a concert. There was something she didn't like in the look of things and Mr Fitzpatrick's vacant smile irritated her very much. However, she said nothing and waited to see how it would end. The concert expired shortly before ten, and everyone went home quickly.

The concert on Thursday night was better attended, but Mrs Kearney saw at once that the house was filled with paper.* The audience behaved indecorously, as if the concert were an informal dress rehearsal. Mr Fitzpatrick seemed to enjoy himself; he was quite unconscious that Mrs Kearney was taking angry note of his conduct. He stood at the edge of the screen, from time to time jutting out his head and exchanging a laugh with two friends in the corner of the balcony. In the course of the evening, Mrs Kearney learned that the Friday concert was to be abandoned and that the committee was going to move heaven and earth to secure a bumper house on Saturday night. When she heard this, she sought out Mr Holohan. She buttonholed him as he was limping out quickly with a glass of lemonade for a young lady and asked him was it true. Yes, it was true.

—But, of course, that doesn't alter the contract, she said. The contract was for four concerts.

Mr Holohan seemed to be in a hurry; he advised her to speak to Mr

---

*That is, the audience has been swelled with free tickets.

Fitzpatrick. Mrs Kearney was now beginning to be alarmed. She called Mr Fitzpatrick away from his screen and told him that her daughter had signed for four concerts and that, of course, according to the terms of the contract, she should receive the sum originally stipulated for, whether the society gave the four concerts or not. Mr Fitzpatrick, who did not catch the point at issue very quickly, seemed unable to resolve the difficulty and said that he would bring the matter before the committee. Mrs Kearney's anger began to flutter in her cheek and she had all she could do to keep from asking:

—And who is the *Cometty* pray?

But she knew that it would not be ladylike to do that: so she was silent.

Little boys were sent out into the principal streets of Dublin early on Friday morning with bundles of handbills. Special puffs appeared in all the evening papers, reminding the music-loving public of the treat which was in store for it on the following evening. Mrs Kearney was somewhat reassured, but she thought well to tell her husband part of her suspicions. He listened carefully and said that perhaps it would be better if he went with her on Saturday night. She agreed. She respected her husband in the same way as she respected the General Post Office,* as something large, secure and fixed; and though she knew the small number of his talents she appreciated his abstract value as a male. She was glad that he had suggested coming with her. She thought her plans over.

The night of the grand concert came. Mrs Kearney, with her husband and daughter, arrived at the Antient Concert Rooms three-quarters of an hour before the time at which the concert was to begin. By ill luck it was a rainy evening. Mrs Kearney placed her daughter's clothes and music in charge of her husband and went all over the building looking for Mr Holohan or Mr Fitzpatrick. She could find neither. She asked the stewards was any member of the committee in the hall and, after a great deal of trouble, a steward brought out a little woman named Miss Beirne to whom Mrs Kearney explained that she wanted to see one of the secretaries. Miss Beirne expected them any minute and asked could she do anything. Mrs Kearney looked searchingly at the oldish face which was screwed into an expression of trustfulness and enthusiasm and answered:

—No, thank you!

The little woman hoped they would have a good house. She looked

---

*Imposing building on Sackville (now O'Connell) Street, near Nelson's Pillar, the geographic center of the city; during the Easter Rising in 1916, Irish rebels took over the G.P.O. as their headquarters.

out at the rain until the melancholy of the wet street effaced all the
trustfulness and enthusiasm from her twisted features. Then she gave a
little sigh and said:

—Ah, well! We did our best, the dear* knows.

Mrs Kearney had to go back to the dressing-room.

The *artistes* were arriving. The bass and the second tenor had already
come. The bass, Mr Duggan, was a slender young man with a scattered
black moustache. He was the son of a hall porter in an office in the city
and, as a boy, he had sung prolonged bass notes in the resounding hall.
From this humble state he had raised himself until he had become a
first-rate *artiste*. He had appeared in grand opera. One night, when an
operatic *artiste* had fallen ill, he had undertaken the part of the king in
the opera of *Maritana*† at the Queen's Theatre.‡ He sang his music
with great feeling and volume and was warmly welcomed by the
gallery; but, unfortunately, he marred the good impression by wiping
his nose in his gloved hand once or twice out of thoughtlessness. He
was unassuming and spoke little. He said *yous* so softly that it passed
unnoticed and he never drank anything stronger than milk for his
voice's sake. Mr Bell, the second tenor, was a fair-haired little man who
competed every year for prizes at the Feis Ceoil.§ On his fourth trial he
had been awarded a bronze medal. He was extremely nervous and extremely jealous of other tenors and he covered his nervous jealousy with
an ebullient friendliness. It was his humour to have people know what
an ordeal a concert was to him. Therefore when he saw Mr Duggan he
went over to him and asked:

—Are you in it too?

—Yes, said Mr Duggan.

Mr Bell laughed at his fellow-sufferer, held out his hand and said:

—Shake!

Mrs Kearney passed by these two young men and went to the edge
of the screen to view the house. The seats were being filled up rapidly
and a pleasant noise circulated in the auditorium. She came back and
spoke to her husband privately. Their conversation was evidently about
Kathleen for they both glanced at her often as she stood chatting to one

---

*That is, God; an example of the Irish strategy of "dodging the curse," substituting
an innocuous word for a profane or irreligious one.

†1845 opera by Irish composer William Wallace.

‡One of Dublin's three major turn-of-the-century theaters.

§Annual Irish music festival, established in 1897; Joyce placed third for his singing
in 1904.

of her Nationalist friends, Miss Healy, the contralto. An unknown solitary woman with a pale face walked through the room. The women followed with keen eyes the faded blue dress which was stretched upon a meagre body. Someone said that she was Madam Glynn, the soprano.

—I wonder where did they dig her up, said Kathleen to Miss Healy. I'm sure I never heard of her.

Miss Healy had to smile. Mr Holohan limped into the dressing-room at that moment and the two young ladies asked him who was the unknown woman. Mr Holohan said that she was Madam Glynn from London. Madam Glynn took her stand in a corner of the room, holding a roll of music stiffly before her and from time to time changing the direction of her startled gaze. The shadow took her faded dress into shelter but fell revengefully into the little cup behind her collar-bone. The noise of the hall became more audible. The first tenor and the baritone arrived together. They were both well dressed, stout and complacent and they brought a breath of opulence among the company.

Mrs Kearney brought her daughter over to them, and talked to them amiably. She wanted to be on good terms with them but, while she strove to be polite, her eyes followed Mr Holohan in his limping and devious courses. As soon as she could she excused herself and went out after him.

—Mr Holohan, I want to speak to you for a moment, she said.

They went down to a discreet part of the corridor. Mrs Kearney asked him when was her daughter going to be paid. Mr Holohan said that Mr Fitzpatrick had charge of that. Mrs Kearney said that she didn't know anything about Mr Fitzpatrick. Her daughter had signed a contract for eight guineas and she would have to be paid. Mr Holohan said that it wasn't his business.

—Why isn't it your business? asked Mrs Kearney. Didn't you yourself bring her the contract? Anyway, if it's not your business it's my business and I mean to see to it.

—You'd better speak to Mr Fitzpatrick, said Mr Holohan distantly.

—I don't know anything about Mr Fitzpatrick, repeated Mrs Kearney. I have my contract, and I intend to see that it is carried out.

When she came back to the dressing-room her cheeks were slightly suffused. The room was lively. Two men in outdoor dress had taken possession of the fireplace and were chatting familiarly with Miss Healy and the baritone. They were the *Freeman* man* and Mr O'Madden

---

*Reporter for the *Freeman's Journal*, a Dublin newspaper.

Burke. The *Freeman* man had come in to say that he could not wait for
the concert as he had to report the lecture which an American priest was
giving in the Mansion House.* He said they were to leave the report for
him at the *Freeman* office and he would see that it went in. He was a
grey-haired man, with a plausible voice and careful manners. He held an
extinguished cigar in his hand and the aroma of cigar smoke floated near
him. He had not intended to stay a moment because concerts and
artistes bored him considerably but he remained leaning against the
mantelpiece. Miss Healy stood in front of him, talking and laughing. He
was old enough to suspect one reason for her politeness but young
enough in spirit to turn the moment to account. The warmth, fragrance
and colour of her body appealed to his senses. He was pleasantly conscious that the bosom which he saw rise and fall slowly beneath him rose
and fell at that moment for him, that the laughter and fragrance and
wilful glances were his tribute. When he could stay no longer he took
leave of her regretfully.

—O'Madden Burke will write the notice, he explained to Mr Holohan, and I'll see it in.

—Thank you very much, Mr Hendrick, said Mr Holohan. You'll see
it in, I know. Now, won't you have a little something before you go?

—I don't mind, said Mr Hendrick.

The two men went along some tortuous passages and up a dark
staircase and came to a secluded room where one of the stewards was
uncorking bottles for a few gentlemen. One of these gentlemen was Mr
O'Madden Burke, who had found out the room by instinct. He was a
suave, elderly man who balanced his imposing body, when at rest, upon
a large silk umbrella. His magniloquent western name was the moral
umbrella upon which he balanced the fine problem of his finances. He
was widely respected.

While Mr Holohan was entertaining the *Freeman* man Mrs Kearney
was speaking so animatedly to her husband that he had to ask her to
lower her voice. The conversation of the others in the dressing-room
had become strained. Mr Bell, the first item, stood ready with his music
but the accompanist made no sign. Evidently something was wrong.
Mr Kearney looked straight before him, stroking his beard, while Mrs
Kearney spoke into Kathleen's ear with subdued emphasis. From the
hall came sounds of encouragement, clapping and stamping of feet.
The first tenor and the baritone and Miss Healy stood together, wait-

---

*Official residence of the Lord Mayor.

ing tranquilly, but Mr Bell's nerves were greatly agitated because he was afraid the audience would think that he had come late.

Mr Holohan and Mr O'Madden Burke came into the room. In a moment Mr Holohan perceived the hush. He went over to Mrs Kearney and spoke with her earnestly. While they were speaking the noise in the hall grew louder. Mr Holohan became very red and excited. He spoke volubly, but Mrs Kearney said curtly at intervals:

—She won't go on. She must get her eight guineas.

Mr Holohan pointed desperately towards the hall where the audience was clapping and stamping. He appealed to Mr Kearney and to Kathleen. But Mr Kearney continued to stroke his beard and Kathleen looked down, moving the point of her new shoe: it was not her fault. Mrs Kearney repeated:

—She won't go on without her money.

After a swift struggle of tongues Mr Holohan hobbled out in haste. The room was silent. When the strain of the silence had become somewhat painful Miss Healy said to the baritone:

—Have you seen Mrs Pat Campbell this week?

The baritone had not seen her but he had been told that she was very fine. The conversation went no further. The first tenor bent his head and began to count the links of the gold chain which was extended across his waist, smiling and humming random notes to observe the effect on the frontal sinus. From time to time everyone glanced at Mrs Kearney.

The noise in the auditorium had risen to a clamour when Mr Fitzpatrick burst into the room, followed by Mr Holohan, who was panting. The clapping and stamping in the hall were punctuated by whistling. Mr Fitzpatrick held a few bank-notes in his hand. He counted out four into Mrs Kearney's hand and said she would get the other half at the interval. Mrs Kearney said:

—This is four shillings short.

But Kathleen gathered in her skirt and said: *Now, Mr Bell*, to the first item, who was shaking like an aspen. The singer and the accompanist went out together. The noise in the hall died away. There was a pause of a few seconds; and then the piano was heard.

The first part of the concert was very successful except for Madam Glynn's item. The poor lady sang *Killarney** in a bodiless gasping voice, with all the old-fashioned mannerisms of intonation and pronunciation

---

*Song from Michael William Balfe's *Innisfallen*.

which she believed lent elegance to her singing. She looked as if she had been resurrected from an old stage-wardrobe and the cheaper parts of the hall made fun of her high wailing notes. The first tenor and the contralto, however, brought down the house. Kathleen played a selection of Irish airs which was generously applauded. The first part closed with a stirring patriotic recitation delivered by a young lady who arranged amateur theatricals. It was deservedly applauded; and, when it was ended, the men went out for the interval, content.

All this time the dressing-room was a hive of excitement. In one corner were Mr Holohan, Mr Fitzpatrick, Miss Beirne, two of the stewards, the baritone, the bass, and Mr O'Madden Burke. Mr O'Madden Burke said it was the most scandalous exhibition he had ever witnessed. Miss Kathleen Kearney's musical career was ended in Dublin after that, he said. The baritone was asked what did he think of Mrs Kearney's conduct. He did not like to say anything. He had been paid his money and wished to be at peace with men. However, he said that Mrs Kearney might have taken the *artistes* into consideration. The stewards and the secretaries debated hotly as to what should be done when the interval came.

—I agree with Miss Beirne, said Mr O'Madden Burke. Pay her nothing.

In another corner of the room were Mrs Kearney and her husband, Mr Bell, Miss Healy and the young lady who had to recite the patriotic piece. Mrs Kearney said that the committee had treated her scandalously. She had spared neither trouble nor expense and this was how she was repaid.

They thought they had only a girl to deal with and that, therefore, they could ride roughshod over her. But she would show them their mistake. They wouldn't have dared to have treated her like that if she had been a man. But she would see that her daughter got her rights: she wouldn't be fooled. If they didn't pay her to the last farthing she would make Dublin ring. Of course she was sorry for the sake of the *artistes*. But what else could she do? She appealed to the second tenor, who said he thought she had not been well treated. Then she appealed to Miss Healy. Miss Healy wanted to join the other group but she did not like to do so because she was a great friend of Kathleen's and the Kearneys had often invited her to their house.

As soon as the first part was ended Mr Fitzpatrick and Mr Holohan went over to Mrs Kearney and told her that the other four guineas would be paid after the committee meeting on the following Tuesday and that, in case her daughter did not play for the second part, the committee would consider the contract broken and would pay nothing.

—I haven't seen any committee, said Mrs Kearney angrily. My daughter has her contract. She will get four pounds eight into her hand or a foot she won't put on that platform.

—I'm surprised at you, Mrs Kearney, said Mr Holohan. I never thought you would treat us this way.

—And what way did you treat me? asked Mrs Kearney.

Her face was inundated with an angry colour and she looked as if she would attack someone with her hands.

—I'm asking for my rights, she said.

—You might have some sense of decency, said Mr Holohan.

—Might I, indeed? . . . And when I ask when my daughter is going to be paid I can't get a civil answer.

She tossed her head and assumed a haughty voice:

—You must speak to the secretary. It's not my business. I'm a great fellow fol-the-diddle-I-do.

—I thought you were a lady, said Mr Holohan, walking away from her abruptly.

After that Mrs Kearney's conduct was condemned on all hands: everyone approved of what the committee had done. She stood at the door, haggard with rage, arguing with her husband and daughter, gesticulating with them. She waited until it was time for the second part to begin in the hope that the secretaries would approach her. But Miss Healy had kindly consented to play one or two accompaniments. Mrs Kearney had to stand aside to allow the baritone and his accompanist to pass up to the platform. She stood still for an instant like an angry stone image and, when the first notes of the song struck her ear, she caught up her daughter's cloak and said to her husband:

—Get a cab!

He went out at once. Mrs Kearney wrapped the cloak round her daughter and followed him. As she passed through the doorway she stopped and glared into Mr Holohan's face.

—I'm not done with you yet, she said.

—But I'm done with you, said Mr Holohan.

Kathleen followed her mother meekly. Mr Holohan began to pace up and down the room, in order to cool himself for he felt his skin on fire.

—That's a nice lady! he said. O, she's a nice lady!

—You did the proper thing, Holohan, said Mr O'Madden Burke, poised upon his umbrella in approval.

GRACE

TWO GENTLEMEN WHO WERE in the lavatory at the time tried to lift him up: but he was quite helpless. He lay curled up at the foot of the stairs down which he had fallen. They succeeded in turning him over. His hat had rolled a few yards away and his clothes were smeared with the filth and ooze of the floor on which he had lain, face downwards. His eyes were closed and he breathed with a grunting noise. A thin stream of blood trickled from the corner of his mouth.

These two gentlemen and one of the curates* carried him up the stairs and laid him down again on the floor of the bar. In two minutes he was surrounded by a ring of men. The manager of the bar asked everyone who he was and who was with him. No one knew who he was but one of the curates said he had served the gentleman with a small rum.

—Was he by himself? asked the manager.

—No, sir. There was two gentlemen with him.

—And where are they?

No one knew; a voice said:

—Give him air. He's fainted.

The ring of onlookers distended and closed again elastically. A dark medal of blood had formed itself near the man's head on the tessellated floor. The manager, alarmed by the grey pallor of the man's face, sent for a policeman.

His collar was unfastened and his necktie undone. He opened his eyes for an instant, sighed and closed them again. One of the gentlemen who had carried him upstairs held a dinged silk hat in his hand. The manager asked repeatedly did no one know who the injured man was or where had his friends gone. The door of the bar opened and an immense constable entered. A crowd which had followed him down the laneway collected outside the door, struggling to look in through the glass panels.

The manager at once began to narrate what he knew. The constable,

*Dublin lingo for "bartenders."

a young man with thick immobile features, listened. He moved his head slowly to right and left and from the manager to the person on the floor, as if he feared to be the victim of some delusion. Then he drew off his glove, produced a small book from his waist, licked the lead of his pencil and made ready to indite. He asked in a suspicious provincial accent:

—Who is the man? What's his name and address?

A young man in a cycling-suit cleared his way through the ring of bystanders. He knelt down promptly beside the injured man and called for water. The constable knelt down also to help. The young man washed the blood from the injured man's mouth and then called for some brandy. The constable repeated the order in an authoritative voice until a curate came running with the glass. The brandy was forced down the man's throat. In a few seconds he opened his eyes and looked about him. He looked at the circle of faces and then, understanding, strove to rise to his feet.

—You're all right now? asked the young man in the cycling-suit.

—Sha, 's nothing, said the injured man, trying to stand up.

He was helped to his feet. The manager said something about a hospital and some of the bystanders gave advice. The battered silk hat was placed on the man's head. The constable asked:

—Where do you live?

The man, without answering, began to twirl the ends of his moustache. He made light of his accident. It was nothing, he said: only a little accident. He spoke very thickly.

—Where do you live? repeated the constable.

The man said they were to get a cab for him. While the point was being debated a tall agile gentleman of fair complexion, wearing a long yellow ulster,* came from the far end of the bar. Seeing the spectacle, he called out:

—Hallo, Tom, old man! What's the trouble?

—Sha, 's nothing, said the man.

The new-comer surveyed the deplorable figure before him and then turned to the constable, saying:

—It's all right, constable. I'll see him home.

The constable touched his helmet and answered:

—All right, Mr Power!

---

*Wool overcoat.

—Come now, Tom, said Mr Power, taking his friend by the arm. No bones broken. What? Can you walk?

The young man in the cycling-suit took the man by the other arm and the crowd divided.

—How did you get yourself into this mess? asked Mr Power.

—The gentleman fell down the stairs, said the young man.

—I' 'ery 'uch o'liged to you, sir, said the injured man.

—Not at all.

—'ant' we have a little . . . ?

—Not now. Not now.

The three men left the bar and the crowd sifted through the doors in to the laneway. The manager brought the constable to the stairs to inspect the scene of the accident. They agreed that the gentleman must have missed his footing. The customers returned to the counter and a curate set about removing the traces of blood from the floor.

When they came out into Grafton Street,* Mr Power whistled for an outsider.† The injured man said again as well as he could:

—I' 'ery 'uch o'liged to you, sir. I hope we'll 'eet again. 'y na'e is Kernan.

The shock and the incipient pain had partly sobered him.

—Don't mention it, said the young man.

They shook hands. Mr Kernan was hoisted on to the car and, while Mr Power was giving directions to the carman, he expressed his gratitude to the young man and regretted that they could not have a little drink together.

—Another time, said the young man.

The car drove off towards Westmoreland Street. As it passed the Ballast Office‡ the clock showed half-past nine. A keen east wind hit them, blowing from the mouth of the river. Mr Kernan was huddled together with cold. His friend asked him to tell how the accident had happened.

—I 'an't 'an, he answered, 'y 'ongue is hurt.

—Show.

The other leaned over the well of the car and peered into Mr Kernan's mouth but he could not see. He struck a match and, sheltering it in the shell of his hands, peered again into the mouth which Mr

*The heart of Dublin's upscale shopping district.
†Type of jaunting car.
‡Headquarters of the Dublin Port and Docks Board.

Kernan opened obediently. The swaying movement of the car brought
the match to and from the opened mouth. The lower teeth and gums
were covered with clotted blood and a minute piece of the tongue
seemed to have been bitten off. The match was blown out.

—That's ugly, said Mr Power.

—Sha, 's nothing, said Mr Kernan, closing his mouth and pulling
the collar of his filthy coat across his neck.

Mr Kernan was a commercial traveller of the old school which believed in the dignity of its calling. He had never been seen in the city
without a silk hat of some decency and a pair of gaiters. By grace of
these two articles of clothing, he said, a man could always pass muster.
He carried on the tradition of his Napoleon,* the great Blackwhite,
whose memory he evoked at times by legend and mimicry. Modern
business methods had spared him only so far as to allow him a little office in Crowe Street, on the window blind of which was written the
name of his firm with the address—London, E. C. On the mantelpiece
of this little office a little leaden battalion of canisters was drawn up and
on the table before the window stood four or five china bowls which
were usually half full of a black liquid. From these bowls Mr Kernan
tasted tea. He took a mouthful, drew it up, saturated his palate with it
and then spat it forth into the grate. Then he paused to judge.

Mr Power, a much younger man, was employed in the Royal Irish
Constabulary Office in Dublin Castle.† The arc of his social rise inter-
sected the arc of his friend's decline, but Mr Kernan's decline was mit-
igated by the fact that certain of those friends who had known him at
his highest point of success still esteemed him as a character. Mr Power
was one of these friends. His inexplicable debts were a byword in his
circle; he was a debonair young man.

The car halted before a small house on the Glasnevin road and Mr
Kernan was helped into the house. His wife put him to bed, while Mr
Power sat downstairs in the kitchen asking the children where they
went to school and what book they were in. The children—two girls
and a boy, conscious of their father's helplessness and of their mother's
absence, began some horseplay with him. He was surprised at their
manners and at their accents, and his brow grew thoughtful. After a
while Mrs Kernan entered the kitchen, exclaiming:

---

*His role model.
†The police force for all of Ireland outside Dublin; "Dublin Castle" here represents
British Rule in Ireland.

—Such a sight! O, he'll do for himself one day and that's the holy alls of it. He's been drinking since Friday.

Mr Power was careful to explain to her that he was not responsible, that he had come on the scene by the merest accident. Mrs Kernan, remembering Mr Power's good offices during domestic quarrels, as well as many small, but opportune loans, said:

—O, you needn't tell me that, Mr Power. I know you're a friend of his, not like some of the others he does be with. They're all right so long as he has money in his pocket to keep him out from his wife and family. Nice friends! Who was he with to-night, I'd like to know?

Mr Power shook his head but said nothing.

—I'm so sorry, she continued, that I've nothing in the house to offer you. But if you wait a minute I'll send round to Fogarty's, at the corner.

Mr Power stood up.

—We were waiting for him to come home with the money. He never seems to think he has a home at all.

—O, now, Mrs Kernan, said Mr Power, we'll make him turn over a new leaf. I'll talk to Martin. He's the man. We'll come here one of these nights and talk it over.

She saw him to the door. The carman was stamping up and down the footpath, and swinging his arms to warm himself.

—It's very kind of you to bring him home, she said.

—Not at all, said Mr Power.

He got up on the car. As it drove off he raised his hat to her gaily.

—We'll make a new man of him, he said. Good-night, Mrs Kernan.

＊   ＊   ＊   ＊   ＊   ＊   ＊   ＊   ＊   ＊

Mrs Kernan's puzzled eyes watched the car till it was out of sight. Then she withdrew them, went into the house and emptied her husband's pockets.

She was an active, practical woman of middle age. Not long before she had celebrated her silver wedding and renewed her intimacy with her husband by waltzing with him to Mr Power's accompaniment. In her days of courtship, Mr Kernan had seemed to her a not ungallant figure: and she still hurried to the chapel door whenever a wedding was reported and, seeing the bridal pair, recalled with vivid pleasure how she had passed out of the Star of the Sea Church in Sandymount,*

---

*Church on the coast in south Dublin.

leaning on the arm of a jovial well-fed man, who was dressed smartly in a frock-coat and lavender trousers and carried a silk hat gracefully balanced upon his other arm. After three weeks she had found a wife's life irksome and, later on, when she was beginning to find it unbearable, she had become a mother. The part of mother presented to her no insuperable difficulties and for twenty-five years she had kept house shrewdly for her husband. Her two eldest sons were launched. One was in a draper's shop in Glasgow and the other was clerk to a tea-merchant in Belfast. They were good sons, wrote regularly and sometimes sent home money. The other children were still at school.

Mr Kernan sent a letter to his office next day and remained in bed. She made beef-tea for him and scolded him roundly. She accepted his frequent intemperance as part of the climate, healed him dutifully whenever he was sick and always tried to make him eat a breakfast. There were worse husbands. He had never been violent since the boys had grown up, and she knew that he would walk to the end of Thomas Street and back again to book even a small order.

Two nights after, his friends came to see him. She brought them up to his bedroom, the air of which was impregnated with a personal odour, and gave them chairs at the fire. Mr Kernan's tongue, the occasional stinging pain of which had made him somewhat irritable during the day, became more polite. He sat propped up in the bed by pillows and the little colour in his puffy cheeks made them resemble warm cinders. He apologised to his guests for the disorder of the room, but at the same time looked at them a little proudly, with a veteran's pride.

He was quite unconscious that he was the victim of a plot which his friends, Mr Cunningham, Mr M'Coy and Mr Power had disclosed to Mrs Kernan in the parlour. The idea had been Mr Power's, but its development was entrusted to Mr Cunningham. Mr Kernan came of Protestant stock and, though he had been converted to the Catholic faith at the time of his marriage, he had not been in the pale[4] of the Church for twenty years. He was fond, moreover, of giving side-thrusts at Catholicism.

Mr Cunningham was the very man for such a case. He was an elder colleague of Mr Power. His own domestic life was not very happy. People had great sympathy with him, for it was known that he had married an unpresentable woman who was an incurable drunkard. He had set up house for her six times; and each time she had pawned the furniture on him.

Everyone had respect for poor Martin Cunningham. He was a thoroughly sensible man, influential and intelligent. His blade of human knowledge, natural astuteness particularised by long association with cases in the police courts, had been tempered by brief immersions in the waters of general philosophy. He was well informed. His friends bowed to his opinions and considered that his fate was like Shakespeare's.

When the plot had been disclosed to her, Mrs Kernan had said:

—I leave it all in your hands, Mr Cunningham.

After a quarter of a century of married life, she had very few illusions left. Religion for her was a habit, and she suspected that a man of her husband's age would not change greatly before death. She was tempted to see a curious appropriateness in his accident and, but that she did not wish to seem bloody-minded, she would have told the gentlemen that Mr Kernan's tongue would not suffer by being shortened. However, Mr Cunningham was a capable man; and religion was religion. The scheme might do good and, at least, it could do no harm. Her beliefs were not extravagant. She believed steadily in the Sacred Heart* as the most generally useful of all Catholic devotions and approved of the sacraments. Her faith was bounded by her kitchen, but, if she was put to it, she could believe also in the banshee† and in the Holy Ghost.

The gentlemen began to talk of the accident. Mr Cunningham said that he had once known a similar case. A man of seventy had bitten off a piece of his tongue during an epileptic fit and the tongue had filled in again, so that no one could see a trace of the bite.

—Well, I'm not seventy, said the invalid.

—God forbid, said Mr Cunningham.

—It doesn't pain you now? asked Mr M'Coy.

Mr M'Coy had been at one time a tenor of some reputation. His wife, who had been a soprano, still taught young children to play the piano at low terms. His line of life had not been the shortest distance between two points and for short periods he had been driven to live by his wits. He had been a clerk in the Midland Railway, a canvasser for advertisements for *The Irish Times*‡ and for *The Freeman's Journal,* a town traveller for a coal firm on commission, a private inquiry agent, a clerk in the office of the Sub-Sheriff, and he had recently become secretary to the City Coroner. His new office made him professionally interested in Mr Kernan's case.

---

*Litany of the Sacred Heart of Jesus, a devotional discipline.
†From the Irish phrase *bean sí* ("fairy woman").
‡The main conservative Dublin paper.

—Pain? Not much, answered Mr Kernan. But it's so sickening. I feel as if I wanted to retch off.

—That's the boose, said Mr Cunningham firmly.

—No, said Mr Kernan. I think I caught cold on the car. There's something keeps coming into my throat, phlegm or—

—Mucus, said Mr M'Coy.

—It keeps coming like from down in my throat; sickening thing.

—Yes, yes, said Mr M'Coy, that's the thorax.

He looked at Mr Cunningham and Mr Power at the same time with an air of challenge. Mr Cunningham nodded his head rapidly and Mr Power said:

—Ah, well, all's well that ends well.

—I'm very much obliged to you, old man, said the invalid.

Mr Power waved his hand.

—Those other two fellows I was with—

—Who were you with? asked Mr Cunningham.

—A chap. I don't know his name. Damn it now, what's his name? Little chap with sandy hair. . . .

—And who else?

—Harford.

—Hm, said Mr Cunningham.

When Mr Cunningham made that remark, people were silent. It was known that the speaker had secret sources of information. In this case the monosyllable had a moral intention. Mr Harford sometimes formed one of a little detachment which left the city shortly after noon on Sunday with the purpose of arriving as soon as possible at some public-house on the outskirts of the city where its members duly qualified themselves as *bona-fide* travellers.* But his fellow-travellers had never consented to overlook his origin. He had begun life as an obscure financier by lending small sums of money to workmen at usurious interest. Later on he had become the partner of a very fat, short gentleman, Mr Goldberg, in the Liffey† Loan Bank. Though he had never embraced more than the Jewish ethical code, his fellow-Catholics, whenever they had smarted in person or by proxy under his exactions,

---

*Alcoholic beverages could be sold outside of regular pub hours to genuine travelers; some determined drinkers "traveled" for the sake of exploiting this loophole of the law.

†The river running west to east through downtown Dublin, dividing it into south and north.

spoke of him bitterly as an Irish Jew and an illiterate, and saw divine
disapproval of usury* made manifest through the person of his idiot
son. At other times they remembered his good points.

—I wonder where did he go to, said Mr Kernan.

He wished the details of the incident to remain vague. He wished his
friends to think there had been some mistake, that Mr Harford and he
had missed each other. His friends, who knew quite well Mr Harford's
manners in drinking were silent. Mr Power said again:

—All's well that ends well.

Mr Kernan changed the subject at once.

—That was a decent young chap, that medical fellow, he said. Only
for him—

—O, only for him, said Mr Power, it might have been a case of seven
days, without the option of a fine.

—Yes, yes, said Mr Kernan, trying to remember. I remember now
there was a policeman. Decent young fellow, he seemed. How did it
happen at all?

—It happened that you were peloothered, Tom, said Mr Cunningham
gravely.

—True bill, said Mr Kernan, equally gravely.

—I suppose you squared the constable, Jack, said Mr M'Coy.

Mr Power did not relish the use of his Christian name. He was not
straight-laced, but he could not forget that Mr M'Coy had recently
made a crusade in search of valises and portmanteaus to enable Mrs
M'Coy to fulfil imaginary engagements in the country. More than he
resented the fact that he had been victimised he resented such low playing of the game. He answered the question, therefore, as if Mr Kernan
had asked it.

The narrative made Mr Kernan indignant. He was keenly conscious
of his citizenship, wished to live with his city on terms mutually honourable and resented any affront put upon him by those whom he
called country bumpkins.

—Is this what we pay rates† for? he asked. To feed and clothe these
ignorant bostooms‡ . . . and they're nothing else.

Mr Cunningham laughed. He was a Castle official only during office hours.

---

*Lending money at excessive rates of interest.
†Taxes.
‡From the Irish word *bastún* ("blockhead").

—How could they be anything else, Tom? he said.

He assumed a thick, provincial accent and said in a tone of command:

—65, catch your cabbage!

Everyone laughed. Mr M'Coy, who wanted to enter the conversation by any door, pretended that he had never heard the story. Mr Cunningham said:

—It is supposed—they say, you know—to take place in the depot where they get these thundering big country fellows, omadhauns,* you know, to drill. The sergeant makes them stand in a row against the wall and hold up their plates.

He illustrated the story by grotesque gestures.

—At dinner, you know. Then he has a bloody big bowl of cabbage before him on the table and a bloody big spoon like a shovel. He takes up a wad of cabbage on the spoon and pegs it across the room and the poor devils have to try and catch it on their plates: *65, catch your cabbage*.

Everyone laughed again: but Mr Kernan was somewhat indignant still. He talked of writing a letter to the papers.

—These yahoos coming up here, he said, think they can boss the people. I needn't tell you, Martin, what kind of men they are.

Mr Cunningham gave a qualified assent.

—It's like everything else in this world, he said. You get some bad ones and you get some good ones.

—O yes, you get some good ones, I admit, said Mr Kernan, satisfied.

—It's better to have nothing to say to them, said Mr M'Coy. That's my opinion!

Mrs Kernan entered the room and, placing a tray on the table, said:

—Help yourselves, gentlemen.

Mr Power stood up to officiate, offering her his chair. She declined it, saying she was ironing downstairs, and, after having exchanged a nod with Mr Cunningham behind Mr Power's back, prepared to leave the room. Her husband called out to her:

—And have you nothing for me, duckie?

—O, you! The back of my hand to you! said Mrs Kernan tartly.

Her husband called after her:

---

*From the Irish word *amadán* ("fool").

—Nothing for poor little hubby!

He assumed such a comical face and voice that the distribution of
the bottles of stout* took place amid general merriment.

The gentlemen drank from their glasses, set the glasses again on the
table and paused. Then Mr Cunningham turned towards Mr Power
and said casually:

—On Thursday night, you said, Jack?

—Thursday, yes, said Mr Power.

—Righto! said Mr Cunningham promptly.

—We can meet in M'Auley's,† said Mr M'Coy. That'll be the most
convenient place.

—But we mustn't be late, said Mr Power earnestly, because it is sure
to be crammed to the doors.

—We can meet at half-seven, said Mr M'Coy.

—Righto! said Mr Cunningham.

—Half-seven at M'Auley's be it!

There was a short silence. Mr Kernan waited to see whether he
would be taken into his friends' confidence. Then he asked:

—What's in the wind?

—O, it's nothing, said Mr Cunningham. It's only a little matter that
we're arranging about for Thursday.

—The opera, is it? said Mr Kernan.

—No, no, said Mr Cunningham in an evasive tone, it's just a little . . . spiritual matter.

—O, said Mr Kernan.

There was silence again. Then Mr Power said, point blank:

—To tell you the truth, Tom, we're going to make a retreat.‡

—Yes, that's it, said Mr Cunningham, Jack and I and M'Coy here—
we're all going to wash the pot.

He uttered the metaphor with a certain homely energy and, encouraged by his own voice, proceeded:

—You see, we may as well all admit we're a nice collection of
scoundrels, one and all. I say, one and all, he added with gruff charity
and turning to Mr Power. Own up now!

—I own up, said Mr Power.

—And I own up, said Mr M'Coy.

---

*Thick, dark Irish beer.

†A grocery and pub.

‡Period of withdrawal for the purpose of spiritual reflection and teaching.

—So we're going to wash the pot together, said Mr Cunningham.

A thought seemed to strike him. He turned suddenly to the invalid and said:

—D'ye know what, Tom, has just occurred to me? You might join in and we'd have a four-handed reel.*

—Good idea, said Mr Power. The four of us together.

Mr Kernan was silent. The proposal conveyed very little meaning to his mind, but, understanding that some spiritual agencies were about to concern themselves on his behalf, he thought he owed it to his dignity to show a stiff neck. He took no part in the conversation for a long while, but listened, with an air of calm enmity, while his friends discussed the Jesuits.†

—I haven't such a bad opinion of the Jesuits, he said, intervening at length. They're an educated order. I believe they mean well, too.

—They're the grandest order in the Church, Tom, said Mr Cunningham, with enthusiasm. The General of the Jesuits stands next to the Pope.

—There's no mistake about it, said Mr M'Coy, if you want a thing well done and no flies about, you go to a Jesuit. They're the boyos have influence. I'll tell you a case in point. . . .

—The Jesuits are a fine body of men, said Mr Power.

—It's a curious thing, said Mr Cunningham, about the Jesuit Order. Every other order of the Church had to be reformed at some time or other but the Jesuit Order was never once reformed. It never fell away.

—Is that so? asked Mr M'Coy.

—That's a fact, said Mr Cunningham. That's history.

—Look at their church, too, said Mr Power. Look at the congregation they have.

—The Jesuits cater for the upper classes, said Mr M'Coy.

—Of course, said Mr Power.

—Yes, said Mr Kernan. That's why I have a feeling for them. It's some of those secular priests, ignorant, bumptious—

—They're all good men, said Mr Cunningham, each in his own way. Irish priesthood is honoured all the world over.

—O yes, said Mr Power.

—Not like some of the other priesthoods on the continent, said Mr M'Coy, unworthy of the name.

---

*Irish dance.

†The Society of Jesus, an order within the Catholic Church founded by Ignatius Loyola (1491–1556); its members are known especially for their learning.

—Perhaps you're right, said Mr Kernan, relenting.

—Of course I'm right, said Mr Cunningham. I haven't been in the world all this time and seen most sides of it without being a judge of character.

The gentlemen drank again, one following another's example. Mr Kernan seemed to be weighing something in his mind. He was impressed. He had a high opinion of Mr Cunningham as a judge of character and as a reader of faces. He asked for particulars.

—O, it's just a retreat, you know, said Mr Cunningham. Father Purdon* is giving it. It's for business men, you know.

—He won't be too hard on us, Tom, said Mr Power persuasively.

—Father Purdon? Father Purdon? said the invalid.

—O, you must know him, Tom, said Mr Cunningham stoutly. Fine, jolly fellow! He's a man of the world like ourselves.

—Ah, . . . yes. I think I know him. Rather red face; tall.

—That's the man.

—And tell me, Martin. . . . Is he a good preacher?

—Munno. . . . It's not exactly a sermon, you know. It's just a kind of a friendly talk, you know, in a common-sense way.

Mr Kernan deliberated. Mr M'Coy said:

—Father Tom Burke,† that was the boy!

—O, Father Tom Burke, said Mr Cunningham, that was a born orator. Did you ever hear him, Tom?

—Did I ever hear him! said the invalid, nettled. Rather! I heard him. . . .

—And yet they say he wasn't much of a theologian, said Mr Cunningham.

—Is that so? said Mr M'Coy.

—O, of course, nothing wrong, you know. Only sometimes, they say, he didn't preach what was quite orthodox.

—Ah! . . . he was a splendid man, said Mr M'Coy.

—I heard him once, Mr Kernan continued. I forget the subject of his discourse now. Crofton and I were in the back of the . . . pit, you know . . . the—

—The body, said Mr Cunningham.

—Yes, in the back near the door. I forget now what. . . . O yes, it was

---

*Fictional character.

†(1830–1883); popular Dominican fundraiser who combined spiritual and nationalist appeals in Ireland.

on the Pope, the late Pope.* I remember it well. Upon my word it was magnificent, the style of the oratory. And his voice! God! hadn't he a voice! *The Prisoner of the Vatican,* he called him. I remember Crofton saying to me when we came out—

—But he's an Orangeman,† Crofton, isn't he? said Mr Power.

—'Course he is, said Mr Kernan, and a damned decent Orangeman, too. We went into Butler's‡ in Moore Street—faith, I was genuinely moved, tell you the God's truth—and I remember well his very words. *Kernan,* he said, *we worship at different altars,* he said, *but our belief is the same.* Struck me as very well put.

—There's a good deal in that, said Mr Power. There used always be crowds of Protestants in the chapel when Father Tom was preaching.

—There's not much difference between us, said Mr M'Coy. We both believe in—

He hesitated for a moment.

—. . . in the Redeemer. Only they don't believe in the Pope and in the mother of God.

—But, of course, said Mr Cunningham quietly and effectively, our religion is *the* religion, the old, original faith.

—Not a doubt of it, said Mr Kernan warmly.

Mrs Kernan came to the door of the bedroom and announced:

—Here's a visitor for you!

—Who is it?

—Mr Fogarty.

—O, come in! come in!

A pale, oval face came forward into the light. The arch of its fair trailing moustache was repeated in the fair eyebrows looped above pleasantly astonished eyes. Mr Fogarty was a modest grocer. He had failed in business in a licensed house§ in the city because his financial condition had constrained him to tie himself to second-class distillers and brewers. He had opened a small shop on Glasnevin Road where, he flattered himself, his manners would ingratiate him with the housewives of the district. He bore himself with a certain grace, complimented little children and spoke with a neat enunciation. He was not without culture.

Mr Fogarty brought a gift with him, a half-pint of special whisky.

---

*Leo XIII (1810–1903; pope 1878–1903).

†A Unionist; one favoring the continued union of Ireland with Great Britain.

‡Wine and spirits merchant.

§Pub.

He inquired politely for Mr Kernan, placed his gift on the table and sat down with the company on equal terms. Mr Kernan appreciated the gift all the more since he was aware that there was a small account for groceries unsettled between him and Mr Fogarty. He said:

—I wouldn't doubt you, old man. Open that, Jack, will you?

Mr Power again officiated. Glasses were rinsed and five small measures of whisky were poured out. This new influence enlivened the conversation. Mr Fogarty, sitting on a small area of the chair, was specially interested.

—Pope Leo XIII., said Mr Cunningham, was one of the lights of the age. His great idea, you know, was the union of the Latin and Greek Churches. That was the aim of his life.

—I often heard he was one of the most intellectual men in Europe, said Mr Power. I mean, apart from his being Pope.

—So he was, said Mr Cunningham, if not the most so. His motto, you know, as Pope, was *Lux upon Lux—Light upon Light.*

—No, no, said Mr Fogarty eagerly. I think you're wrong there. It was *Lux in Tenebris,* I think—*Light in Darkness.*

—O yes, said Mr M'Coy, *Tenebrae.*

—Allow me, said Mr Cunningham positively, it was *Lux upon Lux.* And Pius IX.* his predecessor's motto was *Crux upon Crux*—that is, *Cross upon Cross*—to show the difference between their two pontificates.[5]

The inference was allowed. Mr Cunningham continued.

—Pope Leo, you know, was a great scholar and a poet.

—He had a strong face, said Mr Kernan.

—Yes, said Mr Cunningham. He wrote Latin poetry.

—Is that so? said Mr Fogarty.

Mr M'Coy tasted his whisky contentedly and shook his head with a double intention, saying:

—That's no joke, I can tell you.

—We didn't learn that, Tom, said Mr Power, following Mr M'Coy's example, when we went to the penny-a-week school.

—There was many a good man went to the penny-a-week school with a sod of turf under his oxter,[†] said Mr Kernan sententiously. The

---

*(1792–1878); as pope (1846–1878), he promulgated the dogmas of the Immaculate Conception and papal infallibility.
†A brick of peat (turf) fuel under his arm.

old system was the best: plain honest education. None of your modern trumpery. . . .

—Quite right, said Mr Power.

—No superfluities, said Mr Fogarty.

He enunciated the word and then drank gravely.

—I remember reading, said Mr Cunningham, that one of Pope Leo's poems was on the invention of the photograph—in Latin, of course.

—On the photograph! exclaimed Mr Kernan.

—Yes, said Mr Cunningham.

He also drank from his glass.

—Well, you know, said Mr M'Coy, isn't the photograph wonderful when you come to think of it?

—O, of course, said Mr Power, great minds can see things.

—As the poet says: *Great minds are very near to madness,* said Mr Fogarty.

Mr Kernan seemed to be troubled in mind. He made an effort to recall the Protestant theology on some thorny points and in the end addressed Mr Cunningham.

—Tell me, Martin, he said. Weren't some of the popes—of course, not our present man, or his predecessor, but some of the old popes—not exactly . . . you know . . . up to the knocker?

There was a silence. Mr Cunningham said:

—O, of course, there were some bad lots. . . . But the astonishing thing is this. Not one of them, not the biggest drunkard, not the most . . . out-and-out ruffian, not one of them ever preached *ex cathedra*† a word of false doctrine. Now isn't that an astonishing thing?

—That is, said Mr Kernan.

—Yes, because when the Pope speaks *ex cathedra,* Mr Fogarty explained, he is infallible.

—Yes, said Mr Cunningham.

—O, I know about the infallibility of the Pope. I remember I was younger then. . . . Or was it that—?

Mr Fogarty interrupted. He took up the bottle and helped the oth-

---

*Paraphrase from John Dryden's *Absalom and Achitophel* (1681): "Great Wits are sure to Madness near ally'd."

†From the throne (Latin); the dogma of papal infallibility holds that when the pope speaks about matters of church doctrine, he is infallible.

ers to a little more. Mr M'Coy, seeing that there was not enough to go round, pleaded that he had not finished his first measure. The others accepted under protest. The light music of whisky falling into glasses made an agreeable interlude.

—What's that you were saying, Tom? asked Mr M'Coy.

—Papal infallibility, said Mr Cunningham, that was the greatest scene in the whole history of the Church.

—How was that, Martin? asked Mr Power.

Mr Cunningham held up two thick fingers.

—In the sacred college, you know, of cardinals and archbishops and bishops there were two men who held out against it while the others were all for it. The whole conclave except these two was unanimous. No! They wouldn't have it!

—Ha! said Mr M'Coy.

—And they were a German cardinal by the name of Dolling . . . or Dowling* . . . or—

—Dowling was no German, and that's a sure five, said Mr Power, laughing.

—Well, this great German cardinal, whatever his name was, was one; and the other was John MacHale.[†]

—What? cried Mr Kernan. Is it John of Tuam?

—Are you sure of that now? asked Mr Fogarty dubiously. I thought it was some Italian or American.

—John of Tuam, repeated Mr Cunningham, was the man.

He drank and the other gentlemen followed his lead. Then he resumed:

—There they were at it, all the cardinals and bishops and archbishops from all the ends of the earth and these two fighting dog and devil until at last the Pope himself stood up and declared infallibility a dogma of the Church *ex cathedra*. On the very moment John MacHale, who had been arguing and arguing against it, stood up and shouted out with the voice of a lion: *Credo!*

—*I believe!* said Mr Fogarty.

—*Credo!* said Mr Cunningham. That showed the faith he had. He submitted the moment the Pope spoke.

---

*Johannes Josef Ignaz von Döllinger (1799–1890), far from participating in the First Vatican Council (1869–1870), was excommunicated for his refusal to accept its decrees.

†(1791–1881); Irish archbishop who opposed English influence in Ireland.

—And what about Dowling? asked Mr M'Coy.

—The German cardinal wouldn't submit. He left the church.

Mr Cunningham's words had built up the vast image of the church in the minds of his hearers. His deep, raucous voice had thrilled them as it uttered the word of belief and submission. When Mrs Kernan came into the room, drying her hands, she came into a solemn company. She did not disturb the silence, but leaned over the rail at the foot of the bed.

—I once saw John MacHale, said Mr Kernan, and I'll never forget it as long as I live.

He turned towards his wife to be confirmed.

—I often told you that?

Mrs Kernan nodded.

—It was at the unveiling of Sir John Gray's* statue. Edmund Dwyer Gray† was speaking, blathering away, and here was this old fellow, crabbed-looking old chap, looking at him from under his bushy eyebrows.

Mr Kernan knitted his brows and, lowering his head like an angry bull, glared at his wife.

—God! he exclaimed, resuming his natural face, I never saw such an eye in a man's head. It was as much as to say: *I have you properly taped, my lad.* He had an eye like a hawk.

—None of the Grays was any good, said Mr Power.

There was a pause again. Mr Power turned to Mrs Kernan and said with abrupt joviality:

—Well, Mrs Kernan, we're going to make your man here a good holy pious and God-fearing Roman Catholic.

He swept his arm round the company inclusively.

—We're all going to make a retreat together and confess our sins— and God knows we want it badly.

—I don't mind, said Mr Kernan, smiling a little nervously.

Mrs Kernan thought it would be wiser to conceal her satisfaction. So she said:

—I pity the poor priest that has to listen to your tale.

Mr Kernan's expression changed.

---

*1816–1875; well-known owner of the *Freeman's Journal*; a Protestant, he supported repeal of the Union of England and Ireland; his statue still stands on O'Connell Street.

†1845–1888; Sir John's son, owner of the *Freeman's Journal* and a Nationalist.

—If he doesn't like it, he said bluntly, he can . . . do the other thing. I'll just tell him my little tale of woe. I'm not such a bad fellow—

Mr Cunningham intervened promptly.

—We'll all renounce the devil, he said, together, not forgetting his works and pomps.

—Get behind me, Satan!* said Mr Fogarty, laughing and looking at the others.

Mr Power said nothing. He felt completely out-generalled. But a pleased expression flickered across his face.

—All we have to do, said Mr Cunningham, is to stand up with lighted candles in our hands and renew our baptismal vows.

—O, don't forget the candle, Tom, said Mr M'Coy, whatever you do.

—What? said Mr Kernan. Must I have a candle?

—O yes, said Mr Cunningham.

—No, damn it all, said Mr Kernan sensibly, I draw the line there. I'll do the job right enough. I'll do the retreat business and confession, and . . . all that business. But . . . no candles! No, damn it all, I bar the candles!

He shook his head with farcical gravity.

—Listen to that! said his wife.

—I bar the candles, said Mr Kernan, conscious of having created an effect on his audience and continuing to shake his head to and fro. I bar the magic-lantern business.

Everyone laughed heartily.

—There's a nice Catholic for you! said his wife.

—No candles! repeated Mr Kernan obdurately. That's off!

*   *   *   *   *   *   *   *   *   *

The transept† of the Jesuit Church in Gardiner Street was almost full; and still at every moment gentlemen entered from the side door and, directed by the lay-brother,‡ walked on tiptoe along the aisles until they found seating accommodation. The gentlemen were all well dressed and orderly. The light of the lamps of the church fell upon an assembly of black clothes and white collars, relieved here and there by tweeds, on dark mottled pillars of green marble and on lugubrious canvases. The gentlemen sat in the benches, having hitched their trousers

---

*Jesus' words to Peter in Matthew 16:23.

†Part of a church that crosses the nave at right angles to main length of the building.

‡Member of a religious order who has not taken priestly vows.

slightly above their knees and laid their hats in security. They sat well back and gazed formally at the distant speck of red light which was suspended before the high altar.

In one of the benches near the pulpit sat Mr Cunningham and Mr Kernan. In the bench behind sat Mr M'Coy alone: and in the bench behind him sat Mr Power and Mr Fogarty. Mr M'Coy had tried unsuccessfully to find a place in the bench with the others, and, when the party had settled down in the form of a quincunx,* he had tried unsuccessfully to make comic remarks. As these had not been well received, he had desisted. Even he was sensible of the decorous atmosphere and even he began to respond to the religious stimulus. In a whisper, Mr. Cunningham drew Mr Kernan's attention to Mr Harford, the money lender, who sat some distance off, and to Mr Fanning, the registration agent and mayor maker of the city, who was sitting immediately under the pulpit beside one of the newly elected councillors of the ward. To the right sat old Michael Grimes, the owner of three pawnbroker's shops, and Dan Hogan's nephew, who was up for the job in the Town Clerk's office. Farther in front sat Mr Hendrick, the chief reporter of *The Freeman's Journal,* and poor O'Carroll, an old friend of Mr Kernan's, who had been at one time a considerable commercial figure. Gradually, as he recognised familiar faces, Mr Kernan began to feel more at home. His hat, which had been rehabilitated by his wife, rested upon his knees. Once or twice he pulled down his cuffs with one hand while he held the brim of his hat lightly, but firmly, with the other hand.

A powerful-looking figure, the upper part of which was draped with a white surplice,† was observed to be struggling up into the pulpit. Simultaneously the congregation unsettled, produced handkerchiefs and knelt upon them with care. Mr Kernan followed the general example. The priest's figure now stood upright in the pulpit, two-thirds of its bulk, crowned by a massive red face, appearing above the balustrade.

Father Purdon knelt down, turned towards the red speck of light and, covering his face with his hands, prayed. After an interval, he uncovered his face and rose. The congregation rose also and settled again on its benches. Mr Kernan restored his hat to its original position on his knee and presented an attentive face to the preacher. The preacher turned back each wide sleeve of his surplice with an elaborate large gesture and slowly surveyed the array of faces. Then he said:

---

*Figure of five points: the four corners of a square and the center.
†White vestment with loose sleeves worn by those presiding over church services.

For the children of this world are wiser in their generation than the children of light. Wherefore make unto yourselves friends out of the mammon* of iniquity so that when you die they may receive you into everlasting dwellings.†

Father Purdon developed the text with resonant assurance. It was one of the most difficult texts in all the Scriptures, he said, to interpret properly. It was a text which might seem to the casual observer at variance with the lofty morality elsewhere preached by Jesus Christ. But, he told his hearers, the text had seemed to him specially adapted for the guidance of those whose lot it was to lead the life of the world and who yet wished to lead that life not in the manner of worldlings. It was a text for business men and professional men. Jesus Christ, with His divine understanding of every cranny of our human nature, understood that all men were not called to the religious life, that by far the vast majority were forced to live in the world, and, to a certain extent, for the world: and in this sentence He designed to give them a word of counsel, setting before them as exemplars in the religious life those very worshippers of Mammon who were of all men the least solicitous in matters religious.

He told his hearers that he was there that evening for no terrifying, no extravagant purpose; but as a man of the world speaking to his fellow-men. He came to speak to business men and he would speak to them in a businesslike way. If he might use the metaphor, he said, he was their spiritual accountant; and he wished each and every one of his hearers to open his books, the books of his spiritual life, and see if they tallied accurately with conscience.

Jesus Christ was not a hard taskmaster. He understood our little failings, understood the weakness of our poor fallen nature, understood the temptations of this life. We might have had, we all had from time to time, our temptations: we might have, we all had, our failings. But one thing only, he said, he would ask of his hearers. And that was: to be straight and manly with God. If their accounts tallied in every point to say:

—Well, I have verified my accounts. I find all well.

But if, as might happen, there were some discrepancies, to admit the truth, to be frank and say like a man:

—Well, I have looked into my accounts. I find this wrong and this wrong. But, with God's grace, I will rectify this and this. I will set right my accounts.

---

*Riches.
†Quotation from Luke 16:8–9.

THE DEAD

LILY, THE CARETAKER'S DAUGHTER, was literally run off her feet. Hardly had she brought one gentleman into the little pantry behind the office on the ground floor and helped him off with his overcoat than the wheezy hall-door bell clanged again and she had to scamper along the bare hallway to let in another guest. It was well for her she had not to attend to the ladies also. But Miss Kate and Miss Julia had thought of that and had converted the bathroom upstairs into a ladies' dressing-room. Miss Kate and Miss Julia were there, gossiping and laughing and fussing, walking after each other to the head of the stairs, peering down over the banisters and calling down to Lily to ask her who had come.

It was always a great affair, the Misses Morkan's annual dance. Everybody who knew them came to it, members of the family, old friends of the family, the members of Julia's choir, any of Kate's pupils that were grown up enough, and even some of Mary Jane's pupils too. Never once had it fallen flat. For years and years it had gone off in splendid style, as long as anyone could remember; ever since Kate and Julia, after the death of their brother Pat, had left the house in Stoney Batter* and taken Mary Jane, their only niece, to live with them in the dark, gaunt house on Usher's Island,[†] the upper part of which they had rented from Mr Fulham, the corn-factor[‡] on the ground floor. That was a good thirty years ago if it was a day. Mary Jane, who was then a little girl in short clothes, was now the main prop of the household, for she had the organ[§] in Haddington Road. She had been through the Academy[||] and gave a pupils' concert every year in the upper room of the Antient Concert Rooms. Many of her pupils belonged to the

---

*On the south bank of the Liffey, west of the city center.
[†]A south-bank quay of the Liffey, near Phoenix Park.
[‡]Broker between grower and wholesaler.
[§]Served as organist.
[||]The Royal Irish Academy of Music.

"The Dead"

better-class families on the Kingstown and Dalkey line.* Old as they were, her aunts also did their share. Julia, though she was quite grey, was still the leading soprano in Adam and Eve's,[6] and Kate, being too feeble to go about much, gave music lessons to beginners on the old square piano in the back room. Lily, the caretaker's daughter, did housemaid's work for them. Though their life was modest, they believed in eating well; the best of everything: diamond-bone sirloins, three-shilling tea and the best bottled stout.† But Lily seldom made a mistake in the orders, so that she got on well with her three mistresses. They were fussy, that was all. But the only thing they would not stand was back answers.

Of course, they had good reason to be fussy on such a night. And then it was long after ten o'clock and yet there was no sign of Gabriel and his wife. Besides they were dreadfully afraid that Freddy Malins might turn up screwed.‡ They would not wish for worlds that any of Mary Jane's pupils should see him under the influence; and when he was like that it was sometimes very hard to manage him. Freddy Malins always came late, but they wondered what could be keeping Gabriel: and that was what brought them every two minutes to the banisters to ask Lily had Gabriel or Freddy come.

—O, Mr Conroy, said Lily to Gabriel when she opened the door for him, Miss Kate and Miss Julia thought you were never coming. Goodnight, Mrs Conroy.

—I'll engage they did, said Gabriel, but they forget that my wife here takes three mortal hours to dress herself.

He stood on the mat, scraping the snow from his goloshes, while Lily led his wife to the foot of the stairs and called out:

—Miss Kate, here's Mrs Conroy.

Kate and Julia came toddling down the dark stairs at once. Both of them kissed Gabriel's wife, said she must be perished alive, and asked was Gabriel with her.

—Here I am as right as the mail, Aunt Kate! Go on up. I'll follow, called out Gabriel from the dark.

He continued scraping his feet vigorously while the three women went upstairs, laughing, to the ladies' dressing-room. A light fringe of snow lay like a cape on the shoulders of his overcoat and like toecaps

---

*Train line to the affluent seaside communities of Kingstown (now Dun Laoghaire) and Dalkey, south of Dublin.
†Thick, dark Irish beer.
‡Drunk.

on the toes of his goloshes; and, as the buttons of his overcoat slipped with a squeaking noise through the snow-stiffened frieze, a cold, fragrant air from out-of-doors escaped from crevices and folds.

—Is it snowing again, Mr Conroy? asked Lily.

She had preceded him into the pantry to help him off with his overcoat. Gabriel smiled at the three syllables she had given his surname and glanced at her. She was a slim, growing girl, pale in complexion and with hay-coloured hair. The gas in the pantry made her look still paler. Gabriel had known her when she was a child and used to sit on the lowest step nursing a rag doll.

—Yes, Lily, he answered, and I think we're in for a night of it.

He looked up at the pantry ceiling, which was shaking with the stamping and shuffling of feet on the floor above, listened for a moment to the piano and then glanced at the girl, who was folding his overcoat carefully at the end of a shelf.

—Tell me, Lily, he said in a friendly tone, do you still go to school?

—O no, sir, she answered. I'm done schooling this year and more.

—O, then, said Gabriel gaily, I suppose we'll be going to your wedding one of these fine days with your young man, eh?

The girl glanced back at him over her shoulder and said with great bitterness:

—The men that is now is only all palaver* and what they can get out of you.

Gabriel coloured, as if he felt he had made a mistake and, without looking at her, kicked off his goloshes and flicked actively with his muffler at his patent-leather shoes.

He was a stout, tallish young man. The high colour of his cheeks pushed upwards even to his forehead, where it scattered itself in a few formless patches of pale red; and on his hairless face there scintillated restlessly the polished lenses and the bright gilt rims of the glasses which screened his delicate and restless eyes. His glossy black hair was parted in the middle and brushed in a long curve behind his ears where it curled slightly beneath the groove left by his hat.

When he had flicked lustre into his shoes he stood up and pulled his waistcoat down more tightly on his plump body. Then he took a coin rapidly from his pocket.

—O Lily, he said, thrusting it into her hands, it's Christmas-time, isn't it? Just . . . here's a little. . . .

*Sweet talk.

He walked rapidly towards the door.

—O no, sir! cried the girl, following him. Really, sir, I wouldn't take it.

—Christmas-time! Christmas-time! said Gabriel, almost trotting to the stairs and waving his hand to her in deprecation.

The girl, seeing that he had gained the stairs, called out after him:

—Well, thank you, sir.

He waited outside the drawing-room door until the waltz should finish, listening to the skirts that swept against it and to the shuffling of feet. He was still discomposed by the girl's bitter and sudden retort. It had cast a gloom over him which he tried to dispel by arranging his cuffs and the bows of his tie. He then took from his waistcoat pocket a little paper and glanced at the headings he had made for his speech. He was undecided about the lines from Robert Browning,* for he feared they would be above the heads of his hearers. Some quotation that they would recognise from Shakespeare or from the Melodies† would be better. The indelicate clacking of the men's heels and the shuffling of their soles reminded him that their grade of culture differed from his. He would only make himself ridiculous by quoting poetry to them which they could not understand. They would think that he was airing his superior education. He would fail with them just as he had failed with the girl in the pantry. He had taken up a wrong tone. His whole speech was a mistake from first to last, an utter failure.

Just then his aunts and his wife came out of the ladies' dressing-room. His aunts were two small, plainly dressed old women. Aunt Julia was an inch or so the taller. Her hair, drawn low over the tops of her ears, was grey; and grey also, with darker shadows, was her large flaccid face. Though she was stout in build and stood erect, her slow eyes and parted lips gave her the appearance of a woman who did not know where she was or where she was going. Aunt Kate was more vivacious. Her face, healthier than her sister's, was all puckers and creases, like a shrivelled red apple, and her hair, braided in the same old-fashioned way, had not lost its ripe nut colour.

They both kissed Gabriel frankly. He was their favourite nephew, the son of their dead elder sister, Ellen, who had married T. J. Conroy of the Port and Docks.

---

*(1812–1889); preeminent English poet.

†Thomas Moore's *Irish Melodies*, a popular (and less difficult) alternative to the poetry of Browning.

—Gretta tells me you're not going to take a cab back to Monkstown* to-night, Gabriel, said Aunt Kate.

—No, said Gabriel, turning to his wife, we had quite enough of that last year, hadn't we? Don't you remember, Aunt Kate, what a cold Gretta got out of it? Cab windows rattling all the way, and the east wind blowing in after we passed Merrion.† Very jolly it was. Gretta caught a dreadful cold.

Aunt Kate frowned severely and nodded her head at every word.

—Quite right, Gabriel, quite right, she said. You can't be too careful.

—But as for Gretta there, said Gabriel, she'd walk home in the snow if she were let.

Mrs Conroy laughed.

—Don't mind him, Aunt Kate, she said. He's really an awful bother, what with green shades for Tom's eyes at night and making him do the dumb-bells, and forcing Eva to eat the stirabout.‡ The poor child! And she simply hates the sight of it! . . . O, but you'll never guess what he makes me wear now!

She broke out into a peal of laughter and glanced at her husband, whose admiring and happy eyes had been wandering from her dress to her face and hair. The two aunts laughed heartily, too, for Gabriel's solicitude was a standing joke with them.

—Goloshes! said Mrs Conroy. That's the latest. Whenever it's wet underfoot I must put on my goloshes. To-night even, he wanted me to put them on, but I wouldn't. The next thing he'll buy me will be a diving suit.

Gabriel laughed nervously and patted his tie reassuringly, while Aunt Kate nearly doubled herself, so heartily did she enjoy the joke. The smile soon faded from Aunt Julia's face and her mirthless eyes were directed towards her nephew's face. After a pause she asked:

—And what are goloshes, Gabriel?

—Goloshes, Julia! exclaimed her sister. Goodness me, don't you know what goloshes are? You wear them over your . . . over your boots, Gretta, isn't it?

—Yes, said Mrs Conroy. Guttapercha§ things. We both have a pair now. Gabriel says everyone wears them on the continent.

---

*Affluent coastal suburb south of the city center.
†Merrion Square, fashionable neighborhood east of St. Stephen's Green.
‡Hot cereal.
§A rubber-like material.

—O, on the continent, murmured Aunt Julia, nodding her head slowly.

Gabriel knitted his brows and said, as if he were slightly angered:

—It's nothing very wonderful, but Gretta thinks it very funny because she says the word reminds her of Christy Minstrels.*

—But tell me, Gabriel, said Aunt Kate, with brisk tact. Of course, you've seen about the room. Gretta was saying . . .

—O, the room is all right, replied Gabriel. I've taken one in the Gresham.†

—To be sure, said Aunt Kate, by far the best thing to do. And the children, Gretta, you're not anxious about them?

—O, for one night, said Mrs Conroy. Besides, Bessie will look after them.

—To be sure, said Aunt Kate again. What a comfort it is to have a girl like that, one you can depend on! There's that Lily, I'm sure I don't know what has come over her lately. She's not the girl she was at all.

Gabriel was about to ask his aunt some questions on this point, but she broke off suddenly to gaze after her sister, who had wandered down the stairs and was craning her neck over the banisters.

—Now, I ask you, she said almost testily, where is Julia going? Julia! Julia! Where are you going?

Julia, who had gone half way down one flight, came back and announced blandly:

—Here's Freddy.

At the same moment a clapping of hands and a final flourish of the pianist told that the waltz had ended. The drawing-room door was opened from within and some couples came out. Aunt Kate drew Gabriel aside hurriedly and whispered into his ear:

—Slip down, Gabriel, like a good fellow and see if he's all right, and don't let him up if he's screwed. I'm sure he's screwed. I'm sure he is.

Gabriel went to the stairs and listened over the banisters. He could hear two persons talking in the pantry. Then he recognised Freddy Malins' laugh. He went down the stairs noisily.

—It's such a relief, said Aunt Kate to Mrs Conroy, that Gabriel is here. I always feel easier in my mind when he's here. . . . Julia, there's Miss Daly and Miss Power will take some refreshment. Thanks for your beautiful waltz, Miss Daly. It made lovely time.

---

*Blackface vaudeville entertainers.
†One of Dublin's most elegant hotels, on Upper O'Connell Street.

A tall wizen-faced man, with a stiff grizzled moustache and swarthy skin, who was passing out with his partner, said:

—And may we have some refreshment, too, Miss Morkan?

—Julia, said Aunt Kate summarily, and here's Mr Browne and Miss Furlong. Take them in, Julia, with Miss Daly and Miss Power.

—I'm the man for the ladies, said Mr Browne, pursing his lips until his moustache bristled and smiling in all his wrinkles. You know, Miss Morkan, the reason they are so fond of me is—

He did not finish his sentence, but, seeing that Aunt Kate was out of earshot, at once led the three young ladies into the back room. The middle of the room was occupied by two square tables placed end to end, and on these Aunt Julia and the caretaker were straightening and smoothing a large cloth. On the sideboard were arrayed dishes and plates, and glasses and bundles of knives and forks and spoons. The top of the closed square piano served also as a sideboard for viands* and sweets. At a smaller sideboard in one corner two young men were standing, drinking hop-bitters.†

Mr Browne led his charges thither and invited them all, in jest, to some ladies' punch, hot, strong and sweet. As they said they never took anything strong, he opened three bottles of lemonade‡ for them. Then he asked one of the young men to move aside, and, taking hold of the decanter, filled out for himself a goodly measure of whisky. The young men eyed him respectfully while he took a trial sip.

—God help me, he said, smiling, it's the doctor's orders.

His wizened face broke into a broader smile, and the three young ladies laughed in musical echo to his pleasantry, swaying their bodies to and fro, with nervous jerks of their shoulders. The boldest said:

—O, now, Mr Browne, I'm sure the doctor never ordered anything of the kind.

Mr Browne took another sip of his whisky and said, with sidling mimicry:

—Well, you see, I'm like the famous Mrs Cassidy, who is reported to have said: *Now, Mary Grimes, if I don't take it, make me take it, for I feel I want it.*

His hot face had leaned forward a little too confidentially and he had assumed a very low Dublin accent so that the young ladies, with

---

*Delicacies.

†Dry ale.

‡A carbonated lemon-lime beverage.

one instinct, received his speech in silence. Miss Furlong, who was one of Mary Jane's pupils, asked Miss Daly what was the name of the pretty waltz she had played; and Mr Browne, seeing that he was ignored, turned promptly to the two young men who were more appreciative.

A red-faced young woman, dressed in pansy, came into the room, excitedly clapping her hands and crying:

—Quadrilles! Quadrilles!*

Close on her heels came Aunt Kate, crying:

—Two gentlemen and three ladies, Mary Jane!

—O, here's Mr Bergin and Mr Kerrigan, said Mary Jane. Mr Kerrigan, will you take Miss Power? Miss Furlong, may I get you a partner, Mr Bergin. O, that'll just do now.

—Three ladies, Mary Jane, said Aunt Kate.

The two young gentlemen asked the ladies if they might have the pleasure, and Mary Jane turned to Miss Daly.

—O, Miss Daly, you're really awfully good, after playing for the last two dances, but really we're so short of ladies to-night.

—I don't mind in the least, Miss Morkan.

—But I've a nice partner for you, Mr Bartell D'Arcy, the tenor. I'll get him to sing later on. All Dublin is raving about him.

—Lovely voice, lovely voice! said Aunt Kate.

As the piano had twice begun the prelude to the first figure Mary Jane led her recruits quickly from the room. They had hardly gone when Aunt Julia wandered slowly into the room, looking behind her at something.

—What is the matter, Julia? asked Aunt Kate anxiously. Who is it?

Julia, who was carrying in a column of table-napkins, turned to her sister and said, simply, as if the question had surprised her:

—It's only Freddy, Kate, and Gabriel with him.

In fact right behind her Gabriel could be seen piloting Freddy Malins across the landing. The latter, a young man of about forty, was of Gabriel's size and build, with very round shoulders. His face was fleshy and pallid, touched with colour only at the thick hanging lobes of his ears and at the wide wings of his nose. He had coarse features, a blunt nose, a convex and receding brow, tumid and protruded lips. His heavy-lidded eyes and the disorder of his scanty hair made him look sleepy. He was laughing heartily in a high key at a story which he had

---

*Type of square dance.

been telling Gabriel on the stairs and at the same time rubbing the knuckles of his left fist backwards and forwards into his left eye.

—Good-evening, Freddy, said Aunt Julia.

Freddy Malins bade the Misses Morkan good-evening in what seemed an offhand fashion by reason of the habitual catch in his voice and then, seeing that Mr Browne was grinning at him from the sideboard, crossed the room on rather shaky legs and began to repeat in an undertone the story he had just told to Gabriel.

—He's not so bad, is he? said Aunt Kate to Gabriel.

Gabriel's brows were dark but he raised them quick and answered:

—O, no, hardly noticeable.

—Now, isn't he a terrible fellow! she said. And his poor mother made him take the pledge* on New Year's Eve. But come on, Gabriel, into the drawing-room.

Before leaving the room with Gabriel she signalled to Mr Browne by frowning and shaking her forefinger in warning to and fro. Mr Browne nodded in answer and, when she had gone, said to Freddy Malins:

—Now, then, Teddy, I'm going to fill you out a good glass of lemonade just to buck you up.

Freddy Malins, who was nearing the climax of his story, waved the offer aside impatiently but Mr Browne, having first called Freddy Malins' attention to a disarray in his dress, filled out and handed him a full glass of lemonade. Freddy Malins' left hand accepted the glass mechanically, his right hand being engaged in the mechanical readjustment of his dress. Mr Browne, whose face was once more wrinkling with mirth, poured out for himself a glass of whisky while Freddy Malins exploded, before he had well reached the climax of his story, in a kink of high-pitched bronchitic laughter and, setting down his untasted and overflowing glass, began to rub the knuckles of his left fist backwards and forwards into his left eye, repeating words of his last phrase as well as his fit of laughter would allow him.

*   *   *   *   *   *   *   *   *   *

Gabriel could not listen while Mary Jane was playing her Academy piece, full of runs and difficult passages, to the hushed drawing-room. He liked music but the piece she was playing had no melody for him and he doubted whether it had any melody for the other listeners,

---

*The temperance pledge—that is, to not drink alcohol.

though they had begged Mary Jane to play something. Four young men, who had come from the refreshment-room to stand in the doorway at the sound of the piano, had gone away quietly in couples after a few minutes. The only persons who seemed to follow the music were Mary Jane herself, her hands racing along the keyboard or lifted from it at the pauses like those of a priestess in momentary imprecation, and Aunt Kate standing at her elbow to turn the page.

Gabriel's eyes, irritated by the floor, which glittered with beeswax under the heavy chandelier, wandered to the wall above the piano. A picture of the balcony scene in *Romeo and Juliet* hung there and beside it was a picture of the two murdered princes in the Tower* which Aunt Julia had worked in red, blue and brown wools when she was a girl. Probably in the school they had gone to as girls that kind of work had been taught for one year. His mother had worked for him as a birthday present a waistcoat of purple tabinet,† with little foxes' heads upon it, lined with brown satin and having round mulberry buttons. It was strange that his mother had had no musical talent though Aunt Kate used to call her the brains carrier of the Morkan family. Both she and Julia had always seemed a little proud of their serious and matronly sister. Her photograph stood before the pierglass.‡ She held an open book on her knees and was pointing out something in it to Constantine who, dressed in a man-o'-war suit, lay at her feet. It was she who had chosen the names of her sons for she was very sensible of the dignity of family life. Thanks to her, Constantine was now senior curate in Balbriggan§ and, thanks to her, Gabriel himself had taken his degree in the Royal University.‖ A shadow passed over his face as he remembered her sullen opposition to his marriage. Some slighting phrases she had used still rankled in his memory; she had once spoken of Gretta as being country cute and that was not true of Gretta at all. It was Gretta who had nursed her during all her last long illness in their house at Monkstown.

He knew that Mary Jane must be near the end of her piece for she was playing again the opening melody with runs of scales after every

---

*The two sons of English King Edward IV, rumored to have been murdered in the Tower of London in 1483 by their uncle, Richard III.

†Material like damask, popular for embroidery.

‡Long, narrow mirror.

§Assistant to the parish priest in a seaside resort north of Dublin.

‖An examining college, established in 1879 for the purpose of granting degrees to students of University College Dublin, which Gabriel probably attended, and other Catholic universities.

bar and while he waited for the end the resentment died down in his
heart. The piece ended with a trill of octaves in the treble and a final
deep octave in the bass. Great applause greeted Mary Jane as, blushing
and rolling up her music nervously, she escaped from the room. The
most vigorous clapping came from the four young men in the doorway
who had gone away to the refreshment-room at the beginning of the
piece but had come back when the piano had stopped.

Lancers* were arranged. Gabriel found himself partnered with Miss
Ivors. She was a frank-mannered talkative young lady, with a freckled
face and prominent brown eyes. She did not wear a low-cut bodice and
the large brooch which was fixed in the front of her collar bore on it an
Irish device† and motto.

When they had taken their places she said abruptly:

—I have a crow to pluck‡ with you.

—With me? said Gabriel.

She nodded her head gravely.

—What is is? asked Gabriel, smiling at her solemn manner.

—Who is G. C.? answered Miss Ivors, turning her eyes upon him.

Gabriel coloured and was about to knit his brows, as if he did not
understand, when she said bluntly:

—O, innocent Amy! I have found out that you write for *The Daily
Express.*§ Now, aren't you ashamed of yourself?

—Why should I be ashamed of myself? asked Gabriel, blinking his
eyes and trying to smile.

—Well, I'm ashamed of you, said Miss Ivors frankly. To say you'd
write for a paper like that. I didn't think you were a West Briton.‖

A look of perplexity appeared on Gabriel's face. It was true that he
wrote a literary column every Wednesday in *The Daily Express,* for
which he was paid fifteen shillings. But that did not make him a West
Briton surely. The books he received for review were almost more welcome than the paltry cheque. He loved to feel the covers and turn over
the pages of newly printed books. Nearly every day when his teaching
in the college was ended he used to wander down the quays to the
second-hand booksellers, to Hickey's on Bachelor's Walk, to Webb's or

---

*Another type of square dance.
†An identifiably Irish design.
‡We would say a "bone to pick."
§Dublin newspaper with Unionist leanings.
‖That is, an Irishman whose sympathies were more British than Irish.

Massey's on Aston's Quay, or to O'Clohissey's in the by-street. He did not know how to meet her charge. He wanted to say that literature was above politics. But they were friends of many years' standing and their careers had been parallel, first at the University and then as teachers: he could not risk a grandiose phrase with her. He continued blinking his eyes and trying to smile and murmured lamely that he saw nothing political in writing reviews of books.

When their turn to cross had come he was still perplexed and inattentive. Miss Ivors promptly took his hand in a warm grasp and said in a soft friendly tone:

—Of course, I was only joking. Come, we cross now.

When they were together again she spoke of the University question* and Gabriel felt more at ease. A friend of hers had shown her his review of Browning's poems. That was how she had found out the secret: but she liked the review immensely. Then she said suddenly:

—O, Mr Conroy, will you come for an excursion to the Aran Isles† this summer? We're going to stay there a whole month. It will be splendid out in the Atlantic. You ought to come. Mr Clancy is coming, and Mr Kilkelly and Kathleen Kearney. It would be splendid for Gretta too if she'd come. She's from Connacht,‡ isn't she?

—Her people are, said Gabriel shortly.

—But you will come, won't you? said Miss Ivors, laying her warm hand eagerly on his arm.

—The fact is, said Gabriel, I have just arranged to go—

—Go where? asked Miss Ivors.

—Well, you know, every year I go for a cycling tour with some fellows and so—

—But where? asked Miss Ivors.

—Well, we usually go to France or Belgium or perhaps Germany, said Gabriel awkwardly.

—And why do you go to France and Belgium, said Miss Ivors, instead of visiting your own land?

—Well, said Gabriel, it's partly to keep in touch with the languages and partly for a change.

---

*Debate regarding the proper role of religion and nationalism in Ireland's universities.
†Relatively undeveloped islands off the west coast of Ireland, near Galway.
‡Ireland's western province; the seaport Galway is one of its principal cities.

—And haven't you your own language to keep in touch with—Irish? asked Miss Ivors.

—Well, said Gabriel, if it comes to that, you know, Irish is not my language.

Their neighbours had turned to listen to the cross-examination. Gabriel glanced right and left nervously and tried to keep his good humour under the ordeal which was making a blush invade his forehead.

—And haven't you your own land to visit, continued Miss Ivors, that you know nothing of, your own people, and your own country?

—O, to tell you the truth, retorted Gabriel suddenly, I'm sick of my own country, sick of it!

—Why? asked Miss Ivors.

Gabriel did not answer for his retort had heated him.

—Why? repeated Miss Ivors.

They had to go visiting together and, as he had not answered her, Miss Ivors said warmly:

—Of course, you've no answer.

Gabriel tried to cover his agitation by taking part in the dance with great energy. He avoided her eyes for he had seen a sour expression on her face. But when they met in the long chain he was surprised to feel his hand firmly pressed. She looked at him from under her brows for a moment quizzically until he smiled. Then, just as the chain was about to start again, she stood on tiptoe and whispered into his ear:

—West Briton!

When the lancers were over Gabriel went away to a remote corner of the room where Freddy Malins' mother was sitting. She was a stout feeble old woman with white hair. Her voice had a catch in it like her son's and she stuttered slightly. She had been told that Freddy had come and that he was nearly all right. Gabriel asked her whether she had had a good crossing. She lived with her married daughter in Glasgow and came to Dublin on a visit once a year. She answered placidly that she had had a beautiful crossing and that the captain had been most attentive to her. She spoke also of the beautiful house her daughter kept in Glasgow, and of all the friends they had there. While her tongue rambled on Gabriel tried to banish from his mind all memory of the unpleasant incident with Miss Ivors. Of course the girl or woman, or whatever she was, was an enthusiast but there was a time for all things. Perhaps he ought not to have answered her like that. But she had no right to call him a West Briton before people, even in joke. She had tried to make him ridiculous before people, heckling him and staring at him with her rabbit's eyes.

He saw his wife making her way towards him through the waltzing couples. When she reached him she said into his ear:

—Gabriel, Aunt Kate wants to know won't you carve the goose as usual. Miss Daly will carve the ham and I'll do the pudding.

—All right, said Gabriel.

—She's sending in the younger ones first as soon as this waltz is over so that we'll have the table to ourselves.

—Were you dancing? asked Gabriel.

—Of course I was. Didn't you see me? What row had you with Molly Ivors?

—No row. Why? Did she say so?

—Something like that. I'm trying to get that Mr D'Arcy to sing. He's full of conceit, I think.

—There was no row, said Gabriel moodily, only she wanted me to go for a trip to the west of Ireland and I said I wouldn't.

His wife clasped her hands excitedly and gave a little jump.

—O, do go, Gabriel, she cried. I'd love to see Galway* again.

—You can go if you like, said Gabriel coldly.

She looked at him for a moment, then turned to Mrs Malins and said:

—There's a nice husband for you, Mrs Malins.

While she was threading her way back across the room Mrs Malins, without adverting to the interruption, went on to tell Gabriel what beautiful places there were in Scotland and beautiful scenery. Her son-in-law brought them every year to the lakes and they used to go fishing. Her son-in-law was a splendid fisher. One day he caught a beautiful big fish and the man in the hotel cooked it for their dinner.

Gabriel hardly heard what she said. Now that supper was coming near he began to think again about his speech and about the quotation. When he saw Freddy Malins coming across the room to visit his mother Gabriel left the chair free for him and retired into the embrasure of the window. The room had already cleared and from the back room came the clatter of plates and knives. Those who still remained in the drawing-room seemed tired of dancing and were conversing quietly in little groups. Gabriel's warm trembling fingers tapped the cold pane of the window. How cool it must be outside! How pleasant it would be

---

*Ireland's most important western seaport.

to walk out alone, first along by the river and then through the park!* The snow would be lying on the branches of the trees and forming a bright cap on the top of the Wellington Monument.† How much more pleasant it would be there than at the supper-table!

He ran over the headings of his speech: Irish hospitality, sad memories, the Three Graces, Paris, the quotation from Browning. He repeated to himself a phrase he had written in his review: *One feels that one is listening to a thought-tormented music.* Miss Ivors had praised the review. Was she sincere? Had she really any life of her own behind all her propagandism? There had never been any ill-feeling between them until that night. It unnerved him to think that she would be at the supper-table, looking up at him while he spoke with her critical quizzing eyes. Perhaps she would not be sorry to see him fail in his speech. An idea came into his mind and gave him courage. He would say, alluding to Aunt Kate and Aunt Julia: *Ladies and Gentlemen, the generation which is now on the wane among us may have had its faults but for my part I think it had certain qualities of hospitality, of humour, of humanity, which the new and very serious and hypereducated generation that is growing up around us seems to me to lack.* Very good: that was one for Miss Ivors. What did he care that his aunts were only two ignorant old women?

A murmur in the room attracted his attention. Mr Browne was advancing from the door, gallantly escorting Aunt Julia, who leaned upon his arm, smiling and hanging her head. An irregular musketry‡ of applause escorted her also as far as the piano and then, as Mary Jane seated herself on the stool, and Aunt Julia, no longer smiling, half turned so as to pitch her voice fairly into the room, gradually ceased. Gabriel recognised the prelude. It was that of an old song of Aunt Julia's—*Arrayed for the Bridal.*§ Her voice, strong and clear in tone, attacked with great spirit the runs which embellish the air and though she sang very rapidly she did not miss even the smallest of the grace notes. To follow the voice, without looking at the singer's face, was to feel and share the excitement of swift and secure flight. Gabriel applauded loudly with all the others at the close of the song and loud applause was borne in from the invisible supper-table. It sounded so

---

*Phoenix Park, on the western outskirts of the city; the largest enclosed urban park in the world.

†Large obelisk in Phoenix Park, erected in 1817 in honor of the Duke of Wellington.

‡Sound of musket fire.

§From Vincenzo Bellini's *I Puritani di Scozia* (1835).

genuine that a little colour struggled into Aunt Julia's face as she bent to replace in the music-stand the old leather-bound song-book that had her initials on the cover. Freddy Malins, who had listened with his head perched sideways to hear her better, was still applauding when everyone else had ceased and talking animatedly to his mother who nodded her head gravely and slowly in acquiescence. At last, when he could clap no more, he stood up suddenly and hurried across the room to Aunt Julia whose hand he seized and held in both his hands, shaking it when words failed him or the catch in his voice proved too much for him.

—I was just telling my mother, he said, I never heard you sing so well, never. No, I never heard your voice so good as it is to-night. Now! Would you believe that now? That's the truth. Upon my word and honour that's the truth. I never heard your voice sound so fresh and so . . . so clear and fresh, never.

Aunt Julia smiled broadly and murmured something about compliments as she released her hand from his grasp. Mr Browne extended his open hand towards her and said to those who were near him in the manner of a showman introducing a prodigy to an audience:

—Miss Julia Morkan, my latest discovery!

He was laughing very heartily at this himself when Freddy Malins turned to him and said:

—Well, Browne, if you're serious you might make a worse discovery. All I can say is I never heard her sing half so well as long as I am coming here. And that's the honest truth.

—Neither did I, said Mr Browne. I think her voice has greatly improved.

Aunt Julia shrugged her shoulders and said with meek pride:

—Thirty years ago I hadn't a bad voice as voices go.

—I often told Julia, said Aunt Kate emphatically, that she was simply thrown away in that choir. But she never would be said by me.*

She turned as if to appeal to the good sense of the others against a refractory child while Aunt Julia gazed in front of her, a vague smile of reminiscence playing on her face.

—No, continued Aunt Kate, she wouldn't be said or led by anyone, slaving there in that choir night and day, night and day. Six o'clock on Christmas morning! And all for what?

—Well, isn't it for the honour of God, Aunt Kate? asked Mary Jane, twisting round on the piano-stool and smiling.

---

*She would never take my advice.

Aunt Kate turned fiercely on her niece and said:

—I know all about the honour of God, Mary Jane, but I think it's not at all honourable for the pope to turn out the women out of the choirs* that have slaved there all their lives and put little whippersnappers of boys over their heads. I suppose it is for the good of the Church if the pope does it. But it's not just, Mary Jane, and it's not right.

She had worked herself into a passion and would have continued in defence of her sister for it was a sore subject with her but Mary Jane, seeing that all the dancers had come back, intervened pacifically:

—Now, Aunt Kate, you're giving scandal to Mr Browne who is of the other persuasion.†

Aunt Kate turned to Mr Browne, who was grinning at this allusion to his religion, and said hastily:

—O, I don't question the pope's being right. I'm only a stupid old woman and I wouldn't presume to do such a thing. But there's such a thing as common everyday politeness and gratitude. And if I were in Julia's place I'd tell that Father Healey straight up to his face . . .

—And besides, Aunt Kate, said Mary Jane, we really are all hungry and when we are hungry we are all very quarrelsome.

—And when we are thirsty we are also quarrelsome, added Mr Browne.

—So that we had better go to supper, said Mary Jane, and finish the discussion afterwards.

On the landing outside the drawing-room Gabriel found his wife and Mary Jane trying to persuade Miss Ivors to stay for supper. But Miss Ivors, who had put on her hat and was buttoning her cloak, would not stay. She did not feel in the least hungry and she had already overstayed her time.

—But only for ten minutes, Molly, said Mrs Conroy. That won't delay you.

—To take a pick itself, said Mary Jane, after all your dancing.

—I really couldn't, said Miss Ivors.

—I am afraid you didn't enjoy yourself at all, said Mary Jane hopelessly.

—Ever so much, I assure you, said Miss Ivors, but you really must let me run off now.

—But how can you get home? asked Mrs Conroy.

---

*A decree by Pius X in 1903 forbade women to sing or perform music in church services.

†That is, he is a Protestant.

—O, it's only two steps up the quay.

Gabriel hesitated a moment and said:

—If you will allow me, Miss Ivors, I'll see you home if you are really obliged to go.

But Miss Ivors broke away from them.

—I won't hear of it, she cried. For goodness' sake go in to your suppers and don't mind me. I'm quite well able to take care of myself.

—Well, you're the comical girl, Molly, said Mrs Conroy frankly.

—*Beannacht libh*,* cried Miss Ivors, with a laugh, as she ran down the staircase.

Mary Jane gazed after her, a moody puzzled expression on her face, while Mrs Conroy leaned over the banisters to listen for the hall-door. Gabriel asked himself was he the cause of her abrupt departure. But she did not seem to be in ill humour: she had gone away laughing. He stared blankly down the staircase.

At the moment Aunt Kate came toddling out of the supper-room, almost wringing her hands in despair.

—Where is Gabriel? she cried. Where on earth is Gabriel? There's everyone waiting in there, stage to let, and nobody to carve the goose.

—Here I am, Aunt Kate! cried Gabriel, with sudden animation, ready to carve a flock of geese, if necessary.

A fat brown goose lay at one end of the table and at the other end, on a bed of creased paper strewn with sprigs of parsley, lay a great ham, stripped of its outer skin and peppered over with crust crumbs, a neat paper frill round its shin and beside this was a round of spiced beef. Between these rival ends ran parallel lines of side-dishes: two little minsters of jelly, red and yellow; a shallow dish full of blocks of blancmange† and red jam, a large green leaf-shaped dish with a stalk-shaped handle, on which lay bunches of purple raisins and peeled almonds, a companion dish on which lay a solid rectangle of Smyrna figs, a dish of custard topped with grated nutmeg, a small bowl full of chocolates and sweets wrapped in gold and silver papers and a glass vase in which stood some tall celery stalks. In the centre of the table there stood, as sentries to a fruit-stand which upheld a pyramid of oranges and American apples, two squat old-fashioned decanters of cut glass, one containing port and the other dark sherry. On the closed square piano a pudding in a huge yellow dish lay in waiting and behind it were three squads of bottles of

---

*Irish for "blessings on you"; good-bye.

†Sweet, white pudding.

stout and ale and minerals,* drawn up according to the colours of their uniforms, the first two black, with brown and red labels, the third and smallest squad white, with transverse green sashes.

Gabriel took his seat boldly at the head of the table and, having looked to the edge of the carver, plunged his fork firmly into the goose. He felt quite at ease now for he was an expert carver and liked nothing better than to find himself at the head of a well-laden table.

—Miss Furlong, what shall I send you? he asked. A wing or a slice of the breast?

—Just a small slice of the breast.

—Miss Higgins, what for you?

—O, anything at all, Mr Conroy.

While Gabriel and Miss Daly exchanged plates of goose and plates of ham and spiced beef Lily went from guest to guest with a dish of hot floury potatoes wrapped in a white napkin. This was Mary Jane's idea and she had also suggested apple sauce for the goose but Aunt Kate had said that plain roast goose without any apple sauce had always been good enough for her and she hoped she might never eat worse. Mary Jane waited on her pupils and saw that they got the best slices and Aunt Kate and Aunt Julia opened and carried across from the piano bottles of stout and ale for the gentlemen and bottles of minerals for the ladies. There was a great deal of confusion and laughter and noise, the noise of orders and counter-orders, of knives and forks, of corks and glass-stoppers. Gabriel began to carve second helpings as soon as he had finished the first round without serving himself. Everyone protested loudly so that he compromised by taking a long draught of stout for he had found the carving hot work. Mary Jane settled down quietly to her supper but Aunt Kate and Aunt Julia were still toddling round the table, walking on each other's heels, getting in each other's way and giving each other unheeded orders. Mr Browne begged of them to sit down and eat their suppers and so did Gabriel but they said there was time enough, so that, at last, Freddy Malins stood up and, capturing Aunt Kate, plumped her down on her chair amid general laughter.

When everyone had been well served Gabriel said, smiling:

—Now, if anyone wants a little more of what vulgar people call stuffing let him or her speak.

A chorus of voices invited him to begin his own supper and Lily came forward with three potatoes which she had reserved for him.

---

*Carbonated nonalcoholic beverages.

—Very well, said Gabriel amiably, as he took another preparatory draught, kindly forget my existence, ladies and gentlemen, for a few minutes.

He set to his supper and took no part in the conversation with which the table covered Lily's removal of the plates. The subject of talk was the opera company which was then at the Theatre Royal.* Mr Bartell D'Arcy, the tenor, a dark-complexioned young man with a smart moustache, praised very highly the leading contralto of the company but Miss Furlong thought she had a rather vulgar style of production. Freddy Malins said there was a negro chieftain singing in the second part of the Gaiety† pantomime who had one of the finest tenor voices he had ever heard.

—Have you heard him? he asked Mr Bartell D'Arcy across the table.

—No, answered Mr Bartell D'Arcy carelessly.

—Because, Freddy Malins explained, now I'd be curious to hear your opinion of him. I think he has a grand voice.

—It takes Teddy to find out the really good things, said Mr Browne familiarly to the table.

—And why couldn't he have a voice too? asked Freddy Malins sharply. Is it because he's only a black?

Nobody answered this question and Mary Jane led the table back to the legitimate opera. One of her pupils had given her a pass for *Mignon*.‡ Of course it was very fine, she said, but it made her think of poor Georgina Burns. Mr Browne could go back farther still, to the old Italian companies that used to come to Dublin—Tietjens, Ilma de Murzka, Campanini, the great Trebelli Giuglini, Ravelli, Aramburo.§ Those were the days, he said, when there was something like singing to be heard in Dublin. He told too of how the top gallery of the old Royal used to be packed night after night, of how one night an Italian tenor had sung five encores to *Let me like a Soldier fall*,|| introducing a high C every time and of how the gallery boys would sometimes in their enthusiasm unyoke the horses from the carriage of some great *prima donna* and pull her them-

---

*Burned down in 1880.
†Another Dublin theater.
‡Popular 1866 opera by Ambroise Thomas.
§Georgina Burns and the others named were notable nineteenth-century operatic singers.
||Song from *Maritana*, an 1845 opera by Irish composer William Wallace.

selves through the streets to her hotel. Why did they never play the grand old operas now, he asked, *Dinorah*,* *Lucrezia Borgia*? † Because they could not get the voices to sing them: that was why."

—O, well, said Mr Bartell D'Arcy, I presume there are as good singers to-day as there were then.

—Where are they? asked Mr Browne defiantly.

—In London, Paris, Milan, said Mr Bartell D'Arcy warmly. I suppose Caruso‡ for example, is quite as good, if not better than any of the men you have mentioned.

—Maybe so, said Mr Browne. But I may tell you I doubt it strongly.

—O, I'd give anything to hear Caruso sing, said Mary Jane.

—For me, said Aunt Kate, who had been picking a bone, there was only one tenor. To please me, I mean. But I suppose none of you ever heard of him.

—Who was he, Miss Morkan? asked Mr Bartell D'Arcy politely.

—His name, said Aunt Kate, was Parkinson.§ I heard him when he was in his prime and I think he had then the purest tenor voice that was ever put into a man's throat.

—Strange, said Mr Bartell D'Arcy. I never even heard of him.

—Yes, yes, Miss Morkan is right, said Mr Browne. I remember hearing of old Parkinson but he's too far back for me.

—A beautiful, pure, sweet, mellow English tenor, said Aunt Kate with enthusiasm.

Gabriel having finished, the huge pudding was transferred to the table. The clatter of forks and spoons began again. Gabriel's wife served out spoonfuls of the pudding and passed the plates down the table. Midway down they were held up by Mary Jane, who replenished them with raspberry or orange jelly or with blancmange and jam. The pudding was of Aunt Julia's making and she received praises for it from all quarters. She herself said that it was not quite brown enough.

—Well, I hope, Miss Morkan, said Mr Browne, that I'm brown enough for you because, you know, I'm all brown.

All the gentlemen, except Gabriel, ate some of the pudding out of compliment to Aunt Julia. As Gabriel never ate sweets the celery had been left for him. Freddy Malins also took a stalk of celery and ate it with

---

*1859 opera by Giacomo Meyerbeer.
†1833 opera by Gaetano Donizetti.
‡Enrico Caruso (1873–1921), the most famous operatic tenor of his day.
§Identity uncertain.

his pudding. He had been told that celery was a capital thing for the blood and he was just then under doctor's care. Mrs Malins, who had been silent all through the supper, said that her son was going down to Mount Melleray* in a week or so. The table then spoke of Mount Melleray, how bracing the air was down there, how hospitable the monks were and how they never asked for a penny-piece from their guests.

—And do you mean to say, asked Mr Browne incredulously, that a chap can go down there and put up there as if it were a hotel and live on the fat of the land and then come away without paying anything?

—O, most people give some donation to the monastery when they leave, said Mary Jane.

—I wish we had an institution like that in our Church, said Mr Browne candidly.

He was astonished to hear that the monks never spoke, got up at two in the morning and slept in their coffins. He asked what they did it for.

—That's the rule of the order, said Aunt Kate firmly.

—Yes, but why? asked Mr Browne.

Aunt Kate repeated that it was the rule, that was all. Mr Browne still seemed not to understand. Freddy Malins explained to him, as best he could, that the monks were trying to make up for the sins committed by all the sinners in the outside world. The explanation was not very clear for Mr Browne grinned and said:

—I like that idea very much but wouldn't a comfortable spring bed do them as well as a coffin?

—The coffin, said Mary Jane, is to remind them of their last end.

As the subject had grown lugubrious it was buried in a silence of the table during which Mrs Malins could be heard saying to her neighbour in an indistinct undertone:

—They are very good men, the monks, very pious men.

The raisins and almonds and figs and apples and oranges and chocolates and sweets were now passed about the table and Aunt Julia invited all the guests to have either port or sherry. At first Mr Bartell D'Arcy refused to take either but one of his neighbours nudged him and whispered something to him upon which he allowed his glass to be filled. Gradually as the last glasses were being filled the conversation ceased. A pause followed, broken only by the noise of the wine and by unsettlings of chairs. The Misses Morkan, all three, looked down at the

---

*The Abbey of St. Bernard de Trappe, in County Waterford; Freddy is heading there to "dry out."

tablecloth. Someone coughed once or twice and then a few gentlemen patted the table gently as a signal for silence. The silence came and Gabriel pushed back his chair and stood up.

The patting at once grew louder in encouragement and then ceased altogether. Gabriel leaned his ten trembling fingers on the tablecloth and smiled nervously at the company. Meeting a row of upturned faces he raised his eyes to the chandelier. The piano was playing a waltz tune and he could hear the skirts sweeping against the drawing-room door. People, perhaps, were standing in the snow on the quay outside, gazing up at the lighted windows and listening to the waltz music. The air was pure there. In the distance lay the park where the trees were weighted with snow. The Wellington Monument wore a gleaming cap of snow that flashed westward over the white field of Fifteen Acres.*

He began:

—Ladies and Gentlemen,

—It has fallen to my lot this evening, as in years past, to perform a very pleasing task but a task for which I am afraid my poor powers as a speaker are all too inadequate.

—No, no! said Mr Browne.

—But, however that may be, I can only ask you to-night to take the will for the deed and to lend me your attention for a few moments while I endeavour to express to you in words what my feelings are on this occasion.

—Ladies and Gentlemen, it is not the first time that we have gathered together under this hospitable roof, around this hospitable board. It is not the first time that we have been the recipients—or perhaps, I had better say, the victims—of the hospitality of certain good ladies.

He made a circle in the air with his arm and paused. Everyone laughed or smiled at Aunt Kate and Aunt Julia and Mary Jane who all turned crimson with pleasure. Gabriel went on more boldly:

—I feel more strongly with every recurring year that our country has no tradition which does it so much honour and which it should guard so jealously as that of its hospitality. It is a tradition that is unique as far as my experience goes (and I have visited not a few places abroad) among the modern nations. Some would say, perhaps, that with us it is rather a failing than anything to be boasted of. But granted even that,

---

*Misleading name for a 200-acre portion of the 1,760-acre Phoenix Park, used for military exercises.

it is, to my mind, a princely failing, and one that I trust will long be cultivated among us. Of one thing, at least, I am sure. As long as this one roof shelters the good ladies aforesaid—and I wish from my heart it may do so for many and many a long year to come—the tradition of genuine warm-hearted courteous Irish hospitality, which our forefathers have handed down to us and which we in turn must hand down to our descendants, is still alive among us.

A hearty murmur of assent ran round the table. It shot through Gabriel's mind that Miss Ivors was not there and that she had gone away discourteously: and he said with confidence in himself:

—Ladies and Gentlemen,

—A new generation is growing up in our midst, a generation actuated by new ideas and new principles. It is serious and enthusiastic for these new ideas and its enthusiasm, even when it is misdirected, is, I believe, in the main sincere. But we are living in a sceptical and, if I may use the phrase, a thought-tormented age: and sometimes I fear that this new generation, educated or hypereducated as it is, will lack those qualities of humanity, of hospitality, of kindly humour which belonged to an older day. Listening to-night to the names of all those great singers of the past it seemed to me, I must confess, that we were living in a less spacious age. Those days might, without exaggeration, be called spacious days: and if they are gone beyond recall let us hope, at least, that in gatherings such as this we shall still speak of them with pride and affection, still cherish in our hearts the memory of those dead and gone great ones whose fame the world will not willingly let die.

—Hear, hear! said Mr Browne loudly.

—But yet, continued Gabriel, his voice falling into a softer inflection, there are always in gatherings such as this sadder thoughts that will recur to our minds: thoughts of the past, of youth, of changes, of absent faces that we miss here to-night. Our path through life is strewn with many such sad memories: and were we to brood upon them always we could not find the heart to go on bravely with our work among the living. We have all of us living duties and living affections which claim, and rightly claim, our strenuous endeavours.

—Therefore, I will not linger on the past. I will not let any gloomy moralising intrude upon us here to-night. Here we are gathered together for a brief moment from the bustle and rush of our everyday routine. We are met here as friends, in the spirit of good-fellowship, as colleagues, also to a certain extent, in the true spirit of *camaraderie,* and as the guests of—what shall I call them?—the Three Graces* of the Dublin musical world.

The table burst into applause and laughter at this allusion. Aunt Julia vainly asked each of her neighbours in turn to tell her what Gabriel had said.

—He says we are the Three Graces, Aunt Julia, said Mary Jane.

Aunt Julia did not understand but she looked up, smiling, at Gabriel, who continued in the same vein:

—Ladies and Gentlemen,

—I will not attempt to play to-night the part that Paris played on another occasion. I will not attempt to choose between them. The task would be an invidious one and one beyond my poor powers. For when I view them in turn, whether it be our chief hostess herself, whose good heart, whose too good heart, has become a byword with all who know her, or her sister, who seems to be gifted with perennial youth and whose singing must have been a surprise and revelation to us all to-night, or, last but not least, when I consider our youngest hostess, talented, cheerful, hard-working and the best of nieces, I confess, Ladies and Gentlemen, that I do not know to which of them I should award the prize.

Gabriel glanced down at his aunts and, seeing the large smile on Aunt Julia's face and the tears which had risen to Aunt Kate's eyes, hastened to his close. He raised his glass of port gallantly, while every member of the company fingered a glass expectantly, and said loudly:

—Let us toast them all three together. Let us drink to their health, wealth, long life, happiness and prosperity and may they long continue to hold the proud and self-won position which they hold in their profession and the position of honour and affection which they hold in our hearts.

All the guests stood up, glass in hand, and turning towards the three seated ladies, sang in unison, with Mr Browne as leader:

> *For they are jolly gay fellows,*
> *For they are jolly gay fellows,*
> *For they are jolly gay fellows*
> *Which nobody can deny.*

Aunt Kate was making frank use of her handkerchief and even Aunt Julia seemed moved. Freddy Malins beat time with his pudding-fork

---

*In Greek mythology, the daughters of Zeus and Eurynome—Aglaia (brilliance), Thalia (bloom), and Euphrosyne (joy)—embodied refinement.

and the singers turned towards one another, as if in melodious conference, while they sang with emphasis:

> *Unless he tells a lie,*
> *Unless he tells a lie.*

Then, turning once more towards their hostesses, they sang:

> *For they are jolly gay fellows,*
> *For they are jolly gay fellows,*
> *For they are jolly gay fellows,*
> *Which nobody can deny.*

The acclamation which followed was taken up beyond the door of
the supper-room by many of the other guests and renewed time after
time, Freddy Malins acting as officer with his fork on high.

      *   *   *   *   *   *   *   *   *

The piercing morning air came into the hall where they were standing so that Aunt Kate said:

—Close the door, somebody. Mrs Malins will get her death of cold.

—Browne is out there, Aunt Kate, said Mary Jane.

—Browne is everywhere, said Aunt Kate, lowering her voice.

Mary Jane laughed at her tone.

—Really, she said archly, he is very attentive.

—He has been laid on here like the gas, said Aunt Kate in the same
tone, all during the Christmas.

She laughed herself this time good-humouredly and then added
quickly:

—But tell him to come in, Mary Jane, and close the door. I hope to
goodness he didn't hear me.

At that moment the hall-door was opened and Mr Browne came in
from the doorstep, laughing as if his heart would break. He was dressed
in a long green overcoat with mock astrakhan* cuffs and collar and wore
on his head an oval fur cap. He pointed down the snow-covered quay
from where the sound of shrill prolonged whistling was borne in.

—Teddy will have all the cabs in Dublin out, he said.

---

*Material made from the wool of young lambs.

Gabriel advanced from the little pantry behind the office, struggling into his overcoat and, looking round the hall, said:

—Gretta not down yet?

—She's getting on her things, Gabriel, said Aunt Kate.

—Who's playing up there? asked Gabriel.

—Nobody. They're all gone.

—O no, Aunt Kate, said Mary Jane. Bartell D'Arcy and Miss O'Callaghan aren't gone yet.

—Someone is fooling at the piano anyhow, said Gabriel.

Mary Jane glanced at Gabriel and Mr Browne and said with a shiver:

—It makes me feel cold to look at you two gentlemen muffled up like that. I wouldn't like to face your journey home at this hour.

—I'd like nothing better this minute, said Mr Browne stoutly, than a rattling fine walk in the country or a fast drive with a good spanking goer between the shafts.

—We used to have a very good horse and trap at home, said Aunt Julia sadly.

—The never-to-be-forgotten Johnny, said Mary Jane, laughing.

Aunt Kate and Gabriel laughed too.

—Why, what was wonderful about Johnny? asked Mr Browne.

—The late lamented Patrick Morkan, our grandfather, that is, explained Gabriel, commonly known in his later years as the old gentleman, was a glue-boiler.

—O, now, Gabriel, said Aunt Kate, laughing, he had a starch mill.

—Well, glue or starch, said Gabriel, the old gentleman had a horse by the name of Johnny. And Johnny used to work in the old gentleman's mill, walking round and round in order to drive the mill. That was all very well; but now comes the tragic part about Johnny. One fine day the old gentleman thought he'd like to drive out with the quality to a military review in the park.

—The Lord have mercy on his soul, said Aunt Kate compassionately.

—Amen, said Gabriel. So the old gentleman, as I said, harnessed Johnny and put on his very best tall hat and his very best stock collar and drove out in grand style from his ancestral mansion somewhere near Back Lane, I think.

Everyone laughed, even Mrs Malins, at Gabriel's manner and Aunt Kate said:

—O, now, Gabriel, he didn't live in Back Lane, really. Only the mill was there.

—Out from the mansion of his forefathers, continued Gabriel, he drove with Johnny. And everything went on beautifully until Johnny came in sight of King Billy's statue:* and whether he fell in love with the horse King Billy sits on or whether he thought he was back again in the mill, anyhow he began to walk round the statue.

Gabriel paced in a circle round the hall in his goloshes amid the laughter of the others.

—Round and round he went, said Gabriel, and the old gentleman, who was a very pompous old gentleman, was highly indignant. *Go on, sir! What do you mean, sir! Johnny! Johnny! Most extraordinary conduct! Can't understand the horse!*

The peals of laughter which followed Gabriel's imitation of the incident was interrupted by a resounding knock at the hall door. Mary Jane ran to open it and let in Freddy Malins. Freddy Malins, with his hat well back on his head and his shoulders humped with cold, was puffing and steaming after his exertions.

—I could only get one cab, he said.

—O, we'll find another along the quay, said Gabriel.

—Yes, said Aunt Kate. Better not keep Mrs Malins standing in the draught.

Mrs Malins was helped down the front steps by her son and Mr Browne and, after many manoeuvres, hoisted into the cab. Freddy Malins clambered in after her and spent a long time settling her on the seat, Mr Browne helping him with advice. At last she was settled comfortably and Freddy Malins invited Mr Browne into the cab. There was a good deal of confused talk, and then Mr Browne got into the cab. The cabman settled his rug over his knees, and bent down for the address. The confusion grew greater and the cabman was directed differently by Freddy Malins and Mr Browne, each of whom had his head out through a window of the cab. The difficulty was to know where to drop Mr Browne along the route, and Aunt Kate, Aunt Julia and Mary Jane helped the discussion from the door-step with cross-directions and contradictions and abundance of laughter. As for Freddy Malins he was speechless with laughter. He popped his head in and out of the window every moment to the great danger of his hat, and told his mother how the discussion was progressing, till at last Mr Browne shouted to the bewildered cabman above the din of everybody's laughter:

—Do you know Trinity College?

—Yes, sir, said the cabman.

---

*Statue of King William III, which stands on College Green, in front of Trinity College.

—Well, drive bang up against Trinity College gates, said Mr Browne, and then we'll tell you where to go. You understand now?

—Yes, sir, said the cabman.

—Make like a bird for Trinity College.

—Right, sir, said the cabman.

The horse was whipped up and the cab rattled off along the quay amid a chorus of laughter and adieus.

Gabriel had not gone to the door with the others. He was in a dark part of the hall gazing up the staircase. A woman was standing near the top of the first flight, in the shadow also. He could not see her face but he could see the terra-cotta and salmon-pink panels of her skirt which the shadow made appear black and white. It was his wife. She was lean-ing on the banisters, listening to something. Gabriel was surprised at her stillness and strained his ear to listen also. But he could hear little save the noise of laughter and dispute on the front steps, a few chords struck on the piano and a few notes of a man's voice singing.

He stood still in the gloom of the hall, trying to catch the air that the voice was singing and gazing up at his wife. There was grace and mystery in her attitude as if she were a symbol of something. He asked himself what is a woman standing on the stairs in the shadow, listening to distant music, a symbol of. If he were a painter he would paint her in that attitude. Her blue felt hat would show off the bronze of her hair against the darkness and the dark panels of her skirt would show off the light ones. *Distant Music* he would call the picture if he were a painter.

The hall-door was closed; and Aunt Kate, Aunt Julia and Mary Jane came down the hall, still laughing.

—Well, isn't Freddy terrible? said Mary Jane. He's really terrible.

Gabriel said nothing but pointed up the stairs towards where his wife was standing. Now that the hall-door was closed the voice and the piano could be heard more clearly. Gabriel held up his hand for them to be silent. The song seemed to be in the old Irish tonality and the singer seemed uncertain both of his words and of his voice. The voice, made plaintive by distance and by the singer's hoarseness, faintly illu-minated the cadence of the air with words expressing grief:

> *O, the rain falls on my heavy locks*
> *And the dew wets my skin,*
> *My babe lies cold . . .*

—O, exclaimed Mary Jane. It's Bartell D'Arcy singing and he wouldn't sing all the night. O, I'll get him to sing a song before he goes.

—O, do, Mary Jane, said Aunt Kate.

Mary Jane brushed past the others and ran to the staircase, but before she reached it the singing stopped and the piano was closed abruptly.

—O, what a pity! she cried. Is he coming down, Gretta?

Gabriel heard his wife answer yes and saw her come down towards them. A few steps behind her were Mr Bartell D'Arcy and Miss O'Callaghan.

—O, Mr D'Arcy, cried Mary Jane, it's downright mean of you to break off like that when we were all in raptures listening to you.

—I have been at him all the evening, said Miss O'Callaghan, and Mrs Conroy, too, and he told us he had a dreadful cold and couldn't sing.

—O, Mr D'Arcy, said Aunt Kate, now that was a great fib to tell.

—Can't you see that I'm as hoarse as a crow? said Mr D'Arcy roughly.

He went into the pantry hastily and put on his overcoat. The others, taken aback by his rude speech, could find nothing to say. Aunt Kate wrinkled her brows and made signs to the others to drop the subject. Mr D'Arcy stood swathing his neck carefully and frowning.

—It's the weather, said Aunt Julia, after a pause.

—Yes, everybody has colds, said Aunt Kate readily, everybody.

—They say, said Mary Jane, we haven't had snow like it for thirty years, and I read this morning in the newspapers that the snow is general all over Ireland.

—I love the look of snow, said Aunt Julia sadly.

—So do I, said Miss O'Callaghan. I think Christmas is never really Christmas unless we have the snow on the ground.

—But poor Mr D'Arcy doesn't like the snow, said Aunt Kate, smiling.

Mr D'Arcy came from the pantry, fully swathed and buttoned, and in a repentant tone told them the history of his cold. Everyone gave him advice and said it was a great pity and urged him to be very careful of his throat in the night air. Gabriel watched his wife, who did not join in the conversation. She was standing right under the dusty fanlight* and the flame of the gas lit up the rich bronze of her hair, which he had seen her drying at the fire a few days before. She was in the same attitude and seemed unaware of the talk about her. At last she turned towards them and Gabriel saw that there was colour on her cheeks and that her eyes were shining. A sudden tide of joy went leaping out of his heart.

---

*Decorative window above the front door of a home.

—Mr D'Arcy, she said, what is the name of that song you were singing?

—It's called *The Lass of Aughrim,* said Mr D'Arcy, but I couldn't remember it properly. Why? Do you know it?

—*The Lass of Aughrim,* she repeated. I couldn't think of the name.

—It's a very nice air, said Mary Jane. I'm sorry you were not in voice to-night.

—Now, Mary Jane, said Aunt Kate, don't annoy Mr D'Arcy. I won't have him annoyed.

Seeing that all were ready to start she shepherded them to the door, where good-night was said:

—Well, good-night, Aunt Kate, and thanks for the pleasant evening.

—Good-night, Gabriel. Good-night, Gretta!

—Good-night, Aunt Kate, and thanks ever so much. Good-night, Aunt Julia.

—O, good-night, Gretta, I didn't see you.

—Good-night, Mr D'Arcy. Good-night, Miss O'Callaghan.

—Good-night, Miss Morkan.

—Good-night, again.

—Good-night, all. Safe home.

—Good-night. Good-night.

The morning was still dark. A dull, yellow light brooded over the houses and the river; and the sky seemed to be descending. It was slushy underfoot; and only streaks and patches of snow lay on the roofs, on the parapets of the quay and on the area railings. The lamps were still burning redly in the murky air and, across the river, the palace of the Four Courts* stood out menacingly against the heavy sky.

She was walking on before him with Mr Bartell D'Arcy, her shoes in a brown parcel tucked under one arm and her hand holding her skirt up from the slush. She had no longer any grace of attitude, but Gabriel's eyes were still bright with happiness. The blood went bounding along his veins; and the thoughts went rioting through his brain, proud, joyful, tender, valorous.

She was walking on before him so lightly and so erect that he longed to run after her noiselessly, catch her by the shoulders and say something foolish and affectionate into her ear. She seemed to him so frail that he longed to defend her against something and then to be alone with her. Moments of their secret life together burst like stars upon his memory. A

---

*Complex of legal buildings on the north side of the Liffey.

heliotrope envelope was lying beside his breakfast-cup and he was caressing it with his hand. Birds were twittering in the ivy and the sunny web of the curtain was shimmering along the floor: he could not eat for happiness. They were standing on the crowded platform and he was placing a ticket inside the warm palm of her glove. He was standing with her in the cold, looking in through a grated window at a man making bottles in a roaring furnace. It was very cold. Her face, fragrant in the cold air, was quite close to his; and suddenly he called out to the man at the furnace:

—Is the fire hot, sir?

But the man could not hear with the noise of the furnace. It was just as well. He might have answered rudely.

A wave of yet more tender joy escaped from his heart and went coursing in warm flood along his arteries. Like the tender fire of stars moments of their life together, that no one knew of or would ever know of, broke upon and illumined his memory. He longed to recall to her those moments, to make her forget the years of their dull existence together and remember only their moments of ecstasy. For the years, he felt, had not quenched his soul or hers. Their children, his writing, her household cares had not quenched all their souls' tender fire. In one letter that he had written to her then he had said: *Why is it that words like these seem to me so dull and cold? Is it because there is no word tender enough to be your name?*

Like distant music these words that he had written years before were borne towards him from the past. He longed to be alone with her. When the others had gone away, when he and she were in the room in the hotel, then they would be alone together. He would call her softly:

—Gretta!

Perhaps she would not hear at once: she would be undressing. Then something in his voice would strike her. She would turn and look at him. . . .

At the corner of Winetavern Street they met a cab. He was glad of its rattling noise as it saved him from conversation. She was looking out of the window and seemed tired. The others spoke only a few words, pointing out some building or street. The horse galloped along wearily under the murky morning sky, dragging his old rattling box after his heels, and Gabriel was again in a cab with her, galloping to catch the boat, galloping to their honeymoon.

As the cab drove across O'Connell Bridge[7] Miss O'Callaghan said:

—They say you never cross O'Connell Bridge without seeing a white horse.

—I see a white man this time, said Gabriel.

—Where? asked Mr Bartell D'Arcy.

Gabriel pointed to the statue, on which lay patches of snow. Then he nodded familiarly to it and waved his hand.

—Good-night, Dan, he said gaily.

When the cab drew up before the hotel, Gabriel jumped out and, in spite of Mr Bartell D'Arcy's protest, paid the driver. He gave the man a shilling over his fare. The man saluted and said:

—A prosperous New Year to you, sir.

—The same to you, said Gabriel cordially.

She leaned for a moment on his arm in getting out of the cab and while standing at the curbstone, bidding the others good-night. She leaned lightly on his arm, as lightly as when she had danced with him a few hours before. He had felt proud and happy then, happy that she was his, proud of her grace and wifely carriage. But now, after the kindling again of so many memories, the first touch of her body, musical and strange and perfumed, sent through him a keen pang of lust. Under cover of her silence he pressed her arm closely to his side; and, as they stood at the hotel door, he felt that they had escaped from their lives and duties, escaped from home and friends and run away together with wild and radiant hearts to a new adventure.

An old man was dozing in a great hooded chair in the hall. He lit a candle in the office and went before them to the stairs. They followed him in silence, their feet falling in soft thuds on the thickly carpeted stairs. She mounted the stairs behind the porter, her head bowed in the ascent, her frail shoulders curved as with a burden, her skirt girt tightly about her. He could have flung his arms about her hips and held her still, for his arms were trembling with desire to seize her and only the stress of his nails against the palms of his hands held the wild impulse of his body in check. The porter halted on the stairs to settle his guttering candle. They halted, too, on the steps below him. In the silence Gabriel could hear the falling of the molten wax into the tray and the thumping of his own heart against his ribs.

The porter led them along a corridor and opened a door. Then he set his unstable candle down on a toilet-table and asked at what hour they were to be called in the morning.

—Eight, said Gabriel.

The porter pointed to the tap of the electric-light and began a muttered apology, but Gabriel cut him short.

—We don't want any light. We have light enough from the street.

And I say, he added, pointing to the candle, you might remove that handsome article, like a good man.

The porter took up his candle again, but slowly, for he was surprised by such a novel idea. Then he mumbled good-night and went out. Gabriel shot the lock to.

A ghastly light from the street lamp lay in a long shaft from one window to the door. Gabriel threw his overcoat and hat on a couch and crossed the room towards the window. He looked down into the street in order that his emotion might calm a little. Then he turned and leaned against a chest of drawers with his back to the light. She had taken off her hat and cloak and was standing before a large swinging mirror, unhooking her waist. Gabriel paused for a few moments, watching her, and then said:

—Gretta!

She turned away from the mirror slowly and walked along the shaft of light towards him. Her face looked so serious and weary that the words would not pass Gabriel's lips. No, it was not the moment yet.

—You looked tired, he said.

—I am a little, she answered.

—You don't feel ill or weak?

—No, tired: that's all.

She went on to the window and stood there, looking out. Gabriel waited again and then fearing that diffidence was about to conquer him, he said abruptly:

—By the way, Gretta!

—What is it?

—You know that poor fellow Malins? he said quickly.

—Yes. What about him?

—Well, poor fellow, he's a decent sort of chap, after all, continued Gabriel in a false voice. He gave me back that sovereign I lent him, and I didn't expect it, really. It's a pity he wouldn't keep away from that Browne, because he's not a bad fellow, really.

He was trembling now with annoyance. Why did she seem so abstracted? He did not know how he could begin. Was she annoyed, too, about something? If she would only turn to him or come to him of her own accord! To take her as she was would be brutal. No, he must see some ardour in her eyes first. He longed to be master of her strange mood.

—When did you lend him the pound? she asked, after a pause.

Gabriel strove to restrain himself from breaking out into brutal language about the sottish Malins and his pound. He longed to cry to her from his soul, to crush her body against his, to overmaster her. But he said:

—O, at Christmas, when he opened that little Christmas-card shop in Henry Street.

He was in such a fever of rage and desire that he did not hear her come from the window. She stood before him for an instant, looking at him strangely. Then, suddenly raising herself on tiptoe and resting her hands lightly on his shoulders, she kissed him.

—You are a very generous person, Gabriel, she said.

Gabriel, trembling with delight at her sudden kiss and at the quaintness of her phrase, put his hands on her hair and began smoothing it back, scarcely touching it with his fingers. The washing had made it fine and brilliant. His heart was brimming over with happiness. Just when he was wishing for it she had come to him of her own accord. Perhaps her thoughts had been running with his. Perhaps she had felt the impetuous desire that was in him, and then the yielding mood had come upon her. Now that she had fallen to him so easily, he wondered why he had been so diffident.

He stood, holding her head between his hands. Then, slipping one arm swiftly about her body and drawing her towards him, he said softly:

—Gretta, dear, what are you thinking about?

She did not answer nor yield wholly to his arm. He said again, softly:

—Tell me what it is, Gretta. I think I know what is the matter. Do I know?

She did not answer at once. Then she said in an outburst of tears:

—O, I am thinking about that song, *The Lass of Aughrim.*

She broke loose from him and ran to the bed and, throwing her arms across the bed-rail, hid her face. Gabriel stood stock-still for a moment in astonishment and then followed her. As he passed in the way of the cheval-glass* he caught sight of himself in full length, his broad, well-filled shirt-front, the face whose expression always puzzled him when he saw it in a mirror, and his glimmering gilt-rimmed eyeglasses. He halted a few paces from her and said:

—What about the song? Why does that make you cry?

She raised her head from her arms and dried her eyes with the back of her hand like a child. A kinder note than he had intended went into his voice.

---

*Full-length mirror with a pivot through its central axis.

—Why, Gretta? he asked.

—I am thinking about a person long ago who used to sing that song.

—And who was the person long ago? asked Gabriel, smiling.

—It was a person I used to know in Galway when I was living with my grandmother, she said.

The smile passed away from Gabriel's face. A dull anger began to gather again at the back of his mind and the dull fires of his lust began to glow angrily in his veins.

—Someone you were in love with? he asked ironically.

—It was a young boy I used to know, she answered, named Michael Furey. He used to sing that song, *The Lass of Aughrim*. He was very delicate.

Gabriel was silent. He did not wish her to think that he was interested in this delicate boy.

—I can see him so plainly, she said, after a moment. Such eyes as he had: big, dark eyes! And such an expression in them—an expression!

—O, then, you are in love with him? said Gabriel.

—I used to go out walking with him, she said, when I was in Galway.

A thought flew across Gabriel's mind.

—Perhaps that was why you wanted to go to Galway with that Ivors girl? he said coldly.

She looked at him and asked in surprise:

—What for?

Her eyes made Gabriel feel awkward. He shrugged his shoulders and said:

—How do I know? To see him, perhaps.

She looked away from him along the shaft of light towards the window in silence.

—He is dead, she said at length. He died when he was only seventeen. Isn't it a terrible thing to die so young as that?

—What was he? asked Gabriel, still ironically.

—He was in the gasworks, she said.

Gabriel felt humiliated by the failure of his irony and by the evocation of this figure from the dead, a boy in the gasworks. While he had been full of memories of their secret life together, full of tenderness and joy and desire, she had been comparing him in her mind with another. A shameful consciousness of his own person assailed him. He saw himself as a ludicrous figure, acting as pennyboy for his aunts, a nervous, well-meaning sentimentalist, orating to vulgarians and idealising his own clownish lusts, the pitiable fatuous fellow he had caught a glimpse of in the mirror. Instinctively he turned his back more to the light lest she might see the shame that burned upon his forehead.

He tried to keep up his tone of cold interrogation, but his voice when he spoke was humble and indifferent.

—I suppose you were in love with this Michael Furey, Gretta, he said.

—I was great with him at that time, she said.

Her voice was veiled and sad. Gabriel, feeling now how vain it would be to try to lead her whither he had purposed, caressed one of her hands and said, also sadly:

—And what did he die of so young, Gretta? Consumption, was it?

—I think he died for me, she answered.

A vague terror seized Gabriel at this answer, as if, at that hour when he had hoped to triumph, some impalpable and vindictive being was coming against him, gathering forces against him in its vague world. But he shook himself free of it with an effort of reason and continued to caress her hand. He did not question her again, for he felt that she would tell him of herself. Her hand was warm and moist: it did not respond to his touch, but he continued to caress it just as he had caressed her first letter to him that spring morning.

—It was in the winter, she said, about the beginning of the winter when I was going to leave my grandmother's and come up here to the convent.* And he was ill at the time in his lodgings in Galway and wouldn't be let out, and his people in Oughterard† were written to. He was in decline, they said, or something like that. I never knew rightly.

She paused for a moment and sighed.

—Poor fellow, she said. He was very fond of me and he was such a gentle boy. We used to go out together, walking, you know, Gabriel, like the way they do in the country. He was going to study singing only for his health. He had a very good voice, poor Michael Furey.

—Well; and then? asked Gabriel.

—And then when it came to the time for me to leave Galway and come up to the convent he was much worse and I wouldn't be let see him so I wrote him a letter saying I was going up to Dublin and would be back in the summer, and hoping he would be better then.

She paused for a moment to get her voice under control, and then went on:

—Then the night before I left, I was in my grandmother's house in

---

*Convent school.

†Small town about 20 miles outside Galway.

Nuns' Island, packing up, and I heard gravel thrown up against the window. The window was so wet I couldn't see, so I ran downstairs as I was and slipped out the back into the garden and there was the poor fellow at the end of the garden, shivering.

—And did you not tell him to go back? asked Gabriel.

—I implored of him to go home at once and told him he would get his death in the rain. But he said he did not want to live. I can see his eyes as well as well! He was standing at the end of the wall where there was a tree.

—And did he go home? asked Gabriel.

—Yes, he went home. And when I was only a week in the convent he died and he was buried in Oughterard, where his people came from. O, the day I heard that, that he was dead!

She stopped, choking with sobs, and, overcome by emotion, flung herself face downward on the bed, sobbing in the quilt. Gabriel held her hand for a moment longer, irresolutely, and then, shy of intruding on her grief, let it fall gently and walked quietly to the window.

She was fast asleep.

Gabriel, leaning on his elbow, looked for a few moments unresentfully on her tangled hair and half-open mouth, listening to her deep-drawn breath. So she had had that romance in her life: a man had died for her sake. It hardly pained him now to think how poor a part he, her husband, had played in her life. He watched her while she slept, as though he and she had never lived together as man and wife. His curious eyes rested long upon her face and on her hair: and, as he thought of what she must have been then, in that time of her first girlish beauty, a strange, friendly pity for her entered his soul. He did not like to say even to himself that her face was no longer beautiful, but he knew that it was no longer the face for which Michael Furey had braved death.

Perhaps she had not told him all the story. His eyes moved to the chair over which she had thrown some of her clothes. A petticoat string dangled to the floor. One boot stood upright, its limp upper fallen down: the fellow of it lay upon its side. He wondered at his riot of emotions of an hour before. From what had it proceeded? From his aunt's supper, from his own foolish speech, from the wine and dancing, the merry-making when saying good-night in the hall, the pleasure of the walk along the river in the snow. Poor Aunt Julia! She, too, would soon be a shade with the shade of Patrick Morkan and his horse. He had caught that haggard look upon her face for a moment when she was singing *Arrayed for the Bridal*. Soon, perhaps, he would be sitting in that same drawing-room, dressed in black, his silk hat on his knees. The blinds would be drawn down and Aunt Kate would be sitting beside him, crying and blowing her nose and telling him how Julia had died. He would cast about in his mind for some words that might console her, and would find only lame and useless ones. Yes, yes: that would happen very soon.

The air of the room chilled his shoulders. He stretched himself cautiously along under the sheets and lay down beside his wife. One by one, they were all becoming shades. Better pass boldly into that other world, in the full glory of some passion, than fade and wither dismally with age. He thought of how she who lay beside him had locked in her heart for so many years that image of her lover's eyes when he had told her that he did not wish to live.

Generous tears filled Gabriel's eyes. He had never felt like that himself towards any woman, but he knew that such a feeling must be love. The tears gathered more thickly in his eyes and in the partial darkness he imagined he saw the form of a young man standing under a dripping tree. Other forms were near. His soul had approached that region where dwell the vast hosts of the dead. He was conscious of, but could not apprehend, their wayward and flickering existence. His own identity was fading out into a grey impalpable world: the solid world itself, which these dead had one time reared and lived in, was dissolving and dwindling.

A few light taps upon the pane made him turn to the window. It had begun to snow again. He watched sleepily the flakes, silver and dark, falling obliquely against the lamplight. The time had come for him to set out on his journey westward. Yes, the newspapers were right: snow was general all over Ireland. It was falling on every part of the dark central plain, on the treeless hills, falling softly upon the Bog of Allen* and, farther westward, softly falling into the dark mutinous Shannon† waves. It was falling, too, upon every part of the lonely churchyard on the hill where Michael Furey lay buried. It lay thickly drifted on the crooked crosses and headstones, on the spears of the little gate, on the barren thorns. His soul swooned slowly as he heard the snow falling faintly through the universe and faintly falling, like the descent of their last end, upon all the living and the dead.

---

*Large (370-square-mile) turf (peat) bog west of Dublin; near Clongowes Wood School, which Stephen Dedalus attends in *A Portrait of the Artist as a Young Man*.
†The estuary of the River Shannon, on the southwestern coast of Ireland.

ENDNOTES

A Portrait of the Artist as a Young Man

1. (p. 4) *Michael Davitt . . . Parnell:* Socialist thinker Michael Davitt (1846–1906) founded the Irish Land League, a group dedicated to winning a measure of independence for the Irish. Charles Stewart Parnell (1846–1891), sometimes called "the Chief" or "the uncrowned king of Ireland," was the public face of the movement for Irish independence; he was a member of the British parliament (1875–1891), until an adultery scandal (the subject of much acrimony in the Christmas dinner scene, below) forced him from office.

2. (p. 10) *the higher line fellows:* Students at Clongowes were placed by age into three groups. The higher line was further divided into poetry and rhetoric; the lower line, into second and first grammar. The third line, for the youngest boys (including Stephen), comprised elements and third of grammar.

3. (p. 23) *he had got those three cramped fingers making a birthday present for Queen Victoria:* This quip is based in Joyce's family history. A family friend, forced to pick oakum (recycled hemp) while imprisoned for political activism, became crippled in three fingers of his right hand.

4. (p. 31) *The Paris Funds! Mr Fox! Kitty O'Shea:* The "Paris funds" were funds under the control of the Irish National League (the successor to the Irish Land League) that Parnell was accused of misusing. "Mr Fox" was a pseudonym used by Parnell to hide his affair with Kitty O'Shea, wife of Captain William Henry O'Shea. When Parnell was named in a divorce action by Captain O'Shea, on Christmas Eve, 1899, his political career quickly began to unravel.

5. (p. 35)—*Didn't the bishops of Ireland betray us. . . . And didn't they dishonour the ashes of Terence Bellew MacManus?:* Mr Casey provides a catalog of Catholic clergy who, he believes, betrayed their country; compare, on p. 28, Mr Dedalus's slurs on two archbishops. Terence MacManus (1823–1861) was an Irish nationalist deported for treason; his body was returned to Ireland for burial by the Fenians, a gesture opposed by the church (in particular, Cardinal Paul Cullen; see just below).

6. (p. 54) *The Count of Monte Cristo:* In this 1844 romantic novel by Alexandre Dumas père, Edmond Dantes, prevented by intrigues from marrying Mercedes, returns as the Count of Monte Cristo to avenge his dispossession. Vowing not to eat in the house of his enemy, he refuses Mercedes's offer of muscatel grapes.

7. (p. 69)—*Here. It's about the Creator and the soul. . . . I meant* without a possibility of ever reaching: Stephen's heresy is in suggesting not that the soul can never reach the Creator: This is an orthodox position, affirming our inability

to effect our own salvation without God's grace. But Stephen more radically suggests that we can never draw nearer to God through our own efforts, which contradicts Catholic teaching.

8. (p. 69) *Cardinal Newman:* John Henry Cardinal Newman (1801–1890), a convert to Catholicism, wrote *Apologia pro vita sua* (1864; *A Defense of His Life*) and *The Idea of a University* (1873). He served as rector of University College Dublin, which Stephen later attends, from 1854 to 1858.

9. (p. 91) . . . *the fountains of sanctifying grace having ceased to refresh his soul*. . . . *he might hope wearily to win for himself some measure of actual grace:* Sanctifying grace is the habitual, "background" grace against which the Christian's life plays out; actual grace is displayed in specific moments of God's reaching out to aid the sinner.

10. (p. 92) *Quasi cedrus exaltata sum . . . quasi myrrha electa dedi suavitatem odoris:* This is a quotation from Ecclesiasticus 24:17–20: "I was exalted like a cedar in Lebanon, and as a cypress tree on Mount Sion. I was exalted like a palm tree in Gades, and as a rose plant in Jericho. As a fair olive tree in the plains, and as a plane tree by the water in the streets was I exalted. I gave a sweet smell like cinnamon and aromatical balm. I yielded a sweet odor like the best myrrh" (Douay version).

11. (p. 94) *first beatitude . . . second beatitude:* The beatitudes are the blessings pronounced by Jesus in the Sermon on the Mount (Matthew 5:3–4): "Blessed are the poor in spirit: for theirs is the kingdom of heaven. Blessed are the meek: for they shall possess the land" (Douay version).

12. (pp. 95–96)—*Remember only thy last things and thou shalt not sin for ever:* The citation is wrong: The verse occurs not in Ecclesiastes, but in Ecclesiasticus, an Old Testament book that is held to be apocryphal by Protestants but that appears in the Douay (Roman Catholic) version of the Bible. Joyce adapted a good deal of the text for these retreat sermons from Italian Jesuit Giovanni Pietro Pinamonti's *Hell Opened to Christians, to Caution Them from Entering into It* (1688).

13. (p. 123) *confessionals:* In the Roman Catholic Church, booths called confessionals are set apart for the hearing of confessions by the priest. Commonly, the booth is divided into three sections, with the priest sitting in the middle compartment, and penitents kneeling in either of the outside compartments; the priest listens to the confession of one penitent by sliding open a wooden divider, exposing a screen between himself and the penitent. The priest respects the anonymity of the penitent by focusing his eyes straight ahead, rather than looking through the screen.

14. (p. 134) *the Dominican and Franciscan orders:* The Dominicans, or Order of Friars Preachers, was founded by Saint Dominic, around 1215, for the salvation of souls. The Franciscans, or Order of Friars Minor, was founded by Saint Francis of Assisi in 1209; its members take a vow of poverty.

15. (p. 141) *fall:* To "fall" is to move from a state of grace, in which salvation is se-

cured, to one of damnation, through sin. The story of the Garden of Eden in Genesis 3 is the story of the archetypal Fall of humankind, "man's first disobedience," as Milton puts it at the start of *Paradise Lost*.

16. (p. 148) *his strange name seemed to him a prophecy:* Both Stephen's given and family names are rich with allusion. Stephen is the name of the first martyr of the Christian church, who was stoned to death for his adherence to the teachings of Christ. Dædalus was the legendary Greek labyrinth-maker, who crafted wax wings for himself and his son, Icarus, to escape from their imprisonment on Crete; Icarus flew too close to the sun, where his wings melted, and he plummeted to his death in the sea.

17. (p. 166) *with the same eyes as the elder brother in the parable may have turned on the prodigal:* Luke 15:11–32 gives the story of the prodigal son. In the parable, told by Jesus, the older brother who has remained faithful to his father is infuriated when the dissolute, or "prodigal," younger brother is welcomed back to the home with open arms, all his misbehavior forgiven.

18. (p. 187) *Goethe and Lessing.* Donovan is referring to German poet and dramatist Johann Wolfgang von Goethe (1749–1832) and German critic and dramatist Gotthold Ephraim Lessing (1729–1781). Together, the two represent the Romantic and classical poles in art and criticism. *Laocoon* (1766) is Lessing's influential tract on aesthetics.

19. (p. 204)—*The Forster family . . . the Blake Forsters:* This is a hodgepodge of information and misinformation about royal European lineages. Between Baldwin I (c.1058–1118) and Baldwin IX (Baldwin the Forester), an impostor who was executed by the French in the thirteenth century, many of those named were involved in ruling the area now known as Belgium.

20. (p. 215)—*Jesus, too, seems to have treated his mother with scant courtesy in public but Suarez . . . has apologised for him:* Jesus sometimes treated his mother in a seemingly somewhat discourteous fashion, as in Mark 3:31–35 and John 2:1–4. Francisco Suarez (1548–1617), a Spanish Jesuit theologian, attempted to explain away these passages.

21. (p. 217)—Et tu cum Jesu Galilæo eras: Thou also wast with Jesus the Galilean (Latin). This charge is made against Peter by a bystander in Matthew 26:69 (Douay version).

22. (p. 221) *Puzzled for the moment by saint John at the Latin gate:* In his musing, Stephen brings together an image of the beheaded John the Baptist and of another John, Saint John the Evangelist, who escaped persecution by miraculously passing through the locked Latin Gate in Rome. The Feast of St. John at the Latin Gate is celebrated on May 6; it also celebrates the dedication of the Basilica of St. John Lateran in Rome, which is dedicated to both St. John the Baptist and St. John the Evangelist.

Dubliners

1. (p. 245) *the poetry of Thomas Moore or the works of Sir Walter Scott and Lord Lytton:* The reference is to three popular writers of the Romantic period. London-based Irish poet Thomas Moore (1779–1852) wrote the popular *Irish Melodies.* Novelist Sir Walter Scott (1771–1832) was the author of many popular romances. Edward Bulwer-Lytton (1803–1873) was a poet and a prolific novelist.

2. (p. 314) *The next-door girls put some saucers on the table and then led the children up to the table, blindfold:* In the game being played, a blindfolded girl is led to three saucers, and her hand descends upon one of them. In the original version of the game, the saucers contained water (meaning a journey by sea), a ring (marriage within the year), or soil—"clay" (death). In the polite version of the game, a prayer book was substituted for the soil, representing entrance into a convent.

3. (p. 332) *hillsiders and fenians:* The reference is to the Fenian Brotherhood, founded in 1858 by James Stephens; a revolutionary group dedicated to winning Irish independence, it was the forerunner of the contemporary Irish Republican Army (I.R.A.). Because of their guerrilla tactics, the fenians were sometimes called "hillside men."

4. (p. 357) *pale:* Here the word means "dominion" or "jurisdiction." Historically, the Pale was the area around Dublin that the English held securely against the "wild Irish." Metaphorically, to be "within the pale" is to be within safe limits; to be "beyond the pale" is to be outside the bounds of polite or civil society.

5. (p. 366) *His motto . . . as Pope . . . to show the difference between their two pontificates:* Popes do not have a motto. This is a hodgepodge of information, misinformation, and bastardized Latin.

6. (p. 375) *Adam and Eve's:* This is the Dubliner's name for the Church of the Immaculate Conception, a Franciscan church on the Liffey in the city center. During the suppression of the Catholic Church, the Franciscans served the people, in secret, from the Adam and Eve Tavern, located nearby.

7. (p. 405) *O'Connell Bridge:* This primary north–south bridge over the River Liffey leads into Sackville (now O'Connell) Street. At the south end of O'Connell Street stands a large statue in honor of "Dan"—Daniel O'Connell—primary architect of Irish Catholic emancipation in the nineteenth century.

INSPIRED BY *A PORTRAIT OF THE ARTIST AS A YOUNG MAN* AND *DUBLINERS*

Film

Joseph Strick, known for his 1967 film adaptation of Joyce's *Ulysses*, adapted *A Portrait of the Artist as a Young Man* for the screen in 1977. Strick emphasized the autobiographical nature of the novel, virtually creating a film about Joyce himself. Bosco Hogan, wearing Joycean wire-framed glasses, plays the role of Stephen Dedalus as he struggles to define himself. An authentically Irish film, *Portrait* brings to life the Catholicism and traditional education of Joyce's country, along with the author's richly colloquial language.

In 1987 legendary filmmaker John Huston released his final film, an adaptation of Joyce's elegiac story "The Dead." Mirroring the story, Huston devotes much of the film to Aunt Julia and Aunt Kate's party, then delves into the spiritual upset of Gretta Conroy and the epiphany of her husband, Gabriel. Eerie throughout, the film was shot by Huston as if he had prescient knowledge of his own impending death. With an Academy Award–nominated screenplay adaptation by son Tony Huston and with daughter Anjelica Huston playing the part of Gretta Conroy, "The Dead" serves as a triumphant coda to Huston's illustrious career.

Theater

Fitting for a story imbued with music, "The Dead" opened on Broadway in January 2000 as the musical play *James Joyce's "The Dead."* Winning a Tony Award for the book by Richard Nelson, it featured music by Shaun Davey, with whom Nelson wrote the lyrics. The two received a Tony nomination for their original score, which they derived from nineteenth-century Irish parlor music, ballads, and poetry. The cast featured Christopher Walken as Gabriel, Blair Brown as Gretta, and Stephen Spinella as Freddy Malins in an understated production. After a short but successful run in New York, the play was well received in Los Angeles, Washington, D.C., and Chicago before closing.

Literature

The artistic work most directly linked with *Portrait* is Joyce's own autobiographical *Stephen Hero*. Joyce began writing what was to become *Stephen Hero* in his teens and abandoned the project halfway through. *Portrait* represents his second effort at autobiography, a rewriting. *Stephen Hero*, the book finally published in 1944 after Joyce's death, is what survives of the early manuscript. Considerably longer than *Portrait*, *Hero* takes the reader through only the latter third of Stephen's development as presented in *Portrait*.

Though artistically inferior, *Stephen Hero* allows readers to chart Joyce's magnificent progress as a writer. Even at a very early age, Joyce had clear ideas about his writing style, approaches that would define his entire career. The following passage taken from *Stephen Hero* sheds light on Joyce's use of the "epiphany":

> *By an epiphany he meant a sudden spiritual manifestation, whether in the vulgarity of speech or of gesture or in a memorable phase of the mind itself. He believed that it was for the man of letters to record these epiphanies with extreme care, seeing that they themselves are the most delicate and evanescent of moments.*

Another work by Joyce connected with both *Portrait* and *Dubliners* is his 1922 masterpiece *Ulysses*, widely described as the greatest novel of the twentieth century. Joyce originally thought of his Odyssean cycle as a short story to be included in *Dubliners*, but he recognized its true scope once he began committing it to paper. The finished, lengthy novel comprises a single day, June 16, 1904, and imbues daily modern life with epic as well as ironic implications. *Ulysses* centers on Leopold Bloom, a Jewish advertising salesman, who is Joyce's Odysseus, but also makes use of several familiar faces from the pages of *Dubliners* and gives particular attention to the further development of *Portrait*'s Stephen Dedalus. Stephen, now a full-fledged writer and teacher, corresponds to the Telemachus figure from the *Odyssey*, in that he is a spiritual son to Bloom. A rich tapestry that gains in complexity and meaning with each reading (followers of the prose stylist call repeated readings "re-Joycing"), *Ulysses* stands as a major hallmark of modern literature.

Stream of Consciousness

Among novels in English, *A Portrait of the Artist as a Young Man* pioneered the use of the stream of consciousness writing technique, which eliminates the mediation of the narrator, providing a direct, unadulterated view of a character and the actual process of his or her thought formation. For example, the opening chapter of *Portrait* is not solely the account of a third-person narrator who describes or interprets the inner thoughts of young Stephen Dedalus; instead, this outside perspective alternates with an interior one, emerging from Stephen's mind and revealing the thoughts themselves in all their fragmented, incoherent variety.

The phrase "stream of consciousness" was coined by psychologist and philosopher William James, elder brother of writer Henry James, in *The Principles of Psychology* (1890). Joyce cited a French novel as his inspiration for employing the idea as a writing technique; he first read Édouard Dujardin's *Les Lauriers sont coupes* (1888; published in English as *We'll to the Woods No More*) when he was in self-imposed exile in Paris in 1902. Joyce expanded his use of stream of consciousness in *Ulysses* and *Finnegans Wake* (1939).

British writer Virginia Woolf was well known for her ability to enter the minds of her characters with stream of consciousness writing, notably in *Mrs. Dalloway* (1925), *To the Lighthouse* (1927), and *The Waves* (1931). Woolf said in a letter to painter Jacques Raverat that it was "precisely the task of the writer to go beyond the 'formal railway line of sentence' and to show how people 'feel or think or dream.'" Among Americans, William Faulkner wrote his tale of Southern degeneracy, *The Sound and the Fury* (1929), with almost no narrative intrusion, making it one of the most complex and experimental novels to emerge in twentieth-century America.

COMMENTS & QUESTIONS

In this section, we aim to provide the reader with an array of perspectives on the texts, as well as questions that challenge those perspectives. The commentary has been culled from sources as diverse as reviews contemporaneous with the works, letters written by the author, literary criticism of later generations, and appreciations written throughout the works' histories. Following the commentary, a series of questions seeks to filter James Joyce's A Portrait of the Artist as a Young Man *and* Dubliners *through a variety of points of view and bring about a richer understanding of these enduring works.*

Comments

JAMES JOYCE

The Dublin papers will object to my stories as to a caricature of Dublin life. . . . At times the spirit directing my pen seems to me so plainly mischievous that I am almost prepared to let the Dublin critics have their way.

—from a letter to Stanislaus Joyce (July 19, 1905)

H. G. WELLS

It is no good trying to minimize a characteristic that seems to be deliberately obtruded. Like Swift and another living Irish writer, Mr. Joyce has a cloacal obsession. He would bring back into the general picture of life aspects which modern drainage and modern decorum have taken out of ordinary intercourse and conversation. . . .

Like some of the best novels in the world [*A Portrait of the Artist as a Young Man*] is the story of an education; it is by far the most living and convincing picture that exists of an Irish Catholic upbringing. It is a mosaic of jagged fragments that does altogether render with extreme completeness the growth of a rather secretive, imaginative boy in Dublin. The technique is startling, but on the whole it succeeds. Like so many Irish writers from Sterne to Shaw Mr. Joyce is a bold experimentalist with paragraph and punctuation. He breaks away from scene to scene without a hint of the change of time and place; at the end he passes suddenly from the third person to the first; he uses no inverted commas to mark off his speeches. The first trick I found sometimes tiresome here and there, but then my own disposition, perhaps acquired at the blackboard, is to mark off and underline rather fussily, and I do not know whether I was so much put off by the thing itself as anxious, which after all is not my business, about its effect on those others; the second trick, I will admit, seems entirely justified in this particular instance by its success; the third reduces Mr. Joyce to a free use of dashes. One conversation in this book is a superb success, the one in which Mr. Dedalus carves the Christmas turkey; I write with all due deliberation that Sterne himself could not have done it better; but most of the talk flickers blindingly with these dashes, one has the same wincing feeling of being flicked at that one used to have in the early cinema shows. I think Mr. Joyce has failed to discredit the inverted comma.

The interest of the book depends entirely upon its quintessential and unfailing reality. One believes in Stephen Dedalus as one believes in few characters in fiction. And the peculiar lie of the interest for the intelligent reader is the convincing revelation it makes of the limitations of a great mass of Irishmen. Mr. Joyce tells us unsparingly of the adolescence of this youngster under conditions that have passed almost altogether out of English life. There is an immense shyness, a profound secrecy, about matters of sex, with its inevitable accompaniment of nightmare revelations and furtive scribblings in unpleasant places, and there is a living belief in a real hell. The description of Stephen listening without a doubt to two fiery sermons on that tremendous theme, his agonies of fear, not disgust at dirtiness such as unorthodox children feel but just fear, his terror-inspired confession of his sins of impurity to a strange priest in a distant part of the city, is like nothing in any boy's experience who has been trained under modern conditions. Compare its stuffy horror with Conrad's account of how under analogous circumstances Lord Jim wept. And a second thing of immense significance is the fact that everyone in this Dublin story, every human being, accepts as a matter of course, as a thing in nature like the sky and the sea, that the English are to be hated. There is no discrimination in that hatred, there is no gleam of recognition that a considerable number of Englishmen have displayed a very earnest disposition to put matters right with Ireland, there is an absolute absence of any idea of a discussed settlement, any notion of helping the slow-witted Englishman in his three-cornered puzzle between North and South. It is just hate, a cant cultivated to the pitch of monomania, an ungenerous violent direction of the mind. That is the political atmosphere in which Stephen

Dedalus grows up, and in which his essentially responsive mind orients itself. I am afraid it is only too true an account of the atmosphere in which a number of brilliant young Irishmen have grown up. What is the good of pretending that the extreme Irish "patriot" is an equivalent and parallel of the English or American liberal? He is narrower and intenser than any English Tory. He will be the natural ally of the Tory in delaying British social and economic reconstruction after the war. He will play into the hands of the Tories by threatening an outbreak and providing the excuse for a militarist reaction in England. It is time the American observer faced the truth of that. No reason in that why England should not do justice to Ireland, but excellent reason for bearing in mind that these bright-green young people across the Channel are something quite different from the liberal English in training and tradition, and absolutely set against helping them. No single book has ever shown how different they are, as completely as this most memorable novel.

—from *New Republic* (March 10, 1917)

PADRAIC COLUM

Joyce, when I knew him first, was a student in the Old Royal University (since organized as the National University). He was very noticeable among the crowd of students that frequented the National Library or sauntered along the streets between Nelson's Pillar and Stephens's Green. He was tall and slender then, with a Dantesque face and steely blue eyes. His costume as I see him in my mind's eye now included a peaked cap and tennis shoes more or less white. He used to swing along the street carrying an ashplant in his hand for a cane. (That ashplant is celebrated in *Ulysses*; Stephen Dedalus carries it with him all through the day and frequently addresses it.) Although he had a beautiful voice for singing and repeating poetry, he spoke harshly in conversation, using many of the unprintable words that he has got printed in *Ulysses*. Stories were told about his arrogance. Did not this youth say to Yeats, "We have met too late: you are too old to be influenced by me." And did he not laugh in derision when Arthur Symons spoke to him of Balzac? (Balzac at this hour of the day!) We, the fry swimming about in the National Library, looked with some reverence on the youth who already had an article published in the *Fortnightly Review*. He had taught himself whatever Scandinavian language Ibsen wrote in—he used to repeat Ibsen's lyrics in the original—and when *We Dead Awaken* was published in English his essay on it came out in the *Fortnightly*—

William Archer had it published as a sort of preface to his translation. . . .

After I had made his acquaintance he went to Paris for a while and then returned to Dublin. It was then that he wrote the stories that are in *Dubliners* and began the writing of *Portrait of the Artist* (Dublin 1904—Trieste 1914). After he had begun that book he went abroad to take a place as a teacher of English in a Berlitz school. A few years later I met him when he was back in Dublin. He had his son, a little boy, with him, of whom he was very proud. He was more mellowed than I had ever known him before. It was then that he told me the title of the book he was writing—the book that was being referred to in Dublin as "Joyce's Meredithian novel." It was *Portrait of the Artist as a Young Man*—a book that is by no means Meredithian.

He was glad he had left Dublin—he was glad to be away from a place where "the reformed conscience" had left its fetter and away from the fog of Anglo-Saxon civilization. His little boy went to all the operas in the Italian city they lived in, and he would not be brought up to speak English.

. . . I am reminded of an incident that might find a place in *Dubliners* or in *Ulysses*—an incident that seems a parody on the plans that now and again occurred to him. He came to me one day and asked me for that rare coin with student Publiners—a golden half sovereign. By a miracle I had one. A financial scheme was involved in its use.

Joyce had been given a pawnticket by a medical student. Now, to any one else a pawnticket would be a minus quantity, but to Joyce it was something realizable. The ticket was for books, and 6 shillings was the amount they were in for. They were medical books, for a certainty, and valuable. And we would take them to our friend George Webb on the Quays and sell them and make 50, or even 100, per cent.

It was an attractive proposition. We handed in 7 and 6, and the redeemed parcel came across Terence Kelly's counter to us. Hastily we undid the wrappings! And behold! The books were Walter Scott's, an unsellable edition of the Waverley Novels, with one volume missing!

There was a wan hope in going to Webb's. That most knowing of all booksellers received Joyce cordially, for he had his eye on the Italian books that Joyce was then selling. We opened the parcel and exhibited the wretched, papier-mâché bound set! Very loftily, indeed, did Joyce talk to the incredulous Webb—"Webb, I have brought you some particularly good books." He would not believe that Joyce was serious. "You have some Italian books with you, haven't you, Mr. Joyce?" he kept on saying. When he gathered that Joyce was serious and that he had released the books on the prospect of selling them, he had them wrapped up for us. "There is only one thing to do, boys," he said. "Take them back to Terence Kelly. Pawn them again, and he may let you have 6 shillings on them." So we did.

—from the *New York Times* (June 11, 1922)

Questions

1. While thinking about the title of Joyce's first novel, would you emphasize *A Portrait of the Artist* or would you emphasize *as a Young Man*? Do you think Joyce was justified in writing "portrait of *the* artist" rather than "portrait of *an* artist"?

2. Compare the conclusion of "Araby" with the conclusion of "The Dead." In the first story, the young man sees himself as a "creature driven and derided by vanity" (p. 254). In "The Dead," Gabriel "saw himself as a ludicrous figure, . . . orating to vulgarians and idealising his own clownish lusts" (p. 409). What have they done to deserve this self-criticism? Is Puritanism involved? Are these male characters unmanly, too self conscious to make it in life? Should we approve or disapprove of—or just discover—their overreaction to a disappointment that is not their fault? Or is it?

3. Joyce said he wrote *Dubliners* "to betray the soul of that hemiplegia or paralysis which many consider a city." Do the stories suggest either the cause of or cure for this paralysis? Consider the conclusion of "Eveline."

4. At the very end of *Portrait*, Stephen vows "to forge in the smithy of my soul the uncreated conscience of my race." Assuming that by "race" Stephen means "countrymen," how can writing *fictions* create their conscience? Can you think of any writer of any nation whose fictions created the conscience of his or her race?

5. Padraic Colum portrays Joyce as convinced of his own genius at an early age. Is this related to the character of Stephen Dedalus? How do you think Joyce's persona, as described by Colum, resembles the heroes and heroines of his stories and novels?

FOR FURTHER READING

Also by James Joyce

Chamber Music, 1907
Exiles, 1918
Ulysses, 1922
Pomes Penyeach, 1927
Finnegans Wake, 1939
Stephen Hero, 1944 (posthumous)

Biography

Bradley, Bruce. *James Joyce's Schooldays*. New York: St. Martin's Press, 1982.
Ellmann, Richard. *James Joyce*. Revised edition. New York: Oxford University Press, 1982.
Kenner, Hugh. *Dublin's Joyce*. Bloomington: Indiana University Press, 1956.

Criticism

Attridge, Derek, ed. *The Cambridge Companion to James Joyce*. Cambridge and New York: Cambridge University Press, 1990.
Benstock, Bernard. *Narrative Con/Texts in "Dubliners."* Urbana: University of Illinois Press, 1994.
Bidwell, Bruce, and Linda Heffer, eds. *The Joycean Way: A Topographic Guide to "Dubliners" and "A Portrait of the Artist as a Young Man."* Baltimore, MD: Johns Hopkins University Press, 1982.
Bloom, Harold, ed. *James Joyce's "Dubliners."* New York: Chelsea House, 1988.
Buttigieg, Joseph A. *A Portrait of the Artist in Different Perspective*. Athens: Ohio University Press, 1987.
Dettmar, Kevin J. H. *The Illicit Joyce of Postmodernism: Reading Against the Grain*. Madison: University of Wisconsin Press, 1996.
Jackson, John Wyse, and Bernard McGinley, eds. *James Joyce's "Dubliners": An Illustrated Edition with Annotations*. New York: St. Martin's Press, 1995.

Joyce, James. *Critical Writings.* Edited by Ellsworth Mason and Richard Ellmann. New York: Viking, 1959.

———. *Stephen Hero: Part of the First Draft of "A Portrait of the Artist as a Young Man."* Revised edition. Edited by Theodore Spencer. London: Cape, 1969.

Kershner, R. Brandon. *Joyce, Bakhtin, and Popular Literature: Chronicles of Disorder.* Chapel Hill: University of North Carolina Press, 1989.

Norris, Margot. *Suspicious Readings of Joyce's "Dubliners."* Philadelphia: University of Pennsylvania Press, 2003.

Scholes, Robert, and Richard M. Kain, eds. *The Workshop of Daedalus: James Joyce and the Raw Materials for "A Portrait of the Artist as a Young Man."* Evanston, IL: Northwestern University Press, 1965.

Seidel, Michael. *James Joyce: A Short Introduction.* Oxford: Blackwell, 2002.

Torchiana, Donald T. *Backgrounds for Joyce's "Dubliners."* Boston: Allen and Unwin, 1986.

Wollaeger, Mark A., ed. *James Joyce's "A Portrait of the Artist as a Young Man": A Casebook.* Oxford and New York: Oxford University Press, 2003.